Praise for Vince Flynn

'Flynn perfectly measures all the ingredients for a fast and furious read' *Publishers Weekly*

'Sizzles with inside information, military muscle and CIA secrets. Vince Flynn remains the king of high-concept intrigue' Dan Brown

'Vince Flynn is Tom Clancy on speed. He grabs you by the scruff of the neck on page one and doesn't let you go until the end' Stephen Leather

'A fast-paced rollercoaster with a razor-sharp edge' *Lads Mag*

'Mitch Rapp is a great character who always leaves the bad guys either very sorry for themselves or very dead' *Guardian*

'An action-packed page-turner . . . makes Tom Clancy look like a limp-wristed pinko wimp' *Sydney Sun Herald*

Vince Flynn is an international No. 1 bestseller, published in 20 countries. He lives in Minneapolis with his wife and three children. Visit his website at www.vinceflynn.com.

Also by Vince Flynn

American Assassin
Pursuit of Honour
Extreme Measures
Protect and Defend
Act of Treason
Consent to Kill
Executive Power
Separation of Power
The Third Option
Transfer of Power
Term Limits

VINCE FLYNN

MEMORIAL DAY

SIMON &
SCHUSTER

London · New York · Sydney · Toronto · New Delhi

A CBS COMPANY

First published in Great Britain by Simon & Schuster UK Ltd, 2004
A CBS COMPANY

This paperback edition first published, 2011

9 10 8

Simon & Schuster UK Ltd
1st Floor
222 Gray's Inn Road
London WC1X 8HB

www.simonandschuster.co.uk

Simon & Schuster Australia, Sydney
Simon & Schuster India, New Delhi

A CIP catalogue record for this book is available from the British Library

ISBN 978-1-84983-581-7

Printed and bound by CPI Group (UK) Ltd, Croydon, CR0 4YY

To the men and women who serve

ACKNOWLEDGMENTS

As always I must first thank my best friend and love of my life, my wife, Lysa. As my friends are fond of pointing out, I definitely overachieved when I married you. To my editor, Emily Bestler, and my agent Sloan Harris, thank you once again for all of your guidance and friendship. I can't imagine working with anyone else in the business. To Sarah Branham and Katherine Cluverius, thank you for putting up with me. To Jack Romanos and Carolyn Reidy at Simon & Schuster, two of the smartest people in publishing, a sincere thanks for all of your support. To Judith Curr and Louise Burke, your enthusiasm and humor are two of the many reasons why I enjoy being published by Atria and Pocket Books. To Paolo Pepe for his creativity, Seale Ballenger for his commitment and hard work, and as always, to the entire S&S sales force. To John Attenborough and all of the folks at S&S Australia, thank you for showing my wife and me your lovely country. We can't wait to come back. Also, a special thanks to Jeffrey Berg at ICM for taking such a personal interest in *Memorial Day*.

One of the best parts of my job is getting to meet the people I base my fiction on. At the CIA I'd like to thank

Bill Harlow, Chase Brandon, Robert Richer, Michael Tadie, and all of the people at the CTC who gave me such a warm reception last year. At the FBI I'd like to thank Brad Garret, Pat O'Brien, and Jay Rooney. I admire the commitment and sacrifice that all of you make. To Larry Johnson, again, thank you for your always unique take on national security. To Kat, your frank advice and humor are always welcome. And to Carl Pohlad, thank you for all your generosity and friendship.

To Larry Mefford, who recently left the FBI for greener pastures and hopefully a little less stress—you are a true gentleman and a professional who will be missed. To Paul Evancoe, a real shooter, thank you for taking the time to explain to me the intricacies of the Nuclear Emergency Support Teams and all things technical. Your career is a story worth telling, and when you get it down on paper I can't wait to read it. Thank you for your commitment to service and country, and best of luck with your new endeavor. Lastly, to all of my sources who wish remain anonymous, thank you for your insights.

PRELUDE

M itch Rapp stared through the one-way mirror into the dank, subterranean cement chamber. A man, clothed in nothing more than a pair of underwear, sat handcuffed to a small, ridiculously uncomfortable-looking chair. A naked lightbulb hung from the ceiling, dangling only a foot or so above him. The stark glare of the light combined with his state of near total exhaustion, caused the man's head to droop forward, leaving his chin resting on his chest. He was dangerously close to losing his balance and toppling over, which was exactly what they wanted.

Rapp checked his watch. He was running out of time and patience. He'd just as soon shoot this piece of human refuse and get it over with, but the present situation was more complicated than that. He needed the man to talk, that was the point of this endeavor. They all talked eventually, of course, that wasn't the problem. The trick was to get them to tell you the truth. This one was no exception. So far he was sticking to his story, a story Rapp knew to be an outright lie.

The CIA counterterrorism operative hated coming to this place. It literally made his skin crawl. It had all the charm of a mental hospital without the barred windows and the beefy orderlies stuffed into their white uniforms. It was a place intentionally designed to starve the human mind of stimuli. It was so secret, it didn't even have a name. The handful of people who knew of its existence referred to it only as the Facility.

It was off the books, not even listed in the black-intelligence budget submitted in secret to Congress every year. The Facility was a relic from the Cold War. It was located near Leesburg, Virginia, and looked just like all the other horse farms dotting the countryside thereabouts. Situated on sixty-two beautiful rolling acres, the place had been purchased by the Agency in the early fifties, at a time when the CIA was given far more latitude and discretion than it was today.

This was one of several sites where the CIA debriefed Eastern Bloc defectors, and even a few of the Agency's own who were snared in the net of James Angleton, the CIA's notoriously paranoid genius who was in charge of rooting out spies during the height of the Cold War. Very nasty things had been done to people in this crypt. This was where the CIA would have likely taken Aldrich Ames if they had caught him before the FBI did. The men and women who were charged with pro-tecting Langley's secrets would have given almost anything for the chance to put the screws to that traitorous bastard, but they were unfortunately denied the opportunity.

The Facility was not a pleasant place, but it was a neessary evil in a world chock-full of sadistic deeds and misguided, brutal men. This was something Rapp was more than aware of, but that didn't mean he had to like it. He was neither delicate nor squeamish. Rapp had killed more men than he could even attempt to count, and he'd employed his craft in a variety of imaginative ways that spoke to the sheer depth of his skill.

He was a modern-day assassin who lived in a civilized country where such a term could never be used openly. His was a nation that loved to distinguish itself from the less refined nations of the world. A democracy that celebrated individual rights and freedom. A state that would never tolerate the open recruiting, training, and use of one of its own citizens for the specific purpose of covertly killing the citizens of another country. But that was exactly who Rapp was. He was a modern-day assassin who was conveniently called an *operative* so as to not offend the sensibilities of the cultured people who occupied the centers of power in Washington.

If those very people knew of the existence of the Facility they would fly into an indignant rage that would result in the partial or complete destruction of the CIA. These haters of America's capitalistic muscle wanted to analyze what we had done to evoke such hatred from the terrorists, all the while missing the point that they were using the logic of a seedy attorney defending a rapist. The woman had on a short skirt, sexy top, and high heels—maybe she was asking for it? America was a rude and arrogant country run by selfish, colonialist men who were out to exploit the resources of lesser countries—maybe we were asking for it?

Under their narrow definition the Washington elite would call this place a torture chamber. Rapp, however, knew what real torture was, and it wasn't this. This was coercion, it was sensory deprivation, it was interrogation, but it wasn't real torture.

Real torture was causing a person so much unthinkable pain that he or she begged to be killed. It was hooking alligator clips to a man's testicles and sending jolts of searing electricity through his body, it was gang-raping a woman day after day until she slipped into a coma, it was forcing a man to watch as his wife and children were sodomized by a bunch of thugs, it was making a man eat his own excrement. It was monstrous, it was barbaric, and it could also be wildly ineffective. Time and time again such methods proved that most prisoners would say or do almost anything to stop the pain, sign any confession, create terrorist plots that didn't exist, even turn on their own parents.

Rapp was a practical man, however, and the prisoner sitting cuffed to the chair on the other side of the glass knew firsthand what real torture was. The organization he worked for was notorious for its treatment of political prisoners. If anyone was deserving of a good beating it was this vile bastard, but still there were other things to consider.

Rapp didn't like torture, not only because of its effect on the person being brutalized, but for what it did to the person who sanctioned and carried it out. He had no desire to sink to those depths unless it was a last resort, but unfortunately they were quickly approaching that point. Lives were at stake. Two CIA operatives were already dead, thanks to the duplicitous scum in the other room, and many more lives were in the balance. Something was in the works, and if Rapp didn't find out what it was hundreds, maybe thousands, of innocent people would die.

The door to the observation room opened and a man approximately the same age as Rapp entered. He walked up to the window and with his deep-set brown eyes looked at the handcuffed man. There was a certain clinical detachment in the way the man carried himself. His hair was elegantly cut and his beard trimmed to

4

perfection. He was dressed in a dark, well-tailored suit, white dress shirt with French cuffs, and an expensive red silk tie. He owned two identical sets of the outfit, and in an effort to keep his subject off balance, it was the only thing he had worn in front of the man since his arrival three days ago. The outfit was carefully chosen to convey a sense of superiority and importance.

Bobby Akram was one of the CIA's best interrogators. He was a Pakistani immigrant and a Muslim, who was fluent in Urdu, Pashto, Arabic, Farsi, and, of course, English. Akram had controlled every detail of every second of his prisoner's incarceration. Every noise, variation in temperature, morsel of food and drop of liquid had been carefully choreographed.

The goal with this specific subject, as with any subject, was to get him to talk. The first step had been to isolate him and strip him of all sense of time and place by immersing him in a world of sensory deprivation until he craved stimuli. Akram would then throw the man a lifeline; he would begin a dialogue. He would get the man to talk, not even necessarily to divulge secrets, at least not at first. The secrets would come later. To do the job thoroughly and properly took a great deal of time and patience, but those were luxuries they did not possess. Intelligence was time sensitive and that meant things had to be expedited.

Turning to Rapp he said, "It shouldn't be much longer."

"I sure as hell hope not," grumbled Rapp. Mitch Rapp was many things, but patient was not one of them.

Akram smiled. He had great respect for the legendary CIA operative. The two of them were on the front line of this war against terrorism, allies with a mutual enemy. For Rapp it was about protecting innocent people against the aggressions of a growing threat. For Akram it was about saving the religion he loved from a group of fanatics who had twisted the words of the great prophet so they could perpetuate hatred and fear.

Akram checked his watch and asked, "Are you ready?"

Rapp nodded and looked again at the exhausted, bound man. He mumbled a few curses to himself. If word got out about this, all of his accomplishments and connections wouldn't be able to save him. He was way off the reservation with this little hunt, but he needed answers and running things through the proper channels was sure to get him bogged down in a quagmire of politics and diplomacy.

There were too many varying interests at play, without even getting into the issue of leaks. The man bound and drugged in the other room was Colonel Masood Haq of the dreaded Pakistani Inter-Services Intelligence or ISI. Without telling anyone at Langley, Rapp had hired a team of freelancers to snatch the man and bring him here. The brutal murders of two CIA operatives, and a growing fear that al-Qaeda had reconstituted itself, had given Rapp the impetus to take action without authorization.

Akram pointed at their prisoner as he began to nod off. "He's going to fall over any second. Are you sure you want to go forward with your plan right now?" Akram crossed his arms. "If we wait another day or two I'm very confident I can get him to talk."

Rapp shook his head and answered firmly. "My patience has run out. If you don't get him to talk, I will."

Akram nodded thoughtfully. He was not opposed to using the good cop/bad cop technique of interrogation.

On the right person the results could be quite satisfactory. Akram himself, however, never resorted to violence, he was careful to leave that to others.

"All right. When I get up and leave that's your cue."

Rapp acknowledged the plan, and kept his eyes on the bound man as Akram left the room. The prisoner had no idea how long he had been here, how long he had been in the hands of his captors, or who his captors even were. He had no idea where he was, what country, let alone what continent. He had heard only one man speak, and that was Akram, a fellow Pakistani by birth.

He would, of course, assume that he was being held in his own country, probably by the ISI's chief competitor, the IB, and because of that he would hold out as long as he could in the belief that the ISI would come to his rescue. He had been drugged and deprived of all sense of time and routine. He was an exhausted man awash in a sea of sensory deprivation. He was ready to break, and when he saw Rapp enter the room, his hopes would crumble.

As Akram had predicted, the man had finally dozed off long enough to lose his balance and topple over. He hit the floor fairly hard, but didn't bother attempting to get up. Having been in this hopeless position countless times during his incarceration, he knew it was impossible.

Akram entered the room with two assistants. While they righted the prisoner, Akram pulled up a chair and told his assistants to remove the man's restraints. When the prisoner was free to move his arms and legs, Akram handed him a glass of water. The two assistants went and stood in the shadows by the door in case they were needed.

"Now, Masood," Akram said in the man's native

language, "would you like to start telling me the truth?"

The man glared at his interrogator with bloodshot eyes, "I have been telling you the truth. I am not a supporter of the Taliban or al-Qaeda. I deal with them only because it is my job to keep tabs on them."

"You know that General Musharraf has made it very clear that we are to stop supporting the Taliban and al-Qaeda." Akram had maintained the fiction that he was a fellow Pakistani from the moment he'd met Haq.

"I keep telling you," the man replied firmly, "the only reason I still meet with my contacts is to keep tabs on them."

"And you're still sympathetic to their cause, aren't you?"

"Yes, I'm . . . I mean no! I'm not sympathetic to their cause."

Akram smiled. "I am a devout Muslim, and I am sympathetic to their cause." He tilted his head to the side. "Are you not a devout Muslim?"

The question was a slap in the intelligence officer's face. "Of course I am a devout Muslim," he blurted indignantly, "but I am . . . I am an officer in the ISI. I know where my allegiance lies."

"I'm sure you do," said a skeptical Akram. "The problem is that I do not know where your allegiance lies, and I'm running out of patience." There was no malice in his voice as he said this, merely regret.

The man buried his face in his hands and shook his head. "I don't know what to say. I am not the man you say I am." He lifted his head and stared past the bright light at his interrogator. His eyes were glassy and pleading. "Ask my superiors. Ask General Sharif. He will tell you I was following orders."

Akram shook his head. "Your superiors have

forsaken you. You are nothing but a plague to them. They claim to know very little about what you've been up to."

"You are a liar," spat Haq.

This was exactly what Akram was after. Uncontrollable mood swings. Desperate and pleading one second and then angry and antagonistic the next. Raising his hands in surrender, Akram's expression spoke of a sad resolve that he could do no more. "I have been very patient with you, and all you do is reward me with more lies and insults."

"I have told you the truth!" Haq said far too quickly.

Akram gave him an almost paternal stare. "Would you say that I have been kind to you?"

The lack of sleep and drugs caused Haq to slip. He opened his arms and looked around the room. "Your hospitality leaves much to be desired." In a defiant tone he said, "I want to speak with General Sharif immediately!"

"Let me ask you, Masood, how do you treat your prisoners?"

The Pakistani intelligence officer lowered his eyes to the floor, deciding it was better to ignore the question.

"Have I laid a hand on you since you've been here?"

Haq shook his head reluctantly.

"Well . . . all of that is about to change." This was the first time Akram had threatened violence, either implicitly or explicitly. Their conversations up until now had consisted of Haq talking about his contacts, and going over and over the same well-rehearsed story, Haq slipping up on a few details here and there, but for the most part holding his ground.

Akram studied his subject intently and said, "There is someone here who would like to see you."

Haq looked up, his eyes glimmering with hope.

"No." Akram shook his head and laughed ominously. "I don't think you want to see this man. In fact," Akram stood, "he is probably the last person on the planet you want to see right now. He is someone who I cannot control, and someone who knows for a fact that you are a liar."

"I am telling you the truth," Haq shrieked and reached out for his interrogator's arm.

Akram caught his wrist and twisted it with just enough pressure to send the man a clear signal not to touch him again. He looked down at the wide, pleading eyes and said, "You had ample opportunity to tell the truth, but chose not to. It is now out of my hands." With that Akram released the man's wrist and left the room.

RAPP DID NOT enter right away. Akram told him it was best to let the tension build. They watched through the one-way mirror as Haq began nervously pacing back and forth along the far wall. He grew more agitated by the minute, until finally the bright overhead lights came on and Rapp entered the room.

The look on Haq's face was at first one of disbelief and then dawning horror. The arrival of the infamous American intelligence officer changed everything. Things began to fall into place, and Haq instantly knew he was in much more trouble than he could ever have imagined.

Pointing at the uncomfortable chair, Rapp barked, "Sit!"

Haq did so without hesitation. Rapp grabbed a small square table by the wall and dragged it over, placing it in front of the Pakistani. Looking up at the two guards he said in English, "I can handle him by myself."

As the guards left, Rapp laid a letter-sized manila envelope on the table and then slowly took off his jacket revealing his holstered 9mm FNP-9. He draped the jacket over the back of the chair and began yanking at his tie.

"Do you know who I am?" Rapp placed the tie on top of his jacket.

Haq nodded and swallowed nervously.

Rapp retrieved two photos from the envelope and laid them on the table. "Do these people look familiar to you?" He began rolling up his sleeves.

The Pakistani intelligence officer looked reluctantly at the photos. He knew exactly who the two people were, but also knew it was exceedingly dangerous to admit such a thing. Haq had been on the giving end of enough interrogations to know that he had to stay the course and stick with his story. Slowly he shook his head. "No."

Even though Rapp had anticipated the answer, it still infuriated him. He placed his right hand on the table and brought his left hand around with blinding speed, slapping Haq so hard he knocked him out of his chair and sent him sprawling across the floor.

"Wrong answer!" Rapp screamed as he stepped around the table, his closed fist raised and ready to come down on Haq like a sledge-hammer.

Haq lay stunned on the floor. It was the first time one of his captors had touched him. Panic set in and he threw his hands up to block the blow. "All right! All right! I know who they are, but I had nothing to do with their deaths!"

Rapp grabbed him by the throat, and even though Haq was a good twenty pounds heavier, he yanked him off the floor and slammed him against the wall like he was a rag doll. "Do you want to live or die?"

Haq looked at him with honest confusion on his face, so Rapp repeated the question, this time screaming it directly into his ear. "Do you want to live or die?"

Haq croaked his answer. *"Liiiive."*

"Then you'd better get smart fast." Rapp threw him back toward the desk and shouted, "Sit your ass back down, and look at those photos!"

Rapp circled around behind him, his fists clenched and his face flushed with anger. "Now, Masood!" he shouted the man's first name. "I'm only going to ask you this one time. I know more about you than you can possibly imagine." Rapp pointed at the two black-and-white photos. Did you have any hand, either directly or indirectly, in the murder of these two CIA employees?"

This time Haq brought his hands up before he answered. "No." His eyes were wide with terror as he scrambled to come up with an answer, any answer that would keep this animal at bay. "I don't think so."

I don't think so, was better than an outright denial. "You don't think so," mocked Rapp. "Masood, I think you can do a whole lot better than that."

"I don't know . . ." he said nervously. "This is a dangerous part of the world. People disappear all the time."

"Yeah . . . like you. You stupid piece of crap." Rapp turned his neck toward the ceiling and yelled, "Play cut one." A second later Haq's voice came over the speaker system. Although Rapp was fluent in both Arabic and Farsi, he didn't know Urdu well enough to understand what was being said. He'd read the translation enough times, though, to know it by heart. The tape was of a phone call placed by Haq to an unknown person requesting a meeting. When the short recording was over, Rapp asked for the second cut to be played. It was this second cut and its references to some sort of big event in the near future that had chilled Rapp to the bone.

Rapp grabbed another photo from the envelope and let it fall into Haq's lap. "Recognize this?"

Haq looked at the photo of himself having coffee with Akhtar Jilani, a high-ranking member of the Taliban. He remembered the meeting well, and as he listened to the audio of their conversation he suddenly felt nauseated.

As the voices played from the speakers Rapp announced, "Pretty sloppy work for a guy who's in the business of spying." Rapp placed three small photos on the table in very deliberate fashion. One was of an infant and the other two were toddlers. "Any idea who they are?"

Haq shook his head nervously.

"They are the children of the two men you had killed." Rapp let his words hang in the air uncomfortably so the reality of what Haq had done could sink in. Then in the same manner as before he placed five more photographs on the table. They were black and white surveillance photos, the cute faces of Haq's five children framed perfectly in each one. Rapp stared down menacingly at the man and watched in silence as Haq began to weep.

Through sniffles and sobs Haq pleaded, "Please . . . I beg of you, don't do anything to my children. This is my fault . . . not theirs."

Rapp's face twisted into a grimace of disgust. "I don't kill children, you piece of shit." Tapping the photos of the three American kids he said, "They will never see their fathers again." Rapp began circling the table. "Look at their faces!" he screamed. "Tell me why your kids should ever see you again?"

Haq fingered the photos of his children and began sobbing uncontrollably. While Haq continued to weep, Rapp drew his 9mm FNP-9 and began screwing into place a thick black silencer. When the silencer was attached, he extended the weapon and grabbed the well-oiled slide, pulling it back and letting it slam forward with a resounding metal on metal clank.

With a hollow-tipped round in the chamber, Rapp pointed the weapon at the Pakistani intelligence officer's head and said, "I am a man of my word, Masood. If you ever want to see your children again, you'd better give me a reason to let you live. I want to know everything you know about the Taliban and al-Qaeda. I want to know what this bold plan is that you and Jilani made reference to and if at any point I find out you're lying to me, the deal is off, and I'll blow your brains all over the floor."

Rapp flicked the safety off and pulled the hammer all the way back into the cocked position. "So what's it going to be, Masood? Do you want to go to work for me and see your children grow up, or do you want to die?"

lecture. The dark-haired man had showed up at sunrise with a single bag and in clipped English told the captain to get underway. There was no greeting, no introduction, and he declined Scott's offer to help him with his bag.

The man had gone straight down to the cabin and closed the door. Now, an hour and a half out of port, Scott was beginning to wonder if he planned to stay below for the entire voyage. The passenger was either an incredible snob, which in the world of luxury yachts was very possible, or he was so hungover he couldn't even muster basic good manners.

Scott scanned the bright horizon. It was too nice a day, and he was captaining too fine a boat, to let the rudeness of his passenger ruin the moment. The Brit reached out with his right hand and placed his palm on the twin chrome throttles. In a tempered gradual motion he pushed them all the way forward, the diesels roaring to their full power, the wind whipping through Scott's sun-bleached hair. He grinned to himself as he stood gripping the wheel, and thought that it might be a very nice trip indeed if his passenger stayed below.

MUSTAFA AL-YAMANI was prostrate, his arms stretched out in front of his head, in a near trancelike state as he supplicated himself to his Creator, asking for guidance and bravery. It had been more than a week's time since he had prayed, and for al-Yamani, who had communed with his God at least five times a day for as long as he could remember, this self-imposed exile from Allah had been the most difficult aspect of the trip. With the boat's engines droning and the door to the private cabin locked, this was quite possibly the last chance he would have to pray properly before he became a *shaheed,* a martyr for his people.

Al-Yamani had worked diligently to avoid the counterterrorism net of the United States intelligence community and its allies. He had first flown to Johannesburg, South Africa, and from there to Buenos Aires, Argentina. He stayed one day in Buenos Aires, changing his identity and making sure he wasn't being followed, and then it was on to Caracas and a short hop to Havana. That was where the boat had been waiting for him, along with provisions and a captain whose only instructions were to ferry the passenger to Grand Bahama. As for the boat itself, a wealthy sponsor had arranged for the use of it. The owner did not know the full intent of the group he was lending it to, but he was sure to have guessed it wasn't for a simple pleasure cruise. In the end it would be all that much better if the man was implicated.

The physical journey to this part of the world had taken only five days, but in a metaphysical sense the journey had taken a lifetime. The forty-one-year-old Saudi Arabian had been preparing himself for this mission since the age of nine when he had been sent to a madrasa in Mecca to study the Koran. By the age of fifteen he was fighting in Afghanistan against the godless Soviets and honing his skills as a mujahid, a warrior who fights for Islam. Every cause needed its fighters, its mujahideen, and for al-Yamani there was no more noble cause than that of Islam.

Al-Yamani finished his supplication and moved into a sitting position, placing his hands on his thighs. In a voice not much more than a whisper he proclaimed, *"Allahu Akbar." God is great.* Al-Yamani repeated himself two more times and then rose to his feet. It was time. He walked over to the bed nestled into the prow of the boat and retrieved an object from the side pocket of his bag. Al-Yamani lifted up the tails of his loose-fitting silk shirt and slid the object into the waist of his pants. He looked every bit the wealthy vacationer, from his floral patterned shirt, to his khaki pants, to his sandals. He'd even donned a wedding ring and a fake Rolex for the trip, and the most difficult thing of all . . . he'd shaved his beard for the first time since puberty.

Al-Yamani took one last look at himself in the mirror to make sure nothing would tip off the captain. With a deep breath he straightened his shoulders and headed for the cabin door. He would make this quick. No games. The captain was a nonbeliever. He meant nothing. Al-Yamani unlocked the small door and slid it up into the open position. He was instantly greeted by the blinding daylight of the Caribbean.

He paused for a second, shielding his eyes from the sun with his left hand, wondering if he should give himself some time to let his eyes adjust to the brightness. He decided to press on and climbed the three steps quickly. Under his left hand he could make out the silhouette of the captain standing at the helm.

Al-Yamani could hear the man talking to him but couldn't make out what he was saying. They were going much faster than he'd realized, and the wind was howling over the bow of the boat. Al-Yamani made no effort to try and understand the man. He had surprise on his side, and everything would be over in a few seconds. Moving past the helm, al-Yamani slid his right hand under his shirt while he brought his left hand up and placed it on the shoulder of the captain. He leaned in as if he was going to ask a question, and as his lips began to part, his left hand clamped down tightly on the captain's shoulder. His right hand came thrusting upward, sending a six inch stainless-steel blade into the man's back.

Thomas Scott arched his back in pain, his hands instantly gripping the wheel, his mind scrambling to comprehend what had just happened. Suddenly, he was yanked away from the helm and spun across the deck. Frantically he tried to reach behind himself to get a grip on whatever it was that was causing him such pain. Before he had time to react, he was up against the side of the boat and losing his balance. He could feel himself going overboard. Blue sky filled his vision and then he hit the water hard.

Al-Yamani watched the Brit disappear under the boat's churning wake, and then scrambled to the helm. He looked down at the high-tech dashboard and squinted to read the dials and digital readouts. Bending close, he noted his speed, heading, and GPS location. He'd spent a week studying the owner's manual and knew the controls well enough to do what needed to be done. After scanning the horizon quickly he began slowly turning the wheel, bringing the boat around on a new northerly heading.

With the vessel pointed in the right direction al-Yamani relaxed a bit. He turned around and looked at the boat's long curving white wake. Bringing his hand up to shield his eyes from the bright sun, he strained to see any sign of the man whose life he had just taken. He thought he saw something for a second, but then it vanished. Al-Yamani wasn't worried. They were thirty miles from the nearest piece of land, and he had stabbed his victim in the heart. If by some miracle he wasn't already dead, he would be shortly.

Al-Yamani turned his attention to what lay ahead, a

confident look of anticipation on his face. He had waited his entire life for this opportunity. It was his destiny to come to America, and it was his providence to strike a blow for Allah. Al-Yamani was not alone. There were others, and they were at this very moment converging on America from all points of the compass. Before the week was over, the arrogant and hedonistic Americans would be dealt a crippling blow.

TWO

The new Joint Counterterrorism Center, or JCTC, was located near Tyson's Corner west of downtown D.C. The facility housed the CIA's Counterterrorism Center, the FBI's Counterterrorism Division, and the newly created Terrorist Threat Integration Center, or TTIC. The reason for putting all three under one roof was to create better analysis of the information collected on terrorists. On paper many people in Washington thought it was a great idea, but in reality it was proving a bit more difficult, at least from Rapp's perspective.

Rapp slid into the high-tech conference room and tried to keep a low profile, which was not easy considering his reputation. He did not plan on staying. The long table was ringed with directors, deputy directors, and assistant directors from various key federal agencies and departments. Every single one of them knew of Rapp's exploits to one degree or another, and he made many of them nervous.

The conference room had opened only in the last week, and it was Rapp's first time inside. The first thing he noticed were the photographs that dominated the wall directly across from him. Twenty-two faces stared back at him. He knew their names by heart, as well as where they'd grown up and where they'd received their training. They were the twenty-two terrorists that the FBI and the Department of Justice would most like to apprehend, put on trial, and incarcerate. Rapp simply wanted to hunt them down and put a bullet in each one of their heads.

That more than anything summed up the problem Rapp had with the Joint Counterterrorism Center. They had too many rules, and they were in a war against an enemy who had none. He understood why they had to operate within the confines of the law and the courts. The Bill of Rights was not something to be taken lightly, but there were times when expediency saved lives.

Rapp was only marginally surprised to hear that this was the exact topic being discussed. Some woman from the Department of Justice was railing against the Patriot Act, and warning everyone that it was only going to cause them problems down the line. He caught his boss's eye and gestured for her to step into the hallway with him.

When Director Kennedy had joined him in the hallway, she asked, "What's up?"

Rapp looked around suspiciously. "I don't want to talk about it out here."

"Understood." Kennedy led him to the elevator where they went up several floors to the CIA's portion of the building. After passing through several cipher locks, they entered a vacant conference room and closed the door.

Rapp handed Kennedy a file. "I think you're going to find this very interesting."

Without saying a word, Kennedy took the file and

sat. She undid the red string and opened the top secret folder as if she had done it thousands of times before, which she had.

She skimmed the first page, and based on the thickness of the file said, "Why don't you take a seat?"

"Don't feel like it." Rapp clasped his hands behind his back and flexed his knees. He was in no mood to sit. "I've got a plane waiting to take me to Kandahar."

The director of the CIA continued reading and said, "Aren't you getting a little ahead of yourself?"

"That's what I'm paid for."

She looked up at him over the top of her glasses and shook her head. Rapp was like a brother to her, which at times could be a problem.

Impatiently, Rapp watched her read the hastily compiled file. His mind was already racing ahead, going over what he would need to pull off an operation of this magnitude.

Colonel Haq had given Rapp the information he was looking for and then some. The man had proved himself a virtual fountain of intelligence, and for that reason alone he was still alive. If he continued to cooperate, Rapp would keep his promise, and the Pakistani would see his children again. Haq had turned on his fellow ISI members who were Taliban sympathizers, and he'd given them crucial information on al-Qaeda and its reconstituted leadership. But most importantly, he had given them the location of al-Qaeda's base of operations.

In a sense, for Rapp, the planning and execution of his next step were easy. But getting permission for that next step in a town like Washington, with all of its competing interests, was a bit trickier. He usually preferred to limit involvement to the Agency and a few highly trained special forces' outfits, but this one was going to have to go all the way to the top. The operation was complicated. It involved snubbing a very important ally, and it wasn't "black," meaning the international community and the press would find out about it five minutes after it was over.

Whether the mission was a success or a failure, Rapp and the CIA would need the cover of the Oval Office, and that meant the president would have to be brought into the loop. Rapp was woefully inept at reading the constantly shifting political landscape of Washington, but Kennedy excelled at interpreting the wants and desires of America's most insatiable egos.

Kennedy continued to read. Rapp watched her flip through the pages in half the time it had taken him to read the report, and he'd written most of it. A near photographic memory was one of her many assets. When she finished the last page she flipped it over and closed the file.

With a pensive look on her face she leaned back and removed her reading glasses. She glanced up at her prized recruit with a thoughtful frown, almost spoke, but then decided against it.

Rapp, lacking his boss's well-known patience, said, "It's a no-brainer."

She didn't answer right away. As she'd already noted, Rapp was getting ahead of himself. Kennedy was privy to the most sensitive intelligence one could imagine, yet Rapp's report was filled with details she had never seen before, and none of them was attributed to a source. There was a saying in the spy business that information was only as good as its source.

"Where did you get this?"

"You don't want to know," answered Rapp in a flat tone.

Kennedy raised a questioning brow. "Is that so?"

Rapp held his ground. He knew she would press him on this point, but for her own good he had to keep her in the dark. "Irene, trust me when I tell you this . . . you don't want to know how I got my hands on this intel."

Kennedy stared at him, trying to guess where he could have come up with such vital information. There were several possibilities, and they all pointed in a direction that was fraught with danger. She glanced down with the report and said, "You're convinced this is accurate?"

"Yes. You could say I obtained it firsthand."

She believed him, but wanted to make sure he'd thought this through all the way. "If this doesn't work, people are going to demand answers . . . and not just the press. We're talking Congressional hearings, cameras, grandstanding politicians, careers destroyed . . . you've seen it all before."

"Yeah, and I'm not afraid. That's why I'm not going to tell you where or how I got this information. If they ever call me up to testify, I'll fall on my sword like a good soldier."

Kennedy knew Rapp would never implicate her or the president, but she also knew he would never go quietly. He would be a formidable adversary for any congressman or senator who chose to lock horns with him. "Well . . . your timing is interesting."

"How so?"

"There are some other things going on . . ." She paused briefly. "Some things that have me concerned."

"Is any of it related to this?"

Kennedy shrugged. "I'm not sure."

"Well," stated a sarcastic Rapp, "we sure as hell aren't going to find out sitting here." He pointed at the file and said, "That's just a start. Give me the green light and I'll tell you within seventy-two hours exactly what they're up to."

It was a familiar refrain from the director's top counterterrorism advisor. Action! Rapp had spent twelve rough years in the field operating without official cover in some of the most inhospitable places in the Middle East and Southwest Asia. Despite his relative youth, at thirty-four he was a throwback, a believer in putting boots on the ground and taking risks. That was what her job ultimately came down to—weighing the risks versus the rewards.

"Irene," Rapp pressed, "opportunities like this don't come along very often."

"I know."

"Then let's do it," he pleaded.

"And your role in this?"

He knew where she was going, and took a half step back. "It's all right there in the report."

"I've heard that before," Kennedy said in a cynical voice.

"I'm going to be monitoring this thing from high in the sky. The Task Force boys will get to have all the fun. I'm just there to make sure no one screws up, and ask a few pointed questions when it's over."

Kennedy nodded. Many of the president's fears would be allayed by Rapp's involvement. "And your wife?"

Rapp almost told Kennedy that was none of her business, but managed to resist the impulse. "She left yesterday for her family's cabin in Wisconsin."

"I know that, and I also know about the promises you've made her . . . as well as the ones you've given me." Kennedy locked eyes with him to make sure there would be no misunderstanding on this point. "So no more cowboy crap this time. All right?"

"Yes, ma'am," Rapp replied with a healthy bit of aggravation in his voice.

Kennedy ignored his tone and his intentional use of the word *ma'am*. At forty-two she was only eight years older than Rapp.

It was time to take some risks. The director of the CIA stood and grabbed the file. "You have my approval. Get moving, and please bring yourself back unscathed."

"And the president?"

"I'll take care of the president. Just make sure you get what we're after, and then get the hell out of there."

THREE

The corner office she was heading for was perhaps the most impressive in all of Washington, even more impressive than the oval-shaped one just up the street. The tall blonde walked right past two administrative assistants and the security detail and entered without asking permission. Once inside she closed the heavy wood door and approached her boss's aircraft carrier–sized desk. The woman had a definite air of confidence about her, a sense of purpose in each step. She was as aware of her surroundings as she was of herself.

There was no middle ground for Peggy Stealey. She'd graduated from the University of Washington's Law School thirteen years ago, and she'd been fighting ever since. One case and one cause after another. Some of them she'd been less passionate about than others, but she'd given every one of them her all. Peggy Stealey hated to lose more than she liked to win, and that more than anything was the key to understanding how she ticked.

While some men found her irresistible, there were perhaps an equal number who found her harsh and a bit intimidating. She was a statuesque six feet tall with the legs of an all-American 400-meter hurdler, and the cheekbones of a Nordic goddess. She tended to dress conservatively; lots of pants suits and skirts that stopped just above the knee, and she almost always wore her blond hair pulled back in a low ponytail, but when she wanted to, when she felt it would give her an advantage, she was not afraid to sex up her look. That was as far as she went, though.

She'd slept with only one coworker since graduating from law school and that had been back in Seattle more than twelve years ago. She hated to admit it, but she'd been naïve. Only a few months out of school, she was overworked, lonely, and sleep deprived. She'd let down her guard and slept with the law firm's rising star, a partner sixteen years her senior. The affair had been torrid, some of the best sex she'd ever had, and definitely the best sex he'd ever had.

It had ended abruptly when he'd been tagged by several of Seattle's business leaders, and the party's chief power broker, to be the next U.S. senator from the state of Washington. Her entire image of him changed almost overnight when the wimp didn't even have the guts to break it off with her himself.

He'd scheduled a lunch with her and in his place his mother, of all people, showed up. He was married, of course, with two children. Important people had already ponied up large sums of money, the announcement had already been made, the race was underway, and the party needed to win. The old dragon had told her that she was not the first and probably wouldn't be the last woman her son would have a dalliance with. It seemed that her son, like his grandfather, which was where all the money came from, had a problem keeping his organ in his pants. The matriarch of the family had hinted at some sort of financial compensation while she picked at her salad. Peggy had dismissed the offer without hesitation. She may have been naïve at the time, but she still had her pride.

By the time their main course was served, Peggy had recovered enough to state assuredly that she had no desire to see herself dragged down in a scandal that might ruin her career. No one, other than her son's opponent, would gain by the information being made public, so a deal of a different kind was made, a deal to ensure that Peggy Stealey's star would continue to rise.

And it had. Still in her thirties, Stealey was now the deputy assistant attorney general in charge of counter-terrorism, and she was standing before the man whose job she planned on someday having. She listened to the attorney general's phone conversation long enough to ascertain that he was talking to neither the president nor his wife, and then made a very stern gesture for him to hang up the phone.

Attorney General Martin Stokes frowned at his subordinate, but did as she wished and cut the director of the FBI off in mid-sentence. Stokes knew Stealey well enough to know that it would not be out of character for her to reach across his desk and end the call herself. He sometimes wondered why he put up with her, but he already knew the answer. Stealey was smart and motivated, and she got things done. She'd given him great advice over the years, whether he wanted to hear it or not, and for that she was invaluable.

Sycophants were as common in politics as lawyers, and in that sense Peggy Stealey's straightforward approach was refreshing. She was like a violent spring thunderstorm: You could see her coming, your excitement and fear growing with the anticipation of the awesome spectacle that was about to commence. If the storm blew through quickly, it was a rather enjoyable experience. The brief downpour cleaned things up and the lightning turned the grass that rich shade of green. But if it hovered or stalled, basements were flooded, trees were toppled, and personal property was damaged.

That was Peggy Stealey. If she dispensed her insightful opinions with brevity, it could be a rather pleasant thing to experience, but if she decided to really unload, it was like a destructive storm; at some point it was a good idea to stop watching and go hide in the basement.

Stokes put the handset back in the cradle and hoped this would be brief. Before he could ask what was on her mind, she started in.

"This Patriot Act is a *fucking* disaster!" She chopped her hand through the air as if she was about to cut his desk in half. "And if you're still holding on to that fantasy of yours that you're going to occupy the White House someday, you'd better get your shit together and figure out that it makes you look like a Goddamn fascist. And in case you haven't noticed, Americans don't elect fascists . . . at least not Demo-cratic fascists."

There it was. She'd got it all out in one breath. On the surface he agreed with much of what she said, except the last part. With the exclusion of the nationalistic component, the Democrats had their fair share of fascist tendencies, but right now that wasn't important. Tropical storm Peggy was in his office and she looked like she could grow into a hurricane any second if he didn't do something.

Nodding he said, "Your timing couldn't be better. I've been sweating over what's going to happen when one of these cases gets kicked up to the Supreme Court."

"Happen?" She scoffed. "They're going to pull down our pants and spank our asses until our butt cheeks are fire engine red, and then the entire legal community is going to stand up and cheer, and then you can kiss the White House good-bye."

She liked to beat him over the head with the White House thing. She knew it got his attention. Stokes didn't bother asking her to sit. In a calm but firm voice he asked, "What do you think we should do?"

With that, she was off again, a six-foot-tall blond-haired, blue-eyed Teutonic goddess, karate-chopping the air with one hand and then the other, expressing herself with efficient, forceful, clipped precision. This was when she really turned him on, when his thoughts returned to having sex with her, but it was not to be. He'd made one foolish effort to try and rekindle their affair after he'd been safely elected senator. Her response had been swift and definite. She'd delivered a blow to his solar plexus that had left him curled up on the floor like an infant.

FOUR

D r. Irene Kennedy stood off to the side and watched as the photographers clicked away. It was a beautiful spring day in the capital. Normally she would have enjoyed the ride into the city from McLean, but not this morning. Her crack of dawn meeting with Rapp, combined with some other things she knew, had her worried. Waiting idly for the president to finish his photo op wasn't helping, but there wasn't much she could do. An antsy, stressed-out director of the CIA was not the type of thing the White House Press Corps should see.

The official start of summer was a week away, and the president was in an extremely good mood. He was posing for a photo with WWII veterans, members of the Congressional leadership, and two of Hollywood's most influential stars. They were all gathered in the Rose Garden to kick off a week of festivities that would lead up to the dedication of the new WWII memorial on the National Mall on Saturday.

Veterans groups had been struggling for decades to get the monument built, and they'd had almost no success until the big hitters from Hollywood had gotten on board. With star power attached to the cause, the politicians in D.C. lined up to get on board, and now they were marching in a very patriotic lockstep toward the dedication ceremony.

The cheerful weather and festive mood only served to heighten Kennedy's sense of foreboding. As the director of the Central Intelligence Agency, Kennedy was always privy to information that made it difficult for her to take a joyous outlook on life. And now something was about to happen, and she and her people didn't have a clue as to what it was. The warning bells started to go off on Friday of the previous week. At first there was a spike in phone and e-mail intercepts hinting that something big was in the works, and then there were some strange trends in the financial and currency markets, and then Rapp showed up in her office confirming her worst fears—that al-Qaeda had something in the works. Something that involved a bomb. How big a bomb they didn't know, but they needed to find out quick.

Kennedy had been tracking terrorists for over twenty years. She had developed a sense for when things were about to happen, and this was one of those times. It had been too quiet for the last six months. The remnants of al-Qaeda had been regrouping and were on the move. What they were up to specifically, Kennedy did not know, but she feared the worst. Her team needed more to go on and they needed it quick, or she and the rest of the country would find out the hard way.

The director of the CIA checked her watch and kept her composure. The photo op was already fifteen minutes over schedule, and although Kennedy didn't show it, her nerves were frayed. If her deepest fears were true, they needed to move quickly. More than anything, though, they needed additional information and a lucky break, and they weren't going to get either sitting in Washington collecting satellite intercepts. She needed to get the president alone so he could sign off on Rapp's plan and get the Pentagon involved.

Kennedy relaxed slightly as the president's press secretary stepped in and told the photographers that the event was over. She stood patiently while the president shook some hands and thanked everybody for coming out. Like almost all politicians at this level President Hayes was very good at making people feel appreciated. He laughed, slapped a few shoulders, and then waved good-bye as he walked up the lawn toward the Oval Office.

As he approached Kennedy his expression turned a bit more serious. Not wanting to discuss anything outside, he simply said, "Aren't you a little early this morning, Irene?"

"Yes, sir."

Hayes frowned. He doubted she was here to report good news. He continued up the slight slope and waved for her to join him.

Kennedy hesitated for a second and looked past the president in search of his chief of staff. She was pleased to see her hanging back in order to bask a while longer in the aura of two Hollywood big hitters. Valerie Jones and Rapp couldn't stand each other. Kennedy had little doubt that, given the opportunity, Jones would use every ounce of influence to dissuade her boss from signing off on the operative's aggressive plan.

Kennedy followed the president into his office past the Secret Service agent standing post by the door. Hayes walked straight to his desk and looked at his schedule. After a moment he asked, "How much time do you need?"

"Fifteen minutes . . . uninterrupted."

Hayes nodded thoughtfully. Kennedy was not the type of person to waste his time. He pressed the intercom button on his phone and said, "Betty, I need fifteen minutes."

"Yes, Mr. President."

Hayes came out from behind his desk and walked across the office. He unbuttoned his suit coat and sat on one of the couches by the fireplace. Looking up at the director of the Central Intelligence Agency he said, "Let's hear the bad news."

Kennedy sat next to him and brushed a strand of brown hair behind her ear. "As you know since 9/11 we've developed some fairly elaborate statistical models for tracking certain economic indicators. We've identified key banks, brokerage houses, and financial services institutions that handle money we have reason to believe is linked to terrorism. In addition to that our Echelon system tracks millions of e-mails and phone calls on a daily basis. Due to the sheer volume of data that we're talking about, and the fact that much of it is encrypted, we're not able to track these trends real-time."

"What's the lag?" asked the president.

"The financial trends we usually have a pretty good handle on by the end of the business day, but Echelon intercepts can sometime take a week to decipher, and then up to a month to translate. Although if we're targeting a specific e-mail account or phone number, the information can be decrypted and translated in near real-time."

"So what have you noticed that has given you cause to worry?"

"It started at the end of Friday with the financials.

The first trend we picked up on was the price of gold closing up four dollars and twenty-six cents. This by itself is nothing to get alarmed about, but the next trend we noticed was that the dollar closed down eight cents. The Dow was off by fifty-six and the Nasdaq closed down sixteen. None of this on the face of it is an unusual day in the financial markets, but when we began to look at the specific institutions that we think have ties to terrorism . . . some unsettling trends showed up."

Kennedy pulled a piece of paper from a folder and handed it to the president. She pointed to the first line with her pen. "The jump in gold was started by a bank in Kuwait that sold two hundred eighty million dollars in U.S. stocks and bonds and dumped all of it into Swiss gold. Over the weekend we discovered four other accounts at various institutions that had liquidated their U.S. investments and purchased gold. Those accounts represented nearly two hundred million dollars."

The president studied the sheet of paper. "What are the chances that all five of these accounts are getting the same financial advice?"

"It is a remote possibility, but it assumes that there is a respected financial advisor out there who would suggest a wholesale conversion of assets at a time when there are no economic indicators that would necessitate such a drastic move. My people tell me the chance of this is extremely unlikely."

Hayes frowned at the sheet of paper. "So that gets us back to the fact that five flagged accounts all placed bets last Friday that the U.S. economy is about to take a hit."

"Correct," nodded Kennedy. "In addition, we also discovered another handful of smaller flagged accounts that made similar but less drastic moves."

Hayes stared at the sheet of paper, reading the various names and countries. "Anything else?"

"Yes." She cleared her throat. "Mitch has come across some very valuable intel." From her bag Kennedy retrieved the file that Rapp had given her only hours ago. She laid it on the glass coffee table that sat between the two couches and opened it to display a sheet with the faces of five bearded men on it. "I know you've been shown these photos before, but to refresh your memory they are all on the FBI's most wanted list. They represent what we think is the reconstituted leadership of al-Qaeda."

Kennedy flipped the page, revealing a map of the Afghanistan-Pakistan border. "For the last six months we have been tracking several of these individuals as they've traveled through the mountainous region of Pakistan. A few weeks ago two of them met up in Gulistan." Kennedy pointed to the city on the map. "From there they were tracked to a small village eighteen miles to the west."

She turned the page again, to a satellite photo that showed a village of approximately one hundred dwellings plus outbuildings. The town was spread out along the base of the mountain with one main road leading in and several cutting across the axis. "The village has been watched day and night for the last five days. Yesterday this convoy pulled into town."

A new image appeared, showing eight pickup trucks and several SUVs. Four of the pickups had large anti-aircraft guns mounted in the beds, and all of them were overflowing with heavily armed men. "Four hours ago we had a high-altitude reconnaissance drone circling at forty thousand feet, and we were lucky enough to get the following pictures. These three individuals getting out of the trucks we believe to be Hassan Izz-al-Din, Abdullah Ahmed Abdullah, and Ali Saed al-Houri."

The president picked up the black-and-white photograph and stared at the three faces circled in red. These reconnaissance photos were rarely completely clear to him, but he knew there was a small army of analysts and a supercomputer that somehow made sense of it all.

"All of them had a hand in 9/11," Kennedy added.

The president took a second hard look at the photograph. "You're sure these are the same men?"

"Mitch has an asset in the region who told him this meeting would be taking place."

Hayes set the photo down and took off his reading glasses. "They're in this village right now?"

"Yes, sir."

The president grinned. "So I assume you want me to call General Musharraf and get him to go clean out this rat's nest."

Kennedy shook her head emphatically. "Absolutely not, sir. General Musharraf is a good man, but he has too many radical fundamentalists in his government . . . especially up in the tribal areas, to trust with something this important. Mitch thinks that the second we bring the Pakistanis in, these men will be alerted and disappear into the mountains."

The president suddenly saw where she was going and his demeanor turned cautious. "Are you suggesting we handle this *without* talking to the Pakistanis?"

"That's correct, sir."

"And what am I to tell General Musharraf when he calls to find out what American troops are doing conducting operations in his country without his permission?"

Hayes had known Kennedy, though, he'd never heard her talk like this.

He took in a deep breath and then said, "You have my approval, but tell Mitch to get in and out as quickly as possible. I'd like to be able to play this off as a border skirmish rather than a full-blown operation."

FIVE

LOS ANGELES

The Qantas 747-400 floated downward, flaps extended, its four powerful General Electric engines throttled almost all the way back. The tarmac at LAX shimmered in the May heat as planes maneuvered to and from the gates picking up and disgorging passengers. From the air it looked like absolute chaos to Imtaz Zubair. In the upper business-class cabin he closed his eyes and silently muttered the word *Alhumdulillah* over and over to himself. The phrase meant, *Praise be to God,* and was part of a *tasbihs,* or Muslim rosary. They had taken his beads away from him, so he rubbed his thumb and forefinger together as if he was holding the well-worn, dark wooden instrument of prayer in his hand. They had told him to show no signs of his faith in public until he had completed his mission, but he could not help himself.

Zubair was a wreck, a ball of frayed nerves with a stomach full of bubbling acid that had resulted in a scorching pyrosis. Even though he was a man of science, he hated flying. His education was rooted in the comforting, ordered logic of mathematics and physics, but it failed him here. Wing mass created lift, engines provided thrust, and planes flew. It was all proven theory, and it was applied thousands of times all over the world every day, but the scientist still fretted. He couldn't accept it, and so he tucked it away deep down with all of his other phobias.

When one of his bosses had told him once that he needed to seek therapy, Zubair had been deeply offended. He was a genius; he knew things, sensed things that very few people could even attempt to grasp. Who was to say that his phobias weren't simply caused by a heightened sense of awareness and a deep understanding of the universe and his relationship with Allah? Zubair suspected things. He talked to God and looked into the future. His role in the battle for his religion was one of great importance. He'd never discussed this with his fellow scientists, for they were too one-dimensional. Religion was a farce to them, a way for simple people to cope with their mundane lives. But not to Zubair; science was proof to him that his God existed. Such magnificence could only have been created by his God.

The touchdown was so gentle that Zubair didn't even realize they were on the ground until the front landing gear was rolling along the tarmac, and the large plane began to slow. He opened his eyes and looked out the window, relieved they were out of the sky. With a smile on his face he muttered a quick prayer of thanks. Unfortunately, his calm didn't last long. As the plane neared its gate, Zubair's smile vanished and his thoughts turned to his next obstacle.

Imtaz Zubair's native country had forsaken him, so he had returned the favor. A math prodigy, Zubair was educated at Pakistan's finest schools and then sent on to Canada and China for his postgraduate work. He was on the path to greatness. Even Dr. A. Q. Khan, the man who had developed and tested Pakistan's first nuclear

45

bomb, had told him that he was the brightest star of his generation of Pakistani scientists. Zubair thought his skills alone would carry him to his chosen field, but they had not.

He found that politics and family connections were more important, and that his deep devotion to his religion created jealousy among his peers. He did not deny the fact that he lacked even the most basic social skills, but to his mind genius was what mattered, not one's ability to politic. Still, they had all turned against him and conspired to deny him his dream of working with Dr. Khan.

He'd still held out hope that his personal relationship with Dr. Khan would carry the day, but those hopes died the day General Musharraf and his band of military officers seized power in a bloodless coup. Musharraf was a secular pig and a lapdog of the Americans. Bowing to pressure from his patrons, Musharraf set about to cleanse true believers from the Pakistani nuclear scientific community.

Zubair had been one of the first to go, exiled to the dreadful Chasnupp nuclear power plant in Central Pakistan, where he was worked like a dog seventy, sometimes eighty hours a week. With his dreams dashed he grew increasingly bitter. He was near his breaking point when providence intervened. A messenger from Allah traveled to the remote region for the sole purpose of contacting him. He was leaving his ramshackle mosque one Friday afternoon when the robed visitor had come to him as if he were the angel Gabriel himself. Allah had a mission of great importance for Zubair, and he was to leave with the stranger immediately.

It had been the beginning of a pilgrimage that had taken him to Iran and the Caspian Sea, Kazakhstan, and a poisonous desert, and then on to Southeast Asia, Australia, and now America. He was not a worldly man, but as with all of the difficulties in his life, the stresses of travel had brought him closer to Allah. He had witnessed firsthand the decadence of the secular world, and it comforted him that his cause was just.

The plane rolled to a stop, and almost instantly Zubair felt the resumption of his stomach's volcanic action. A film of sweat appeared on his forehead and upper lip. The scientist mopped his brow and then his upper lip with a handkerchief. He felt naked without his mustache, but they had made him shave that also. They wanted him to assimilate, to blend in as much as possible. His hair was cut short and styled for the first time in his life. His glasses had been replaced with contacts, and they had purchased for him a new set of clothes and expensive Tumi luggage in Australia.

The passengers began standing, opening compartments and gathering their things. Afraid to move and give away his nervousness, Zubair was in no hurry. Once most of the other passengers were gone, he retrieved his computer bag and made his way down the narrow stairs to the main body of the plane. He half expected to see a group of men in suits waiting for him, but thankfully there were none. He'd been warned that the Americans had gotten much better at intercepting people who were trying to illegally enter their country.

Two female flight attendants with whorish makeup and skirts that were far too short stood by the door. They thanked him for flying Qantas. Despite what his trainers had told him, Zubair ignored the women, refusing to look them in the eye. Fortunately for him his diminutive stature made him seem shy rather than hostile. Zubair was just five and a half feet tall, and weighed a svelte 142 pounds. With his mustache shaved he easily passed for someone five to ten years younger than his twenty-nine years.

He stepped into the Jetway, joining the stampede for baggage claim and customs and sandwiched between the business-class and economy customers. The stress of the situation and the heat of the enclosed Jetway triggered the scientist's sweat glands, sending them into overdrive. Within seconds salty perspiration dampened every inch of his skin.

Zubair felt trapped, as if he was on a conveyor belt headed toward his own execution. There was no turning back. Passengers continued to pour off the plane, pushing forward, moving through the confined tunnel toward U.S. Customs agents who would ask probing questions. Zubair suddenly wished he had taken the sedative that they had given him to calm his nerves. He had thrown the pills away at the Sydney airport. Allah would never approve of him taking a mood-altering drug. Now he desperately wished he'd kept the little pills, just to get him through this part.

They left the Jetway and at least for a moment things got better. The extra space and cooler air of the terminal felt less confining. The stampede of people continued down a set of stairs to a boxed-in area where they began to cue up in multiple lines to present passports and port of entry/declaration forms to U.S. Customs agents. Zubair got in one of the lines being handled by a man. As long as he had the choice he would not deal with a woman.

When it was his turn he stepped up to the counter, his wheeled black carry-on bag in tow, and handed the agent his passport and paperwork. The man eyed the passport first, flipping through several pages to see where the visitor had been over the past few years.

"First time to America?"

"Yes," Zubair answered with his accented English.

"How long have you been an Australian citizen?"

"Three years."

"And your occupation?" The agent flipped through the paperwork for verification.

"I'm a computer programmer."

"Purpose of your visit?" the man asked in a no-nonsense tone.

Zubair couldn't believe his luck. So far the man hadn't even bothered to look at him. "I'm here for business."

"Traveling alone?"

"Yes."

The agent stamped the passport and handed it back to Zubair, for the first time giving him a good look and noticing the beads of perspiration on his upper lip and forehead. "Are you feeling all right?"

"Ah . . . yes," answered Zubair, mopping his brow with his handkerchief. "I just don't like to travel."

The Customs agent studied him for a moment longer. He then handed Zubair his passport and paperwork with his right hand, and with his left, he pressed a button letting his colleagues in the watch room know that he had someone they should run through the facial recognition system. It was nothing alarming. Just a standard precaution.

Zubair took his documents and proceeded to the baggage carousel where his one piece of luggage with its bright orange business-class tag was already waiting for him. He grabbed the bag and went to the next checkpoint where he was met by a woman several inches taller than him.

She gestured for him to go the right and said, "Please place your bags on the table and remove any locks."

Zubair did as he was told, with the sickening feeling that he was about to be discovered. He'd been told there was a good chance that they would ask him to open his bags, but there were others who were being allowed to pass by this checkpoint without any inspection at all. Why couldn't he be one of them?

He stood nervously as the woman began looking through each compartment of his two cases. He reminded himself that there was nothing for her to find. The only items that could implicate him were several encrypted files on his laptop, but they would need someone from their notorious National Security Agency to decipher those. After several minutes the woman closed the bags and told Zubair he was free to go.

Astonished, Zubair grabbed his bags and handed his paperwork to another agent. The man then gestured for him to leave the secure area. Zubair placed his passport in his pocket, and looked down the long hallway in front of him. Up ahead he could see daylight. As he wheeled his bags down the hallway he could barely believe he'd made it through customs. Giddy with excitement he quickened his pace. He'd defeated the gauntlet of American security, and there was nothing they could do to stop him now. He was free to roam America and do his work. *Youmud Deen,* the day of judgment, was fast approaching, and Zubair would strike a mighty blow for Islam.

SIX

Four super-quiet MH-6 Little Bird helicopters wound their way through the craggy canyon at seventy miles per hour in near total darkness. Sixteen of the most highly trained and seasoned soldiers the world had ever seen rode two on each side of the small agile helicopters, their scuffed and worn combat boots dangling in the cool mountain air, their eyes protected by clear goggles. The uniforms varied slightly; some wore flight suits, while others had chosen the desert camouflage version of the U.S. army's standard battle dress, or BDUs. They all wore body armor, knee and elbow pads, and a specialized cut-down helmet with night-vision goggles affixed in a pop-down pop-up mode.

They carried an arsenal of weapons, ranging from pistols, to shotguns, to sniping rifles, to light and heavy machine guns. None of them had bothered to bring silencers. Their presence would be known within seconds of their arrival, and once they hit the ground there was a chance they'd need every extra bullet and grenade they could carry. They were heading directly into the thick of things.

The nimble helicopters ducked and bucked their way

through the cool mountain air like some sadistic amusement park ride, but the men sitting on the specially designed platforms were used to it. They were miles away from civilization in a foreign land that was among the most desolate and inhospitable places on earth, and every last one of them was eagerly anticipating the battle that lay ahead.

A voice crackled over their earpieces announcing that they were one minute out from the target. In the resulting flurry of activity, optic rifle sights, red laser dot pointers, and night-vision goggles, or NVGs, were turned on, gear was shifted, and those who weren't already cocked and locked did so.

The pilots had warned all the men in the premission briefing what would happen next. The helicopters banked sharply around a turn in the mountain pass and accelerated into a steep dive, hugging the terrain as the face of the mountain gave way to a valley approximately 3,000 feet below.

The isolated village rushed up to meet them. There was no sign of life at this early hour. The pilot in the lead chopper marked the target and began to pull up while the other three Little Birds continued their ground-hugging ride in a race against the clock to deliver their deadly warriors before the enemy could respond and put up a fight.

GENERAL KEVIN HARLEY focused intently on the grainy screen before him. He had three to choose from, but for now his attention was on the middle one. The other two screens wouldn't have anything important on them for another minute or so. The four helicopters came into view at precisely the expected moment. Harley watched as the Little Birds decreased speed and broke formation. Three of them hugged the deck while the fourth gained altitude. It was hard to tell from looking at his screen since the image was being shot by a small reconnaissance drone circling 10,000 feet above the village, but it was Harley's battle plan and he knew every minute detail.

General Harley was wearing a bulky in-flight headset so he could communicate with his people over the loud General Electric engines growling just a few feet above his head. In the thin mountain air the engines had to work extra hard to keep the command-and-control bird from dropping like the 12,000-pound stone that it was. The UH-60 Blackhawk was aglow in a wash of modern circuitry and flat-screen monitors. The floor of the bird was covered with bulletproof Kevlar panels, and each man wore a flak vest, even though their intent was to stay out of the action in order to orchestrate the modern military ballet from above. The advanced airborne command-and-control bird had become a second home to five of the six men strapped into the troop compartment.

Several of them had been stationed in Afghanistan for nearly two years logging countless hours at their airborne consoles. They'd hunted al-Qaeda members, the Taliban, drug dealers, and bandits—anyone who tried to undermine the authority of the new U.S.-backed government, but most of all they hunted al-Qaeda.

Members of al-Qaeda were at the top of these soldiers' lists, the rightful targets of genuine retribution and hatred. To a man, their reasons were both personal and patriotic. While their fellow Americans went on with their lives, these Special Forces operators were on the other side of the planet stoically settling a score. To refer to them as simple vigilantes would be an insult to their level of sophistication and training, but even they would admit that they were on a mission of revenge. They were here to send a very clear message that America would not tolerate the slaughter of 3,000 of its citizens.

The sixth passenger in the troop compartment was an outsider, but a welcome one, and a man they all respected. Mitch Rapp had heard of this outfit before. Men and women from the CIA's Directorate of Operations (DO) would return from Afghanistan and tell stories about Task Force 11, an amalgamation of Special Forces bad-asses from the various branches of the U.S. military. They were well funded, well equipped, exquisitely trained, highly motivated, and feared by anyone with enough sense to understand that they were quite possibly the most seasoned, potent, mobile fighting force in action today.

The DO operatives, no shrinking violets themselves, were in awe of the bravado and skill this group brought to bear against the enemy. Their fighting spirit was buoyed by the knowledge that their abilities as a unit were unmatched, they feared no one, and held nothing back, for their enemy only understood one thing— brute force. Their kill ratio was off the charts. Having lost only a handful of men since their deployment, they had done serious damage to their enemies, inflicting casualties in the thousands.

The task force had operated in relative anonymity until someone in Washington decided the PR was too much to pass up. Their accomplishments were leaked, and after that the job had gotten a little more difficult. Reporters began nosing around, wanting to know how the group operated. Politicians and Pentagon officials wanted briefings, and a few even made the effort to travel to Afghanistan.

All of it was a distraction from Task Force 11's mission. Fortunately for the group, everyone's attention soon shifted to Iraq. Shortly after the war started an innocuous statement was released by the Pentagon stating that Task Force 11 was being disbanded. A few of their assets were actually transferred to the new theater of war, enough to give credibility to the story but not enough to harm the group's effectiveness. With the attention of the world focused elsewhere, Afghanistan turned into the perfect place for the Special Forces to hone their skills—and General Harley and his men had done exactly that.

Rapp had never met the general before, but the two clicked almost immediately. As soon as Kennedy had given him the go-ahead, Rapp was on the phone to the Joint Special Operations Command telling them what he needed. By the time he landed in Afghanistan, Harley and his men were ready to go. Harley was skeptical of Rapp's plans at first. He'd been in Southwest Asia for the better part of two years and had been rebuffed so many times for asking to cross the border into Pakistan that his superiors back at MacDill Air Force Base told him to cease and desist, or he'd be reassigned.

Rapp suspected that sometime between his departure from Washington and arrival in Kandahar, Harley had realized that this was probably going to be his one and only chance to set foot in Pakistan. The operation that Harley had drawn up for him was far more than a simple snatch and grab—it was a full-blown assault. Rapp had been involved in enough of these types of operations to understand that it was never a bad idea to take into account what the military commander thought was the best way to crack a nut, but he'd been thinking of something smaller, something less complex. Harley's plan was neither. It involved a force five times what Rapp had imagined and it was absolutely ballsy.

The Special Forces community, more than any other asset in the American military, was forced to constantly refine their abilities and strategies. They looked for ways to either avoid repeating mistakes or to minimize the effect of things they could not control. This zeal to avoid repeating the mistakes of those who had gone into battle before them meant that no single modern engagement had been analyzed more thoroughly than the incident in Somalia in 1993 where nineteen Army Rangers and Delta Force operators were killed in a daytime raid that had spun disastrously out of control. There wasn't a special forces commander on active duty who hadn't studied every last detail of that Mogadishu operation, and they'd all come away with the same conclusion: never operate during daylight if you don't have to, and if you're not sure what you're up against, don't go in without close air support, or armor, or both.

For political reasons the close air support that Harley wanted to bring along wasn't an option. They were supposed to get in and out without alerting the Pakistanis, and if Harley brought in an AC-130U Spooky gunship it would immediately be picked up by radar. The mountainous terrain and the brevity of the mission dictated that armor also was not an option. That left General Harley in the difficult position of trying to launch a helicopter assault into a hostile village numbering approximately 1,000 people without armor and without fixed-wing close air support. And this wasn't just any village. According to intelligence reports from the CIA and the Defense Intelligence Agency, this was an al-Qaeda stronghold. These people were not going to simply hide in their huts and wait for the Americans to leave. They would put up a serious fight.

General Harley's solution to the problem at first seemed a bit much to Rapp, but as the general walked him through each element of his plan, Rapp began to see the true tactical genius behind it. Kennedy had gone to the president and received permission to launch a covert strike across the border into Pakistan. General Harley had decided to use the broadest definition of the word *strike,* looking at this operation as his one and only chance to clean out a vipers' nest, and Rapp wasn't about to stand in his way.

SEVEN

Ali Saed al-Houri was sleeping peacefully for a change. He was only in his mid-fifties, but he had endured an incredibly hard life. With his stooped posture, his limp, and his graying beard he was often mistaken for someone much older. He was Egyptian by birth but no longer claimed that part of his ancestry. Al-Houri was a Muslim, and Allah had no borders. Nationality was for pagans, and al-Houri was a true man of God.

One of the original members of the Egyptian Muslim Brotherhood, al-Houri had been imprisoned twice by his government and brutally tortured by the Mukhabarat, or the Egyptian secret police. This was the source of his limp and of his nightmares. Al-Houri had been implicated in the assassination of Egyptian President Anwar Sadat, and in the subsequent crack-down he was rounded up along with hundreds of other members of the Muslim Brotherhood and tortured mercilessly.

They all broke eventually. Some of them told the truth, others said anything to stop the pain, and there were a lucky few who died due to mistakes made by overzealous and inexperienced torturers. Several of his fellow captives went insane and there were a weak few who left the cause, but there were many more, like al-Houri, who grew closer to Allah.

Sitting alone in his filthy cell, with no bed, blanket, or pillow, he sweated his way through the days, too tired to brush away the flies that pestered his battered body, and shivered his way through the chilly nights. During this excruciating state of physical and mental anguish, al-Houri had grown to understand his God on a truly mystical plane. Allah had spoken to him and told him what must be done.

Islam was under assault, yet again. And this time it was not by conventional armies. The West was waging a coward's war using technology and commerce to eat away at the very fabric of the Islamic faith. They were poisoning the minds of Muslim children and leading them astray. The Arab people were in the midst of another holy war, and they didn't even know it. It was al-Houri's mission to spread the word, to pick up the sword in defense of his people, his religion, and his way of life and to protect them all against the infidel.

The torture, the hardship, the expulsion from his place of birth, the last two years on the run, were all worth it. Al-Houri and his people were about to strike a mighty blow for Islam. This was the thought that comforted him as he slept. Allah had given them a great gift. Very soon America would pay for its colonialism and corruption of the children of Allah.

Al-Houri was not normally a sound sleeper, but he found the remoteness and fresh air of this mountain village refreshing. He'd traveled here frequently over the past half year, and this quiet town had turned into his base of operations for what was to be the greatest attack ever launched against America. Al-Houri had split his time between the village and the dirty and overpopulated city of Quetta, the capital of Pakistan's southwestern Balochistan Province. Whenever he came to the village he would dream of the noises the city made. There was a faint rumbling in the distance. In his dream al-Houri couldn't quite place it. Was it a train? The noise continued to grow until it was punctuated by several louder cracks.

Al-Houri's eyes snapped open, and he struggled to focus. He began to sit up, his body still stiff from sleep. The wind was howling outside, buffeting the house, whipping dirt and pebbles into the air, peppering the small bedroom window. Was a storm upon them? There was another noise, eerily familiar, but not loud enough to be that of his worst fear.

Then came a noise he knew all too well, the distinctive sound of an AK-47 machine gun firing on full automatic. The burst was followed by several quieter pops. As another few precious seconds ticked away al-Houri shook the sleep from his brain and realized what was happening. He looked to the bedroom door, urging it to burst open. Closing his eyes, he whispered the name of his bodyguard Ahmed. The Afghani had been a loyal servant for seven years. His orders were specific. Al-Houri knew too much. They could not allow him to be captured alive.

There was a muted explosion followed by a thunderous bang from the other room. Light flashed under the crack at the bottom of the door and more guns joined the battle. Al-Houri cursed himself for having been lulled into a false sense of security in this isolated village. How could this have happened? There were many believers in the Pakistani military and government. They would have risked their lives to alert him to such treachery. He continued to stare at the door, praying his bodyguard would burst forth at any moment. Where was Ahmed?

Finally, the door to the bedroom opened with a crash. As if Allah had answered his prayers, it was Ahmed and not some American mercenary. Ahmed had his weathered Kalashnikov in his hands and was lifting the muzzle, a pained expression on his face, his eyes filled with dread over carrying out his sworn duty.

Al-Houri smiled in relief at the man who had become a son to him. He closed his eyes and welcomed his death and destiny knowing that the Americans themselves were about to be dealt a mortal blow.

EIGHT

The four helicopters had swooped down on the sleepy village like predatory hawks, making little more noise than a strong gust of wind. Thirty-two well worn boots had dangled in the air, eagerly waiting to touch the ground. As they had passed over the flat rooftops of the dark village each man looked through his night vision goggles for potential targets. From the lack of activity below it appeared they'd caught the enemy by surprise.

Approximately one hundred yards from the target they came under fire. A Delta Trooper dangling from the first Little Bird dispatched the guard with two quick shots from his M4A1 carbine. Seconds later two of the Little Birds landed in front of the target, their flexible landing skids carving fresh tracks into the dirt road. A third landed behind the target, and the fourth and final bird came in more slowly to drop its troopers on the roof.

Master Sergeant Todd Corrigan was in charge of the sixteen-man assault platoon. The stocky thirty-four-year-old Corrigan was an eight-year veteran of Delta Force. Before joining Delta he'd done two tours with the famed 101st Airborne Division. He was one of the most respected and decorated NCOs in the entire armed forces. Tonight General Harley was relying heavily on Corrigan and his men. The sixteen troopers were being dropped into the middle of a hostile environment where they were guaranteed to draw heavy enemy fire.

As soon as his bird touched down, Corrigan yanked free his Velcro restraint and was off, his weapon up and trained on his specific area of responsibility. His men all moved swiftly into their preplanned positions without uttering a word. All sixteen of the soldiers were able to talk via a secure internal radio link consisting of an earpiece and lip mike, but any communication was to be kept to an absolute minimum.

The Little Birds did not loiter. They were too vulnerable on the ground, so as soon as the shooters were clear each bird increased power and climbed back into the dark night, kicking up a maelstrom of dust and rocks.

The team's demo man rushed to the front of the target house and slapped two thin adhesive ribbon charges on the front door. He carefully linked them together with a loop of orange Primadet cord and stepped back, pressing his body up against the wall. "Breaching charge ready."

Corrigan listened as the other two elements of his team checked in and then gave the thumbs up signal to his door breacher.

"Fire in the hole!"

The eight troopers in front of the house lowered their heads as the charges were tripped, blowing the wooden door off its hinges. The point man already had the pin on his flash-bang grenade pulled and wasted no time. He chucked the pyrotechnic through the open, smoking doorway and yelled, "Flash-bang away!"

Every trooper sealed his eyes shut in anticipation of the blinding white hot light of the grenade. At the sound of the thunderous explosion the team moved, storming the house in a well-orchestrated maneuver. The point man entered the house first and immediately swept the room to the right as the second man came in and swept it to the left. Both men found tangos and let loose a single round, striking their targets in the head. The third man pressed through the doorway with Corrigan right on his heels. They went straight for the back of the house not knowing the exact layout, but assuming that's where the bedrooms would be.

A man came out of a room on the left with a rifle in his hand and let go a poorly aimed burst. The trooper in front of Corrigan hit the man with two rounds in the face and they both kept moving. As the trooper peeled off into the open doorway that the gunman had come out of Corrigan moved quickly for the back of the house knowing that four more of his troopers were right behind him, and that the other two elements were covering the back of the house and the street. The only hope they had of getting live prisoners was to take the building down fast.

At the end of the hallway a man crossed from one room to another. Corrigan squeezed off a burst and kept moving. He wasn't sure if he'd hit his mark or not. Assured that his back was covered he ran down the hallway and swung his weapon into the room where the man had just gone. Looking through the narrow tunnel of his night-vision goggles, Corrigan was surprised to find the man with his back to him and standing only a few feet away. He had his weapon raised in the firing position. Without hesitation the master sergeant sent a

When he entered the steakhouse, there was a flurry of activity. Holmes was tall, just under six and a half feet, and in relatively good shape, considering how much he liked food and drink. He was in his early fifties with a slight double chin and a bit of gut that was well disguised by tailored dress shirts and handmade suits.

The ass kissing ensued almost immediately. The general manager was on hand at the front of the restaurant as well as the head chef, the wine steward, and a buxom blond hostess who was Holmes's favorite. It was nothing for Holmes to drop five or ten grand in an evening. He liked his wine and he liked it expensive.

"Patrick," the general manager thrust his hand forward, "thank you for gracing us with your presence."

"My pleasure, David." Holmes had a gift for remembering people's names. He said hello to the other two men and then gave the hostess a big hug and a kiss on the cheek.

"Still only two of you tonight?" asked the general manager.

"Yes, in fact here comes my dinner partner right now."

Peggy Stealey came walking across the bar in high-heel shoes, chic black pants, and a sapphire blouse. She held a glass of chardonnay in one hand and her purse in the other. Her blond hair was pulled back in a ponytail that called attention to her high cheekbones and aqua blue eyes. Practically every guy in the place stopped what he was doing and watched her move across the room.

Holmes extended his hands and placed them on her cheeks, as Stealey pursed her lips and offered them to the chairman of the Democratic National Committee. Holmes gave her mouth a quick peck and then turned to make sure his guest had met everyone. She had, on at least three other occasions, but it didn't bother her that Holmes didn't remember. It was his nature to bring people together as part of the Pat Holmes festival of life. He befriended everyone from the busboys to the president. Holmes loved people and they loved him back.

The hostess led them to Holmes's usual table. It offered just enough privacy while still affording the chairman a good view of the restaurant. Along the way Holmes slapped backs, shook hands, said hello to a few of the wait staff, and introduced Stealey to several lobbyists.

The man did not know how to have a bad time. People were drawn to him. There were some, for sure, who disagreed with his party of choice and thought him a bit gluttonous, but his champions far outweighed his detractors. Holmes was a breath of fresh air for a party that was desperately in need of new ideas and new leadership. Unfortunately, that was not why he'd been pegged to oversee the upcoming national election. First, and foremost, running the DNC was about raising money, and Holmes had both New York and L.A. covered. Secondly, it was about settling disputes and massaging egos, and there were no bigger egos than the ones on Capitol Hill. Holmes knew how to make people feel valuable. Lastly, the job involved kicking some ass, and although Holmes was a pretty level-headed guy, he was results-oriented and if you didn't get him what he wanted he showed you the door.

Holmes sat down and looked at Stealey's nearly finished glass of wine. "Am I late?"

"No. It was a long day, and I needed a drink, so I got here a little early."

"Nothing wrong with that." Holmes loved to imbibe. On cue a waiter showed up at the table with the chairman's usual; a lowball glass filled with ice, Belvedere vodka, and three olives. Holmes thanked the man graciously and then raised his glass. Stealey followed suit. "To you and your continued success."

"And to a successful national campaign this year," added Stealey.

Holmes rolled his eyes and took a big gulp of the smooth Belvedere. This year was a presidential election. In addition to that, one third of the Senate was up for reelection, as well as the entire House of Representatives and a handful of key democratic governors. Fortunately, he had already hit all of their financial targets. Unfortunately, the Republicans had raised more money than they'd projected, so now he had to go back around and start asking the unions and the big hitters for further contributions.

"Aren't things going as well as you'd like?" asked Stealey.

Holmes took another sip of vodka and tried to think of the most positive way to put it. "Our opponents keep raising the bar on fund-raising but . . . that's not the problem."

"What is?"

Holmes looked around to make sure no one was eavesdropping. "The party hacks are driving me nuts. They would rather sit around and piss and moan than go out and do something about it."

With a knowing nod Stealey said, "They've never worked in the private sector."

Holmes pointed at her and said, "Bingo. They have this trench warfare mentality, and they're deathly afraid of change or new ideas. All they want to do is kiss the unions' asses and beg me for more money."

"Well, if it makes you feel any better, the other side is the same way. They've both been running off the same playbook for a hundred years."

"Except we have more fun, right?" Holmes recited the party's line and held up his drink.

Stealey laughed. "Correct."

The wine steward approached the table with his extensive list, but before he could open it, Holmes stopped him. Looking at his guest he asked, "Are you going to stick with white or have some red?"

"I'll drink red with my meal."

"Good. George," he said to the wine steward, "You know what I like. Why don't you go ahead and select something on the lighter side." The man gave a half bow and retreated.

When the two of them were alone, Holmes leaned in and asked, "Let's get business out of the way. Why did you suggest we have dinner tonight?"

Stealey gave him a coy smile. "Do I have to have a reason to want to have dinner with a handsome, fabulously wealthy, powerful man?"

Holmes's response was a mix of primal grunt and laughter. "Oh, Peggy, you know I'd screw your brains out in a New York minute, but we both also know you're a dick tease. So unless you've decided that tonight's the night we consummate this little friendship, let's just keep our attention above the table."

"That won't be any fun." She gave him a pouty look.

"Seriously, I can't afford another set of sore balls from all your games. I've got too much to do tomorrow."

She reached out for his hand. "I've been very up front with you. Sleeping with men in this town can be very dangerous. Women's careers have a way of petering out, so to speak, right after the man has his last orgasm."

Holmes squeezed her hand and then quickly let go. "That's fine. I'm not that hard up that I'm going to beg for it. Either we sleep with each other, or we don't, but no more jerking my chain."

Stealey acted as if her next words were heartfelt, but they weren't. She'd used the same excuse hundreds of times to keep men at bay, but also keep them interested. "I'm very attracted to you, it's just that there's someone else right now, and it's kind of complicated."

"Anyone I know?"

"No. He doesn't travel in your circles."

Holmes grinned. "One of those gun-toting G-men you've been working with?"

"I would prefer not to talk about it."

"That's fine." In truth, Holmes thought Stealey was a bit of a nutbag, but he was too far into this game to lose interest, even if he was trying to act like he didn't care. He'd sealed more business deals by getting up and walking away from the table than by any other tactic. Stealey would come around sooner or later, and until then, she offered great insights into how Washington worked and what was going on at the Justice Department.

"So back to my question. What's on your mind?"

She frowned and shook her head. "That damn Patriot Act."

"What about it?" asked Holmes.

"I know you like to joke that the only reason you became a Democrat is that they have more fun, but you need to be more aware of the issues that affect the base."

"And you think the Patriot Act is one of them?"

"Yes," Stealey answered forcefully.

Holmes, unconvinced, rolled his eyes.

"Pat, I'm serious. This entire war on terror has been blown out of proportion. A gang of ragtag militants got lucky, and now we've picked a fight with half the damn world to prove that we're not going to take it, and in the process we're crapping all over our Bill of Rights. It doesn't matter if its the Republicans who dreamed this thing up, we're the ones who are defending it."

He took a sip of Belvedere. "I'd say you're simplifying it just a bit."

"Am I?" she asked sarcastically. "You're way up here, Pat." Stealey put her hand above her head. "I'm down in the trenches. I hear what the foot soldiers at the Justice Department are saying. I see the briefs that are filed on a daily basis challenging the constitutionality of that deeply flawed piece of legislation. I see the fear in the eyes of the people who are going to have to go before the Supreme Court and defend it."

"And how," asked Holmes a bit underwhelmed, "is this going to affect the election?"

"You don't want any bad press the last four months before the election, and that is exactly when these challenges are going to go before the court."

"Peggy, I know you're passionate about this, but the majority of the voting public could give a rat's ass if some suspected terrorist doesn't get read his Miranda rights and is denied a lawyer."

"But the base does."

Holmes had learned the hard way that the base of his party meant the 10 percent who were so far to the left they were completely out of touch with the values of the vast majority of middle America. If they had it their way, they would lead the party right over the edge of a cliff and into the great abyss of fanatical liberalism.

"What are they going to do . . . go vote for whoever the Republicans put up?"

"No, they just won't vote, and you know what happens if the base doesn't turn out."

He had to reluctantly admit that she was right. It was an unnerving reality of his job. Holmes was a pro-business Democrat, and if he had it his way he'd jettison the crazy lefties and send them packing to the Green Party, but that was an untenable solution.

He shook his head. "You're ruining a perfectly good evening and we're only five minutes into it."

Stealey remained intense. "I'm telling you right now the activists who are steering these challenges over the constitutionality of that stupid piece of legislation are going to time this so they get maximum exposure. They're going to beat this drum all the way up to the election. And you and I both know who's going to take the hit."

"Hayes?"

"No," Stealey frowned. "He may eventually, but it's going to start with my boss AG Stokes . . . and I'm not going to sit back and let it happen." As a not so subtle threat she added, "and neither will he."

Holmes was slowly beginning to see that he might have a problem on his hands. Attorney General Martin Stokes was a rising star in the Democratic Party. There was even talk of having the president dump his worthless vice president and replace him on the ticket with Stokes. The man came from big money, and like Holmes he was pro-business and pro-defense. He was the type of man who could neutralize the Republicans.

"Peggy, I'm not going to say I agree with you on this, but you've at least piqued my interest." He looked down into his glass and snagged an olive. Holmes popped it in his mouth and said, "Knowing you as well as I do, I assume you have a plan of action."

"I do," said Stealey confidently, "but it's not going to get us anywhere unless you can get the president to play ball."

Holmes had significant pull with the president, and he had to admit as of late he thought the pendulum was swinging a bit too far in favor of the law enforcement, defense, and intelligence communities. "Let me hear your idea and I'll see what I can do."

TEN

The two AH-64 Apache helicopters arrived on station one minute after the takedown. One began flying cover over the village while the other moved to secure the landing field. The two attack helicopters carried a combined total of 120 rockets, 16 hellfire missiles for hardened targets, and their eviscerating 30mm nose cannons. In addition to their firepower they were equipped with the most advanced navigation, weapons system, and electronic countermeasures of any helicopter in the world. They were General Harley's solution to not being able to use fixed-wing air cover.

A lone Pave Hawk helicopter, an advanced version of the Blackhawk, came through the mountain pass and sped over the city well out of RPG range, but still within shot of antiaircraft guns and shoulder-launched missiles. In the premission briefing, they'd been shown the reconnaissance photos of the truck-mounted anti-aircraft guns, called technicals, and were also warned that there was a real chance the enemy might have surface-to-air missiles.

Having no desire to encounter either, the two pilots continued well past the town and banked hard to come back in and drop off their payload. As they descended toward the open field the pilot kept his focus on the patch of land that was punched into the advanced avionics computer, and the instruments that relayed his speed, altitude, and attitude. The copilot scanned the horizon and kept a nervous eye on the missile warning system. Even though visibility was good the door gunners called out their descent and searched the landing area for any hostiles.

As the Pave Hawk landed on the open field, a ten-man Air Force Special Tactics Squadron kicked their hundred-pound packs from the troop compartment and hit the ground running. After sprinting a short distance and fanning out, the men hit the dirt, taking up their defensive positions while the Pave Hawk lifted off, struggling to gain altitude in the thin mountain air.

When the helicopter had reached a safe altitude, the squadron went to work. Retrieving their packs, four of the six men lumbered across the field to secure the main road and cut the phone line while the others consulted their handheld GPS computers and began laying out a precise grid of infrared strobes. Across the field, only a half mile away, they could hear the gun battle building, the cracks of rifle fire spurring them to complete their task as quickly as possible.

They weren't quite finished laying out the grid when they heard a rumbling in the distance. The noise continued to grow as if it was a herd of stampeding cattle headed up the valley. Then the ground started to shake. The six men quickly laid down the remaining strobes and headed off at a near full sprint to their rallying point where they were to set up an aid station and act as forward combat air controllers.

★

General harley's command-and-control bird arrived over the village and began circling at ten thousand feet. Rapp had his eyes closed and his hands cupped over his headset as he strained to hear the chatter between Sergeant Corrigan and his men. There was already conflicting reports as to whether they had two or three of the big honchos. Rapp would be ecstatic if they had nabbed all three, but if it turned out one of them was killed in the takedown and two of them were alive to be interrogated, he certainly wouldn't shed any tears.

They were barely five minutes into the op, and it was apparent from the movement below that the town had woken up. As they'd predicted, it was no sleepy mountain village. Rapp opened his eyes and looked at the image on the screen before him. A quarter of the moon was out and with the clear sky, the night-vision systems were providing relatively clear pictures. Sergeant Corrigan's position was in the center of the screen. Rapp could make out hostiles moving toward him from all four directions. The numbers weren't alarming yet, but it was still early. As long as the enemy didn't throw anything heavy at them, Corrigan and his team should have no trouble holding out until the reinforcements arrived.

Movement at the far left of the screen caught Rapp's attention. He still hadn't deciphered what it was when the mission's air commander sitting across from him spoke in an even but urgent voice.

"Raptor One, we have a *technical* on the move approaching Team one's position . . . engage immediately."

★

ONE BLACKHAWK and six massive, lumbering MH-47E Special Operations Aircraft made their way into the valley from a different direction than the initial strike force. Loaded down, the large helicopters were too vulnerable to risk flying directly over the village when they weren't sure what they were up against. The pilots had to fly an extra forty-two circuitous miles to reach the target, but none of them complained.

The roar of their twin rotors and powerful turbine engines shook the entire valley and sent a clear signal to every person in the village that something bad was on its way. Thanks to the Air Force Special Tactics Squadron the landing area was lit up like a Christmas tree with infrared strobes that shone bright on the chopper's FLIR screens.

Two of the big choppers came in first and set down, their aft ramps already lowered. Within seconds a pair of Desert Patrol Vehicles (DPVs) eased their way down the ramps and tore across the bumpy field in search of the road that led into the village. The low-slung vehicles were capable of speeds up to eighty mph and could be outfitted with an array of powerful weapons systems. Each carried a crew of three U.S. Navy SEALs; a driver, a vehicle commander, and a gunner who sat in an elevated position behind the other two men.

For tonight's mission the DPVs were armed with big .50-caliber machine guns, 40mm grenade launchers, 7.62mm machine guns, and two AT4 antitank missiles per vehicle. The storage compartments on the sides of the vehicles were packed with extra ammunition and could also be configured to carry stretchers if need be. The vehicles were a potent weapon in open terrain, but in an urban environment they were vulnerable. They lacked the armor that was needed to sit tight and sock it out with opposing forces, so tonight they would use hit-and-run tactics to keep the enemy off balance until the bulk of the force arrived.

As the Desert Patrol Vehicles disappeared into the night a pair of ATVs rolled down the ramps of the Chinooks pulling trailers laden with crates and other equipment. The drivers of each small off-road vehicle cleared the landing zone and headed off to set up the command post and several mortar positions. A dozen Rangers in heavy gear struggled to keep up as they hoofed it over the patchy ground.

The two Chinooks, with their loads delivered, cleared the landing area to make room for their sister ships that were already on approach. Four of the big dull-green transports came in, breaking their single-file formation as they lined up with their marked landing zones. As each bird touched down, Rangers streamed from the aft ramps, breaking off into different-sized groups and heading off to various rallying points. What looked like chaos to the uninitiated was actually a highly orchestrated battlefield deployment of a reinforced U.S. Army Ranger company.

They were the sledgehammer that General Harley intended to wield in routing the Taliban and al-Qaeda fighters from their mountain stronghold. The Rangers were part of the 75th Ranger Regiment, 2nd Battalion. The company had rotated into Afghanistan four months ago, and had already seen plenty of action.

They were trained to fight in every environment, climate, and terrain that could be thrown at them. They excelled at direct-action missions—seizing airfields or capturing key facilities or towns. Using mobile fire-power, agility, and speed, they were trained to

ELEVEN

Corrigan walked to the front of the house and poked his head past the splintered and mangled doorframe just in time to hear a bullet whistle past and slap into the side of the mud-brick house. The bearded Corrigan didn't even flinch. He turned in the direction the shot had come from and shouldered his rifle, but before he had the chance to fire, one of his men on the roof took care of the problem for him.

The amount of incoming fire was building steadily. So far none of his men had been hit, but if this kept up it was only a matter of time. He'd put four more shooters on the roof to bolster the two snipers and two light machine guns that were already in place, and all eight of them were busy. It was quickly becoming a target-rich environment, and inside one hundred yards, Delta shooters didn't miss very often, even when the targets were moving.

The potshots weren't what had Corrigan worried. Brave men with machine guns assaulting a team of entrenched Delta Force shooters was little more than suicide, but these were battle-hardened soldiers who'd been in a state of perpetual war for two decades. It wouldn't take long for them to get organized and come up with a better strategy—a strategy that would probably involve bigger guns and rocket-propelled grenades.

The call came over the unit's internal radio link. "Cor, it's Lou . . . I think you'd better come back here and take a look at something."

Corrigan poked his head around the door frame and looked down the street through his AN/PVS-17 night sight. Two blocks away a tango came around the corner and took up position to fire an RPG. "Hold on a second, Lou."

Corrigan moved reflexively. The PEQ-2 laser designator mounted at the front of his weapon painted the man's chest with a bright red dot and Corrigan squeezed the trigger. The tango crumpled to the ground. Almost immediately, another man scrambled from the cover of the building and reached down to pick up the RPG. Corrigan painted the man's head, dropped him with a single shot, and then ducked back into the house.

"What's up, Lou?"

"I think I found something back here."

Corrigan edged his way up to one of the broken windows and took a quick look outside. He saw two men dart across the street about eighty yards away. One of them made it and the other didn't.

"Can it wait?" he asked, as he surveyed the situation.

Before the man could answer, the thunderous reports of a heavy-caliber machine gun boomed above the din of the steadily building rifle fire. A fist-sized hole was punched in the wall a few feet from Corrigan. The master sergeant hit the floor instantly as chunks of the dry mud brick rained down on him. He crawled back to the front door swearing under his breath.

Thumbing the switch on his radio for the command net, he said in an angry growl, "Condor Five, this is Rattle Snake, where is my air cover?"

"Air cover is on its way in, Rattle Snake. Sit tight."

The voice was calm and professional and it irritated Corrigan to no end. It was easy to stay cool when you were safely above the fray circling at five thousand feet. Come down here on the street and get your ass shot at and see if your voice takes on a more urgent tone.

"I've got a heavy-caliber machine gun firing on my position from the east!"

"I see it, Rattle Snake. Raptor One is inbound."

Before Corrigan could ask for an ETA he heard the telltale "whoosh" of aerial rockets passing overhead. A split second later there was a series of thunderous explosions.

CAPTAIN MILT Guerrero stood at the edge of his hastily established forward command post and looked out across the field through a pair of night vision binoculars. He and his command staff had come in on a Blackhawk and landed at the forward command post set up by the Air Force STS Team. He watched his three platoons, 144 men strong, rush across the open field. Even with their heavy gear they would cover the distance to the edge of the town in five minutes or less. If they ran into any resistance, that estimate could easily double or even triple, but the company commander had contingencies ready in case the enemy put up an unexpected early fight.

General Harley's original plan had called for the Rangers to march immediately to Rattle Snake One's position and create a secure perimeter for the exfiltration of the Delta Team and any prisoners, but after studying the objective, and the surrounding terrain further, General Harley came up with a bolder plan—a plan that was more reminiscent of the way Rangers fought in WWII. They were too far afield to fight with one hand tied behind their backs, and Harley had no desire to lose any of his men due to limited rules of engagement.

For an American officer, however, the desire for force protection always had to be balanced against the lives of innocent civilians. In almost any battlefield situation this was an area as murky as a Louisiana swamp, but here in Southwest Asia the lines between innocent civilian and guerrilla fighter were almost completely indistinguishable. Virtually everybody carried a weapon of some sort, even the young boys. A farmer was rarely a simple farmer. This village was an al-Qaeda and Taliban stronghold used to ferry men and supplies across the border into Afghanistan. Those supplies were used to kill American soldiers. There wasn't an adult in this village who didn't know what was going on.

The brutal reality of war in this violent, fanatical region was that every child over the age of ten was a potential threat, as were their mothers. If they didn't move decisively, if they didn't shock the enemy and keep them off balance, they could quickly find themselves bogged down in a house-to-house fight where they would be outnumbered—an entrenched street-by-street battle against a well-seasoned force that was not known for taking prisoners. If that happened they would have to call in the A-10 Warthogs and possibly a Spooky gunship that would undoubtedly lead to many more civilian deaths. Guerrero bought into the General Patton creed: engagements, battles, wars that were fought quickly, decisively, and with brute force saved lives in the long run. Patton knew well after fighting in WWI what happened when forces got bogged down.

The loss of innocent life was to be avoided if possible, but not if it meant risking the life of a Ranger. Quick and decisive force on the front end would save lives in the end. It was Captain Guerrero who had pushed for the battle's more traditional rules of engagement. Anyone seen running toward the battle carrying a weapon, man, woman, or child, was to be considered hostile and engaged, and any house or structure that was used to fire upon American forces was to be pulverized.

That was worst case and they were hoping to avoid it completely by separating the proverbial wheat from the chaff. Guerrero had a great respect for General Harley that bordered on reverence. Harley had studied the enemy, had gone back and read the history of the country. He'd talked with Soviet officers who had fought and lost in Afghanistan. Harley knew the enemy well, and he knew with relative certainty what they would do when confronted with a surprise attack in the dead of night.

"Sir," a young lieutenant approached the company commander, "the mortar teams are ready."

Part of General Harley's ingenious plan for tonight's operation was to reinforce the young captain's two 60mm mortars. "Have sections one, two, and three begin laying down a barrage at the southern edge of the town, have sections four and five coordinate with Rattle Snake One on where they'd like them dropped, and have section six look for targets of opportunity as directed by the forward observers."

The lieutenant snapped off a salute, glad to hear that the plan hadn't changed. He and his mortar teams had worked diligently to prepare precise coordinates for virtually every intersection and target of potential interest in the village. They had already been in contact with the Air Force forward observer who had reached the edge of town, and one of the Delta shooters on the roof of the target building. The mortar teams were eager to show their stuff. Working in conjunction with forward observers, and using their M-23 mortar ballistic computers, they could drop their 60mm rounds through the sunroof of a parked car. Twelve of the lethal tubes stood ready with enough rounds to level the entire town if necessary.

CORRIGAN LOOKED AT the twisted, blazing hunk of metal that had almost blown his head off only a few moments ago. Not wanting to diminish his vision he then turned away from the burning wreck and told himself he'd have to remember to buy the boys flying the Apache a cold one.

"Rattle Snake One." The scratchy voice came over his radio. "This is Mustang One. We're going to be at your front door in about thirty, coming in from the west. Do you have any targets for us?"

The SEALs were on their way in with their fast Desert Patrol Vehicles. Great news as far as Corrigan was concerned. The sergeant didn't like a fair fight. He glanced up and down the street. Now that the rocket strike by the Apache had passed he could see the enemy was renewing their efforts. Several rounds struck the road in front of Corrigan, kicking up geysers of dirt. He casually stepped back into the house. "Nothing specific, but watch out for the rooftops."

Corrigan called out for a quick "sit rep" from his team. One by one each man checked in. There were a few minor scrapes, but nothing serious, and his machine gunners asked for some more ammunition for their M240B medium machine guns. Corrigan knew they weren't critically low on ammo, but the plan was for the Desert Patrol Vehicles to drop off some extra supplies and two light machine guns in case the Rangers got held up.

Corrigan looked out onto the street just in time to see the two low-slung dune buggies come skidding around the corner, guns blazing, their big .50-calibers chewing up the rooftops on either side of the street.

The first vehicle pulled right up to the door, its fat knobby tires gripping the packed dirt road like claws. The second vehicle swung out into the intersection and stopped in the middle of a right-hand turn. The crews in the two vehicles began furiously pumping rounds into anything that moved. Corrigan set his weapon down and grabbed a couple of extra ammo pouches from the vehicle. He tossed them back in the house and grabbed an M249 SAW and more ammo.

The vehicle commander, a chief and a perpetual smart-ass, yelled to Corrigan over the roar of the guns, "Once again, it's the Navy to the rescue!"

Corrigan grabbed his weapon and yelled back, "Rescue my ass! You wanna change spots?"

The Navy SEAL shook his head vigorously. "No thanks! I don't like staying in one place if I don't have to." With his left hand up in the air he gestured wildly for the driver to move out. Turning back to Corrigan, he smiled again and yelled as the driver gunned the engine, "We'll be in the neighborhood! Just call if you need us!"

The two crews were in contact via radio and as soon as the one vehicle began to move, the one holding the corner took off. As per the plan, they were now to drive around the back of the house and drop off more ammunition and another machine gun, and along the way knock the enemy back a bit. After that they were to proceed to the western edge of town where they were to look for targets of opportunity and hold the flank. If needed, they were also in reserve to evacuate any seriously wounded. The six SEALs knew the key to their effectiveness was to hit and move. If they stayed in any one place for too long they might be the ones needing a medical evac.

TWELVE

Circling directly over the town at 10,000 feet, Rapp watched the fight taking shape on the screens and resisted the urge to ask Rattle Snake One for an ID on the prisoners. Right now the Delta boys were busy using their well-honed skills to make sure the engagement didn't turn into their own private Alamo. General Harley's plan was proceeding as they'd expected, but military engagements had a way of changing in the blink of an eye. If the enemy could get organized, there was still a very real possibility that they could overrun Rattle Snake One and his men, but Harley had bet the farm that the enemy would opt for another strategy, especially now that the other assets were joining the battle.

For thousands of years the people in the village below and their ancestors had used the mountains to hide from invaders. They were masters at guerilla warfare. Hit the enemy and then disappear into the mountains where the inhospitable terrain and climate could wear down the best that the conquering armies could throw at them. Most recently, the Soviet Union had learned this modern military axiom: don't use conventional forces to fight a guerilla war. There was a major difference, however, between the war with the Soviets and what was going on now. Back in the eighties, the CIA and U.S. Special Forces provided crucial training and supplies that helped turn the tide against the communist aggressors. Most notably the mujahideen was given the highly effective Stinger surface-to-air missile.

The Taliban and al-Qaeda had the misfortune this time of going up against the same benefactor who had supported them against the Soviet aggression. Those high-tech Stinger missiles were now old technology. Every helicopter and plane under Harley's command was equipped with state-of-the-art missile counter-measure systems more than capable of defeating all but the newest and most advanced surface-to-air missiles. The few Stingers that were still in the Taliban's arsenal had deteriorated over time and were highly unstable.

That meant the enemy had to try and use more antiquated methods to bring down the American helicopters—antiaircraft guns and RPGs. Both were all but useless against the sturdy American helicopters unless they were caught in a low hover, and even then, with the firepower the helicopters could bring to bear, it was all but suicide for the man firing the weapon. Harley had no desire to lose a bird, so he constantly changed tactics and kept his helicopters above two thousand feet and moving at a good clip whenever possible.

The general and his task force were beating the Taliban at their own game. They were using guerilla warfare tactics coupled with air mobility and firepower to choose the time and location of the battle. They harassed their opponent, and then retreated to their base hundreds of miles away, frustrating the enemy and inflicting massive casualties. Harley and his warriors were wearing the bad guys down.

Rapp listened to the chatter amongst the various officers in the command-and-control bird who were directing the action below. The Apache flying cover had destroyed another mounted gun and several buildings at the far end of town, and the Ranger's mortar barrage had just commenced, peppering the southern edge of town with bright flashes. After another minute the Rangers would begin marching their mortar fire through the village in a slow methodical pounding, intersection by intersection. The idea was to leave the enemy only one direction to flee—toward the mountains. The homes were not to be targeted unless individual Ranger units called in a strike. The Rangers would then sweep in and take the entire village one block at a time. General Harley wanted, if at all possible, to separate the terrorist and Taliban thugs from the noncombatants.

Harley knew his enemy, and had told Rapp they would do what they had done for centuries— they would flee to the mountains, and that was where the general had one more surprise waiting for them. Rapp couldn't help feeling satisfied at the hand he'd had in bringing this about. These were the fighters who smuggled weapons and explosives and fresh recruits across the border. These were the men who ambushed U.S. troops who were building roads and hospitals and bringing sanitary drinking water to people for the first time in their lives. These were zealots who hated America, and hated freedom whether it was religious, political, or otherwise.

They had miscalculated, thinking they were safe sitting on the Pakistani side of the border. Once again they had underestimated their enemy. They thought America lacked the courage and resolve to take them on. They were bullies and thugs blinded by their misguided righteousness. War was the only thing that would ever dissuade them of their ways, and they'd picked a fight with the wrong enemy.

THE FIRST 60MM mortar shell came inbound, its high-pitched, ominous whistle giving anyone experienced enough in battle a second or two to find cover. Corrigan was one such man and he got small quick, hitting the ground and curling up in a ball. The Ranger mortar teams were good, but until they were zeroed in on a target anything could happen. Fire support and close air support were the number one cause of fratricide amongst American forces.

Thankfully the shell exploded three full blocks away. There was a brief pause followed by the cry of a second round on its way in. This explosion was a bit closer and was followed a few seconds later by yet another one. Corrigan raised himself up to one knee and looked out the window in time to see the light show swing into full gear. The mortar teams were zeroed in and were bracketing his position with lethal indirect fire.

For the briefest of moments the sergeant felt sorry for the men on the receiving end of the barrage. War was infinitely unpleasant with all of its hardships and death and mayhem, but to a foot soldier, there were few things more frightening than being shelled. The entire method of indirect fire was frustrating. Someone who was far away, too far away to shoot back at, was dropping high explosives on your position. With no way to fight back, your instinct for survival kicked in and your brain told you to run.

There was only one problem, however. If you tried to run you'd almost certainly get cut to shreds by shrapnel, if not pulverized by a direct hit, so you were left to wrestle with one of your strongest survival instincts. You had to learn to ignore and override thousands of years of human evolution and stay right where you were. If possible, you had to try to squeeze your body into some depression or behind a heavy object. Crawl if you must, but never stand up and run.

Corrigan saw a muzzle flash across the street and down a ways. He shouldered his rifle and looked through his night vision sight. The scope was able to pierce the shadows just enough to catch some movement, and he let loose with a three-round burst, knowing that the guy on the receiving end was either dead or seriously wounded. Not wanting the same thing to happen to him, Corrigan moved to the other side of the window.

Over the rooftop of the building across the street the sky was alight with strobelike flashes from the mortar barrage that was hitting the southern edge of town. Between the explosions he could make out the building staccato of gunfire that meant the Rangers were joining the battle.

Corrigan relaxed just a notch, taking comfort that things were proceeding as planned. Then his momentary relief vanished when he heard one of his men let loose with a string of expletives. The sergeant craned his neck skyward to look up at the ceiling. The swearing didn't sound like it had come from inside the house and he thought he recognized the voice. "Brian," he called out over his radio, "what's going on up there?"

The reply came back as a torrent of profanity that ended with the dreaded phrase, "I'm hit."

Before Corrigan could respond, Danny Goblish, one of the two medics that was with the team said, "I'm on it, Cor."

"How serious is it?"

"Direct hit to the shoulder. I'll know more in a minute."

"Roger. Keep me in the loop." Corrigan took a sip of water from his camel pack and walked back to the front door.

"Hey, boss, it's Lou."

"What's up?" asked Corrigan.

"I think one of these tangos was trying to get at a trap door in the floor before I pasted him."

Corrigan frowned, momentarily wondering if any of these houses were connected by tunnel. That could be a problem. "I'll be right there."

The master sergeant looked at the other troopers in the front room. All three of them flashed him the thumbs up sign. "I'll be back in a minute," he snapped, as he headed down the dark hallway.

THIRTEEN

Rapp watched as the rifle teams moved into the city, leapfrogging their way from one building to the next. The forty-two Rangers that made up the first platoon were in the middle, out in front of the other two platoons. Their mission was to head straight for Rattle Snake One's position and secure a perimeter. In the process they were also supposed to secure a two-block corridor from the target house to the southern edge of the village. The other two platoons were to act as flanking forces driving just one block into the village and then digging in. Each platoon had one squad in reserve to use as a reaction force if a particular area of the battle got too hot, but ideally the mortar teams would take care of any stiff resistance.

The first sign of an exodus was reported by the Apache pilot as he made a quick pass over the northern edge of the town. Men were seen moving on foot for the mountain pass. Rapp checked one of his monitors, and could just make out the shapes of people walking up a trail. As he looked at the streets of the village he counted another dozen or so individuals making their way toward the mountains. The general's prediction was proving true.

Rapp watched his monitor as the lead element of the Ranger force cut through the village with little trouble. It took them no more than two minutes to reach Rattle Snake One's position, where they quickly set up a perimeter. Rapp smiled with satisfaction. If things stayed on course, they would begin evacuating the prisoners shortly.

Individual units began reporting in that their sectors were secure, and as the enemy resistance began to fade, the exodus for the mountains gained momentum. Rapp was caught slightly off guard when he heard himself referenced over the command net. It was Master Sergeant Corrigan talking to General Harley.

"Eagle Six . . . Rattle Snake One here. We've found something down here that I think our visitor might want to take a look at."

General Harley looked at Rapp and asked, "What've you got, Rattle Snake?"

"We found a room under the house. A couple of computers, a lot of videos, some files, and a couple of maps."

General Harley was surprised by none of this. They almost always found stuff on these raids. As to why the master sergeant thought Rapp would want to take a look, he was not sure. "Why would our visitor be interested in what you've found?"

Corrigan's answer caused Harley and Rapp to exchange nervous glances. "Say again, Rattle Snake."

The Delta trooper repeated himself more loudly this time. As soon as he was done Rapp covered his lip mike and yelled at the general, "You need to set this bird down right now."

Harley didn't argue, and within seconds the Blackhawk was headed for the landing field.

★

By the time they touched down the two Fast Attack Vehicles were waiting for them. Rapp hit the ground and Harley followed him. The two men ran clear of the spinning blades to the waiting vehicles. Rapp jumped into the recently vacated passenger seat of the second one. The Navy SEAL standing next to it offered Rapp his helmet. He declined the helmet but took the man's clear ski goggles. While Rapp buckled himself in, General Harley leaned on the cage.

Shouting above the noise of the idling Blackhawk, Harley said, "No dicking around, Mitch. You get in, take a look and then I want you the hell out of there. I've got a schedule to keep. The sun's going to be up in a couple hours, and I want all of my men back across the border before then."

Rapp nodded. "Don't worry, general, I have no intention of hanging around."

Harley stepped away from the vehicle and yelled, "And don't get shot!" He jerked his thumb toward the village, "Now get the hell out of here and hurry up!" With that the two vehicles tore off across the field and onto the main road.

The mortar teams had taken the fight out of the enemy and they were in a full retreat toward the mountain pass where a very nasty surprise was waiting for them. A platoon of Navy SEALs was lying in wait ready to spring an ambush. Individual Ranger units were reporting sporadic potshots from the enemy, but any concerted effort to try and launch a counterattack was gone. The Rangers had created a safe corridor around Rattle Snake One's position that they alone controlled. This made the ride into the village very uneventful. Neither of the Fast Attack Vehicles drew or fired a shot.

They stopped in front of the bullet-riddled house, and Rapp was met immediately by Corrigan. The master sergeant brought him inside. Rapp ignored the bound-and-hooded prisoners on the floor and followed Corrigan down the hallway to a bedroom. The Delta trooper turned on a flashlight and pointed it into the subterranean room.

"We gave it a quick check for booby traps, but be careful."

Rapp nodded and took the flashlight from Corrigan. Dropping to the floor he swung his feet into the hole and took one last look before putting the flashlight in his mouth. Leaning forward he grabbed onto the other side of the opening with both hands and let himself drop down until his feet found the damp earth floor. Rapp grabbed the flashlight and slowly did a full turn. There were several com-puters, along with a number of boxes and files stacked haphazardly all around the room. He found what he was looking for on the last wall and froze, a combination of fear and disbelief coursing through his veins.

He moved closer, studying the map that he knew all too well. The rivers, roads, parks, and landmarks were all infinitely familiar to him. Finding such a map in this remote village was enough to give him pause, but in and of itself, it was not enough to explain his growing alarm. That was caused by what had been drawn over the map. Concentric circles emanated from the center, each one with two numbers written next to it. One was a temperature and the other a body count. The margins were filled with notes written in Arabic analyzing the weather patterns for the region in question.

Rapp stepped back, wondering how much time he had, his head swimming with disastrous possibilities. He had seen this type of map before. It was used to measure the destructive power of a nuclear weapon, and it appeared Washington, D.C., was the target.

FOURTEEN

Some 8,000 miles away, as nightfall descended on the eastern coast of Florida the forty-four-foot power yacht made its way between the channel buoys and headed for the inlet of the Merritt Island National Wildlife Refuge. It had been a long day for al-Yamani. After killing the captain of the boat, he'd traveled 360 miles, stopping only once in Fort Pierce to top off the fuel tanks. Fortunately, the weather had cooperated and he'd been able to engage the autopilot for at least a third of the journey. Still, the bright sun and wind had beaten his senses relentlessly for twelve hours straight and left him a bit off-kilter.

Now with the boat moving at just under five knots through the calm narrow inlet he was met with an eerie silence punctuated only by the occasional nocturnal cry of animals he couldn't even begin to identify. Al-Yamani was not a man of the sea. He'd grown up in the al-Baha Province of Saudi Arabia, and until recently, he couldn't even swim. His knowledge of boats had been gained entirely in the last year as he'd helped transfer his martyrs on the Caspian Sea from Northern Iran to Kazakhstan. He'd paid close attention to their Iranian captain and how he maneuvered their decrepit flat-bottomed barge. After much cajoling, the captain had agreed to teach the Muslim warrior the ways of the sea, for even then al-Yamani knew he would have to find an unconventional way to enter the United States.

The twin diesel engines purred while the exhaust ports gurgled at the water line and al-Yamani prayed yet again that he would avoid running into any alligators. The thought of such an encounter sent a shiver down his spine. He was a brave man, but he had grown up in the barren landscape of Saudi Arabia and such reptiles gave him near fits. He'd already heard several splashing noises and could imagine the scaly beasts following him up the narrow canal.

He had the running lights on but resisted the urge to use the bright search light. He would have preferred dousing the lights entirely, but if he by chance happened to stumble across some local law enforcement officer, or worse, a DEA agent, he didn't want them to think he was running drugs. His purpose was far more noble than the importing of an illicit substance. It was part of an ongoing battle between his people and the nonbelievers. A battle that had been waged for more than a thousand years.

Al-Yamani kept one hand on the throttle and the other on the wheel while he consulted the GPS readout on the dash. He had memorized all the coordinates. Satellite maps had been purchased on the black market from a retired Russian intelligence officer in the northern Pakistani town of Peshawar. The Russian even helped him pick the point at which he should come ashore. The 140,000-acre refuge was owned and operated by NASA. For years the KGB had moved people in and out of the refuge so they could monitor what the Americans were up to in the race for space.

Mustafa al-Yamani was a cautious man by nature, but when he was pitted against an enemy with almost endless resources, like America, his instincts bordered on paranoia. Before embarking on this mission, he had sent encrypted e-mails to followers who had been in place for years. None of them knew the face or name of the man they were told to meet, only a time and place and that their mission was of the highest order. There were two more locations to be used as backup if something went wrong.

The FBI had increased its surveillance of American Muslims significantly, so they had to be careful. That meant using contacts who did not adhere to the strict Islamic teachings of the Wahhabi sect, which was most unfortunate. Al-Yamani was used to working with those who were truly devoted—men who were willing to martyr themselves without question. He had known many such men over the years and in the past months he had seen dozens of them forfeit their lives to a silent killer they could neither see nor understand. It had happened in a Godforsaken land on the northern edge of the Caspian Sea where the earth was so poisonous only a few mutated forms of life could survive.

Al-Yamani's days were numbered. He too had been exposed to the lethal levels of radiation, but not to the extent of his brave mujahideen. He took pills that helped fight off the nausea and fever, but there was no cure. Mustafa al-Yamani was a dead man walking, but he had just enough life left in him to strike a glorious blow for Islam.

America was a large country with more shoreline than it could ever realistically defend. It was the Great Satan's one glaring weakness, and al-Yamani was planning to exploit it in every phase of his operation.

His importance was known to the Western intelligence agencies. A price of ten million dollars had been placed on his head. Several of his own people had been tempted by the bounty, and if not for moles inside both the Pakistani and Saudi intelligence services who had tipped him off, he would now be rotting inside a dungeon somewhere, never to see the light of day again. Instead he was about to unleash the ultimate terror weapon on the arrogant Americans.

Al-Yamani consulted the GPS again and pulled back on the throttles, slipping the engines into neutral. The small bridge where he was to meet his contact was not far up ahead. In the faint glow of the moonlight he could just barely make it out. The retired KGB officer had told him that the canals of the refuge were sometimes only navigable during high tide. Based on the draft of the forty-four-foot Rivarama, he'd calculated that he had a one-hour window to wait for his contact. After that he'd have to leave or risk getting stuck.

Deftly, he slipped the engines back into gear and goosed the sleek craft forward. A short while later he could clearly see the small bridge. With about fifty feet to go he pulled the throttles back and killed the engines. The boat slowly glided forward, while al-Yamani strained to hear the noise of an approaching car or anything suspicious. There was nothing other than the cacophony of nocturnal animals going about their business.

The bow slid under a steel girder, and al-Yamani reached up to grab hold. The windscreen cleared the rusted support with barely a foot to spare. Al-Yamani stopped the slow forward progress of the boat and then set about turning it around in case he had to race back out to sea. When he had it pointed back in the direction he'd come from, he tied the boat up and looked for a spot to go ashore. There wasn't enough light to see anything with great detail, and al-Yamani couldn't shake the thought that somewhere in the reeds an alligator lay in wait. He stood near the back of the boat wracked by indecision. He could either blindly jump into the grass or he could grab a flashlight. While he stood gripped with the fear of the unknown, something moved in the tall grass, and that decided it for him.

He ducked down below and grabbed a flashlight and can of soda from the fridge. Pointing the light down he turned it on and threw the can into the tall grass. Something moved quickly, and al-Yamani caught a glimpse of it with his light as it scurried into the water. It was a furry creature of some kind. Definitely not an alligator. He growled to himself and grabbed his bag. Whatever was out there, with the exception of the alligators, was likely more afraid of him than he of it. Standing atop the engine compartment he took one last look around and leaped for the shore.

He landed on one leg and then stumbled for a second before catching himself. One of the chief reasons why al-Yamani couldn't simply disguise himself and enter the U.S. by plane was that he wore a prosthetic from the knee down on his right leg. At the age of sixteen the young Saudi had gone to fight the Soviets in Afghanistan. After stepping on a land mine he returned home minus the lower half of his right leg. With the help of a prosthetic, there was little that al-Yamani couldn't do, but passing through a metal detector at an airport was not one of them. One of their moles inside Saudi intelligence had told him that the Americans knew all about him. Al-Yamani was on all their watch lists, and it wasn't that hard to pick out an Arab man missing part of his leg.

After collecting himself he started up the bank in a low crouch. When he reached the top he stayed in the tall grass and peered down the road in both directions. As expected it was empty. The road was called Black Point Drive, part of a seven-mile loop used by tourists and nature lovers to get a closer look at the refuge's wildlife.

He could see the glow of an approaching car but could not hear it yet. His heart quickened and his palms became moist. The car rounded the bend and headed straight for him. Al-Yamani laid flat on his stomach and kept his head down. The noise of the vehicle grew and then it came to a stop. Al-Yamani could hear the idling engine and then as per his instructions the headlights were extinguished and the car was turned off. If the car had remained running, al-Yamani would have taken it as a signal that the man thought he was being followed.

He lifted himself up just enough to get a look through the tall grass. On the opposite side of the road he saw the silver Ford Taurus he'd expected. The driver's door opened, and a man stepped out and lit a cigarette. So far so good. Al-Yamani watched him for a little while and then stood grabbing his bag.

The man did not see him at first as he stepped from the grass. Al-Yamani was half way across the road when he softly said, "*Allahu Akbar.*"

The man spun nervously, almost dropping his cigarette. With his eyes wide he repeated the phrase in a less than steady voice.

Al-Yamani was pleased. If the young man was nervous, that meant he was taking this seriously. In Arabic he asked, "Are you sure no one has followed you?"

"Yes. I have not been to my mosque in two months, just as you ordered."

Al-Yamani nodded with satisfaction and embraced his colleague. For now he would let him live.

FIFTEEN

Irene Kennedy had just spent the last two hours helping her son with his homework. It was late, she was tired, and they both needed to go to bed. Tommy was a first grader for three more days and immensely proud of the fact that he was about to move up in the pecking order of his grade school. Kennedy was just happy that he would no longer have Mrs. Johnson as a teacher. It was the last week before summer, and she was still handing out homework like it was college midterms.

Kennedy sent her son into his bathroom to brush his teeth, and then headed down the hall to draw a bath for herself. By the time she got back, he was already under the covers. He had undoubtedly cut a few corners on brushing his teeth, but Kennedy was too tired to make an issue out of it. He was a good kid who was polite and respectful, got perfect grades, and stayed out of trouble. An occasional cavity wouldn't kill him.

Begin the day on a positive note and end the day on a positive note. That was her motto, at least at home. The other stuff she couldn't control: the politicians on the Hill, the president and his advisors, the press, and even some of her own people at Langley. Kennedy listened to Tommy say his prayers and then kissed him on the forehead.

"I love you, honey."

He rolled away from her and said, "I love you too."

She was losing him. It seemed like yesterday that she used to carry him to bed, and not too long ago he would look her in the eyes and tell her he loved her. Now he was entering that goofy stage where girls, including mothers, were weird. Kennedy rubbed his back and then got up and left.

Her child taken care of, she could now turn her attention to herself. A nice long hot bath sounded like just the thing. She would lose herself in thoughts of nothing but the trivial for a good half hour. She entered her small walk-in closet and took off her clothes. She put her silk blouse in her dry cleaning bag and then made her way into the bathroom. The old-fashioned claw-foot tub was half full and steaming. Kennedy added some bath oil and then shut off the water. All she had to do was get through the next three days and they'd have a nice relaxing long weekend together. She and Tommy and her mother had plans to visit cousins at the shore. It would be a weekend of sun, surf, and fun. The perfect way to kick off the start of summer. At least she hoped it would be, even though she knew there was a good chance duty would call and her mother and Tommy would spend the weekend at the shore without her.

She was just about to ease her foot into the water when the serenity of the moment was shattered by a distinctive ringing noise. Kennedy, a normally unflappable person, turned and glared at the white phone and its blinking red light. Her secure telephone had no voice mail. If she didn't answer it, they would simply call the agent in charge of her security detail, and he would politely come upstairs and knock on her bedroom door.

She snatched her robe from the hook on the door and walked over to her bedside table. Without her glasses she struggled to read the small display. She made out the first word and decided it was the CIA's Global Ops Center. Kennedy grabbed the handset and in a tired, but composed voice said, "DCI Kennedy."

The voice on the other end sounded somewhat scratchy and far away. "Irene, it's Mitch."

Kennedy looked at the bedside clock. It was nearing ten in the evening, which meant it was almost six in the morning where Rapp was. "Is everything all right?"

"Yeah . . ."

"Where are you?"

"We're on our way back across the border. Listen, I don't want to alarm you, but we found some serious intel in this village. I need you to get the Southwest Asia CTC people back into the office, and call the station chief in Kandahar and tell him to give me complete carte blanche on anything I ask for, especially translators."

Kennedy's brow furrowed. "Just how time sensitive is this stuff?"

"I'm not sure."

"Then what's the big rush?" Kennedy didn't like going into action without a solid reason.

"Just trust me when I tell you we have to move quickly on this stuff."

Kennedy sensed something in his voice. "Mitch, you sound a little ruffled. What's going on?"

Rapp didn't answer right away. "Listen, I don't want to alarm everyone until we have a chance to look at everything more closely, but we found a room under the target house."

"What kind of room?" Kennedy was now standing.

"It was filled with files. Most of it in Pashtu, but some of it in Arabic. There were also several computers and a few maps."

"And?" asked Kennedy knowing there had to be more for Rapp to make this urgent call.

There was a long pause and then Rapp said, "One of the maps was of D.C. and it showed the effects of a nuclear blast."

"Jesus Christ." Kennedy sat back down, her thoughts turning to her worst fear.

"Irene, do what you need to do to cover your ass, but give me a few hours to look into this before everyone flies off the handle and gets in my way."

Kennedy's head was swimming with possibilities, none of them good. There were the financial movements of last Friday, the intercepts that something big was in the works, and now this. "I don't know if I can sit on this, Mitch, even for a minute."

"All I'm asking for is a few hours." Rapp knew what was going through her mind. He had seen the plans for what they called continuity of government. It involved alerting thousands of people in the first hour alone. "Once this genie's out of the bottle there's no putting her back. Just give me some time to study our take, and find out if it's all a fantasy, or if they've actually got the goods."

Kennedy had stopped listening, her mind stuck on the fact that the president, vice president, speaker of the House, pro tem of the Senate, secretary of state, and secretary of the treasury were all in town. Some people needed to be moved.

"Irene, it's a Tuesday night. You know how these guys work. They want maximum exposure. If they do this, it'll be during broad daylight when downtown is filled with people."

Kennedy pinched the bridge of her nose. "You might be right, but I can't take that chance." There were plans in place, protocol to be followed.

"If they have a bomb, our number one priority should be to make sure they don't detonate it. To do that I need some time. Just hold off on doing anything crazy for a few hours. That's all I'm asking."

His voice was less than clear, but she could still hear his pleading tone. Finally, she said, "You'll get everything you need, Mitch. Just work fast, and call me as soon as you learn more. I need to go."

Kennedy held on to the handset and disconnected the call. Her mind was racing, trying to factor in everything she'd just heard with the information she already knew. She was reminded of a similar situation where very powerful people in Washington missed all of the signs that an attack was imminent. Tragically, their inaction led to the deaths of thousands. The director of the CIA reached her tipping point, and decided on a course of action. She was about to walk a very fine line, but given the circumstances she saw no other way.

SIXTEEN

The president's private study was located on the second floor of the Executive Mansion. President Hayes had his shoes off, his feet up, a drink in one hand, and a book in the other. An early riser, he was looking forward to finishing his drink and heading off to bed.

There was a firm knock on the door, but before Hayes could answer, it opened. Beth Jorgenson, the Secret Service agent in charge of the shift detail, walked in.

"I'm sorry to interrupt, sir, but something has come up." Jorgenson strode purposefully across the room to the president's desk and picked up his secure phone. She handed Hayes the handset and said, "Director Kennedy needs to speak with you."

Hayes was still holding on to his book and drink, and didn't move at first. Something out of the ordinary was happening, and he had the peculiar feeling that is was not good. He set the drink down slowly and took the phone. "Irene."

"Mr. President, we have a situation that you need to be aware of." Kennedy relayed the intel Rapp had given her and repeated the information that she'd briefed the president on the morning before.

When she was done, Hayes didn't answer right away. After some hesitation he stated the obvious, "This doesn't sound good."

"No, it doesn't, sir." Kennedy paused. She knew the president would not like her next suggestion, but she had to make it. "As a precaution I would like you and the First Lady to spend the evening in the bunker."

The president thought about the cement tomb underneath the Executive Mansion. He'd spent a dismal few days there once before and had no desire to set foot back in the place. "Slow down a minute, Irene. One map doesn't give us a whole lot to go on."

"No it doesn't, sir, but it's more than just the map."

Three more Secret Service agents entered the room and Hayes began to get the idea that something was already in the works. "Irene, before you get ahead of yourself, please tell me you haven't authorized any evacuations."

"No, I have not, sir, even though I have the authority to do so without seeking your approval." Kennedy chose her words carefully. She had the power to implement a continuity of government plan that would evacuate certain key decision makers from the city. The implementation of such a plan was not to be undertaken lightly, for it was widely agreed that shortly after it went into effect, the press would be all over the story and nationwide panic might follow.

"What are you saying, Irene?"

"Sir, I'm saying that as of yet I am not prepared to implement Operation Ark, but I think it would be prudent for you and the First Lady to go downstairs and spend the night there."

"Irene, I think you're moving too fast."

Kennedy was not to be deterred. "Sir, we have a real

problem. Both you and the vice president are in town, as well as the speaker of the House, the president pro tem of the Senate, and your entire cabinet with the exception of the secretary of the interior."

"Oh . . . I see." If a nuke took out DC, the secretary of the interior would become president, and although he was a decent enough fellow, he was not the type of man who would instill confidence in a time of national tragedy.

"Sir, I agree that it might be premature to start pulling people out of restaurants and beds. Mitch tells me he'll know more in the next couple hours. Until then, I would feel much better if I knew you were less of a target." She intentionally chose the word target.

After an uncomfortable silence Hayes responded in a tone that left no doubt that he was in charge, "I'm going to wander down to the Situation Room and keep an eye on this."

They'd been over this possibility on their threat assessments. The Situation Room was not a bunker, but it had enough reinforced concrete to withstand a truck bomb parked in front of the building. It was better than nothing. She knew she'd pushed it about as far as she could for now, and she couldn't very well stop him from doing his job.

"What about the First Lady?"

"Irene . . . you know her well enough to understand, no one, not even yours truly is going to get her to go spend the night in that bunker."

"Will you at least ask her, sir?"

"I'll give it a shot, and I'll call you in fifteen for an update." Hayes hung up the phone and looked at his yet unfinished drink. He hated to waste good bourbon, but it might be a long night. He left it there on the small end table and went and told his wife he was going over to the Situation Room for a bit. Despite his promise to Kennedy he didn't waste any breath asking her to spend the night in the bunker.

SEVENTEEN

Rapp had asked for more time to sift through the intelligence gold mine they'd found under the house while they were right there, but General Harley had denied his request. Disengaging from the enemy in foreign terrain was not an easy thing, and the general wanted it done right, and on schedule. Harley sent one of the ATVs into the village and Rapp, with the help of the Delta boys, filled the undersized trailer with the maps, files, and computers from the small room under the house.

Talking to Kennedy had made several things clear. Rapp had to move fast, and that meant he would have to break some rules. He made his arrangements before they landed at the Kandahar Air Base. That was the way it had to be. The military had too many rules, and more than enough Good Samaritans, Bible thumpers, and people who in general thought their mission in life was to do everything by the book. The course that Rapp was about to set could not be done by the book. There could be no record of it.

Rapp had explained the situation to General Harley, and the warrior had then said to the other officers in the command-and-control helicopter, "You know what to do." They all nodded. The mission's tapes needed to be erased, or at a bare minimum sanitized; the Delta boys would keep their mouths shut without ever having to be told; and the Rangers would know enough not to ask questions. That left the thousands of other personnel on the base they were headed for who were prone to gossip and rumor mongering. The mere presence of a character like Rapp was enough to get people going, so he was going to have to be careful.

The five men who lay bound, gagged, and hooded on the floor of one of the Chinook helicopters no longer existed as far as the U.S. military was concerned. Rapp knew, however, that they were very much alive—at least for now, and that he would be the one who would decide if any or all of them remained that way. Based on the plan he was going to implement, it was almost certain that at least one of them was going to die, though.

The sun was barely up when the command-and-control Blackhawk landed at the base back in Kandahar. Rapp saw the man he was looking for standing in front of a Toyota 4 Runner. As soon as the door to the Blackhawk was open, Rapp was out of the helicopter and running across the Tarmac.

Jamal Urda was a former Marine and eight-year veteran with the CIA. The son of Iranian immigrants, and a Muslim by birth, he had exceptional language skills, and an intuitive understanding of the Persian and Arab cultures. Urda had been one of the first people to arrive in the Taliban controlled country after 9/11. He had entered from the north with a group of heavily armed former special forces operators and bundles of American cash. Over the ensuing months, Urda and several others just like him negotiated deals with

Afghanistan's far-flung and powerful warlords. The warlords were presented with a simple choice: either get onboard and help destroy the Taliban, in which case Uncle Sam will provide you with a suitcase filled with crisp hundred-dollar bills, or say no, and we'll drop a 2,000-pound laser-guided bomb on your house.

Urda had been very successful in his negotiations, and in turn the CIA's director of operations had made him his point man in Kandahar. Rapp had met him only briefly on several other occasions. Urda had a reputation as a man who wasn't always easy to deal with. The word was he did not like people from headquarters looking over his shoulder. Rapp hoped Kennedy had greased the skids, because he didn't have time to dance with this guy.

As Rapp approached, Urda didn't move. He stood with his feet a shoulder width apart and his hands on his hips. He was short, a good five inches less than Rapp's six-foot frame, and a bit stocky. Rapp could tell by the look on his bearded face that he was not in a good mood.

Rapp didn't bother offering his hand. "Jamal, thanks for getting out here on such short notice."

"Cut the bullshit, Rapp. I heard you were in-country yesterday. Thanks for the fucking calling card." Urda folded his arms across his chest. The handles of his two .45-caliber pistols bulged beneath his biceps. "You know, professional courtesy among spooks and all that shit."

Rapp suppressed his initial reaction, which was to tell Urda what he could go do with himself, and tried to look at it from his perspective. He needed Urda, and his people, and he'd rather have them as willing participants than have to threaten them with losing their jobs. Rapp was so used to running closed ops that the thought of alerting the Agency's man in Kandahar that he was going to be running an op in his backyard hadn't even occurred to him.

In very uncharacteristic fashion Rapp said, "I'm sorry I didn't give you a heads-up, but this thing came down fast."

"So fast you couldn't pick up the phone?" Urda scratched his heavy black beard and waited for a reply.

Rapp had given it this one weak effort to act humble, and it wasn't working. He was hungry, tired, and not really in the mood for anything other than people following his orders. He looked over his shoulder and saw the base's medical staff racing forward to take care of the wounded. The one seriously injured trooper had been evacuated more than an hour ago and was already in surgery. The surgeon said he'd make it, but the young man's days as a Delta Force operator were probably over. There were nine others who were in need of medical treatment, though fortunately, none of the injuries was life threatening. Rapp, however, had planned on using the confusion of the postmission triage to quietly load the prisoners into Urda's two trucks. Which meant that he could ill afford to waste time arguing with this capable man who just might have a Napoleon complex.

"Jamal, I have five prisoners in the back of that Chinook over there." Rapp pointed to one of the large twin rotor birds. Six tired and dirty Delta Troopers were standing guard at the ship's aft ramp. "One of those men is Ali Saed al-Houri."

Rapp watched Urda's demeanor change instantly at the mention of one of al-Qaeda's top lieutenants. "I flew eight thousand miles and, in one day, did what you've been trying to do for almost two years. So don't give me this shit about professional courtesy. I don't know you, and I don't give a shit if I get to know you. All I care about is whether or not you're good at your job and whether you get me the results I'm looking for. Now, if you have a problem taking orders from me, let me know right now, and I'll make sure your ass is on the next plane back to the States. I'm sure I can get the director to find a nice desk job for you somewhere."

Rapp paused long enough for Urda to get a clear picture of himself sitting at the desk in question, and just how embarrassing it would be for him to get sent packing back to Langley, and then he offered the man an out. "I admire the sacrifice you've made, and I'd prefer to have you involved in this . . . especially since we don't have a lot of time. So do me a favor. Take your two trucks, pull them around to the back of that Chinook, and let's load these prisoners up and get the hell out of here."

Urda looked at the helicopter and then back at Rapp. "I heard you could be a real prick."

"I heard the same thing about you." Rapp gave the man a wry grin and said, "Let's go."

EIGHTEEN

Finding a CIA station in a new town was a little bit like looking for a Catholic cathedral. Scan the horizon for the highest point and that was most likely where you would find it. Kandahar was no different, except there were no cathedrals, or even churches—only mosques. The Agency had set up shop at a villa that overlooked the entire town. The place had been built and occupied by a wealthy Afghan family who had fled like all the other well to do families when the Soviet Union had invaded their country. During the eighties the compound had been occupied by the Soviets and then in the nineties by the Taliban, and now it was the Americans.

The recently paved road to the station snaked its way up the hillside to a checkpoint manned by U.S. Marines. The Toyota 4 Runners did not turn off on the road, though. Rapp had told Urda of his plans, and his fellow CIA officer thought it best if they steered clear of both official and unofficial types of U.S. installations. There was a place a little further down the road that Urda knew of. Rapp didn't bother to ask him how he knew of it, or if he'd actually used it. There was no need to ask prying questions in their profession. They only led to liabilities and answers that one was better off not knowing. At the CIA the attitude toward torture was a little bit like the military's policy on homosexuality: don't ask, don't tell.

Rapp was perhaps more comfortable with this state of intentional ignorance than anyone at the Agency. His entire recruitment into the CIA was part of a plan launched by the then director of operations Thomas Stansfield. Stansfield had been a member of the CIA's precursor, the Office of Strategic Services, or OSS. He'd distinguished himself during WWII when he became a highly effective and decorated operative, serving behind enemy lines in both Norway and France. After the war, when the CIA was formed, Stansfield became one of the Agency's first employees.

Stansfield was on the ground in Europe during the Cold War and had been the strategist behind some of America's greatest intelligence coups. During the Church Commission hearings on Capitol Hill in the seventies, when some of the CIA's biggest dunderheads were exposed, he was grateful to be ensconced behind the Iron Curtain. He was hopeful that the Agency would rebound from the hearings as an organization more focused and clear in its mission, but it was not to be. Stansfield watched his once great spy organization slide further into decline during the Iran–Contra fiasco, and saw long before anyone else what political correctness would do to the effectiveness of the CIA.

In the late eighties he reacted by creating a covert organization called the Orion Team. Its mission was to take the war to the terrorists. Stansfield understood, possibly more than any person in Washington at the time, that fighting religious fanatics by civilized means was a doomed endeavor, and ignoring them simply wasn't an option.

The twenty-two-year-old Rapp had been Stansfield and Kennedy's prized recruit. An international business major fluent in French, Rapp was an All-America Lacrosse star for the Syracuse Orangemen. During his junior year thirty-five of his fellow classmates were killed while returning from a semester abroad. The Pan Am Lockerbie terrorist attack had changed Rapp's life irrevocably. His high school sweetheart, the woman he planned on marrying some day, had been on the plane.

The pain from that tragedy had fueled Rapp's motive for revenge, and over the next decade he was honed into the most effective counterterrorism operative in America's arsenal. All of this was done without the official knowledge of either the Executive or Legislative branches of the government. There were certain key people in Washington who knew of the Orion Team, several esteemed senators and congressmen, but the specifics had been known only to Stansfield. These elder statesmen knew a full decade before the rest of their colleagues that there was a war on terrorism, and they also understood that neither their colleagues nor the American public had the stomach for what it would take to fight the rise in fanaticism.

Calling Rapp a counterterrorism operative was essentially a polite way of ducking the truth. When everything was stripped away, the reality was that he was an assassin. He had killed, and killed often, for his country, and in his mind 9/11 was proof that he hadn't killed enough. These zealots would stop at nothing to impose their narrow interpretation of the Koran, and that included the detonation of a nuclear warhead in the center of a civilian population. Rapp did not look forward to what he had to do, but he certainly wasn't squeamish about it either. There was a very real possibility that the men he had taken from the village possessed information that could save thousands of lives—possibly even hundreds of thousands, and Rapp would do whatever it took to ferret out what they knew.

NINETEEN

The vehicles turned onto a rutted and dusty road. After several minutes they came upon a series of ramshackle buildings. Rapp was a little taken aback to see that the place was occupied, but not as surprised as he was when he spotted a Soviet-made T-72 tank parked next to the largest of the buildings.

Sensing Rapp's unease, Urda turned to him and said, "Northern Alliance. My allies in this crazy war against the Taliban."

Rapp nodded and looked through the smeared and pitted windshield. "They going to be all right with this?"

"They hate these religious nuts more than you can possibly imagine. My boys," Urda pointed to the other vehicle that his two Afghani bodyguards were in, "are fiercely loyal to me. Good kids who lost their parents in the war. The Taliban did a lot of nasty shit to a lot of people. Consequently, they have no shortage of enemies."

Rapp had already noted that Urda's two locals looked as if they were still in their mid-teens, which didn't do a lot to instill confidence.

Urda gripped the wheel and brought the SUV

around the side of one of the buildings. "Whenever I have someone who doesn't want to do things the nice way I bring 'em out here, and let these guys get it out of them."

Rapp chose not to respond. This was not a part of his job that he enjoyed.

The two Toyota 4 Runners stopped next to a fenced-in pen of some sort. Rapp stepped out of the vehicle and was hit with the pungent smell of animal waste. He looked over the top of the fence and saw several dozen pigs lying in their own excrement.

Urda lifted the tailgate of the SUV, revealing three bound and hooded prisoners. He looked at his two Afghani bodyguards and said, "Hoods off and up and over the top."

The two Northern Alliance mercenaries grinned at each other and slung their rifles over their shoulders.

Rapp looked at him, somewhat puzzled.

"Pigs!" said Urda. "They freak these guys out. They think if they touch one before they die they won't go to heaven. You know, the whole ninety-nine virgins and all that shit."

Rapp grinned, "You mean seventy-seven houri." Rapp used the Arabic word for the beautiful young virgins who supposedly awaited the Muslim martyrs when they arrived in heaven.

"Yeah . . . whatever."

Rapp actually laughed for the first time in days. He watched as they tore the hood off the first man and tossed him over the fence with no care whatsoever as to how he landed. Rapp turned to Urda. "Tell them not to drop them on their heads. Especially the old man. I need them alive . . . at least for a while."

He glanced into the pen and watched the man

struggle against his bonds as pigs sniffed and licked him. His eyes were wide with fear rather than anger, and his shouts were stifled by his filthy gag. Rapp thought he'd seen it all, but this took the cake. He shook his head and walked away from the pen, fishing out his satellite phone. After flipping the large antennae into the upright position he punched in the number General Harley had given him.

A duty officer answered and Rapp asked for the general. Five seconds later Harley was on the line. "Mitch."

"General, have you ID'd the other two prisoners?" With reasonable certainty Rapp had already identified Hassan Izz-al-Din, Abdullah Ahmed Abdullah, and Ali Saed al-Houri.

"Not yet, but we're working on it."

"What about Langley?"

"As per your request, we're scanning documents as fast as we can and sending them back to the CTC."

"Have your guys, or Jamal's guys, found anything I can use?"

"Oh, there's stuff here," Harley said confidently, "it's just a question of getting it organized. We've got financial records, names, documents on WMD, plans for terrorist attacks . . . my J2 is telling me we hit the mother lode."

"Good." Time was critical, however. Word would get out quickly that al-Qaeda's command structure had been compromised. Bank accounts would be emptied, people would disappear, and plans would change.

"Listen, General, I can't stress enough how time-sensitive this information is. Have your people made any progress on the computers?"

"Not yet."

"Shit." Rapp ran a hand through his thick black hair. "Does the CTC have Marcus Dumond on it?"

"Let me check."

Rapp looked back at the pen in time to see another body tossed in. Marcus Dumond was the little brother he'd never wanted. A bona fide computer genius and hacker extraordinaire, the social misfit had been personally recruited by Rapp to work for the counter-terrorism center at Langley.

The general came back on the line. "They haven't been able to track him down."

Rapp's face twisted into an irritated frown. It was approaching midnight back in the states, and knowing Marcus he was probably hanging out at some cyber café with his friends. "Listen, General, I have to start inter-rogating these guys, so I need your people to work really fast. The second you learn anything, I want you to call me."

"Roger."

Rapp put the phone away and went back to the pen. His five prisoners were all on their backs writhing in agony as the dirty swine defiled their supposedly purified martyred bodies. He looked to Urda and said, "Have your boys bring them inside."

Rapp then gestured for Urda to follow him. The two men walked a safe distance away from any prying ears. Rapp looked around at the dusty hardscrabble landscape, and asked, "Off the record, how rough have you had to be?"

Urda shrugged. "Afghanistan is a rough place . . . hell, it shouldn't even be a place. It should be four or five countries. We've got communists, war lords, or drug dealers . . . however you want to describe them, we've got the Taliban, we've got people who want democracy, and we have a lot of nice men and women who just want to live their lives, and the other assholes who won't let them do it, so what we've got is one gigantic fucking mess."

"You didn't answer my question." Rapp kept his eyes fixed on Urda's. "How rough have you had to be?"

Urda returned his stare with equal intensity. "You mean have I tortured people?"

"Yeah."

He looked back toward the warehouse, obviously not wanting to answer the question. "There have been times where I have let the locals get physical, but I prefer to stay out of it as much as possible."

Watching every twitch of the man's bearded face, Rapp decided he was lying to him, or at least not telling the whole story. A notoriously impatient man, he said, "Jamal, let's cut the shit. I'm guessing you're a pretty straight shooter, but you don't want to say too much because I'm a little too high up on the totem pole."

Urda shifted his weight from one foot to the other, clearly uncomfortable with this line of questioning. Finally he said, "Those pricks back in Washington have no idea how ugly it is over here. They want us to act like we're cops . . . everything by the book." He spit on the ground, then threw his arms out gesturing at the harsh landscape. "There is no fucking rule book over here."

Rapp nodded. He understood. Having worked in the field for so many years he had very little affinity for the people back in Washington who tried to tell him how to do his job. Before he took this next step, however, he needed to make absolutely certain that he and Urda were of the same mind. "Listen, I'm about to go in there and do something that is so far off the reservation it can never be discussed with anyone . . . and I mean anyone."

Urda looked away, obviously uncomfortable.

Rapp reached out and grabbed his arm. "I haven't told you the whole story yet. This is not going to be your typical interrogation. We don't have the time to do it properly."

"Why?"

"Because we have reason to believe these guys are planning to detonate a nuclear weapon in Washington, D.C., and we have absolutely no idea how close they are to doing it, or if the little raid we conducted last night will cause them to move up their timetable." Rapp watched the expression change on Urda's face, and he let go of his arm.

"That's right . . . a nuke," repeated Rapp. "We're talking casu-alty rates that you and I can't even begin to calculate and the clock is ticking."

Urda's jaw hung slack for a moment and then he said, "My ex-wife and kids live just outside the city."

Not for the first time Rapp thought how lucky he was that his wife was visiting her parents in Wisconsin.

Urda shook his head as if struggling to comprehend the full enormity of the situation. "How big a bomb are we talking?"

"I don't know. That's one of the things I need to find out, and we don't have a lot of time. I need your help. My Arabic and Farsi are good but my Pashto and Urdu are nonexistent."

Rapp pointed toward the pen where the soiled prisoners were being dragged away from the squealing pigs. "I know two of these guys are fluent in Arabic, English, and Pashtu, and one of them speaks only Pashtu and a little bit of Arabic. I don't know what the other two speak. I'm going to need your help translating, but more importantly, I'm going to need your eyes and ears, because we are going to interrogate all five of them together."

Urda turned his attention away from the prisoners and back to the notorious CIA operative. As far as Urda knew, there was only one reason why someone would want to interrogate all five of the prisoners at the same time. His lips twisted into a pensive expression. "There are people who will do this for us," he offered.

Rapp began shaking his head before Urda had finished his sentence. "Nope. It's too important to trust to some warlord's thugs." He pointed at the bound prisoners as they shuffled single file into the building. "The fourth man in line is none other than Ali Saed al-Houri. He helped plan and execute the 9/11 attacks, and if he doesn't start singing like a bird I'm going to kill him right here and now, and I can tell you honestly that I won't lose a wink of sleep over it."

Urda let out a long sigh and looked at the ground as if the burden of what was about to happen was too much.

Rapp's jaw tightened. "I am going to do whatever it takes to get those men to talk. Make no mistake about it." Rapp moved his head to make sure Urda was looking directly at him. "And I mean whatever it takes, so before we go in there I need to know without a doubt that you're going to have the stomach for this, and that when all is said and done, you will never breathe a word of it to anyone."

Urda's thoughts returned to his ex-wife and three children. He pictured all them in their beds, in the house that he used to live in before this job destroyed his marriage. He thought of the reasons why he'd picked his career over his family: his sense of duty, the feeling that he could make a difference in this crazy war on terror, and that someone had to man the ramparts. It was as if all of those previous decisions had led to this one defining moment. The moment where his actions really could make the difference. If there was ever a time to ignore the rule book, this was it.

A resolute look crept onto his face, and Urda said with confidence, "I'm in."

TWENTY

The concrete floor could be seen only in patches, mostly where it was cracked and heaved upward. The rest of the floor was covered with a matted layer of gummy brown dirt. The building was approximately thirty feet wide by eighty feet long with large doors at each end to accommodate vehicles pulling in to drop off and pick up product. In this case the product was opium, both the bane and blessing of the Afghani people. Great wealth was derived from the opium poppy, and with that wealth came tribal rivalries that made the infamous prohibition–era Chicago gang-land wars seem infantile. These people didn't simply use machine guns to settle disputes, they used heavy armor, as was evidenced by the Soviet–made main battle tank parked outside.

The warlords who oversaw the growth, production, and distribution of opium were fabulously wealthy, ruthless men who had proven time and time again that they would use whatever force they had at their disposal to settle disputes. And that force was significant. Each had his own militia comprised of seasoned fighters, and almost endless funds to resupply his troops with the best that the former Soviet Union and her satellites had to offer, including guns, artillery, armor, and even heli-copters in a few cases.

For now a partnership of sorts had been struck with the Americans. For their part, the warlords had agreed to join forces with the Americans to rout the Taliban and al-Qaeda. In return the Americans were to turn a blind eye to the once again burgeoning opium trade. As always the CIA had been asked to take the lead on making and maintaining this Faustian alliance. Kennedy felt that this arrangement would eventually bite the CIA in the ass, but for now it was the most reasonable course.

Despite the inevitable criticism and probable Congressional investigation that would someday be launched by political opportunists, the alliance had worked. The Taliban had been thrashed in just months, and with minimal loss of American lives, and the country, while still not safe by Western standards, was as secure as it had been in over twenty years.

As Rapp stood in the dark corner of the poorly lit warehouse, he had accepted all of this and more. He eyed the bags of opium stacked to the rafters and briefly wondered how much it was all worth. He quickly decided he didn't want to know the answer. The potential for corruption among government-salaried CIA operatives was enormous. They worked in an alluring world of opium, cash, spies, drug lords, illegal arms shipments, and blackmail. Simply being in this building could cause him problems he didn't need.

Rapp wondered if this was the right place to conduct the interrogation, but he knew he had neither the time nor the resources to do anything else. The job had to be done and done quickly. Immediate results were paramount. Any fallout, he would have to suffer later.

America was at a distinct disadvantage in this war. International aid groups and reporters were keen to jump on any story about Americans committing atrocities, while they were seemingly numb to the day-to-day horrors perpetrated by the holy warriors on the other side. In the safe and sterile newsrooms, in the marble halls of Congress, it was easy to second-guess decisions and find fault. Out here on the field of battle things were far less certain. Moral ambiguity, rather than clarity, was the norm. What Rapp was about to do would be seen as barbaric by many of the same people whose lives he was trying to save. This was the sad irony of his life—that he would have to kill to save.

At his request the five prisoners were lined up on their knees in the middle of the warehouse. They were still bound and gagged. Rapp asked Urda to tell the two guards to wait outside, then retrieved a pair of earplugs from his black bulletproof tactical vest. He compressed the soft foam and inserted one plug into his left ear. Then he stepped from the shadows.

As he approached the five kneeling men he wondered if any of them would recognize him. During Kennedy's confirmation hearing, Rapp's cover had been blown by a senator who was seeking to derail Kennedy's nomination by exposing Rapp as a free-lancing assassin in the employ of the CIA. The president stepped in and let much more be known. For the first time, Rapp's role in several major counter-terrorism operations was acknowledged, most notably one that had saved the lives of hundreds, including that of the president himself. The president had dubbed Rapp America's first line of defense in the war on terror, and the press bit hard, publishing and broadcasting countless stories, replete with photographs. The fanatical Muslim clerics in turn dubbed Rapp enemy number one and demanded that he be killed.

As Rapp stepped into the faint light, he could tell by the expression on one of the younger man's faces that he did indeed recognize him. Rapp removed the man's gag and in Arabic told him to tell the others who he was.

The prisoner looked to the ground, afraid to stare into the eyes of the man standing before him. Rapp repeated his order, this time more firmly.

The man vacillated and then after clearing his throat and gaining some courage said, *"Malikul Mawt."*

Rapp smiled. The man had just told the others that Rapp was the angel of death. "That is right. My name is Azra'il, and today is *Yaumud Deen."* The day of judgment.

Urda had joined him in front of the five captives. Rapp pointed to one of the men and said, "Take his gag off."

Urda did so and then remained standing next to the gray-bearded man.

Having looked forward to this day for some time Rapp studied the grizzled face and said, "Ali Saed al-Houri, I have seen the *Sijjin* and your name is on it." The *Sijjin* was a scroll where the names of all those who will be sent to Hell are recorded.

The weathered features twisted with defiant rage and let loose a gob of spit. Rapp had expected nothing less and stepped effortlessly out of its way.

"You are a liar," al-Houri yelled in Arabic. "You are not even a true believer. You are nothing more than an assassin."

Rapp shook his head sadly. It was all part of an act he planned for the other four men. The CIA had an extensive file on al-Houri, much of it compiled by the

Egyptian secret police back in his days as a member of the Muslim Brotherhood. His faith was unshakable even then, and it was sure to have been strengthened over the years. That meant he would be exceptionally difficult to break, even if Rapp had all the time in the world to work on him.

"I am not a liar," Rapp replied without malice. "Allah does not hold in favor men who kill innocent women and children. Your name is on the list, and I am here to send you to Hell."

Al-Houri laughed in Rapp's face. "The tide is turning. We are about to strike a great blow for Allah, and you will pay dearly."

Rapp dropped to a squat so he could look al-Houri directly in the eye. "I found your little room under the house." Rapp paused to let this little surprise sink in. "Interesting plan . . . it's too bad it won't work."

The old man smiled. "You cannot stop us. There is not enough time."

Rapp could tell the smile was not false bravado. Out of fear, he almost asked a question, but stopped himself. There was no way the old man would answer it. No matter what Rapp said to al-Houri, his faith and confidence in his chosen path would remain unshaken. This made him dangerous. His conviction would give the others strength. He had to be removed to get the rest to talk.

Rapp stood and slowly walked around behind the prisoners. He approached Urda and whispered something in his ear. Urda nodded and handed over one of his Kimber .45-caliber pistols. Rapp took the heavy and exceptionally loud pistol and stood behind al-Houri who was trying to make eye contact with the other prisoners. With the weapon in his left hand he pulled the hammer back into the cocked position and covered his right ear with his free hand.

Rapp placed the stainless-steel barrel a mere two feet from his head and said, "Ali Saed al-Houri, your deeds have dammed you to Hell, and that is where I am sending you." There would be no last-minute confession, only orders for the others to stay true to their cause, so before al-Houri had a chance to utter a single word, Rapp squeezed the trigger.

TWENTY-ONE

Mitch Rapp wasn't sure if he believed in hell, but if such a place truly existed, Ali Saed al-Houri was on his way. Rapp rolled him over so the others could get a good look at what was in store for them. The force of the hollow-tipped .45-caliber round had punched a fist-sized hole through the terrorist's head, leaving a gaping wound where his nose and upper lip once were.

As Rapp looked down at him he didn't feel the slightest bit of regret or guilt. Al-Houri was one of the organizers of the worst terrorist attack in American history. He had cheered and gloated over the deaths of 3,000 peaceful men and women, and he was planning to kill thousands more. He was a vile and demented religious zealot, deserving of the bullet that had just ripped a large portion of his brain from his head.

Rapp paced back and forth in front of the remaining four prisoners. Not one of them dared raise his eyes and look at him. He knew their ears were ringing from the blast of the powerful .45-caliber Kimber so he shouted in Arabic, "Which one of you wants to go to hell next?"

Rapp told Urda to repeat everything he said in Pashtu. He went on to talk about the *Sirat;* the bridge over hell that all Muslims walk to find out if they will make it to *Jannah,* or paradise. He recited verses from the Koran that condemned the killing of innocent civilians. He screamed about the need to be in a purified state to be accepted into heaven. He spat verse after verse at them to drive doubt into their narrow minds that they were true martyrs and thus deserving of paradise. He got right in their ears and shouted that they were about to spend the rest of their days in endless torment, and then he offered them a chance to repent. A chance to be cleaned and purified. When he had set everything up as best as time would allow, it was time to separate the prisoners and begin questioning them one by one.

Urda's bodyguards came back into the warehouse and dragged three of the men out, leaving behind the one Rapp had chosen. He was the youngest of the lot, the man who had recognized Rapp. He was one of two wild cards. Rapp did not even know his name. It would have been ideal to know exactly who he was, to have a full briefing on him so he knew where to apply pressure and probe, but that was out of the question.

Rapp grabbed a couple of empty white five-gallon buckets and turned them upside down. As he walked around behind the prisoner, the man flinched. That was a good sign. Rapp took hold of him under the arms and hefted him onto the bucket. Moving the other bucket a little closer, he sat and looked into the eyes of the young man only a few feet away. The lifeless body of al-Houri lay beside them, the blood draining from his head and snaking its way toward the bare feet of the prisoner. It served as a vivid reminder of where this interrogation could lead.

For the first time, Rapp scrutinized the man's face. He had a beard, of course, and on the surface did not look

Arab or Persian. The young man was probably Afghani or Pakistani and looked to be in his mid-twenties.

"Do you speak English?" Rapp asked in an easy tone.

The prisoner would not raise his head and look at him. "Yes," he offered quietly.

The answer was more telling than one would think. It was common for English to be taught as a second language in both Afghanistan and Pakistan, but not in the mountainous border region. That meant the young man was more than likely from a larger city. "What is your name?"

"Ahmed."

"Do you have a last name?" Rapp asked.

The prisoner did not answer at first.

"It is only a name," Rapp prodded gently. "You know mine."

He answered reluctantly, "Khalili."

"How old are you?" Rapp wanted to start with the basics.

"Nineteen."

Rapp was surprised to hear how young the man was. It spoke to the harsh life that they lived that he could have easily passed for someone ten years older. Rapp looked up at Urda and held his hand up to his ear as if he was making a phone call. Urda nodded and started for the door. Rapp doubted they'd find the nineteen-year-old's name in their data base, but it was worth a try.

"Are you married, Ahmed?"

"Not yet."

The boy still wouldn't look him in the eye.

"Where are you from?" Rapp maneuvered his head to try and get him to look at him.

He chose not to answer, and kept his eyes fixed on the floor before him.

Rapp got up and walked behind the man, adding to the already tense mood. "I said, where are you from?"

"Karachi," the man answered, his shoulders tense with fear.

The large city in southern Pakistan. The young man was likely the product of one of the many Saudi-funded religious schools where children were indoctrinated into the strict Wahhabi sect of Islam.

Rapp continued walking around the man until he was once again standing in front of him. "Were you an orphan?"

The young man nodded.

It was an all-too-common occurrence in the region and beyond. The Wahhabis were taking in the orphans and street children of these large impoverished cities and filling their heads with their firebrand rhetoric.

Rapp felt a slight touch of sympathy for the person sitting before him. He no longer saw a young man, he saw a child who had been brainwashed. Rapp nudged the bucket forward even farther and sat again. He reached out and lifted the boy's face. "I am not the angel of death, Ahmed, and I am not going to kill you." Rapp noted the gleam of intelligence in the boy's gaze.

Ahmed's hazel eyes began to fill with tears, and he pulled his chin away from Rapp. "You are a liar." His gaze rested on the dead body lying on the dirty floor. He closed his eyes tightly and shook his head in defiance.

"I did not say you won't die, you just won't do so by my hand." Rapp nodded toward the door. "Those two Afghanis who threw you in the pigpen . . . their entire families were murdered by the Taliban. They wanted to do awful things to you, even before they knew you were a Pakistani. Things that I wouldn't even dream of."

Pointing to the bloody corpse on the floor, Rapp said, "That is the easy way out. He will be tormented in Hell for eternity, to be sure, but at least he didn't have to suffer the indignity of being forced to eat his own genitalia."

The young man began to whimper.

"If you do not talk to me," continued Rapp, "I will have no choice but to turn you over to them, and then you will lose any hope of setting things straight before you pass."

"I have done nothing wrong," the boy said defensively.

"Can you be sure of that? Do you pretend to know what Allah wishes? Can you be absolutely certain that those men who gave you your religious instruction know the full intent of the prophet?" Rapp lifted Khalili's chin again. "Ahmed, I'm guessing you're smart . . . smarter than the others. Have you never read the Koran and wondered how the imams derive such hate from a book that is so filled with peace and beauty?"

The boy did not try to pull away this time. Rapp released his chin and placed his hand on his shoulder. "I can help you if you let me, Ahmed. I will take you away from this place and make sure no harm comes to you. You will meet other Muslims who are enlightened. Muslims who will tell you that the people who have taught you are false prophets, sick men who are blinded by bigotry and hate for their fellow man. There is a plane waiting only miles from here. A hot shower, a change of clothes, and a prayer rug for you to begin making things right. That is one path. The other one is several days, perhaps weeks, even months filled with pain and humiliation you can't even begin to comprehend.

Rapp withdrew his hand. "The choice is yours, but you must show me you are willing to cooperate, or I will turn you over to the Afghanis." He studied the boy, and watched as his breathing seemed to settle. Rapp did not want to give him too much time to think of his answer. He was sure the voices of his religious instructors were ringing in his head telling him that their version of Islam was the only true one. The Muslims, who disagreed with him had gone astray and been perverted over the centuries.

Rapp stood and took a step toward the door. Over his shoulder he said, "I will take your silence as an unwillingness to cooperate."

He had barely taken three steps when he heard the beaten voice of his prisoner say something that he could barely make out. He forced himself to turn around more slowly than he would have liked. "What did you say?"

"They are planning to kill your president."

"How?"

He shook his head. "I do not know."

Rapp studied the slumped figure for a few seconds. "Ahmed, if this is going to work, you have to tell me everything."

"I do not know how," he said more adamantly this time.

"A bomb."

"There has been mention of a bomb."

Rapp felt his heart quicken. "A nuclear bomb?"

The boy looked up at the question. "I have not heard them talk of a nuclear bomb."

"Ahmed, you cannot lie to me."

"I only arrived the day before yesterday. I have not been involved in this part of the operation."

Rapp returned to the bucket and sat. "What else did they say about the bomb? Repeat everything."

"I overheard them saying it was very big." Ahmed looked down as if he was ashamed. "They said it would kill thousands. All of your politicians and generals."

Rapp's jaw hung slack with disbelief at the revelation. There was only one bomb that he could think of that killed thousands. "Ahmed, do you know how many Muslims live in Washington, D.C.?"

"No."

"Thousands. These bombs don't simply kill politicians and generals. Do you think Allah will show forgiveness to anyone who kills that many of his flock?"

"I don't know."

"Yes, you do, Ahmed," snapped Rapp, "yes, you do." The sheer lunacy of the entire mess left Rapp at a momentary loss. These bastards were finally going to do it.

"When is the attack to take place?"

"I don't know."

"Come on . . . you must have some idea."

"Soon, is all I know."

"How soon?" demanded Rapp.

"I do not know."

Rapp gave his prisoner an ominous look.

"I swear to you I do not know! I only follow orders. This Friday past, Waheed Abdullah told us we were to leave Karachi and make our way to the mountains."

"Why?"

"Because of the crackdown that will take place after the bomb goes off."

Rapp buried his face in his hands. These idiots had no idea of the Pandora's box they were about to open.

After a moment he regained his composure. So far he believed Ahmed, but he needed to talk to the others and see if he could confirm this story. More importantly, he needed to find out if the others knew more. He was willing to bet that two of them did for sure.

Rapp grabbed Ahmed under the arm and pulled him to his feet. "Let's go, and I don't want you talking to the others. Don't even look at them!" They walked toward the door, Rapp pulling the shackled prisoner along. When they reached the rickety door, Rapp shoved it open, and they were momentarily blinded by the bright morning sun. Rapp brought a hand up to shield his eyes and pushed Ahmed toward Urda.

"Gag him and sit him down over there by the trucks."

Urda was on his mobile phone. He held up a finger signaling to Rapp that he needed a second. He walked a few steps away and continued to listen. "All right. Thanks for the update. Call me as soon as you learn anything else."

Urda flipped the phone closed and approached Rapp. The other three prisoners were kneeling on the ground bound and gagged about fifty feet away. Urda hooked Ahmed by the arm and said to Rapp, "Follow me."

The three of them walked over by the trucks where Urda deposited Ahmed. He fastened the gag over his mouth and grabbed a smelly burlap hood to throw over his head.

Rapp stopped him. "He doesn't need the hood."

Urda threw the hood on the ground and gestured for

Rapp to follow him. He led him around the corner of the building and in a voice barely loud enough for Rapp to hear said, "That was one of my guys calling from the base. They found a couple of interesting dossiers on some guys who we've been looking for. Care to take a guess who?"

Rapp was not in the guessing mood. He'd allowed his thoughts to wander briefly and was thinking of the city of his youth. The place he called home. The faces of innocent people going about their honest lives. They were all in jeopardy. "I have no idea."

"You know those missing Pakistani nuclear scientists we've been trying to track down?"

All Rapp could do was shake his head. "This just keeps getting worse."

"The dossiers are detailed. Filled with surveillance of their activities going back five years in one case. They were recruited by agents at the local mosques where the scientists were posted . . . just like we thought."

"Any more good news?" he asked sarcastically.

"No."

Rapp leaned back around the corner and checked on Ahmed. "Khalili says he left Karachi last Friday when Abdullah ordered them to pack up and head for the mountains."

"The mountains?"

"Reprisals. They think those damn mountains will actually protect them."

Urda looked off to the south. From this distance the mountains looked like a distant wall of clouds. "Those mountains have protected them for centuries."

"Not this time, Jamal. If they've got a nuke, and they set it off in D.C., the mountains will become their tomb." Rapp stepped around the corner and looked at the three prisoners he had yet to interrogate. He could feel the rage building, which wasn't always a good thing, but considering the time constraints they were up against there was no delicate way to handle the situation.

"Follow me," he said to Urda, "And let's get this over with."

TWENTY-TWO

Rapp dragged Hassan Izz-al-Din into the room by his long black hair. The man's personal hygiene left a lot to be desired, and that was before he'd been rolled around in pigshit. Al-Din's gag was still in place, so the curses he was trying to fling at Rapp weren't getting very far. Rapp deposited the Yemeni-born extremist like a bag of garbage on top of his dead comrade. Al-Din struggled wildly against his bonds while simultaneously trying to writhe his way off his dead friend.

He squirmed his way clear of the corpse just in time for Urda to deposit Waheed Ahmed Abdullah in the space he had just vacated. Abdullah's reaction to being placed on top of his lifeless friend was much the same as al-Din's.

Rapp pulled al-Din to his knees, and as soon as Abdullah had rolled clear he yanked him off the ground by his hair. The two men were left kneeling side by side with the body of al-Houri in front of them. Rapp took one man's gag off and then the other. The curses flew forth in furious Arabic. The dignity of Rapp's mother was assaulted right off the bat, and then their attention turned to his wife.

Rapp just stood there, arms folded, watching the bearded mongrels spew their hatred. He wanted them to get all of this off their chests and then he would react. Finally, Rapp asked in Arabic, "Are you done?"

The men spat in his direction and launched into a second tirade every bit as vituperative as the first. Many of the same insults were used, only uttered with redoubled vigor, but as before, they ran out of steam and grew a bit bewildered at Rapp's refusal to engage.

Rapp knew a fair amount about each man. He knew from where they hailed, and where they'd received their religious indoctrination. Although he couldn't recall all the names, he also knew the CIA had a list of their family members.

"Are you done?" he asked again.

This time they only muttered a few curses before stopping.

"Good," replied Rapp in a satisfied tone. He drew his 9mm FNP-9 from his thigh holster, pulled the hammer back into the cocked position, and leveled it at al-Din. Without a question, or word of warning, he squeezed the trigger once, a loud pop and muzzle flash erupting from the weapon. Before Abdullah could react, Rapp brought the weapon to bear on him and fired again.

The entire thing happened in less than a second, with both men toppled over screaming in pain but unable to clutch their shattered kneecaps.

Rapp stepped over the dead body of al-Houri and looked down at the two agonized faces. "You didn't really think it was going to be that easy, did you?"

Through a jaw clenched in pain al-Din tried to assail him with more insults, although they'd lost the intensity they'd had only a moment earlier. Abdullah reacted just as Rapp thought he would. He just lay there on the dirty floor and whimpered to himself.

Rapp had decided to take a calculated risk and make an assumption based on what he already knew. He lowered his weapon and said, "So tell me about the bomb."

Abdullah started to speak, but was stopped by al-Din. "Silence! Don't say another word to him."

Looming over the two men, Rapp reacted instantly and without malice. He grabbed Abdullah by the hair and shoved his face next to al-Din's. He extended his pistol and pointed it at the head of al-Din, the man who he had already guessed would be more difficult to break. The men had their faces pressed tightly together. Rapp squeezed the trigger and sent a hollow-tipped bullet into the Yemeni's face. Al-Din's entire body convulsed at impact and then settled, with only his fingers twitching. Abdullah was left gasping for air, his eyes stinging from the muzzle blast and his face covered with blood and flesh.

Rapp knew that al-Din had been born into an impoverished Yemeni household and at the young age of fifteen had joined the fight against the Soviets in Afghanistan. He was battle hardened and the less likely of the two to break. He had also been in charge of the terrorist training camp that produced seven of the 9/11 hijackers, and for that reason alone Rapp felt no remorse for putting a bullet in his head.

Abdullah, on the other hand, had come from a wealthy Saudi family, and having shown no real skill or interest in business, he was shipped off at the age of twelve to receive religious instruction at one of the grand Wahhabi madrasas in Mecca. Abdullah was a firebrand Muslim, but a pampered one.

"So," Rapp straddled the Saudi and pointed the barrel of the FNP-9 at his head. "You and I were talking. Tell me about the bomb."

Abdullah's face was contorted in pain from the gunshot to his knee. He looked over at the twitching hand of his dead comrade. A second later he shut his eyes and said, "I do not know about any bomb."

"Wrong answer." Rapp brought his gun up. He would not kill Abdullah, at least not yet, but the man did not need to know that.

"No . . . no . . . I am telling you the truth!" Abdullah closed his eyes tightly as if that would somehow slow the impact of the bullet. "It wasn't my part of the operation."

"Abdullah, listen very carefully to me. If you don't tell me everything I want to know I am going to kill you, and then I am going to track down your entire family and kill each one of them. Now, for the last time . . ." Rapp leaned over, placing the hard steel of the FNP-9 against Abdullah's temple and forcing his head onto the dirty floor. "Is the bomb nuclear?"

Abdullah's face was twisted in fright. "Yes."

"How big?"

"I do not know," he pleaded. "Honestly."

"Bullshit!"

"I swear I don't know. All I've been told is that it will destroy the entire city."

"What city?"

"Washington."

Rapp squeezed the grip of his FNP-9. "When are you planning on setting it off?"

"This week some time . . . I think."

Rapp leaned on the gun and yelled, "What do you mean some time?"

"I do not know. I was only told it would happen this week."

"Where is the bomb right now?"

"I don't know."

Rapp removed the pistol from the Saudi's temple and shoved it into his groin. "I'm going to blow your balls off, Abdullah! Where the hell is the bomb?"

"Don't shoot!" the man pleaded. "It was supposed to arrive yesterday."

"Where?"

A bewildered expression spread across Abdullah's face. "I truly don't know. I only know that it was coming in by plane."

"What kind of plane?"

Abdullah closed his eyes. "A cargo plane."

"What carrier, and from where?"

"I do not know."

Rapp kept the pistol firmly in place. It was unclear how much, if any, of what he'd just been told was true, but either way he had to report it to Kennedy immediately. An idea popped into his head and he decided to go with it. He stood, reached down to grab a handful of his prisoner's hair, and started dragging him across the floor.

He looked at Urda and said, "Load the other two up. We're going back to the base." When he reached the door he held it open with one hand while he pulled his prisoner across the threshold. Then, in a moment of inspiration, he decided to stop and slam the door into the terrorist's shattered knee.

Abdullah shrieked in pain. Rapp waited a few seconds and slammed the door into his knee again. Abdullah's eyes rolled back into his head, and he began to hyperventilate.

Rapp bent down and growled into his ear, "Guess where we're going?"

Abdullah either didn't hear the question or was in too much pain to answer so Rapp yanked his hair and screamed the question a second time.

"I don't know," Abdullah answered, with tears streaming from his dark brown eyes.

"Ground zero, you stupid prick." Rapp pulled him out into the bright sunlight. "I'm going to strap your ass to the Washington Monument so you can have a front-row seat."

Rapp began pulling Abdullah toward the waiting vehicles. He couldn't even attempt to remember the last time he'd been so enraged. It had finally come to this. These nutbags were actually going to plunge the world into chaos.

"Hey, Abdullah," Rapp said in a sarcastic voice, "maybe I'll have your mom and dad picked up along with all of your brothers and sisters and nieces and nephews." Rapp pulled him roughly over a crumbled wall. "The whole Abdullah clan. That's what I'm going to do. I'll call my buddy the crown prince and have them sent over."

"The crown prince," hissed Abdullah, "is no friend of yours."

"Sure he is," replied Rapp in a jovial voice. "He owes me a big favor, actually." Rapp reached the back of one of the vehicles and let go of his prisoner's hair.

Abdullah's head hit the ground hard. With an angry face he said, "This proves you are a liar. I know the crown prince." Abdullah wheezed in pain and added, "He is a true believer, and he would never ever speak to someone like you."

Rapp laughed. "The crown prince believes in Allah, but he does not buy into all that Wahhabi crap."

"Liar!"

"Remember fat Omar . . . his half brother? Sure you do. Omar used to send you money to wage your little twisted jihad." Rapp squatted down and pointed to himself. "I was the one who killed him in Monaco last year, and the crown prince thanked me personally for saving him the trouble."

The look on his captive's face was beyond priceless.

Rapp popped the tailgate. "Yeah, I'll have to make that call. That way your family can thank you in person for getting them all killed. Every last member."

TWENTY-THREE

I rene Kennedy stood at the back of the Global Ops Center on the seventh floor of the Old Headquarters Building at Langley. She slowly placed the handset of the secure phone back in its cradle. She didn't move or speak for close to a minute. Around her the room buzzed with every manner of modern communication available. All of it—every voice, beep, whir, churn, and tap of a keyboard—blended into a seamless thrum of background noise, and she blocked it out.

The national security of America was serious business, and Dr. Irene Kennedy had never thought otherwise. The specter of a nuclear attack, however, did strange things to people. She was not incapacitated by fear. On the contrary. She was merely trying to comprehend the full importance of what Rapp had just told her, for she knew there was no turning back once she took the next step. There would be no standing down, at least not for the next few hours. This would likely be her last chance to make a calm assessment of the situation before a myriad of people and agencies got involved: secretaries, undersecretaries, directors, deputy directors, generals, admirals, and of course the president himself and the grab bag of political advisors who came with him. Some of these people were good at keeping secrets, but most of them were not.

Kennedy looked up at the three massive TV screens that dominated the front wall of the room. They were all tuned to twenty-four-hour cable news networks. There was no big news at present, and she hoped that would remain the case for the next twenty-four hours until they could get a handle on this thing.

Somewhat reluctantly, Kennedy picked up the handset of the secure phone. She scanned the numerous buttons for the proper speed-dial label and found it. Several seconds later the duty officer for the Secret Service's Joint Operations Command answered.

"This is Director Kennedy. Patch me through to Agent Warch ASAP."

After several seconds and a few clicks a tired voice came on the line. "Warch here."

Kennedy knew the special agent in charge of the president's Secret Service detail well. "Jack, it's Irene. Sorry to bother you at such an awkward hour, but we have a situation."

Warch's voice was suddenly less tired. "What's up?"

"I'm about to implement Operation Ark, and it's not a drill." Kennedy imagined that the agent was now sliding out of bed. Operation Ark, the code name for the evacuation of key government officials from the city had only been set into motion one other time that the two of them could remember.

"Okay. What's the threat?"

"We have reason to believe a WMD might be in the city."

"What kind?" Warch's voice was suddenly a bit tighter.

"This goes no further, Jack. I haven't even told the Pentagon yet."

"I understand, but I need to know what I'm dealing with."

"The intel right now points to a nuclear weapon."

"Jesus Christ."

"Jack, this needs to be done very low key, but fast. No Marine One. Put him in the limo and take him up to Camp David as quickly as possible without making a scene. Bring the First Lady with, and don't take no for an answer from either of them."

"Roger."

"Call me with confirmation as soon as they're in the limo and on their way. I can be reached at the Global Ops Center for the next fifteen minutes."

"Understood."

Kennedy ended the call and turned to Carl Benson, the director of the Ops Center. He was fully briefed on the evening's developments and was waiting for further direction.

"Have my helicopter warmed up, and lock this place down. I don't want any personal calls in or out."

Benson nodded and went about carrying out Kennedy's orders.

The director of the CIA did not grab the phone immediately. The next call would unleash a torrent of warning bells, waking people from their sleep and beckoning them to secure federal facilities strategically placed around Washington, D.C. Many of them would leave disoriented spouses and children left to guess at what might be happening. By morning, thousands of people would know that something serious was going on and the press would begin to dig. The facts that Mitch Rapp had just unearthed would be exceedingly difficult to hide from the public, and once they knew them, pandemonium would follow.

This was the conundrum they were confronted with. If they wanted to stop these terrorists, they would have to use all of America's national security assets, but at the same time, hope that they didn't tip their hand to the terrorists themselves. It would be an impossible secret to keep, but there was no other choice but to try.

TWENTY-FOUR

The Secret Service was exceedingly good at its job for a variety of reasons. The selection process by which agents were chosen was one of the most stringent in all of law enforcement, but it was the level of their training and its frequency that separated them from virtually every personal protection detail anywhere in the world. Scenarios were constantly scripted and run through with new agents assigned to the presidential detail, as well as veterans.

At their state-of-the-art training facility in Beltsville, Maryland, the agents were taught to shoot with pinpoint accuracy, and they rehearsed ad nauseam motorcade procedure and how to handle a crowd when their charge decided to get out of the car and walk the rope line. In addition they went through countless dry-run exercises at the White House, Camp David, and Andrews Air Force Base. All of this training took place for one specific reason. When a crisis hit, seconds mattered, and a single hesitation by just one agent could be the difference between the president living or dying.

To make matters even more difficult, the men and women they were asked to protect tended to be anything other than docile. Instead, they were almost always intelligent, independent minded people who were used to being in charge. They did not like being told what to do, and very often resisted the suggestions put forth by the Secret Service concerning the proper level of security.

All of this figured into how the Secret Service did their job. So while Director Kennedy would have preferred a quiet orderly evacuation of the first couple, with as few people knowing about it as possible, that just wasn't the way it was done. If there was even a whiff of a nuclear weapon in the nation's capital Warch wanted the president far away, locked up in a secure bunker.

Seconds mattered, and since it would take Warch twenty minutes to get to the White House, the detail's shift leader would have to be the one to execute the evacuation. Warch was left with two options, the first would be to call Beth Jorgenson and utter a single phrase that would in turn set into motion a well-rehearsed preplanned evacuation that would take no more than sixty seconds to complete. Or he could call Jorgenson and tell her that he would like her to calmly and quietly pack up the president and the First Lady and drive them up to Camp David without making any scene.

The problem with the latter option was that there was a fifty-fifty chance the president would choose not to comply in a timely manner, and a ninety-nine percent chance that the First Lady would outright refuse to go. The president would want specifics, and then he would want to talk to his advisors and try to reach a consensus. Warch decided his nerves couldn't take the latter. If there was any fallout he would just have to deal with it later.

★

WHEN THE CALL came out over the detail's secure radio net, agents and officers alike sprang into action. In the basement of the West Wing, eight men who were part of the counterassault team or CAT, jumped to their feet. Dressed in black tactical jumpsuits and laden with ballistic body armor, the men quickly grabbed their helmets, automatic rifles, and machine guns. They poured out of the West Wing and onto the South Lawn setting up a perimeter around "Stage Coach," the presidential limousine.

On the second floor of the mansion two agents, one female the other male, burst into the first family's bedroom without knocking. The agents apologized to the First Lady for the intrusion, but made no effort to explain further why they were awaking her after midnight. The covers were thrown back and Mrs. Hayes was plucked from the king-size bed and offered a robe. Before it was knotted she was being hustled from the room on her toes, an agent on each arm. Across the hall the elevator was waiting, doors open. The First Lady was deposited in the lift and the doors closed like a vise for the quick trip to the ground floor.

The president was in the Situation Room with his feet up on the long shiny conference table watching Sports Center and thinking about going to bed when the heavy soundproof door opened with a thud. Beth Jorgenson entered the room with three other agents.

"Mr. President, please come with us."

Understandably so, the president looked a little shaken. "What is going on?"

"We've been ordered to take you to Camp David, sir."

Two linebacker-sized agents grabbed the president under the arms and yanked him to his feet. Jorgenson led the way out of the Situation Room, down the hall and up the stairs. The agents ignored the president's questions, and stayed focused on the task at hand. They burst onto the colonnade outside the West Wing and began jogging down the path to the driveway that arched its way through the South Lawn.

The tanklike presidential limo was waiting, engine running, its passenger-side doors open. An ominous looking black suburban was also waiting behind it. An agent stood at each corner of the vehicle. Two of them were holding their FNH Five-Seven tactical pistols at the ready while the other two were holding FNP-90 submachine guns.

The First Lady was unceremoniously brought out of the basement door, her robe billowing open, her bare legs on display. Fortunately there was no one around to witness it. She arrived at the limousine seconds before the president. One of the agents who had more or less carried her along the way placed his hand on top of her head as if she were a perp being stuffed into the back of a squad car, and tossed her into the backseat so they could get out of the way of the quickly approaching president and the agents who were helping him. President Hayes was given the same treatment.

Normally, they would have the backup limousine and a half dozen other vehicles as part of the motorcade, but not during a quick evacuation. Those vehicles were at this very moment being fired up at the Secret Service's garage only a few blocks away. Out of necessity four agents piled into the back with the president and the First Lady. Jorgenson climbed into the front seat with the driver, and two more agents got in the jump seats behind her and the driver.

As soon as the doors to the limousine were shut, the

counterassault team piled into the back of the Suburban. The two armor-plated vehicles raced out the heavy gate and onto West Executive Drive where they were met by two Secret Service Uniformed Division sedans. One pulled out in front and the other followed. Six blocks later the backup limousine joined the formation as well as a communication van bristling with antennas. The entire evacuation had taken exactly fifty-two seconds.

TWENTY-FIVE

The warehouse was not located in the best part of town, but that was to be expected. Good real estate in Atlanta was expensive, and the men who had invested in this small trucking company were not looking for a long-term investment. They simply wanted entry into a business that would pay dividends of a different sort. The previous owner, a seventy-two-year-old man who could no longer drive, was more than eager to retire.

They gave him the terms he wanted. He received a cash payment of $80,000 up front and would get an additional $5,000 a month for three years. When the new owners first took over, six of the trucks were in decent shape, and two of them needed some work. That was thirteen months ago. Now only three trucks were running, and the owners had no intention of repairing the others. If things went according to plan they would no longer be in business after Memorial Day.

Ahmed al-Adel mopped his brow with a cloth and cursed the oppressive humidity of Atlanta. The warehouse was not air-conditioned. Only a few more days and he would finally return home. Al-Adel had immigrated to America in 1999, and scarcely a day had passed that he hadn't regretted his decision to come to this godless country. He'd been told Atlanta had a large Muslim population, that it would be easy for him to make friends, and hopefully find a wife. He had two uncles and many cousins in the area. Al-Adel was a gifted man in the sense that he was smart and well educated, even if he lacked physical stature. In his mind, it was infinitely better to have brains.

Al-Adel was shocked that his relatives even bothered to call themselves Muslims. They had been so corrupted by America and its vices that he was certain every last one of them was on the express lane to Hell. Al-Adel had been ready to return home to Saudi Arabia when his glorious brothers had flown the planes into the towers in New York and the military's headquarters in Washington. He had watched the events unfold in his one bedroom apartment, and cheered the successes of the brave Muslim warriors.

Their heroics had given al-Adel the courage to stay and fight. It was not long after the attack that he had started to find others who felt the way he did—that America was a disgusting, decadent place. Even young Muslim women here no longer honored their parents the way they should. They went out in public unaccompanied by male relatives and made no effort to cover their faces. Many of them had even taken to driving.

Al-Adel had expressed his disapproval to one of his uncles and the man had done nothing. His female cousins made fun of him behind his back. They made fun of his slight physical stature and his traditional ways. They did not think he noticed, but he heard their whispers and snickers. They were like a flock of cackling hens, who had no idea of their place in this world. That was all about to change. Al-Adel and his fellow warriors were about to ignite a spark that would lead to a global jihad.

Al-Adel stepped out into the yard and walked across the pock-marked asphalt toward his idling truck. Two men were standing by the truck talking to each other. One of them came toward al-Adel and enveloped him in a warm embrace.

"Allahu Akbar." God is great.

Al-Adel repeated the greeting. *"Allahu."*

"I checked everything personally. It will take you to your destiny and beyond."

"Thank you." Al-Adel clapped him on the shoulders. "Hopefully, we will meet again in our homeland."

"If not, then in paradise," the man said with a proud grin.

"Yes." Al-Adel beamed with satisfaction. "Remember the instructions I gave you. If you do not hear from me by ten this morning I want you to call the number I gave you."

The man nodded. "I know exactly what to do. Now get going."

The two men hugged one more time, and then al-Adel climbed behind the wheel of the big rig. The third man got in the passenger seat of the cab, a pistol bulging from the waist of his pants. Al-Adel gunned the engine several times and then forced it into gear.

The man standing on the ground cupped his hands around his mouth and yelled, "Be careful."

Al-Adel gave him a toothy smile and nodded. He had gotten quite good at driving the big rigs. For nearly a year now he had made three round trips a week from Atlanta to the port of Charleston. None of those trips had been as important as this one, but this time Allah would be keeping an even closer eye on him.

TWENTY-SIX

WASHINGTON, D.C.

Peggy Stealey was in the middle of a rather violent dream. She had just delivered a crushing blow to her karate instructor's groin, but that wasn't enough. With great speed and precision she moved on to his solar plexus, throat, and then finally nose. The last blow was a textbook palm strike and sent the man to the mat, blood dripping from his flattened nose. She saw herself standing over him, her hair a disaster, her cheeks flushed, and her skin glistening with sweat. A look of profound accomplishment spread across her face, and then something happened. A stimuli that wasn't supposed to be in her dream.

Her eyelids flickered and then opened. She looked over at her bedside clock, things still not quite registering. The blue letters told her it was 2:28 in the morning. She realized her victory was only a dream and was pissed. It was the best one she'd had in months. She laid her head back down and closed her eyes. She should have known that kicking her sadist instructor's butt was too good to be true. She told herself if she fell back asleep fast enough she might be able to pick up where she'd left off.

Seconds later Stealey figured out what had pulled her

from her dream. Her pager over on her dresser was vibrating. Stealey grabbed a pillow and clamped it down on her head. She wanted to return to her dream. Weren't twelve-hour days enough? She was almost always up by five, never asleep past six, and always brought work home with her. She was lucky if she got five hours a night, so was it too much to ask for them not to bother her between midnight and when the sun came up?

Stealey whipped her pillow across the room, and cursed herself for not having the courage to ignore the damn siren call of work. No wonder she couldn't find a steady boyfriend. There wasn't time for herself, let alone anyone else.

She swung her long, toned legs from under the covers and walked over to the nightstand. When she reached out for the pager, she realized why she had been dreaming about throttling her karate instructor. Stealey winced as she was reminded of her sore left breast. Always pushing herself to get better, Stealey, a third-degree black belt, had gotten overly aggressive while sparring with her instructor. She had landed a glancing blow to the older man's head, but in the process left herself wide open. Master Jing, not one to let such a mistake go unpunished, responded with a lighting-quick strike that knocked her clean off her feet. Stealey could still picture Master Jing standing over her, chiding her for such a foolish mistake. She would have attempted a reply if it wasn't for the fact that there was no longer any air left in her lungs.

She picked up the pager and looked at the small readout. When she saw the number staring back at her she said, "Oh shit."

Stealey ran from her room. The Department of

Justice had a twenty-four-hour command center, and there were only two reasons why they would be calling her in the middle of the night. She reached the kitchen, where she immediately noticed the blinking message light on her answering machine. Stealey pressed play and grabbed her cell phone to turn it on. She kept a fan on in her bedroom and turned off the ringers at night so she could sleep. The pager was kept in her bedroom on the off chance someone really needed to get hold of her.

The attorney general's voice came out of the small speaker on her answering machine. His only direction was to call him immediately. Even though the message was brief she could tell something was wrong.

She grabbed her phone and dialed his cell phone number. He answered on the first ring. "Peg, are you on a land line?"

"Ah . . . no. I'm on a cordless."

"Where the hell have you been?"

She pulled her hair back trying to think of an excuse and finally told him the truth. "Sleeping."

"Listen to me. I can't discuss this with you over an open line. Get to the Joint Counterterrorism Center immediately and call me back."

Before she could ask what was going on the line went dead.

Stealey just stood there in her kitchen, left dumbfounded and staring at the cordless phone. The new Joint Counterterrorism Center was only a few miles from her apartment. The facility was near Tyson's Corner, on the far western edge of the Beltway, and had just recently opened. The idea behind the top secret facility was twofold. The first was to get the FBI and the CIA working together on the war on terrorism, and the second was to get the FBI's counterterrorism people out of downtown.

The rationale behind that move was pretty straightforward. FBI headquarters was a target of high value for terrorists, and if they succeeded in destroying the building, they would take with it the very agents who were supposed to investigate the attack.

The gravity of what must be going on began to seep in. She was supposed to keep a Go Bag packed at all times for just this type of situation. Stealey cursed herself for not paying more attention during all the exercises.

They'd given her three phones, and two pagers, and instructed her to carry all of them with her at all times. Her feeling had been that the entire thing was overkill. One phone and pager were designated to be used during the normal course of business. The second phone and two-way pager were given top priority on cellular towers, and the last phone, which was still in its box, was an iridium satellite phone to be used if regular service was knocked out.

All she'd wanted was five hours of sleep. She placed the cordless phone back in its cradle and said, "This better not be a damn drill."

Even as she started down the hall to get dressed, she knew it wasn't. Stokes would have told her, plus they didn't wake the attorney general up in the middle of the night for drills. Stealey picked up the pace. She threw on a gray pants suit and stuffed some toiletries and extra garments into the bag she was supposed to have packed, and then headed back to the living room. She took a quick look at herself in the mirror by the door. Her hair was a mess and she still had sleep lines on her face. *Screw it,* she thought. *I'll have to do it in the car.*

Stealey yanked open the front hall closet and started

chucking boxes out of the way until she found the satellite phone they'd given her more than a year ago. She doubted the battery was charged, but she'd bring it anyway. She was almost out the door when she realized she didn't have her purse, so she went back to the kitchen table to get it. She threw the bag over her shoulder, grabbed her purse, and left, forgetting to lock the door. Stealey was already in the garage by the time she realized her mistake and cursed herself up and down. She almost went back and then thought better of it. Something told her now was not the time to worry about unlocked doors.

TWENTY-SEVEN

AFGHANISTAN

The two vehicles arrived back at the base with little fanfare. The Special Forces contingent had their own section of the base and an MP in a Humvee escorted them to General Harley's command tent. Rapp started to get out of the truck before it stopped. He was so sick of listening to Waheed Abdullah scream he'd actually thought of knocking him out. Rapp had been shot before, and there was nothing pleasant about it, but the man had been screaming, moaning, and crying now for close to thirty minutes.

Rapp lifted the back hatch half hoping Abdullah would roll out and hit the ground hard enough to break his jaw. His wish did not come true. The Saudi screamed even louder once he saw his tormentor. Soldiers began spilling out of the command tent, followed by General Harley. Rapp would have liked to avoid this scene, but there'd been a change of plans. Urda and his Afghani bodyguards grabbed the other two prisoners and leaned them against the SUV.

No one, least of all General Harley, noticed, or cared, or more likely dared ask Rapp why he'd left with five prisoners and returned with only three. There were certain things Harley was just better off not knowing.

"You want medical attention for this one?" asked Harley, as he pointed to Abdullah, who was between shrieks and breathing so heavily he looked as if he might pass out.

Rapp wanted to crack him over the head with the butt of his pistol and knock him out, but doing it in front of all these officers would be a real bad idea. Reluctantly, he agreed to the medical attention for Abdullah. Rapp, at any rate, needed to look at the intel they'd seized from the village before he interrogated Abdullah and the others again. Right now he had no way of gauging what was the truth and what were lies.

A medic showed up and quickly assessed the prisoners' wounds. Urda asked Rapp if they should take the other two prisoners away. Rapp told him no. Showing them that their captors could have some compassion was a good thing.

Rapp walked over to the medic and bent down so no one else could hear. "Give him just a little bit of morphine. Enough to last thirty minutes, tops." *The medical treatment might be just the right thing,* thought Rapp. A little bit of morphine to dull the pain temporarily, and then when it started to wear off he might become real talkative.

He stood over Abdullah and quietly spoke to him in Arabic. "I am going to check on what you just told me, and if I find out you've been lying to me; I'm going to start cutting your fingers off one by one."

Rapp straightened up and waved Urda over. The two CIA men huddled with General Harley, and Rapp asked the older man, "You have a place where Jamal can continue interrogating these three?"

"It's all set up and ready to go . . . recording equipment and all. I've also got some Delta boys who are more than eager to assist."

"Good." Rapp turned to Urda, but before he could talk, the general grabbed his arm.

"Listen . . . if you need to get rough with them I don't want anyone other than the Delta guys in the room, and make sure the cameras are turned off."

Both Rapp and Urda nodded.

"And no executions," Harley whispered. Gossip on a military base was as common as morning PT. "You guys need to resort to any of that stuff you take them off base again." The general glared at both men to make sure they were clear on this point.

"Understood," said Rapp. Urda nodded.

Harley nodded with satisfaction and then turned to one of his men. "Captain, would you please escort Mr. Urda and his . . ." Harley almost used the word prisoners, but stopped short. "Would you please take Mr. Urda to the place we discussed."

"Yes, sir."

The Afghani bodyguards grabbed Abdullah, while Urda took hold of the other two by their elbows and they were off.

As Harley watched them leave he said to Rapp in a low tone, "I can't believe they've got a nuke."

Rapp still held out some hope. "We don't know for sure what they have, but we have to assume the worst and work our way back from there. Hopefully, all they've got is a dirty bomb, and they never get the chance to light it."

Harley was silent for a second. His people had found another piece of evidence that he hadn't shared with Rapp yet. "I've got family in D.C."

"They haven't beaten us yet, general."

"No, but I can't even believe they've gotten this far." He waved his arm to the south toward the distant mountains. "We need more men, and I'm not just talking snake eaters." Harley used the slang for Special Forces. "We need three combat divisions and a whole lot of support. We need to go up into those mountains and end this thing."

"Well, if they set a bomb off in D.C., you'll get your wish."

The general shook his head, his sense of foreboding deepening. "If they set off a nuke in D.C., this entire region will be turned into a pile of radioactive rubble."

"Well, let's hope they don't succeed."

Harley didn't seem real optimistic at the moment. He waved for Rapp to follow him. "Let's get started."

They stepped into the large tent and the general walked over to a table set up with food and coffee. "You must be hungry."

"Starved." Rapp grabbed a turkey sandwich and tore at the cellophane. When a large enough portion was free, he took a big bite and then poured himself a cup of black coffee. While Harley explained what they were doing, Rapp continued to eat.

Large rectangular tables were arranged around the room in a horseshoe pattern. A morass of cables and chords connected the various computers, scanners, flat-panel monitors, printers, and fax machines. Most of the men and women were wearing desert BDUs, but a few were in civilian clothes, which meant they were CIA.

"This first group over here is working with your people back in Washington to decipher the data on the computers. The other two groups are pouring through the files and separating them by language. More of it is in Arabic than we originally thought." The general pointed to the last table. "Those are Urda's people. Anything we find written in Urdu or Pashto we immediately kick over to them. We've already found several things of interest. Follow me."

Harley walked over to one of the large bulletin boards that ringed the perimeter of the tent. Pinned to its middle was the map of Washington, D.C., that had everyone so worked up. Next to it was another map that Rapp hadn't seen.

"We found this folded up and stuffed in a file." Harley pointed to the upper portion of the map. "Can you read any of it?"

"Some of it." Rapp studied the map. More than anything he recognized the shape of the large blue body of water in the middle. "It's the Caspian, right?"

"Correct," answered Harley. The map was of the Caspian Sea with Iran to the south and Kazakhstan to the north. "Any idea why they would bother with a map of the Caspian?"

Rapp stared at it for a moment. "None whatsoever."

"Well, neither did we." Harley slid over a bit. "These maps need no introduction," he said, pointing.

One was of the entire eastern seaboard of the United States, and the other one was of Florida and the northern part of the Caribbean.

Harley touched the map and asked, "Do you see what's been circled?"

"New York, Miami, Baltimore, and Charleston."

"That's right. The four busiest ports on the East Coast."

"Shit."

"That's not even the worst of it," replied the general. "Come look at this." He walked Rapp around the outside of the tables to the area where Urda's people were set up. The three bearded men were dressed casually and so focused was their attention that they paid no attention to Rapp and the general.

"These are our Pashto guys. They were the ones who found the names of the missing Pakistani nuclear scientists."

"What else have they discovered?"

"Detailed descriptions on how to shield a nuclear warhead and sneak it past the sensors we have at all the aforementioned ports."

Rapp closed his eyes out of frustration. "What else?"

"A laundry list of materials needed to build the fire set and how to assemble and shape the explosive charge to achieve maximum yield."

The yield was how the explosive power of the bomb was measured. "Have we discovered the yield?"

"According to this right here," Harley tapped a file lying on the table, "twenty kilotons."

"Say again?" asked a somewhat shocked Rapp.

"Twenty kilotons."

"That's no dirty bomb."

"No."

"Any idea where they got this thing? Did they steal it from the Pakistanis?"

"So far we haven't a clue, but all of this is being sent back to the Joint Counterterrorism Center, the Pentagon, and the National Security Council. I would imagine someone very high up in our government will be calling Pakistan any moment and demanding a full accounting of their nuclear arsenal."

"I hope you're right. What else?"

"We have some interesting bills of lading we're trying to decipher, but it's a real jigsaw puzzle."

"What about something arriving by air yesterday?"

Harley asked one of the analysts, and was told no.

"Could it be on one of the computers?" asked Rapp.

The analyst shrugged. He had no idea.

Harley and Rapp walked over to the section that was working on the computers. They were told that so far nothing involving shipping records had been unearthed, but they'd barely scratched the surface.

Rapp wondered if Abdullah had lied to him and thought it might be a good idea to put a few more questions to him. "General, can one of your men bring me to where the interrogations are being conducted?"

Harley called out for one of his aides. He told the junior officer where to take the man from the CIA and then said to Rapp, "If we come up with anything new, I'll send for you."

"All right." Rapp started to leave and then turned. "General, one more favor. Would you have my plane gassed up and ready to go?"

"Consider it done."

TWENTY-EIGHT

WASHINGTON, D.C.

Special Agent Skip McMahon had been with the FBI since the day he'd graduated from Penn State thirty-five years earlier. He'd seen a lot of strange stuff. He'd been involved in more stressful cases than perhaps anyone else at the Bureau, but this one was looking as if it might take the cake. He knew the current situation wasn't a drill because as the man who ran the FBI's Counterterrorism Division, he would have been in on it.

To be rousted in the middle of the night by the shrill ring of his STU-3 secure telephone was never a pleasant experience, but on this particular evening the message he received from the Counterterrorism Watch Center caused him to bolt from his bed and get dressed as fast as his arthritic knees allowed.

Operation Ark had been implemented. The president, his cabinet, the Supreme Court, and the leaders of the House and Senate were all being evacuated from the city. That was part of what they called, "COG," or continuity of government. McMahon was part of "COOP," or continuity of operations. While they fled, it was his job to stay, and try to stop whatever it was that the terrorists were attempting.

At the moment, he was trying to do just that from an elevated glass-enclosed room at the new Tyson's Corner facility. He looked out onto CT Watch, a 24/7 center that monitored terrorist activities around the world. The high-tech room was manned by sixty-two special agents and another twenty-three intelligence analysts from the CIA. The analysts were part of the new Terrorist Threat Integration Center (TTIC). The CIA's Counterterrorism Center was located on a separate floor.

McMahon looked out across the sea of consoles and computers. Something was going on over in Kandahar, Afghanistan. Apparently the CIA, with the aid of the military, had got their hands on some high-level terrorists. Intel was pouring in so fast the translators were struggling to keep up. McMahon saw Jake Turbes, the director of the CIA's Counterterrorism Center, enter the room. He walked hurriedly down the side aisle and joined McMahon in the elevated glass room.

"This just came in." Turbes handed over a piece of paper.

McMahon looked at the list of cities. "These are four of the busiest ports in the world."

"I know, but it's all we have to go on for now."

"In addition to all of the international air-cargo flights?"

"No one ever said it was going to be easy, Skip."

The new Joint Counterterrorism Center wasn't even fully operational and they were getting hit with a scenario that was quickly stretching them to the limits of their capabilities.

"Yeah, I know." McMahon was trying to think of how to deploy his assets. "Any chance you guys are going to be able to narrow this down for us?"

"We're trying."

McMahon dropped the piece of paper on his desk. "I'd better call Reimer and get his people in on this." McMahon was referring to Paul Reimer, who ran the Nuclear Emergency Support Teams for the Department of Energy.

"Good idea." Turbes left the room as quickly as he'd arrived.

McMahon had sixty speed-dial buttons on his secure phone, and Reimer's button was near the top. He pushed it, and a few seconds later the Vietnam vet and retired Navy SEAL was on the line.

Like McMahon, Reimer had also been awakened by the shrill ring of his government issued STU-3 and given instructions to head to the Department of Energy's secure underground facility in Germantown, Maryland.

"Reimer here," he answered in a voice that hadn't quite warmed up.

"Paul, it's Skip. Are your NEST boys ready to go to work?" McMahon was referring to the Department of Energy's Nuclear Emergency Support Team.

"I've already got one of my Search Response Teams doing a random search downtown."

"Great . . . I've also got some ports for you to take a look at."

"How many?"

"Four to start with. New York, Miami, Baltimore, and Charleston."

The list of cities was met with momentary silence and then Reimer said in a sarcastic voice, "As long as you're at it, why don't you just add New Orleans, Houston, and L.A. to the list?"

"I know it's a big job, Paul."

"Big job! You've got to be kidding me."

"Sorry, but right now it's all we've got to go on."

"What about the airports?"

McMahon grabbed the back of his neck. "We've got agents overseas looking into it."

"What if the damn thing's already in the country?"

"The consensus is that the sensors would have picked it up."

The sensors McMahon was referring to were installed in every U.S. port of entry. They were designed to pick up the radiation signature emitted by a nuclear device. The sensors were good at detecting unshielded devices, but were less effective against ones that were shielded properly.

Reimer scoffed at the idea that the sensors would have picked up a device entering the country. "I heard some intel on the Pakistani scientists we've been looking for turned up. Sounds like they got recruited."

"Where did you hear that?" asked a genuinely surprised McMahon.

"I just got an intel dump from CTC. They wanted my technical people to go over some information." Reimer stopped for a second and then added, "Skip, you know as well as I do, if they had any scientific help with this thing, they would have shielded it, which means our sensors at the ports have a significantly reduced chance of detecting it. In fact they have almost no chance at all."

McMahon needed to get a better handle on what they were up against. "Let's hope they aren't that savvy."

"Roger that. For now, I'll call in my RAP teams and have them start looking at these ports." Reimer was thinking about the Department of Energy's Radiological Assistance Program. He had twenty-seven teams dispersed at DOE facilities around the country. They weren't as well equipped as his Search Response Teams, but until they got more specific intel they would have to fill the breach.

"The second you hear anything else let me know."

"I will." McMahon hung up the phone and looked up in time to see a disheveled Peggy Stealey come storming through the Emergency Crisis Center. The near-permanent frown on his face deepened.

This particular legal eagle from the Department of Justice was one tough broad. Smart, aggressive, and pretty damn good-looking if you liked the Amazon type. Ten years ago he would have either clobbered her or slept with her, or maybe both. But now after three decades of working for the Bureau, a divorce, a spin dry through a rehab clinic, and retirement on the horizon, he'd mellowed enough to tolerate her, just barely.

He'd seen her type come and go with each passing attorney general. Almost all of them type-A personalities, they often exerted great control and pressure on the FBI with little concern for the overall effectiveness of the Bureau and its charter. Some wanted to make a name for themselves, while others simply wanted to make sure the FBI didn't embarrass their boss, and in the process stall their own meteoric rise. McMahon never lost sight of their ulterior motives, and he always kept a close eye on them. This particular hotshot was no exception.

Stealey never slowed, laying her shoulder into the heavy door of the bridge. She came up the steps and dropped her bag next to McMahon's desk. "What in the hell is going on?"

McMahon had his flat-panel monitor tilted up so he could remain standing and still read the reports that his team was sending him. He was momentarily relieved to see a flash message alerting all of his people to a link between al-Qaeda and the missing Pakistani nuclear scientists.

He didn't even bother to look up from the monitor. "Nice of you to join us, Peggy."

"You didn't answer my question," she said tersely.

They were not the only two people in the command room. McMahon had already warned Stealey about her obnoxious habit of speaking to coworkers as if she had them on the witness stand. He casually looked at his watch and said, "Peggy, you should have been here an hour ago." He then shifted his gaze from his watch to her deceptively gentle blue eyes. "We're in the middle of a crisis, so check your ego at the door and I'll bring you up to speed as time allows."

McMahon reached down and grabbed his secure phone, leaving Stealey fuming.

"Where is the attorney general?" she asked.

"He's in the secure conference room with Director Roach."

Stealey turned to leave and McMahon said, "You can't go in there right now."

"Excuse me?" snapped Stealey.

"They're about to start a National Security Council meeting, so unless you were given some promotion I'm unaware of, sit your ass down and wait for him to come out of the meeting."

TWENTY-NINE

VIRGINIA

The Ford Taurus made its way north on Interstate 95 with the cruise control set exactly two miles per hour under the speed limit. It exited on U.S. Highway 17 and continued northeast toward Charleston. At a small truck stop just west of the city it stopped for gas. Mustafa al-Yamani awoke when the car pulled under the bright lights of the pumps. He dragged himself up from the backseat and looked at the clock on the dashboard. He'd been asleep for nearly three hours. The nausea hit him almost immediately.

He climbed out of the backseat and headed into the store. Near the back, he found the men's room and entered and locked the door. He popped one of the pills that the doctor had given him in Pakistan, and began dousing his face with cold water. Al-Yamani leaned on the basin and surveyed his bloodshot eyes and irritated skin.

Mustafa al-Yamani did not have long to live. He figured he would be dead in ten days at the most. All he needed were six more days to see everything through. He was at complete peace with the prospect of dying. His faith was strong, so strong that he willed himself to ignore the nausea and intense irritation of his blotchy, burning skin and continue on his mission.

The radiation sickness was in its final stages. The doctor in Pakistan had told him how the disease would progress. At first it would be marked by fatigue and red rashes on the skin that looked like nothing more than a bad case of sunburn. After that would come severe headaches followed by vomiting and diarrhea. Next his hair and teeth would fall out, and if he stayed conscious long enough, he could watch himself bleed to death from the inside out.

He had no intention of letting it get to that point. He would hit the Americans with the ultimate surprise, and then when they least expected it he would hit them again. Al-Yamani left the bathroom and stopped to buy more water and a few soft foods that he hoped he could keep down. He'd already lost ten pounds and he had no appetite whatsoever.

This time he got in the front seat with his driver and they left for the port. The Kuwaiti driving the car was a student at the University of Central Florida. His family was well enough connected to get him a student visa during a time when most of the Arab men his age were being denied the opportunity to go to university in America. He had been instructed not to ask any questions, and so far he had followed his orders. For months the Kuwaiti, Ibrahim Yacoub, had been receiving surreptitious e-mails instructing him on intelligence that should be collected, and items to be purchased. Most importantly, he was told to stay away from his mosque.

Al-Yamani had given him a brief pep talk when they were leaving the nature preserve. He'd told the man they were on a glorious mission for Allah. Like al-Yamani, Yacoub was a Wahhabi, a proud member of

Islam's most radical sect. The man had family in Kuwait and Saudi Arabia that would be thrilled with him when they discovered the path he'd chosen. Al-Yamani could see that his words had the right effect. The Kuwaiti's face beamed with pride as he thought of the reverence he would receive.

Al-Yamani told the student that when the time was right he would reveal to him the entire plan, but for security reasons he could not yet do so. The man was understandably nervous. A lot was at stake and he would just as soon be on his own than trust the mission to a dolt who didn't understand the seriousness of his mission. The boy had asked al-Yamani what he should call him. Al-Yamani told him to call him Mohammed, not because he felt he was the prophet, but because it was the most common of Muslim names.

They continued their drive through Charleston in silence. Every few minutes or so al-Yamani turned around and made a mental note of the types of cars that were behind them. It was only four in the morning and traffic was still light. They drove down near the water by the port. Al-Yamani was slightly surprised by how large the cranes that were used to off-load the cargo were and of the constant stream of ships that entered the port every day of the year. He had seen surveillance photos, but they didn't quite capture the immensity of the bustling port.

As they neared the main gate, al-Yamani asked, "Does anything look unusual?" Trucks were already lined up to enter the yard and pick up their containers.

Yacoub shook his head. "No."

"Have you ever been here at this time of day?" Al-Yamani knew what the answer was supposed to be, but he asked it anyway. He would continue to test the young man right up until the very end.

"Three times."

"And it always looked like this?"

"Yes."

They reached the main gate and Yacoub took his foot off the gas and put it on the brake.

"Don't slow down," al-Yamani said firmly. "We don't want to draw any attention to ourselves."

Yacoub sped up and they continued on. Al-Yamani had seen nothing unusual at the main gate. No extra security. "Take us to the spot you told me about, and we will watch."

There was to be no contact between the two cells, but al-Yamani was in charge of the entire operation. Much of what he would do depended on how successful the first cell was. He would make sure they received the bomb, and then he could focus on the rest of the plan.

THIRTY

MARYLAND

For the last two hours there had been a constant stream of heli-copters and vehicles arriving and departing from the base of Raven Rock Mountain. The mountain straddled the Maryland–Pennsylvania border about an hours drive north of Washington, D.C. Buried deeply beneath it was a highly secure, hardened facility known simply as Site R.

Site R had opened in 1953 and been designated an Alternate Joint Communications Center by the U.S. military. The more blunt description was that it was bunker built to survive a nuclear attack against the United States. There were four ways into Site R. The two main entrances were located one on each side of the mountain. These were guarded by massive blast doors that took ten minutes to open and close. The third was more of an exit to be used for emergency escape, and the fourth, and most secretive of all, was an elevator shaft and tunnel that allowed the president to enter the bunker from Camp David just a few miles down the road.

The president's chief of staff was the last person to arrive at the Camp David entrance, and once she was inside, the immense doors began their unnerving slow grind to their shut position. Once the doors were closed, the inhabitants were safe against all but a direct strike by a large nuclear weapon. Site R was built to house several hundred people for a period of four to six weeks depending on how food and water was dispersed. Most impressive, though, was its exact replica of the National Military Command Center (NMCC) that sits in the bowels of the Pentagon.

The NMCC, which is pronounced "Nimic," is essentially a cavernous war room where the Joint Chiefs and their staffs can monitor and, if need be, run a war that is taking place anywhere in the world. Due to the size of the Pentagon, and the fact that the room sits beneath layer upon layer of reinforced concrete, it is deemed a semihardened facility able to handle anything up to a near strike by a ten kiloton nuke.

Back when the U.S. and the former Soviet Union were in their nuclear arms race, both countries began building these bunkers at a feverish pace. The idea was to create redundancy so that it would be extremely difficult for the opponent to take out your entire command-and-control network. Within several hundred miles of Washington there were six such facilities. In addition, there was the Strategic Air Command, or SAC, in Omaha; the North American Air Defense Command, or NORAD, in Colorado Springs; and a dozen others sprinkled across the vast American landscape.

The Soviets did the same thing, but both nations fell victim to one simple problem. It was easier to build bombs than bunkers. With both sides at their peak having more than 10,000 nuclear warheads, military planners were able to put on the board targeting packages that would hit all of the other side's command-

and-control bunkers with however many nukes it took to destroy each facility. The briefly indestructible bunkers, places built to ensure survivability, began to be viewed by many as tombs.

Psychologically speaking, one thing saved each country: mutually assured destruction, or MAD. The Soviets wanted to live just as much as the Americans did. On those rare occasions when the world was taken to the brink, the leaders on both sides ultimately knew that if they ordered a nuclear strike, they would be not just killing the enemy, they would be signing their own death certificates as well as those of their family and almost everyone they knew.

MAD, despite its ignoble characteristics, had served humanity quite well. The same pragmatism did not apply to the new hostilities, however. There was no rationalizing with religious zealots who were willing to wantonly sacrifice their own lives and those of others. There was no mutually assured destruction, there was only destruction.

Destruction of unimaginable proportions. That was what was on President Hayes's mind as he stood at the glass wall of the conference room looking down into Site R's command center. Military personnel sat at computer consoles or scurried about. Across from the president was a large projection screen that showed the current deployment and readiness of America's armed forces. He watched as designations began to change. Hayes expected it. He'd just given General Flood, the chairman of the Joint Chiefs of Staff, the approval to take the armed forces from their normal peacetime readiness of Defcon 5 to Defcon 4. In addition, plans were already under way to take the Seventh Fleet and Central Command to Defcon 3 if needed. He was told it was standard procedure given the situation. Hayes could already see where this insanity could take them. The hawks at the Pentagon hadn't said it yet, but they would shortly.

If a nuke went off in D.C., they would not just push for retribu-tion, they would demand it, and the president would have a hard time stopping them. The only problem was who, where, and what to strike back at.

Irene Kennedy approached the president. "Sir, we're ready to get started."

Hayes took his spot at the head of the conference table. At the opposite end of the room the large video screen was split in three. The left third showed Secretary of Defense Culbertson and General Flood who were in the NMCC at the Pentagon. The middle portion showed Vice President Baxter, Treasury Secretary Keane, and Secretary of the Department of Homeland Security McClellan. All three men were tucked away at Mount Weather, another secure bunker west of D.C. The last third showed Attorney General Stokes and FBI Director Roach, who were at the new Joint Counter-terrorism Center. In the room with the president was Secretary of State Berg, National Security Advisor Haik, Chief of Staff Jones, and CIA Director Kennedy. The combined assembly made up the president's National Security Council, and more often than not lately they had been conducting their meetings via secure video teleconference.

President Hayes, knowing that much of the group was in the dark as to what was going on, turned to CIA Director Kennedy and said, "Irene, would you please bring everyone up to speed?"

Kennedy began in her typically calm, analytical voice. "As most of you know, starting last week we noticed some trends in the financial markets that gave us concern. In addition to that there was an increase in chatter. On Monday morning we were alerted to a suspected gathering of top al-Qaeda members in a small village near the Afghanistan–Pakistan border. About nine hours ago American Special Forces hit the village."

Before Kennedy could continue Secretary of State Berg asked, "On which side of the border did the village sit?" It was apparent by her tone that she already knew the answer.

"The Pakistani side."

Berg, a much revered and respected former senator, slowly shifted her chilly gaze from Kennedy to the president. "And why wasn't I informed of this?"

Hayes was in no mood to waste valuable time refereeing turf battles. "You weren't told because I didn't want the Pakistanis to know." He looked back to Kennedy. "Continue."

Kennedy cleared her throat. "Three top al-Qaeda members were nabbed in the raid along with several smaller figures. In addition several computers were discovered along with a lot of files. One piece of intel in particular gave us great concern. It was a map of Washington, D.C." Kennedy entered several key strokes and an image of the map appeared on the monitors that were embedded in the surface of the conference table and on the monitors at the other installations.

"For those of you who have seen one of these before, you will recognize the circles that emanate from the National Mall as the blast radius of a nuclear weapon. In addition to the map a bomb damage assessment was found."

"What size bomb are we talking?" asked the president's chief of staff.

"Twenty kilotons," answered Kennedy.

"Is that big?"

Kennedy looked up at the teleconferencing screen and said, "General Flood."

The Chairman of the Joint Chiefs said, "For a nuke it's pretty small, but then again when you're talking about a nuke nothing is really small."

"How much damage?" asked the president.

"That's contingent on whether we're looking at an air burst or ground detonation, and if it's detonated during the middle of the day or in the evening. Immediate casualties could be as low as twenty thousand if it's a ground detonation and could climb to half a million people or more if it's an air burst during the middle of a work day."

An uncomfortable silence fell over the group as individuals grappled with the enormity of the possible carnage. Someone muttered a soft curse, and then General Flood added, "In addition to the casualties the city itself would be uninhabitable for anywhere from thirty to seventy years depending on the radiation fallout."

"Dr. Kennedy," asked Attorney General Stokes, "I'm assuming since you ordered Operation Ark, that there is more to go on than just this map."

"Yes. For some time we have been trying to ascertain the whereabouts of several missing Pakistani nuclear scientists. In the raid, we discovered files that detail the recruitment and defection of these scientists. I've got people pouring through this intelligence as we speak trying to get a more complete picture of what we're up against, but as of right now my team says there is little doubt that these scientists were successfully recruited by al-Qaeda. In addition we also have verbal confirmation from one of the terrorists that the attack on D.C. will employ a nuclear weapon."

"How in the hell," asked Secretary of Defense Culbertson, "did these guys get their hands on a nuclear weapon?"

"We're looking into that right now," answered Kennedy.

"Maybe we should start with the Pakistanis," snapped an angry secretary of defense.

Kennedy looked to the president. They had already discussed this exact point.

"I plan on talking to General Musharraf shortly," responded the president, "but before I do that I would like to get a better handle on the intelligence that's coming out of Kandahar."

"How did they get this thing into the country?" asked the president's chief of staff.

"We're not sure at this point. One report has it coming in by plane, but it's possible it may have come in by ship."

"Do we know when it arrived?" asked Jones.

"As of right now we think it came in yesterday."

"How in the hell did it get past all the sensors?" asked the president's chief of staff.

Kennedy, slightly perplexed, just looked at her. She knew of at least two occasions when they'd sat in the same room while the vulnerability of the detectors was discussed. "There will be time later to figure out exactly how they got the weapon into the country. For now we need to focus our energies on finding this thing, and preparing for the worst."

"What about Washington?" asked Jones. "I thought every bridge and road coming into the city was wired with devices that could detect something like this."

"They are," answered Kennedy, "but they are not foolproof."

"Mr. President," said the Secretary of Homeland Security, "In about two hours this city is going to wake up, and rush hour will begin. If Washington, D.C., is in fact the target, we need to consider shutting down all incoming lanes of traffic. As general Flood pointed out, the quickest way to increase the death toll is to let people come into the city to work."

The president looked to Kennedy for guidance.

"I respectfully disagree," answered the director of the CIA. "Until we have more specific intelligence, any such action would be premature and would likely hinder our search for the device."

The Secretary of Homeland Security frowned at Kennedy's polite rebuke and said, "At a bare minimum, sir, we should begin checking all pickup trucks, box vans, and semi trucks headed into the city. We should also consider shutting down the Metro."

"I would advise waiting another hour," answered Kennedy.

Secretary of the Treasury Keane, who was at the Mount Weather facility with the Secretary of Homeland Security and the vice president, chimed in by saying, "Mr. President, if the slightest whisper of this gets out, we need to be prepared to step in and close the financial markets . . . even before they open."

All at once, the meeting digressed into a free-for-all, with splintered conversations breaking out between the various groups. President Hayes pushed his chair a little further away from the table and for his own part tried to figure out where this madness might lead them.

CIA Director Kennedy leaned closer to the president

and said, "Sir, if you could call the meeting back to order, I'd like to suggest a course of action."

Hayes liked the sound of Kennedy's reassuring voice. "Everyone!" Like all good orators the president knew how to project his voice. He did not have to repeat himself a second time.

"Dr. Kennedy has the floor," he commanded.

Kennedy laid her palms flat on the table and spoke in an even but confident voice. "With each passing minute, we're getting a better handle on this situation. As strange and counterintuitive as it may seem, the best course of action for us right now may be to do nothing. It's a quarter past four in the morning. We have a little time before people begin waking up and heading into work. I propose that for the next hour we allow our counterterrorism people to do what they're trained to do, and stay out of their way. At five thirty we can reconvene, and decide if we need to take further action."

The president didn't wait for anyone else to argue or interject. "We will reconvene at five thirty. In the meantime dust off the contingency plans we have in place, and have your agendas set and prioritized for the next meeting. I want a clear and concise take on everything: intel, military, financial markets, the press . . . and Irene and Beatrice," Hayes pointed to Kennedy and the secretary of State, "I want the two of you to coordinate a strategy on how to deal with Pakistan, and any other allies we might need to put some pressure on."

The president then took in the rest of the room and looked up at the large screen. "I can't stress enough how important it is that we keep a lid on this thing. The last thing we need right now is the press getting wind of this. They'll create a damn panic and this situation will spin out of control before we have the chance to stop it."

THIRTY-ONE

AFGHANISTAN

Rapp stepped into the tent and in the dim light spotted Urda sitting at a small table with one of the prisoners. As he approached and his eyes adjusted he saw it was Ahmed Khalili, the young man from Karachi. Two mugs were sitting on the table in front of them. Khalili's hands were still bound, but in front of him so he could drink. Rapp took all of this as a good sign. As he approached the table the young Pakistani looked away from him.

"Ahmed, don't worry," said Urda, sensing the young man's nervousness at the sight of Rapp. "Nothing will happen to you as long as you continue to cooperate." The CIA's Kandahar man stood. "I'm going to step outside for a second. Continue enjoying your tea, and I'll be right back."

Once the two men were outside Urda said, "He's talking."

"Good, but is he telling us anything useful?"

"I think so. He's their computer guy. That's how he knew who you were, by the way."

"How so?"

"They asked him to get his hands on everything the press wrote about you. They wanted to know about your wife, and he was told to find out where you lived."

A look of proprietary concern spread across Rapp's face. "And did he find out where I live?"

"I don't think so."

Rapp looked back in the tent. None of this came as a surprise to him, but it was still worrisome. He would have to look into it further, but right now there were more important things to deal with. "Did he say anything about where they got this bomb, or how they transported it to the U.S.?"

"Not so far."

"Then what has he been talking about?"

"The cells they have in the U.S." Urda raised an eyebrow.

Rapp liked the sound of this and motioned for Urda to spill the beans.

"He explained how they've been contacting their people in the states via e-mail. He can give us the accounts they were sending the e-mails to, and he said something else very important."

"What?" asked Rapp.

"Supposedly, somebody big was going to America to help carry out the attack."

"Did he tell you who?"

Urda nodded. "Mustafa al-Yamani."

Rapp's hands balled into tight fists upon hearing the man's name. "How and when?"

"They knew they couldn't get him in on a commercial flight so they were going to do it by water."

"How?"

"I haven't got that far yet."

"Let's get back in there and find out."

Urda reached out and grabbed Rapp's arm. "Take it

easy on him. He thinks you're the devil and I'm not exaggerating."

"I'll go easy on him so long as he cooperates."

Urda took his seat at the small table and Rapp grabbed a folding chair, flipping it around backwards and sitting down between the two men. "Ahmed," started Rapp in a calm voice. "As long as you tell me the truth, you have nothing to fear. How did Mustafa al-Yamani plan on entering America?"

"By boat." The young Pakistani slid his trembling hands under the table.

"Do you know when?"

"Yesterday."

Rapp remembered that Abdullah had told him the bomb was to have arrived yesterday. "Was he accompanying the bomb?"

Khalili shook his head.

"Are you sure?" Rapp asked suspiciously.

"Yes. He was to fly to Cuba where he would take a boat and enter Florida somewhere on its eastern coast."

Rapp wanted to know more about al-Yamani, but there was something else of even greater importance he needed to know first. "How was the bomb to enter the country?"

"I'm not sure." The Pakistani looked down and away when he answered this.

Rapp reached out with his right hand and placed it on the table. The move caused the prisoner to flinch. "Ahmed," said Rapp in a stern voice. "Look at me."

Reluctantly, he did so.

"You know more than you are telling us. How were they planning on getting the bomb into the country?"

"I'm not sure," he answered in a shaky voice, "but I think by ship."

"And why do you think that?"

"About three weeks ago it was loaded onto a freighter in Karachi."

If Ahmed was telling the truth, that meant Abdullah was lying to him, that was unless the bomb had been off-loaded at a port somewhere and then transferred onto a plane for the rest of the journey. To Rapp that seemed like more work than it was worth. Why not just put it on a plane to start with?

"Ahmed, an hour ago you seemed to know a lot less. How can I be sure you're telling me the truth?"

He looked up at Rapp with a pleading expression. "These are things I am not supposed to know. Things I overheard the others talking about."

"Did you hear Abdullah talk about any of the details?"

Ahmed, confused, just looked at Rapp.

"Did you hear Abdullah talk about how they were getting the bomb into America?"

"Yes. By ship."

"You're sure?"

"Yes."

Rapp took a moment to study the man's face. "At any point did they talk about putting it on a plane?"

The young Pakistani shook his head. "Not that I heard."

"Did you hear what port they were going to bring the bomb in to?"

"No." He shook his head. "I heard them mention several cities."

"Which ones?"

"New York and Baltimore were the two I remember."

"What about Miami and Charleston?"

"I think those too."

Rapp leaned back and looked at Urda. "I need to go make a call. Maybe you two could discuss how Mr. al-Yamani got into America and who is helping him."

Urda nodded knowingly. As Rapp left the tent, Urda told his young prisoner he was doing a good job and asked him if he wanted more tea.

Outside, Rapp made no effort to retrieve his satellite phone. The call to Kennedy would have to wait until he had the chance to ask Abdullah why he'd lied to him, and this time each lie would cost him a finger.

THIRTY-TWO

Rapp found Abdullah about fifty yards away. They'd placed him in an ammunition storage bunker that was partially underground and surrounded by sandbags. Two Delta troopers were sitting in front of the bunker playing a hand of cards, while Abdullah lay inside on a stretcher. If the medic had given him the right dose of morphine it should be wearing off right about now.

Rapp went down the steps and had to tilt his head so as to not hit the header. Two things were instantly apparent: Abdullah wanted more morphine, and he was not happy to see the man from the CIA. Rapp stood over him for a moment assessing his next move. Even though he told him he'd cut his fingers off if he lied to him, Rapp thought the better approach now would be to dangle the relief of morphine in front of him.

"Waheed," Rapp used his first name. "How does your knee feel?"

The Saudi turned away from Rapp and bit down on his lip.

Looking down at the terrorist, Rapp took the steel toe of his boot and nudged the bloody and bandaged joint. Abdullah let out a scream that was ear-piercing in the confined space. Rapp reacted by bending over and backhanding him in the face. In Arabic he told the terrorist to stop screaming like a woman.

After the Saudi stifled his cries, Rapp asked, "Waheed, would you like more morphine?"

The man did not answer at first, and then finally through a clenched jaw he said, "You know I do."

"Well, that shouldn't be a problem. We have plenty of it."

Abdullah, who was half on his side and turned away from Rapp, opened an eye and looked at his tormentor with a glimmer of hope.

"That's right . . . we have enough morphine to make all the pain go away. It's going to be a long flight back to America, and I want you to be comfortable." Rapp noticed Abdullah had lost his zeal for flinging verbal insults.

"You told me a lie earlier." Rapp lifted up his boot and again nudged Abdullah's bloodied knee. The terrorist screamed in response. When he was done Rapp said, "If you want more morphine, I'm going to have to send someone to get it. It could easily take thirty minutes . . . so the sooner you tell me the truth, the sooner you'll get your shot."

"Thirty minutes?" cried a horrified Abdullah.

Rapp shrugged his shoulders nonchalantly. "I could probably come up with some sooner, but that depends on how forthright you are this time."

"I told you the truth," he moaned.

Rapp wound up this time and sent his steel-toe boot crashing into the Saudi's wounded knee. When Abdullah was done screaming, Rapp said, "The others are talking, Waheed. I know for a fact that you lied to me."

"The others . . . what others?"

"The other two men who came back to the base."

"They know nothing," said Abdullah defiantly. "They were not involved in any of the planning."

"Is that right?" asked Rapp. He dropped down into a squat and grabbed Abdullah's hair. "Would you care to tell me where your friend Mustafa al-Yamani is right now?"

Abdullah's eyes opened wide at the question, but his mouth remained shut.

"This big plan of yours is unraveling," said Rapp. "Those two underlings know a lot more than you think. We know al-Yamani flew to Cuba and then got on a boat for Florida. We're tracing the e-mails that you sent to the cells in America, and the FBI is moving to arrest people right now. This entire thing is falling apart and you're getting left behind." Rapp stood and studied the Saudi for a moment.

"Maybe I should give you more time to think about it. I'll be back in an hour." Rapp started to leave, but before he reached the door Abdullah cried out for him to wait.

"It's not coming into America by plane."

"How is it being transported then?"

"By ship."

"Destined for what port?" Rapp moved to stand over him again.

Abdullah mumbled an unintelligible answer.

"I didn't hear you. What port?"

"I want more morphine first," Abdullah howled.

Rapp put his boot on top of the bad knee and pressed down.

Abdullah began screaming his head off.

Rapp snarled, "I'm not taking my foot off until you tell me what port!"

Abdullah kept screaming.

"What port!" Rapp put almost all of his weight on the bad knee. "What port, Waheed?"

"Charleston! Charleston!" The man's face was covered in sweat and contorted in anguish.

Rapp let up a bit but kept his boot in place. "And when is it due to arrive?"

"Today!"

"You said yesterday when I asked you an hour ago."

"I lied! It's coming today! I swear I'm telling you the truth!"

"What's the name of the ship?"

"I don't know," he screamed with a genuine look of panic on his face.

"Where did it originate from?"

"Karachi!"

"How long ago?"

"Three weeks. Please . . . oh please . . . I'm telling you the truth."

Rapp removed his boot, and grabbed a knife from a scabbard on his right thigh. Bending over, he held the knife in front of Abdullah's face and said, "This is your last chance. I'm going to get you some morphine, but if I find out you've lied to me, I'm going to come back, and not only are you not going to get your morphine . . . I'm going to start lopping off your fingers one by one."

THIRTY-THREE

CHARLESTON

The trip out to Sullivan's Island didn't take long. The island marked the northern entrance to Charleston Harbor. They continued past the main gate to historic Fort Moultrie Park and took a left on Station 12th Street. They parked a half block from the water and got out of the car. al-Yamani asked Yacoub to grab the bag from the trunk, and the two of them walked to the beach. Once out of the car's air-conditioned comfort al-Yamani was again reminded of how foreign humidity was to him. Growing up in an arid land had acclimated him to dry heat, not this smothering wet air.

By the time they reached the sand he could feel rivulets of sweat dripping down his back. Yacoub led the way across the light-colored beach. Visibility was good with a quarter moon and not a cloud in the sky. Out to sea on the horizon the sky was beginning to lighten a bit. The sun would be up in about an hour and a half, and if things went according to plan, not long after that the container would be headed north.

Yacoub pointed out into the harbor and said, "That is Fort Sumter. It is almost one point five kilometers from here to there. The boat will pass right between us."

This is no boat, al-Yamani thought to himself. *It is a ship.* He had been there in Karachi to supervise the packing and loading of the container. Al-Yamani had intentionally chosen the largest vessel he could find. He rationalized that the more containers the ship could carry, the less likely it would be that the Americans would find the lethal one in a random search.

"You can see the channel markers there and there." Yacoub pointed to the red and green lights floating out in the water.

To the right was downtown Charleston. The skyline was nothing stupendous, but al-Yamani knew this was an old city by American standards. The harbor where they had just come from was illuminated by bright flood lights. Even from this vantage al-Yamani could make out the monstrous cranes swinging cargo off the big vessels docked at one of America's busiest ports.

"Here comes a boat now." Yacoub pointed out to sea.

"You mean ship. A boat is little. That is not little." Al-Yamani checked his watch and said, "Binoculars."

Yacoub zipped open the duffel bag and handed the high-powered binoculars over.

Al-Yamani looked through the lenses and found the vessel steaming toward port. It was a container ship. A big one, fully loaded. Beyond it, out to sea, al-Yamani could make out at least two more ships headed in. One of them was his ship, he hoped. A slight breeze blew in from the ocean and it carried with it the sound of engines and churning water.

A minute later the ship passed between their position and Fort Sumter. Al-Yamani read the name on the prow. It was not the ship he was looking for, but he was not surprised. His ship was not due for another ten minutes. He'd checked it on the internet before leaving Cuba. One of their people in Karachi had explained how to do it. Using GPS and transponders, merchant ships were tracked all over the globe. These big container vessels were run by state-of-the-art automated systems that maximized time and fuel efficiency. Barring bad weather or other unforeseen conditions, the arrival time of a vessel at a given port could usually be predicted within minutes.

Al-Yamani grew a bit nervous as the next ship passed and it again wasn't the one he was looking for. There were plenty more lights out on the horizon but he had waited a lifetime for this moment and he didn't want to wait any longer. If the Americans were onto the plan he would know soon enough, for there was no way they would risk letting this cargo enter one of their ports.

The next ship churned its way through the channel, its deck laden with multicolored containers stacked six high over every square foot of the aircraft carrier–sized deck. Its white superstructure was bathed in light and looked like it belonged in the business district of some generic downtown.

Al-Yamani strained to read the barely lit name on the prow and in the faint light he read the first three letters and knew it was the one he was expecting, the *Madagascar*. Al-Yamani lowered the binoculars and exhaled in relief. His ship had arrived.

He turned to his guide, and with genuine happiness he said, "Ibrahim, this is a great day for us."

THIRTY-FOUR

AFGHANISTAN

Rapp left the ammunition bunker, grabbed Urda, and quickly explained to him everything he'd just learned from Abdullah. The two men double-timed it back to the intel tent where Rapp called for everyone's attention. This time he would hold off on contacting Washington until he could corroborate Abdullah's story.

The Saudi's earlier false confession was a setback. How bad a setback Rapp didn't know, but assets had undoubtedly been directed to check international airfreight coming into the U.S. over the last forty-eight hours. Even more harmful, though, would be the loss of confidence by those back in Washington pulling the switches. One more screwup and they would begin to doubt everything Rapp was sending them.

Just as Rapp was about to speak, his sat phone rang. He answered it reluctantly, and listened to Kennedy explain what was going on. The National Security Council was going to reconvene in a little over thirty minutes and decide on a course of action. Kennedy explained that several members of the council were pushing to evacuate the city, or at a bare minimum close all roads leading into the city and cancel Metro service before the morning commute got underway.

Once that happened, Kennedy told him what he already knew. They would have tipped their hand and the terrorists would know what was going on. Kennedy's fear was that if the bomb was already in the country, the terrorists would move up their timetable and detonate the weapon before the NEST teams had a chance to find it. Rapp agreed with his boss, but decided not to tell her what he had just learned from Abdullah. He had thirty minutes to confirm that Charleston was the port of entry for the bomb, and if need be he was going to use every last second. He told Kennedy he'd call her back before the meeting started and put his phone away.

"Everybody listen up," boomed Rapp with Urda and General Harley at his side. "We are looking for any reference to a ship that left Karachi approximately three weeks ago. We think the ship may have been headed for Charleston, South Carolina, due to arrive sometime today."

As Rapp looked out across the silent faces, he saw one of Urda's people sifting quickly through a stack of documents. There was something about the manner in which the man searched the pile that suggested he knew what he was looking for. Rapp's eyes zeroed in on him. He stopped once and licked his fingers. He quickly flipped over several more pages and then looked up triumphantly.

"I've got it right here." He pulled a sheaf of documents from the stack and shook them in the air.

Both Rapp and Urda lunged forward to look at the documents. They were in Urdu, so Rapp understood nothing other than the words *Karachi* and *Charleston*. The analyst translated the rest of the information. The ship was a Liberian container vessel of no great value or significance.

Rapp asked the analyst, "Is this a bill of lading?"

"Yes."

"Is this the only one you remember finding?"

"No." The black-bearded man shook his head, and patted the stack of documents before him. "These are all bills of lading. This one," he shook the prized document in the air, "is the only one I remember originating from Karachi with a destination of Charleston."

"Are there any others that left Karachi approximately three weeks ago?" The smile was now gone from Rapp's face.

"Yes." The man nodded vehemently "Practically the entire stack."

Rapp's jaw clenched. He was once again wondering if Abdullah had lied to him. "How many bills are there, and how many left Karachi three weeks ago?"

The analyst looked down and consulted his notes. "There are seventeen separate bills of lading, with the majority of them leaving from Karachi. Four of those left approximately three weeks ago, and all four are headed for the United States."

"When are they due to arrive?" Rapp asked tensely.

The analyst shook the document he'd already pulled. "This one in Charleston today." He set it down on the table, and began rifling through the stack until he found another one. "This one bound for New York is also due to arrive today, and this one bound for Miami is due to arrive today as well." He shuffled through a few more pages and said, "And this one is due to arrive in Baltimore today."

Rapp began thinking of which finger he would cut off first. "Are there any bills for airfreight?"

"No." The analyst shook his head and gestured at the entire table where Urda's people were working on the documents written in Urdu and Pashto.

"All right listen. Here's what I want you to do. Fax all of these documents to the CTC."

"I already did. About thirty minutes ago."

Rapp was surprised. "Have you spoken to them about this?"

"Yeah, but they don't have anybody on duty right now who can translate Urdu."

"What?" asked an incredulous Rapp.

"We were told to translate these files on the missing Pakistani scientists."

The man wanted to explain further, but Rapp cut him off. "Listen . . . right now I want you to focus your attention on these four bills of lading. Translate them immediately, send the information to CTC and then begin on the others. If you need anyone else to help grab them right now. Good job and get moving!"

THIRTY-FIVE

MARYLAND

The secure video teleconference was up and running. The National Security Council wasn't due to reconvene for another fifteen minutes, but more than half of the principal players were already seated, including the president. On the big screen at the end of the conference room, aides and deputies could be seen coming in and out of the other off-site locations, bringing their bosses information and whispering instructions in their ears. The conference room at Site R was no different. People were coming and going at a feverish pace.

Valerie Jones, the president's chief of staff, was sitting directly across from Kennedy talking on a secure phone and eating a powdered donut. Kennedy watched her with the aim of getting her attention as soon as she hung up. It appeared from the conversation that she was talking to the White House press secretary. Thankfully, it appeared thus far that the media was in the dark. They all agreed, however, that would not last forever. Kennedy doubted sincerely that they would make it to nine o'clock without word somehow leaking out.

Washington, like most centers of power, was an environment dominated by meetings. Breakfast meetings, morning meetings, midmorning meetings, lunch meetings—it went on and on from predawn all the way into the night. A lot of very important people would be missing their breakfast meetings this morning and it would not go unnoticed.

Jones hung up the phone and exhaled in relief. "So far, so good," she said to the president. "That was Tim." Jones was referring to Tim Webber, the White House press secretary, who had been given the unenviable task of pulling duty at the White House. This had been Jones's decision. Most of the TV reporters began showing up around 6:00 a.m. with print media coming in around 9:00 a.m. It would be much easier for Webber to deflect questions and deal with any rumors in person rather than over the phone.

"Not a call from the media yet," the chief of staff added.

The president looked at a string of clocks on the wall and noted the time on the one marked Washington. It was a little past five in the morning. "The media isn't even out of bed yet."

"I know that," retorted Jones, "but they have plenty of sources in your administration. I'm amazed no one has called to tip them off." Jones had a bit of an edge to her, which in a way was a prerequisite for her job. Even when dealing with the president she could be harsh.

Kennedy placed a hand on the president's arm and said, "I need to discuss something with the two of you." She leaned in and the president and Jones followed suit. "I think I know what their endgame is." Like everyone, Kennedy had been stuck in the moment and hadn't really had the time to step back and look at the big picture. Since her last conversation with Rapp, however, something had occurred to her.

"If they in fact have a nuke, it's only logical that they use it for maximum effect. This should be no surprise to you," Kennedy looked at the president, "but one of the terrorists told Mitch that their plan is to kill you. The man also said something strange. He said they wanted to kill you and all the generals. When Mitch told me I thought it sounded a little funny, so I asked him if that was exactly what the man said, and it was. At the time, I wrote it off as one of those statements of exaggerated bravado that Arabs are so fond of making. Taken literally, the statement is ludicrous. Killing all our generals would be impossible, but then I got to thinking that a word that to native English speakers has one meaning in this context might have a subtle but different meaning to them."

"So what did he mean?" asked Jones.

"I think by using the word *general* the man may have been referring to leaders in general."

"What kind of leaders?"

"Yourself, the Congressional leadership, the vice president, your entire cabinet. They want to decapitate our government in one fell swoop."

"How could they be guaranteed to get everyone in the city at the same time?" asked Jones.

Kennedy turned her address book around so the president and his chief of staff could see the calendar. "I'm embarrassed I didn't see it sooner, but here it is. Everyone is in town this week for the dedication of the new World War Two memorial."

The president looked at the calendar. "Memorial Day."

"The festivities actually start on Saturday, and," said Kennedy, "it's already Wednesday, and the heads of Britain, Russia, Canada, Australia, New Zealand, and a

218

dozen other countries are due to begin arriving on Friday. If you wanted to hit us hard, this would be the time to do it."

Hayes looked at the calendar, his eyes locked on Memorial Day. After a few seconds he looked up at Kennedy and said, "How could we have not seen this sooner?"

"Well, at least we have a few days before we have to cancel the damn thing," said Jones.

"We don't have a few days," Kennedy said firmly. "We're going to be lucky if we make it to noon." With a raised brow she added, "The press is going to demand to know where you are, sir."

Hayes understood. "Lying to them won't work and putting them off won't work. They'll just make wild assumptions."

"Logical assumptions," corrected Kennedy. "Why would the president, his cabinet, the supreme court, and the Congressional leadership all be evacuated from the capital in the middle of the night?"

"Only one reason I can think of," said the president.

"We might be able to buy a little more time by appealing to their patriotism," offered Jones weakly.

Hayes shook his head. "We'd be better off if I called the owners of the networks and papers and asked them personally to sit on it."

Kennedy viewed the entire enterprise as rather hopeless. Certain things had been set in motion, and no matter how much clout and power the president had, he would not be able to keep this story from the public. They were quickly headed to a juncture where only one move would calm the press and buy them time. It was a move that was fraught with risk, and one that she didn't dare mention unless it was a last resort.

THIRTY-SIX

Due to the high value of General Harley's mission, he was set up with a secure video teleconference facility so he could interface with his bosses back at Central Command, Special Operations Command, Joint Special Operations Command, and even the Pentagon if needed. Rapp wanted to use the facility. Understanding all too well how Washington worked, and fearing that certain key points would be missed or improperly stated if he didn't contribute, Rapp told Kennedy that in five minutes he wanted to brief the National Security Council himself. Kennedy hesitated, only because she worried about Rapp's famous temper.

Rapp and the president got along well, and he had no problem with General Flood, Secretary of Defense Culbertson, or National Security Advisor Haik, but when it came to the president's chief of staff, the two hated each other. In addition, Rapp had no respect for the vice president, barely tolerated Secretary of State Berg, and did his best to avoid anyone who had anything to do with Homeland Security or the Justice Department. On one hand, having him brief the council could result in a major clash of egos and agendas. On the other hand, due to the gravity of the situation and the time constraints they were up against, Rapp had the potential to cut through all the bullshit and move the president to quick and decisive action.

This was what swayed her, ultimately. The president had publicly acknowledged Rapp's sacrifice and accomplishments, but it went much deeper than that. Rapp was the president's man. When Hayes really needed to get something done, he turned to Rapp. He had proven his worth and effectiveness time and time again, and if there was anyone who could get the president to move decisively and shut out the rest of the clamor it would be Rapp.

Instead of being divided in three the large screen at the front of Site R's command center was now split into six different pictures. Rapp in Kandahar had been added, and at Rapp's request, Skip McMahon and Jake Turbes at the Joint Counterterrorism Center and Paul Reimer at the Department of Energy's Germantown facility were all also included in the meeting.

Kennedy quickly announced the addition of the four new attendees and then told Rapp to begin.

Rapp's attire was strikingly different from the others involved in the meeting. Although no one had had the time to put on a suit or proper business attire, they were all dressed in civilian clothes, with exception of General Flood, whereas Rapp was wearing combat fatigues and a tactical vest. He also hadn't used a razor in more than two days and his face was covered with a thick black stubble.

"Several hours ago," Rapp started, "we were led to believe that a nuclear device was brought into the country yesterday by airfreight somewhere on the East Coast." Rapp paused and held up some documents. "In the face of contrary intelligence, the terrorist who gave us that information has since admitted this was a lie." Rapp wasn't about to get into the specifics of how he got Abdullah to admit this, and he doubted any of these people would want to know the gruesome details.

"We now have good intelligence that the device in question left Karachi, Pakistan, twenty-two days ago by container ship."

"Mitch," said the president, "please tell me this ship hasn't reached our shores."

"General Flood has the Coast Guard checking into that as we speak, sir, but I can tell you that according to the bills of lading we discovered, the ship is due to arrive at the port of Charleston sometime today. In addition," Rapp said quickly before anyone could interrupt, "there are three other ships that have us concerned. All of them originated from Karachi approximately three weeks ago, and all three of them are due to arrive today in Miami, Baltimore, and New York."

Before Rapp could continue, Secretary of Homeland Security McClellan cut him off and said, "Mr. President, we need to shut these harbors down immediately."

"I would agree," seconded Attorney General Stokes.

Rapp had met Secretary McClellan before. The former two-star Marine Corps general was the exact opposite of the notoriously indecisive civil war general whose name he shared.

"Mr. President," interjected Rapp loudly. "That is a terrible idea."

"Excuse me, son?" retorted a red-faced Secretary McClellan.

Rapp had wanted to handle this briefing for two reasons. The first was that he knew how important nuances got lost as information was kicked up the chain of command, and secondly he knew there would be those who would want to use a bulldozer to do a job that required only a shovel.

"The worst thing we could do right now is lock those harbors down."

"I beg to differ," said McClellan. "Our first priority is to protect the American public."

Rapp wasn't even the slightest bit deterred. "And the best way to do that is by letting the NEST people and the FBI locate this device."

"Mr. Rapp," said McClellan in a condescending tone, "you're very good at your job, but you're eight thousand miles away. I don't think you have a very good handle on the situation here in Washington. Now, Mr. President, we have rehearsed this . . ."

"Secretary McClellan," interrupted Rapp, "You're sitting in a damn blast-proof bunker under a mountain two hours outside of Washington." Rapp's bold rebuke took everyone aback. "So don't start telling me you have a better handle on the situation. The situation in Washington is the same as it is every Wednesday morning fifty-two weeks a year. People are going to get up and go to work, and if you try to lock down any of these ports you're going to create a nationwide panic, which is going to, a) interfere with the NEST people trying to find this thing, and b) alert the terrorists that we're onto them."

"Mr. President, if I may." It was Paul Reimer, the former SEAL team commander who ran the Nuclear Emergency Support Teams. "I couldn't agree with Mitch more strongly. Any type of lockdown will only hinder the search."

"Excuse me, everyone." It was General Flood. "The

Coast Guard has just verified the location of the four high interest vessels." Flood was reading from a sheet of paper. "The one headed for Miami and the one headed for New York are still out at sea and aren't expected into port until this afternoon." Flood studied the information. "The vessel destined for Baltimore just entered the Chesapeake and," he looked up with a grim expression, "the fourth vessel is at the docks in Charleston."

THIRTY-SEVEN

In the mayhem that followed the news that the vessel was already docked in Charleston, lots of important people with fancy titles digressed into a free-for-all about what should be done. Mitch Rapp was all but forgotten as the cabinet-level officials forcefully stated their opinions. Fortunately, two individuals with much lower profiles knew what to do, and given the bedlam around them, didn't bother getting approval to act. The first was Skip McMahon, who was sitting in the FBI's Counterterrorism Watch Center.

McMahon turned to one of his deputies and told them to get the Charleston port captain on the line immediately. He then called Dick Schoyer, the special agent in charge of the FBI's Columbia, South Carolina, field office. Schoyer and several of his agents were already on their way to Charleston, an hour and a half from Columbia. Their plan was to meet one of Reimer's RAP Teams that was coming up from the Department of Energy's Savannah River Site to help sweep the port. The good news was their sweep would no longer be random.

McMahon gave Schoyer very explicit instructions on how to deploy his people. By the time he'd finished with Schoyer the harbor master was on the line. McMahon confirmed that the Liberian container vessel *Madagascar* was in fact docked, and further learned that she was due to begin off-loading her cargo shortly. Without getting into details, McMahon told the man that he should expect to see Special Agent Schoyer standing in his office in approximately twenty minutes. Until then the port captain was to under no circumstance allow a single container to be taken off the ship.

The second person to act was Paul Reimer. Technically speaking he was not supposed to deploy one of his Search Response Teams unless he received actionable intelligence from the National Security Council. Reimer had been doing this long enough to know actionable intelligence when he saw it, and he wasn't about to wait for the egos to stop their posturing. The scientists and technicians from the Savannah River Site were still gathering their equipment, and once they were done with that it would take them at least an hour and a half to get to the port.

There was a better option. Reimer's top Search Response Team was sitting on the Tarmac at Andrews Air Force Base in a Gulfstream III ready to go. He called Debbie Hanousek, the senior energy official leading the team, and gave her orders to take off for Charleston Air Force Base immediately. With priority clearance she and her six-person team would be in Charleston in less than an hour.

Back at Site R, Kennedy got the president's attention and whispered something in his ear. When she was done the president called for order and then said, "General Flood, will the navy or coast guard have any problem interdicting the two vessels that are still at sea?"

"No problem at all, sir."

"What about the ship in the Chesapeake? Any ideas?"

Flood quickly conversed with someone off camera and then said, "This intel is being fed to SEAL Team Six as we speak. They're already on alert status down in Little Creek. They can hit the ship and be in control of it before the crew even knows they're on board."

"Are they equipped to handle a nuke?" asked the Secretary of Homeland Security.

"Yes. They're equipped and trained to detect and disable any WMD."

"Have them ready to go as soon as possible, General," said Hayes.

"Yes, sir."

The president began searching the screens for the director of the FBI. "Brian, what's the plan for Charleston?"

"Boss, if I may." It was Skip McMahon asking Roach for permission to field the question. "Mr. President, I just got off the phone with the port captain down in Charleston. The ship we're interested in is the *Madagascar*. I told the port captain that not a single container is to be offloaded until he hears back from me. In addition our special agent in charge of the Columbia office is already on his way to the port with a team of agents. A Department of Energy team is also on its way from the Savannah River Site."

"Correction," said Reimer. "I'm also sending my top search response team. They're leaving Andrews as we speak, and should be there in just under an hour."

"An hour?" asked the president's chief of staff. "A lot can happen in an hour."

"Ma'am," said Reimer with one eyebrow raised in a disapproving frown. "It'll take them half the morning to unload that ship."

"Mr. President," said Secretary McClellan, "We have a DHS Fly Away team ready to go down there and supervise the entire operation. We can have an on-site command post set up in two hours."

Rapp wanted to scream. This entire thing was going to turn into a circus. He desperately wished he was in the room with the president so he could state his case more forcefully. Other than screaming, he had only one other option right now. In an ominous voice Rapp said, "Mr. President, there's something else I haven't told you."

Everyone fell silent almost immediately. "We believe Mustafa al-Yamani, one of the chief architects behind the African embassy bombings, the Cole, and 9/11, entered the U.S. yesterday evening, possibly somewhere along the Florida coast. He came to America in order to personally direct the attack. We're finding evidence that points to multiple cells within the U.S. Financial transfers, e-mails, airline reservations, passport applications for at least a dozen countries . . . we've just barely scratched the surface."

"What's your point?" asked the president's chief of staff.

"It's this . . . let's take a step back and gather ourselves. We have a good handle on these four ships, but there are bills of lading for thirteen other ships that we haven't even begun tracking. There are an undetermined number of terrorist cells operating in the U.S., we have missing Pakistani nuclear scientists, we have one of al-Qaeda's top lieutenants entering the country, and most importantly the terrorists have no idea we're on to them."

"What do you suggest we do?"

"I think we should keep a low profile and see who

shows up at the Port of Charleston to pick this thing up. And then . . ."

"I couldn't disagree more," said the Secretary of Homeland Security. "We could at this very moment have a twenty-kiloton nuclear warhead sitting on the docks of a metropolitan area with a quarter million people. We need to lock that city down and find out what it is exactly that we're dealing with. The Department of Homeland Security is . . ."

"Mr. President," shouted Paul Reimer, the man in charge of the Nuclear Emergency Support Program, "would you mind if I cut through all the bullshit?"

Hayes looked up at the screen. The former SEAL had one of those voices typical of an officer who had led an elite fighting unit. It was efficient and precise and it demanded attention. The president liked his proposal and said, "By all means, please."

"The absolute last thing we need right now is for you to lock down Charleston. Let my people and the feds down there do what they're trained to do. We should give them whatever it is that they need and other than that we should just stay the hell out of their way."

The president found himself nodding in agreement as Reimer spoke. He turned to look at Kennedy, who concurred, and then at his chief of staff who reluctantly did the same.

Hayes stood, signaling to all that the debate was over. "Here's what we're going to do."

THIRTY-EIGHT

CHESAPEAKE BAY

The six helicopters flew across the dark water like a pack of hunting dogs stalking a large beast. They approached from the stern of the ship, skimming the surface of the relatively calm Chesapeake and slowing their speed as they neared the target. The entire horizon to the east was a mind-numbing gray and to the west a blanket of darkness. It was twilight, a time when the water could trick the eye with relative ease.

A quarter of a mile out they reported visual confirmation of the specific high interest vessel and were immediately given the green light to proceed with the takedown. The first two helicopters continued their course and heading, while the other four helicopters broke formation and increased speed. They would encircle their prey, and when everyone was in position they would strike.

The two MH-6 Little Birds moved in almost silently from the stern, the massive container ship towering over them as they approached. Three black-clad SEALs sat on the specially outfitted platforms on each side of the two birds. Each man carried a H&K silenced MP5 submachine gun. The helicopters moved quickly into position, one on the portside and the other on the starboard. No longer able to see each other, the pilots stayed in constant radio communication calling out course, speed, and heading.

They paused for only a second and then the two Little Birds rose simultaneously, passing the rusted hull of the ship and up the towering superstructure to the illuminated bridge. Once they cleared the observation decks on either side of the bridge the pilots did the unthinkable and closed in on the bridge, the rotor blades of their machines coming to within a mere foot of the bridge's glass windows. Matching speed, they expertly set their landing skids down on the observation deck railings, and gave the go word to the men. The pilots were so focused on nursing the controls as each man departed that they didn't even notice the man standing behind the ship's controls a mere forty feet away. Not more than five seconds after the skids had touched the railing their task was accomplished, and each bird deftly slid away from the ship and pealed off.

The officer at the helm of the gigantic container vessel hadn't even noticed the two small helicopters that had set down on his starboard and portside observation decks. Part of this was because prior to this calm morning he didn't think such a feat possible, but it was more directly due to the fact that his attention was focused on something else. A large gray helicopter had suddenly appeared directly amidships, and was noisily hovering above the neatly stacked multicolored containers.

The helicopter's door was open, and two men dressed in black were pointing guns at him. The officer froze, not quite believing what he was seeing. He momentarily thought of changing course, and then noticed a flash of red light on the windscreen of the bridge. The diffused red light tightened and formed a red dot on his chest, and he suddenly realized its significance. Out of fear for his life, he threw himself to the deck, seeking cover behind the controls of the helm.

The HH-60 Seahawk came in and held a position above the cargo area to provide sniper cover for the Little Birds and another helicopter that was coming in at the front of the ship. The fourth helicopter, another matte-gray Seahawk, flared in over the bow of the ship and came to a hover five feet above a relatively small area that was clear of wires and other obstacles. Twelve SEALs leapt the short distance to the deck and took off in pairs to secure preassigned areas of the ship.

Even though they'd had less than thirty minutes to plan the op, each man knew his responsibility and moved with efficiency and assuredness. They had conducted this maneuver hundreds of times on a variety of vessels in both training and real life. The key, as with most things the SEALs did, was to move with lightning speed and overwhelm the opposition before they knew what hit them.

Up on the bridge a man-portable mobile phone jammer was set up and the radio shack was secured and locked down. One of the commandos took the helm while the rest of the strike team began working its way down the superstructure to the crew's quarters. They moved silently, with no shouting and no intent to use lethal force unless they were met with like resistance. Every crew member who was encountered, with the exception of the ship's captain who was brought to the bridge, was forced to lie face down on the deck and bound by the wrists with plastic flex cuffs. In less than five minutes the ship's vital areas were secured and every crew member accounted for.

A fifth helicopter approached the ship out of the darkness at a much safer altitude and speed than the others had. It went into a slow-moving circular pattern a hundred feet or so above the superstructure. The commander of SEAL Team 6 looked down at the ship and surveyed the situation. Now that his men were in control of the ship, he ordered the sniper platform into a holding pattern at a thousand feet. He doubted they would be needed for the remainder of the operation.

Lieutenant Commander Andy Lynch adjusted the microphone arm on his bulky headset and said, "General Flood, the ship is ours, without incident. I'm sending in my WMD team. You can tell the president we should have confirmation for him shortly."

THIRTY-NINE

CHARLESTON

The pilots of the Gulfstream III ran the engines all out to get to Charleston as quickly as the executive jet could fly. When the plane finally touched down just before 6:30 a.m. local time two extremely anxious FBI special agents were waiting. The first person off the plane was Debbie Hanousek, the team leader. The forty-two-year-old health physicist and mother of three hurried down the steps and approached the two agents.

Hanousek was barely five feet tall, with kinky short brown hair. She was dressed casually in jeans and a white T-shirt. A lifelong physical-fitness nut and marathon runner, she extended her hand and sized up the two six-foot-tall bookends. They were dressed in matching FBI windbreakers, and looked fresh out of the FBI Academy in Quantico, Virginia.

The introductions were quick. Hanousek looked them in the eye and gripped their hands firmly. As the six people on her team poured out of the executive jet, laden with equipment, she looked up at the two agents and said, "You guys mind doing me a favor?"

"Yeah . . . sure," one of them answered.

"Lose the windbreakers, and while you're at it lose the ties too."

The two exchanged unsure looks, and then one of them asked, "Are you serious?"

"You guys ever been to the docks before?" They both nodded. "You see a lot of people walking around in ties and FBI windbreakers?"

This time neither man answered.

"The idea here is to keep a low profile," she said. "Get in and locate this thing without anyone knowing we're here. You got it?"

The two bookends nodded.

"Good. Let's load up, and get to the docks."

The members of the Search Response Team stuffed all their gear into the back of the big black Chevy Suburban and the trunk of the Ford Crown Vic and then everyone found a seat and they left for the waterfront.

DICK SCHOYER LOOKED down at the yard through a pair of binoculars and watched as two U.S. Customs officials approached the *Madagascar*. He was standing on the observation deck of a three-story building not far from where the ship was docked. With him were the port captain, the chief of the Port Authority Police, the area port director for Customs and Border Protection, and the commanding officer of the local U.S. Coast Guard station. Schoyer had made it clear to all that no person or thing was to leave that ship until he got the nod from Washington.

As a somewhat standard precaution a Port Authority police officer was put on "gangway watch" to make sure no one left or boarded the ship without their knowledge. The Customs officials made their way past the police officer and up the gangway into the belly of the giant ship. They were under orders to find out the exact location of the container in question and then stall, drag their feet, and in general, do whatever it took for them to buy some time until the Search Response Team arrived.

After twenty tense minutes they radioed the port captain that the container they were interested in was buried in the stacks. Upon consultation with the stevedore it was decided that it would take approximately one hour using two cranes to get to the container, and about forty minutes if they used three cranes. Schoyer made a quick call to McMahon up in Washington, who in turn asked Reimer over at the DOE what they should do. Reimer told him it would be easier for his people to assess the situation if they had access to all four sides of the container. When pressed by McMahon on what to do, Reimer told him to take the container off the ship so that it was waiting for his team.

Two of the giant six-million-dollar cranes went to work almost immediately. Upon confirmation that the Search Response Team had landed at the air force base a third crane joined in. Under the close supervision of Customs officials each container that came off the ship was placed in a specific part of the yard.

Special Agent Schoyer watched all of this with a mix of excitement and dread. He liked his job in every sense of the word. Columbia, South Carolina, was not a glamour posting like New York, Miami, or L.A., but that was just fine with Schoyer. Glamour was something that had really never interested him. He was just competitive enough to rise through the ranks at the FBI, and just smart enough to realize a good thing when he'd found it.

That good thing was Columbia, South Carolina. His government salary went quite a bit further down here than it did in New York or Washington, and his wife and five kids loved the place. The people were nice, the climate was wonderful, and the terrain lush. They'd turned into a golfing family, with the kids caddying on the weekends and during the summer, and he and his wife had joined leagues at a public course that was nicer than most of D.C.'s private clubs. After one year his wife told him if he accepted another promotion he could plan on seeing her and the kids when he came home on the holidays.

Over the past two years he'd grown used to the slower pace of the southeast. He was no longer the action junky that he'd been in his early twenties and thirties. He'd started out as a Detroit cop working nights in one of the worst parts of town. That was when he got hooked on the adrenaline. No job since then had compared. Every night it was something. Usually they were domestic calls, which were wildly unpredictable, often violent, occasionally hilarious, and sometimes deadly. After two years it was on to the Bureau and a different type of action. The job entailed more legwork, paperwork, and patience, but when an investigation hit, the feeling of accomplishment was huge. Locking up bad people for a living was immensely satisfying to the forty-six-year-old agent.

Dick Schoyer liked making a difference. That was why he'd gotten into law enforcement, and as he looked out at the massive container ship that had just traveled from the other side of the world he sincerely hoped they were all going to make a difference today. Whether he liked it or not, he was under a microscope. McMahon had told him the president and his National Security

237

Council were monitoring the situation very closely, and if that wasn't pressure enough, somewhere amidst the maze of metal containers was a possible nuclear weapon that could level the entire historic city of Charleston. Schoyer had no fear of taking on the most hardened criminal, but a nuclear bomb . . . he was out of his depth.

When the Search Response Team showed up at the harbor, he was more than relieved to turn things over to people who actually knew what they were doing. Debbie Hanousek was escorted to the observation deck by one of Schoyer's agents. The introductions were quick and then, thankfully, Hanousek got right to the point.

"I assume," she pointed beyond the observation deck, "this is the high interest vessel that has everyone so excited?"

The port captain handed her his binoculars. "We've been picking around the container for the last ten minutes or so. It's that red one six rows back from the bow sitting all by itself."

"We didn't want to move it until you got here," added Schoyer.

Hanousek nodded. "Well . . . if she didn't blow on a transatlantic ocean crossing she isn't going to blow getting unloaded. Why don't you have the crane grab it and set her down where my people and I will have some room to maneuver."

The Customs official moved in and pointed to a tentlike structure set up in the yard. "We have the VACIS ready to go."

VACIS stood for Vehicle And Container Inspection System. It was a portable system that measured the density of objects. Hanousek shook her head. "I'd rather check it for a radiation signature first."

She turned back to the harbormaster and Schoyer. "Do you have any place where we can look at it away from prying eyes?" She noted the FBI man's windbreaker, but decided it was probably not a good idea to say anything in front of the others.

"Yep." The port captain put a two-way radio up to his mouth and called the stevedore. "Hank, pluck it and have one of the longshoremen drive it over to 105 for inspection." The man in charge of coordinating the unloading confirmed the order and a few seconds later the big crane swung in over the red container.

While the others nervously watched from the observation deck, Hanousek grabbed the agent who had picked her up at the airport and said, "Let's go."

On their way downstairs the agent said, "Aren't you going to give my boss a hard time for wearing his colors?"

Hanousek laughed. "Nope, I know better than that. You guys get a little sensitive about that stuff." They hustled down the first flight. "I was thinking it would go much smoother if you called him, and told him what I said."

Hanousek had found out on the way from the air force base that the young agent was in fact only three months out of the FBI Academy. She could tell he was more than a little nervous about telling his boss to do much of anything but the urge to tease him was irresistible. "I sure hope this damn thing doesn't blow up when they move it."

The guy looked at her with wide eyes as he raced to keep up. "Are you serious?"

Hanousek just laughed and kept going. She could never understand why people got so nervous around nuclear weapons. In comparison to other bombs they were amazingly stable. Well, sort of.

FORTY

The South Carolina Aquarium parking garage afforded the best view of the Columbus Street Terminal. Al-Yamani sat in the front seat of the car and watched what was going on below with great interest. The morning rush hour was in full swing, and the downtown area was teeming with traffic and action, which only served to conceal his presence. Ships and tugs were coming in and out of the port, trucks and trains were bustling through the yard, and the gigantic cranes were moving the omnipresent steel containers around like toy blocks. The sheer volume of commerce was both impressive and comforting to the Saudi-born warrior. In the face of all this frenetic movement, he could not see how the Americans could possibly detect one particular shipment. There was so much happening, so many things coming and going, that the odds were surely in his favor.

Al-Yamani knew that somewhere in the line of trucks waiting to pick up containers were two of his fellow warriors. They had no idea that he was watching them, and he had no intention of alerting them to the fact. So much was riding on this bold plan that he had decided to come to America himself to make sure it worked. None of the cells in America had been alerted to his impending arrival. The others had argued with him, they did not want him to go, but in the end they had relented. He knew it was in part pity for his terminal condition that had caused them to give in, and he felt no shame for that because he believed he was doing the right thing.

Several of them argued that it was too big a risk. If he was captured, the Americans could make him talk. The entire operation would be compromised, and for what? Al-Yamani had greeted this concern with laughter. He'd told the others that he was not afraid to die. The Americans could do their worst and he would not talk. Yes, if they had weeks or perhaps months to work on him they might break him, but al-Yamani would not live long enough for them to get their chance. He had forfeited his life months ago.

No, he had invested too much in this grand plan to simply turn it over to men who he had never met, to men who had proclaimed their devotion to the cause, but who were nonetheless untested. They were Muslims who had been living a much different life in America than their brothers in the cradle of Islam. Yes, they said all the right things and vociferously proclaimed their hatred for America and its lack of modesty and diluted moral behavior, but were they men who would be devoted enough to see the attack through to its glorious and fiery conclusion? It was on this point that the others eventually agreed with al-Yamani. The seriousness of the task at hand, combined with the personal sacrifices that he had made, left the others no choice but to grant his final wish.

Al-Yamani looked down at the yard through the binoculars. Now that the blue cranes were snatching containers from the *Madagascar* he should relax a bit, but he still couldn't quite shake a slight sense of unease. It had started over an hour ago when the ship had docked and then simply sat there. Something didn't seem right. Al-Yamani had asked his Kuwaiti accomplice if this was normal and the young man just shrugged his shoulders. Apparently no one had given him orders to watch how quickly arriving ships were attended to.

Al-Yamani's suspicions grew when a police officer took up position at the bottom of the gangway and then two men boarded the ship. Again the Kuwaiti failed to shed any light on this practice other than the fact that the two men were more than likely customs officials. After almost thirty excruciating minutes the cranes finally swung into action. Al-Yamani told himself all was well, but something was still bothering him.

Yacoub excused himself from the vehicle so he could go to the bathroom. Al-Yamani used the opportunity to get out and stretch. They were parked on the second to the top floor of the aquarium parking ramp. It afforded a good view of the Columbia Street Terminal and the surrounding yard. Al-Yamani leaned up against one of the outer structural supports of the garage and took a sip of water. From this new position he could see a bit more of the yard. He looked out at the endless sea of containers stacked in long rows waiting to be loaded onto either trains or trucks, and some he supposed, back onto ships.

A few hundred meters beyond where the *Madagascar* was berthed, al-Yamani noticed a squat three-story building. He raised his right hand to block out the rising sun and squinted to try and make out the details.

It looked like the building had some type of observation deck on the top floor and there appeared to be several people up there. With a frown, al-Yamani grabbed the binoculars from the car. He held them up and began scanning the yard. A second later he found the building, and a split second after that he was looking at the group of people standing on the observation deck.

Al-Yamani swallowed dryly and counted five of them. Three of the men were in uniforms of some sort and two were in regular clothes. Several of them were talking on phones and all of them, it seemed, had their attention focused on the *Madagascar*. Al-Yamani chastised himself for not noticing them earlier. Lowering the binoculars he looked up and down Concord Street. There were no police cars or any other obvious signs that the Americans knew the lethal cargo had arrived at their doorstep. Using the binoculars he began to search beyond the immediate area of the dock.

He was at a slight disadvantage because he had very little idea what the normal operation of the port consisted of. Other than the policeman standing at the bottom of the *Madagascar*'s gangway and the men on the observation deck nothing appeared unusual, and those two things could be explained easily enough. Al-Yamani checked the men out again. They were still focused on the *Madagascar*. All of them turned around as a man and woman came outside and joined them.

Al-Yamani watched as the woman was introduced to the group. One of the men turned to talk to her and there on his back were three bright yellow letters that caused al-Yamani to grip the binoculars tightly. His breathing ceased as he watched the man wearing the FBI jacket point at the *Madagascar*. The woman listened to him for a moment and then shook her head. After checking out the ship with the binoculars she pointed at the stacks of containers that the cranes were off-loading. One of the other men said something to her, and then he pointed to another spot in the yard. The woman nodded this time and then went back into the building quickly.

Al-Yamani took the binoculars away from his face for a second and took in a deep, tight breath of humid air. He fought off a wave of nausea and brought the binoculars back up to his eyes. This time he zeroed in on the ground level of the building he'd been watching. Almost immediately he didn't like what he saw. A large black SUV was parked in front. One of al-Yamani's chief responsibilities for al-Qaeda had been to conduct research on potential targets. He had looked into assassinating the president and the director of the FBI along with several other key American figures. While checking news footage he found that the Secret Service and the FBI loved to drive these big black SUVs. Never having been to America before, al-Yamani had no idea how common these vehicles were, but there was something about this one and the sedan parked next to it that looked different from the other cars parked near the building.

The woman he had seen on the observation deck exited the building with another man, and they got into the black truck. Al-Yamani followed them as they drove across the yard to one of the warehouses. The car he had noticed followed closely behind. Both vehicles stopped in front of the warehouse and people started getting out. Al-Yamani counted nine total and noted that four of the individuals were carrying guns. Things got worse as he watched them unload a bundle of black cases.

Al-Yamani could scarcely believe what he was watching, but still he held out hope as he watched the people shuttle back and forth, bringing their equipment into the building. Hope was all he had. He had come too far, and sacrificed far too much, to watch things fall apart this late in the attack, but then in a single moment he saw his entire plan crumble.

A truck with a naked chassis pulled to a stop in the area where the cranes were offloading the *Madagascar's* cargo. It was the first time al-Yamani had seen this done all morning. A rusty red container was plucked from the ship's depleted cargo area and delicately placed on the frame of the trailer. A group of men in hard hats locked the container down, and then the truck swung around and eased itself into the warehouse.

The woman with the curly brown hair stood in front of the open warehouse doors talking on a cell phone, watching the truck as it slowly made its way toward her. Once the truck was inside, she stepped out of the morning sunlight and gestured for the doors to be closed.

As al-Yamani watched the large doors inch toward each other, he knew with absolute certainty that the container they had just brought in was his. The very device that had stolen years from his life, the device that dozens of his men had died in the search for, was sitting in that building. Just like that, it was out of his control, and his plan was crumbling before him. For the first time in his adult life al-Yamani felt as if he might cry. How could this happen at his finest moment?

The footsteps of someone approaching from behind pulled him from his morose thoughts. He turned quickly, still holding on to the binoculars with one hand

and reaching for the hilt of his knife with the other, but it was only Yacoub returning from his trip to relieve his bladder.

The Kuwaiti noticed the look of concern on the face of this man he had known for less than a day. "Is everything all right?"

Al-Yamani didn't answer at first. He was still reeling from the harsh realization that somehow his mission had been compromised. Then, concealing his fury and his sudden suspicion of the young man, he said, "Everything is fine."

Yacoub joined him at the wall and looked out across the yard. "It shouldn't be long now. The ship is at least halfway unloaded."

"I think you are right." Al-Yamani offered the man the binoculars. "What is that building over there used for?"

Yacoub took the binoculars and looked through them. "Which one?"

Casually, al-Yamani stepped behind him and pointed over his shoulder to the building with the observation deck on the top floor. "That building right there. The one with the men standing outside." With one hand still pointing, al-Yamani reached under his shirt and grabbed the hilt of his knife again, only this time he drew the weapon from its leather scabbard. The hand that had been pointing was gently placed on the Kuwaiti's shoulder and then without warning it clamped down firmly. Al-Yamani plunged the knife into the unsuspecting man's back with great force.

The binoculars crashed to the hard ground breaking into several pieces. The Kuwaiti's body went rigid in response to the unanticipated assault. He arched his back and his mouth opened wide to let loose a scream of agony, but al-Yamani was too quick, too schooled in the art of killing. His free hand moved from his fellow warrior's shoulder to his mouth, stifling the cry.

The struggle only lasted a few more seconds, and then the Kuwaiti slid to the ground, his eyes open and still seeing, his brain still registering images, struggling to comprehend why this fellow Muslim had just killed him. Al-Yamani loosened his grip and withdrew the knife as the body went limp. He let the man fall the last several feet to the ground and then in a crouch, barely peeking over the roofs of the cars, he quickly scanned the parking garage. He half expected to see a bunch of FBI men rushing toward him, guns drawn, screaming for him to drop the knife, just as they did in the movies. Al-Yamani's mind raced ahead for a way not to escape, but to kill himself before they got their hands on him. He could jump.

But they never came. The seconds passed, and he remained alone on the second to the top floor of the parking garage. Cautiously he bent down on one knee and wiped his weapon on the dead Kuwaiti's shirt. Al-Yamani took a moment to study the dark, innocent-looking eyes, having not the slightest clue if the man he had just killed was guilty of treachery, stupidity, or nothing at all. It didn't really matter.

Everyone was expendable in this just cause, from the greatest of Allah's warriors to the most inconsequential. The facts were stark. Something had gone wrong, what al-Yamani did not know for sure, but it only proved that he needed to be extra vigilant. He would not allow the Americans to capture him, and he couldn't take chances with the Kuwaiti. He was better off on his own. Al-Yamani dragged the body to a corner of the garage where it would be mostly hidden by a parked car. He grabbed the man's wallet and then ran back to the Kuwaiti's car. The most important thing for him right now was to get away from this forsaken city.

FORTY-ONE

"Paul," said Hanousek as the yard tractor rumbled past. She couldn't hear her boss's reply, so she waited a few seconds and said, "We're about to start."

"What's the status?" asked Reimer who was still holed up at the Department of Energy's facility in Germantown, Maryland.

Hanousek walked into the warehouse as the big cargo doors began closing behind her. "The container was just off-loaded and brought into a Customs warehouse." She continued walking through the cavernous space to where her team was setting up their equipment.

Clasps were being popped, cases opened, and equipment unloaded. Hanousek's team had been together almost two years. The many drills, false alarms, and random searches had made this activity routine. Never in those two years, though, had they been given such specific information. They all understood, without saying it, that this one was different. All of Washington had its eyes on them right now, and she could tell by watching her people set up that they were a little tense.

As she neared her team, one of the techs tossed her a headset to plug into her secure satellite phone.

Hanousek caught it with one hand and looped the tiny device over her left ear. After she plugged it into the phone she adjusted the lip mike and clipped the sat phone to her belt.

"We're setting up the secure satcom right now and should have a preliminary reading for you in . . ." Hanousek checked on one of her techs who was donning a backpack that contained a sensitive gamma neutron detector, "about sixty seconds."

Her other five people were busy setting up laptops, unwinding cables, checking on secure com links, and powering up other vital equipment.

"Harry, are you ready to go?" she asked the tech wearing the backpack.

The man fumbled with an earpiece that protruded from the backpack. A moment later he had it in place and flashed her a thumbs-up sign.

Hanousek watched him begin walking the length of the metal box. "Here comes the moment of truth," she told Reimer as the tech slowly marched toward her. At the midway point the man looked over at her and raised a concerned eyebrow.

Hanousek stopped breathing for a second. The tech made it to the end of the forty-foot container and started back. At the midway point he stopped again and listened to his earpiece. After a few excruciating seconds he turned toward his boss.

"I have a gamma nine, a neutron five hit."

Hanousek waved him toward her and repeated the reading to Reimer back in Washington. The news was met with a groan from the former SEAL. She helped the tech take the backpack off and said, "You know what to do."

The man broke off in a near sprint toward the far end

of the warehouse where one of the other techs had already placed the High Purity Germanium Detector (HPGD) so it could begin its background count at a safe distance from the container.

"Debbie," said Reimer over her earpiece, "What do you think about suiting up?"

"It's probably a good idea."

Hanousek strode over to one of the black travel cases and popped the two clasps. "All right, everyone, let's get our Anti C's on."

Normally there would have been a collective groan upon being told that they had to don their anti-contaminant clothing, but not this morning. One by one the team members got into the suits; put on their gloves, boots, and helmets; and duct-taped the seams. By the time Hanousek was done, one of the techs came back with the HPGD in a black computer bag. He handed the device to her and she carefully placed it near the hotspot. Kneeling down she checked to make sure the Palm Pilot controlling the device was recording and relaying the information.

Nuclear scientists from Lawrence Livermore, Sandia, and Los Alamos national laboratories were at this very moment sitting down in front of secure terminals to analyze the gamma spectral data that the HPGD was collecting. The scientists made up what the DOE referred to as the "Home Team."

Hanousek got up and walked back to where her team was set up. Her protective suit was already hot and uncomfortable, but at the moment she was more interested in the information that was being relayed to the two laptop computers. It would take a full fifteen min-utes for the HPGD to get a thorough read on what was inside the trailer.

As the minutes began to tick by, Hanousek stood behind the team's chief scientist and watched the data pour in. Halfway through the process, things were not looking good. The Home Team was a hell of a lot smarter than she was, but even Hanousek could tell, based on what she'd seen so far that they were in big trouble.

"Paul, are you there?" she asked.

"Yes."

"Are you seeing what I'm seeing?"

"Affirmative. I don't understand it, but I'm listening to the Home Team discuss it."

"And?"

"I don't think I've ever heard the *brainiacs* sound this excited."

Hanousek peered through the Plexiglas face mask on her helmet and read the data. "Based on what I'm seeing I think it might be a good idea if we got ready to X-ray this thing."

"I concur. Just keep it low-energy okay?"

"You don't need to tell me," Hanousek laughed nervously. "I'm standing next to the damn thing."

"Sorry." Reimer meant it. If he could change places with her, he'd do it in a second.

"Paul," said Hanousek, "you guys got anybody on their way down here to take care of this thing, or do you expect us to do it?"

"Green is taking off from Bragg as we speak." Reimer was referring to Delta Force's WMD disposal team.

Hanousek relaxed a bit at the news that she would not be expected to defuse and dispose of the bomb if it was active. "All right, I'm going to get ready to X-ray this bad boy."

"Hold on a second, Debbie."

Hanousek could hear Reimer talking to someone else. After about ten seconds he came back on the line. "Debbie, the brain trust is in agreement that we have special nuclear material."

Even though Hanousek knew it was heading in this direction, the news still gave her pause. The faces of her three children and husband flashed before her. A second later she regained her composure and asked, "Is there enough mass to create a yield?"

"Yes."

Hanousek's mouth went bone dry. "How big?"

"Twenty KT."

Twenty kilotons. "Holy shit." Hanousek thought of the explosive force. If this thing went off, the crater alone would be close to a half a mile in diameter.

"Holy shit is right. Listen, Debbie, I have to deliver the good news to the president. Get me an X-ray. I'll be back on the line shortly."

"Roger." Hanousek muted the headset and told the team to get the main portable X-ray machine ready. While everyone else went about their work, she was left standing there staring at the large red steel container. The thought occurred to her, not for the first time, but with new poignancy, that she was severely underpaid.

FORTY-TWO

MARYLAND

The National Security Council had been waiting impatiently for news about the contents of the container in Charleston. Interestingly enough, the vessel that had been boarded by SEAL Team 6 in the Chesapeake Bay seemed to have no weapons aboard. A search of the entire ship with gamma neutron detectors had produced not a single hit. The specific container in question was located in a rather inaccessible area of the hold, but the SEALs were able to lower a gamma neutron detector down between the containers and get a whiff that came up negative. As a precautionary measure the president ordered the vessel turned around and taken back out to sea, where a floating crane and barge would then be used to move the cargo around so they could take a closer look at the container in question.

When Reimer's voice rang out of the secure conference room speakers at Site R, all conversation ceased immediately.

"Mr. President, it's Paul Reimer from NEST. I've got an update for you on Charleston, and I'm afraid it's not good." His voice sounded concerned but not in the least bit panicked.

The president shot Kennedy a glance, and then looked at Reimer's face, which was once again up on the large screen at the far end of the room. "Go ahead."

"It appears the information provided by the CIA is accurate. My team has confirmed that a device of special nuclear material is in fact inside the container in question, and it is large enough to create an estimated yield in the twenty-kiloton range."

No one responded to Reimer's shocking information at first. Uncomfortable glances were exchanged and a few hushed expletives were mumbled by no one and to no one in particular.

Finally, President Hayes asked the obvious. "Is it secured?"

Reimer hesitated for a second and then said, "That's the million-dollar question, sir. In the sense that it is in our possession, yes it is secure. But just how stable it is . . . has yet to be determined."

The president's chief of staff frowned and asked no one in particular, "What in the hell is that supposed to mean?"

"It means that we have it . . . and the terrorists don't." Reimer commented. "At the same time, however, my people haven't had enough time to ascertain the specific configuration of the mass."

Jones waved her hands in front of her face and in an unusually conciliatory tone said, "Mr. Reimer, I'm sorry, but I'm not following you. Could you put this in simple English for those of us who don't have a technical background?"

"Simply put," Reimer sighed, "We don't know if this damn thing is critical and ready to blow or not." He could tell he'd finally got everyone's undivided attention. "We have to move cautiously with it. We can't simply rip open the door of the container and start rummaging around for the device. It could be booby-trapped, so my people are just now getting ready to X-ray the container in an effort to ascertain the configuration and design of the device."

The president cautiously folded his arms across his chest and said, "Give me your best- and worst-case scenarios."

Reimer shrugged, "Best case . . . the thing never got this far."

"But it has," the president said firmly.

"Best case," Reimer shrugged again, "the device has yet to be armed, and it's relatively easy to secure and dispose of. Worst-case scenario . . . someone is waiting for the container in Charleston and they discover that we're onto them."

"And?"

"They remotely detonate the device, sir, and in the blink of an eye the city of Charleston is history."

The president glanced up at his secretary of Homeland Security who had only minutes ago lobbied hard for locking down the city. He made a mental note to himself and addressed Reimer again. "What do you advise we do at this point?"

"Before we do anything, sir, we need to find out exactly what is in that container. That's going to take a little bit of time and a lot of patience. Once we know what we're up against we can deal with it. We've got the Delta Force WMD render safe team on its way down from Fort Bragg, and until they're on site my team is more than capable of conducting diagnostics and design analysis."

"How much time are we talking?" asked Hayes.

"Within thirty minutes my people should have a

pretty complete picture of what we're up against."

"And if it's armed and ticking?"

"We'll have an in extremis situation and Delta's going to have to work real fast, sir."

The president scratched his chin and said, "All right, Mr. Reimer. Good work and let us know the second you find anything else out."

FORTY-THREE

The dissention started almost immediately, and it was no surprise that it originated from Mount Weather, where Vice President Baxter, Secretary of the Treasury Keane, and DHS Secretary McClellan were cloistered. In hindsight, it had been a very bad idea to put the three of them in same location, for each man had a Chicken Little streak in him that under normal circumstances was barely tolerable, but in the midst of a real crisis could manifest itself as near hysteria.

Attorney General Stokes stayed out of it at first. He had been doing a lot of thinking over the last hour, and not just about the immediate events that were going to shape history. He was looking ahead to what the future might hold. The habit had been drilled into him by his mother. Every crisis has a moment where either things slide over the precipice, or disaster is averted. Most people run for cover, panic, overreact, or freeze, but the cunning find opportunity in the midst of chaos, and this crisis was a tectonic event. If this bomb went off, Stokes knew he would be forever associated with a president who didn't act fast enough.

Screw the Department of Homeland Security. The

American people had only a vague concept of what it was supposed to do. The Department of Justice and the FBI were a different story. Citizens knew that domestically it was the president and then the attorney general who were in charge of protecting them.

And presidents were rarely sacrificed, at least not until the next election. Members of the president's cabinet were an entirely different story, however. When a full-blown crisis exploded they were used like vestal virgins in an attempt to satiate some pagan god on a far-flung piece of volcanic rock. First you were fed to the press, piece by piece. Your career and reputation in tatters, you were then sent packing back to wherever it was you came from, where you could count on people who once called you a close friend to treat you as if you had the plague. Yes, in Washington the mighty could fall fast and far, but Attorney General Martin Stokes had no intention of becoming a footnote to some modern-day Greek tragedy.

Always the realist, however, he understood that trying to dodge this particular bullet, this late in the game, would be futile. There was a remote chance that he could throw Secretary McClellan under the bus. Homeland Security was only in its infancy compared to the other cabinet-level departments, but had nonetheless already garnered a reputation as a place staffed by incompetents. Even so, with a disaster of this magnitude, it was likely that it would take more than one cabinet member to appease the wrath that would come down from the Hill, the press, and public in general. No, this thing was too big to get out of the way of. The best play was to cement his relationship with the president and hope that this Reimer fellow and his NEST people were as good as advertised.

The bickering from the Mount Weather facility had been going on for several minutes. Secretary McClellan was once again proposing that Charleston be locked down. Morning rush hour was underway, and with each passing minute, he argued, hundreds if not thousands of people were becoming targets. At a bare minimum he wanted the traffic coming into the city stopped. Secretary of the Treasury Keane said if they shut down Charleston, they would have to shut down the financial markets and get out in front of the likely panic.

Midway through this debate, Stokes noticed the absence of General Flood and Secretary of Defense Culbertson. He supposed they were busy dealing with the other three ships on their list. Stokes was about to jump into the fray when Vice President Baxter made the poor decision to bring politics into the equation.

"Robert," proclaimed Baxter, "We're up for re-election. If this thing goes off, and the press finds out we knew about it, and did nothing to secure the safety of the citizens of Charleston your administration is over."

Stokes knew Vice President Sherman Baxter well enough to know he wasn't a stupid man, so he supposed it was his pride that had finally got the best of him. It was no secret that President Hayes had all but shunned his vice president. The Electoral College had forced them into bed together, and, at first, things went well enough, but not for long. Baxter was from California and, as promised, he filled the campaign coffer and helped deliver the most prized state in the Union. After that, though, things went quickly downhill. Baxter had slowly but surely been isolated. It seemed he'd spent the majority of the last two years either abroad or raising

money. On any issue of importance, he was noticeably absent.

Rumors circulated everywhere that he would be replaced on the ticket, and Stokes supposed he had chosen this as his moment to be heard. Stokes had his own plans, however, and so like a loyal knight, he jumped to the defense of his president.

In an unusually loud and forceful voice Stokes said, "I think everyone needs to *calm the hell down* and leave politics out of this."

The expression on Vice President Baxter's face said it all. He looked like the captain of a ship that had just been broadsided by a torpedo.

Stokes didn't wait long to fill the silent void that followed his admonishment. "If we lock down the *damn* city we'll create a panic, and as Reimer just told us . . . possibly alert the terrorists that we're onto them, which could incite them into detonating this damn thing and vaporize the place. So . . ." Stokes paused and in a more composed voice added, "let's just take a deep breath, relax, and let Reimer and his people, and General Flood and his people, do what they're trained to do, and stay out of their way."

Stokes's reward came only seconds later, when President Hayes smiled approvingly at his attorney general and said, "Well put, Martin."

FORTY-FOUR

CHARLESTON

As someone who usually ran two to three marathons a year, Debbie Hanousek wasn't afraid to break a sweat, but this was ridiculous. It wasn't even midmorning, and the temperature in the warehouse was already pushing an extremely humid ninety degrees. That meant inside her anticontaminant suit it was closer to 100 degrees, but there was no taking the helmet off to wipe the sweat from her face. She and her team had been through enough training exercises and real-life scares to have mastered the fear of suffocating in the suits. She'd never panicked herself, but she'd seen plenty of others do it.

She'd been watching each member of her team for signs of stress. They were well trained and efficient at what they did, but they'd never faced anything like this before. In fact no one in the NEST program had ever faced anything like this. There had been plenty of false alarms; mostly small radiological devices, usually made from medical sources, simply misplaced or forgotten, but nothing of this magnitude—actual bomb-grade nuclear material with enough mass to create a twenty-kiloton yield.

The scientific brain trust located at the various labs

FORTY-FIVE

SOUTHWEST ASIA

The CIA's G-V had already reached a cruising altitude of 41,000 feet and left Afghanistan air space. There was no need for Rapp to bring all the files and maps with him. Everything had already been scanned and placed on a disk. He did, however, bring two of the three prisoners and enough morphine to keep an entire crack house happy for a couple days. He'd taken Waheed Abdullah and Ahmed Khalili, the young man from Karachi. Both were currently bound, sedated, and sleeping. It appeared the third prisoner was nothing more than a bodyguard, but Urda would nonetheless hold on to the man and see what he could get out of him.

Rapp had accomplished what he'd set out to do, and he saw no need to waste a second more than he had to in Southwest Asia. Especially with everything that was going on back in the States. The mere thought of someone like Mustafa al-Yamani loose on American soil was enough to drive him into a fit of rage, which he would gladly take out on Abdullah if he found out the Saudi had lied to him again.

For now he was stuck on hold, waiting for his boss to come on the line. He used the time to pull up the scanned documents on his laptop. Rapp planned on spending most of the long flight back to the States in search of any clue that would help him track down al-Yamani. He would also have to find the time to get a little shut-eye or he would be worthless when they landed.

Kennedy finally came on the line. "Mitch, anything new?"

"No. What's going on with the ships?"

Kennedy told him everything they'd learned since the last time they'd talked, and then she went on to quietly explain the dissention in the National Security Council over how things should be handled in Charleston.

Rapp groaned in frustration. "Irene, listen to me. We don't have a lot of time. I need you to cut through all the bullshit and call Skip directly." Rapp was referring to Skip McMahon, the director of the FBI's Counter-terrorism Division. "Don't go through Director Roach . . . don't even tell the president you're calling him. This thing is about to blow, and I don't mean the bomb . . . I mean the story, and once that happens these terrorists are going to be gone. Skip needs to get some agents to the ports and find out if anybody is waiting to pick up these containers. They might have people working at the docks."

"I was thinking the same thing."

"We're only going to get one chance at this, Irene, and then they're going to be scared off. We need to track the shipments all the way to their final destination and uncover these cells."

"I'll call him right now."

Rapp heard a voice in the background and Kennedy said, "Let me call you back in a minute."

★

REIMER'S VOICE ONCE again filled the room from the overhead speakers, but this time there was something noticeably different about it. Homeland Security Secretary McClellan was the only one in the conference room at the Mount Weather site. Treasury Secretary Keane had gone off to speak to the chairman of the New York Stock Exchange, and Vice President Baxter was off licking his wounds somewhere. General Flood and Secretary of Defense Culbertson were busy handling the situation with the other three ships. So that left the president, Chief of Staff Jones, CIA Director Kennedy, Secretary of State Berg, and National Security Advisor Haik.

Upon hearing Reimer's voice, everyone stopped what they were doing and turned to look at him on the screen.

Reimer's no-nonsense scowl had been replaced with a bit of a grin. "Mr. President, I have some good news to report."

"By all means, let's hear it."

"We've X-rayed the container and believe the device in question to be a naked physics package."

The term was lost on President Hayes, but he assumed by the broad grin on Reimer's usually dour face, that there was something positive in this discovery. "Mr. Reimer, I have no idea what a naked physics package is, but since this is the first time I've seen you smile all morning, I'm going to assume that in this case, naked is better than fully clothed."

"You sure could say that, Mr. President," Reimer laughed.

"So what exactly is a naked physics package?"

"Sir, it's essentially," Reimer held his hands up to

form a circle, "a sphere of weapons-grade nuclear material minus the fire set and explosive material that are used to trigger the implosion."

Hayes thought he followed it. "So this thing is basically the core to a nuclear bomb . . . and nothing else."

"For the most part that is correct, sir."

"So it can't go off."

Reimer thought of explaining the one exception, but the odds of it happening were so small it wasn't worth getting into. "Without the explosives and fire set, sir, there is no way for it to reach any measurable yield."

"So we're in the clear?" asked Valerie Jones.

"That's correct. The nuclear material, as it sits, is no real threat to the city of Charleston."

The room burst into celebration over the good news. There were sighs of relief, nervous laughter, and even a few hugs. The president and the others on the council congratulated Reimer and his people on a job well done. After just a minute things settled down, and Hayes was about to ask Reimer a question when the door to the conference room opened. One of Valerie Jones's people entered the room and walked briskly to the chief of staff's side.

Jones listened for only a second and then grabbed the phone in front of her. She stabbed her forefinger at the blinking red light and said, "Tim." She listened intensely for a full ten seconds. Several times she tried and failed to cut the other person off. Finally she said, "Tim, I get the picture. Have him in your office in fifteen minutes. Tell him I'll talk to him directly."

She listened for another five seconds, shaking her head the entire time. "That's a bunch of crap, Tim, and you can tell him I said that. If he can't wait fifteen minutes, I'll make sure he never gets another interview with anyone involved in this administration again, and then I'll call his boss and have the story stuffed right back down his throat. Now have him in your office in fifteen minutes and call me back."

Jones slammed the phone down and looked up at the president. "The *Times* is about to break the story that you and your entire cabinet were evacuated from the capital last night."

FORTY-SIX

CHARLESTON

As the clock ticked past nine in the morning, Ahmed al-Adel grew increasingly nervous. He'd made hundreds of trips to the yard since taking over the trucking company, but this was without a doubt the most important, and hence stressful. More often than not the trips went smoothly. Al-Adel would leave early from Atlanta so he could avoid the horrendous traffic, and arrive at the port of Charleston before the gates opened at 7:00 a.m.

Everything was legitimate. It had to be that way. Al-Adel was a thorough man, and he'd discovered that the transportation industry was not as rife with corruption as he had once been led to believe. This was not a problem for him, however. Al-Adel planned on playing by their rules right up to the very end.

The international transportation industry was dominated by large multinational corporations with billions of dollars at stake, but as always there was room for small players to carve out a niche. Al-Adel's niche was importing items to Atlanta's burgeoning Muslim population. As long as he paid his bills and followed all the rules laid down by U.S. Customs, the multinationals would continue to ship his goods, and he would continue to pick them up.

He'd done that for a year now. He had a nice little business going for himself. He wasn't turning a profit, but that was because there was no real incentive to. The business was only a short-term cover, so he made almost no effort to get costs under control or expand his distribution. Three times a week he made the trip from Atlanta to Charleston, twice to pick up inbound containers from India and the third time to meet the weekly ship coming from Pakistan.

His fastidiousness had been his salvation. As a Saudi immigrant, and owner of a trucking company that did international business, al-Adel had attracted the attention of the FBI. At first he had cooperated, mostly because he saw no other way, and he knew he had covered his tracks so well he had nothing to hide, but as the FBI's probe into his professional and personal life ground on, al-Adel grew irritated, and then worried that they might actually find something. After many months his Arabic pride emboldened him. He'd lived in America just long enough to understand what to do.

The idea came to him while watching TV one night. There was a panel on one of the cable talk shows and they were discussing the Patriot Act. One of the guests was a civil rights attorney from Atlanta. Al-Adel had heard of him before. The man's name was Tony Jackson, but he was more commonly known by his nickname, the Mouth of the South. A convert to Islam, Jackson loved taking on causes that garnered media attention. After listening to Jackson passionately argue that the Patriot Act was an affront to the Bill of Rights, al-Adel paid him a visit the next day. He explained his situation; that he was an American citizen trying to run a legitimate business, and that the FBI was harassing him at every turn. Jackson took the case and instead of using the courts, he used the media to get the FBI off his client's back.

Al-Adel was very proud of himself for outsmarting the Americans. During his cultural isolation, he had begun to see himself as a solitary, righteous warrior standing up for his faith in the midst of corruption and evil. This feeling of moral clarity and superiority served to sharpen his already quirky awareness of the great cultural and religious divide between his native Saudi Arabia and the decadent American landscape. He would stay one step ahead of the Americans right up to the very end.

He was truly on a mission from God, and he doubted Allah would let him get this far only to fail in the final days of his journey. This thought was foremost in his mind when he was given permission to enter the yard and pick up his container. Al-Adel turned and looked at his companion. Both men exchanged looks of relief. It was so hot and humid they were beginning to worry that the truck might overheat. They had a long drive ahead of them, and the last thing he needed was for the rig to break down on the highway and invite the scrutiny of the police.

The parking brake was released and the truck put into gear. As he drove, al-Adel sat hunched over the large steering wheel and looked around for signs of anything unusual. So far everything appeared normal. The gigantic blue cranes were swinging cargo off the ship, and the rude longshoremen, who were prone to bark at him if he made any wrong move, seemed intent on their own business.

Al-Adel drove through the yard behind another truck

with a naked trailer. Both vehicles eventually came to a stop between some orange cones. Quickly and efficiently one of the big containers was maneuvered into position and al-Adel and his associate watched intently as it was lowered over the chassis of the truck in front of them.

SCHOYER AND HIS men put their plan together on the fly. McMahon had called from D.C. and reiterated Rapp's concern about someone waiting to pick up the nuke. Upon checking with Port officials they discovered that a truck was in fact waiting to pick up the container that had just arrived from Pakistan. Schoyer saw no reason to complicate the matter. A quick surveillance told him that there were two men in the vehicle.

One of his agents suggested calling in a tactical team for backup, but Schoyer dismissed the idea after only a second of thought. He already had six of his own people on-site and another dozen local cops armed with shotguns and submachine guns. If for some reason the two men in question didn't surrender easily Schoyer felt they had enough firepower on-site to handle the situation. Time was the bigger factor. They'd created a backlog of rigs waiting to pick up containers. If they didn't let those trucks in the yard pretty soon, the suspected terrorists might get suspicious and make a break for it.

Schoyer thought his chances of arresting the two men without harming anyone else were best if he let them enter the yard. It would be like letting a bull into the pen. With the cooperation of the harbormaster, a stevedore, and two of the crane operators, a quick plan was devised.

The six FBI agents were waiting out of sight behind containers on either side of the truck lane. Schoyer watched them get into position and then passed on the word to let the trucks enter the yard. From the observation deck Shoyer had watched as the *Madagascar* and another ship to the north were unloaded. The blue cranes that moved the large forty-foot containers were almost impossible to ignore. Their hypnotic movement gave the special agent in charge of the Columbia, South Carolina, field office an idea.

When the first semi stopped in the loading zone, Schoyer brought his digital two-way radio to his mouth and told his people to get ready. What the drivers of the truck couldn't see was that as the vehicle in front of them was being loaded, a second crane was swinging in a container and setting it down behind their empty trailer to pen them in. Schoyer could clearly see the faces of the suspects as they looked skyward watching the container intended for the truck in front of them swing into place.

Schoyer waited until the timing was just right and then told his people to go. Three agents assaulted each side of the truck. The first agent on each side yanked open the door while the next agent in line pulled his man from the cab and threw him to the ground. The third agents on each side covered the other two from a distance of ten feet with their weapons drawn. The two suspects were subdued and cuffed without even the chance to protest.

FORTY-SEVEN

WASHINGTON, D.C.

The Sikorsky S-61 Sea King helicopter raced in over the capital city faster than usual. The pilots of Marine One didn't share the president's confidence that it was safe to return to the White House, but they weren't in the habit of telling the president what to do, so, like the good Marine aviators that they were, they followed their orders and performed their duties to their utmost ability. The Secret Service, however, behaved slightly differently. Jack Warch, the special agent in charge of the presidential detail, had protested fiercely, first to Valerie Jones and then almost as fiercely, but certainly more respectfully, to the president himself.

Warch and the president had a good working relationship. The president almost always listened to the agent's security concerns, and would often do what he could to ease Warch's fears, but on the issue of going back to the White House in the midst of the crisis, the president could not be swayed. Warch put up a fight, but he knew when to quit. Just like the Marine aviators, when the president gave an order, you were expected and conditioned to follow it. Warch did officially state that he thought the move was premature and ill advised, but then went about arranging the president's departure.

Irene Kennedy had watched the proceedings in her usual silent but perceptive way, reading between the lines and looking for the political motive behind each rationale for returning to the White House. Having worked her entire adult life for the CIA, Kennedy believed in keep-ing secrets. There was little doubt in her mind that it would be better if the American people never knew what had just happened down in Charleston. Life was difficult enough for the average person without having to worry about nuclear annihilation.

Unfortunately, burying the entire matter, while a nice thought, was for all intents and purposes no longer an option. The press was onto the story. She herself had implemented Operation Ark with the expectation that they wouldn't make it past noon the next day before the press broke the story, and she was right. Not only had the reporter from The *Times* refused to back down when Jones spoke to him, but two additional reporters were now on the story. Poor Tim Webber, the White House press secretary, had his finger stuck in a dike that was about to lose all structural integrity. If they didn't get back to the White House quickly and help him field questions, there was going to be a flood.

Kennedy was a person with high standards but realistic expectations. Concealing from the press, and the American people, what had taken place over the last twelve hours was hopeless. The more rational course was to get out in front of the story and manage it. This was where Kennedy agreed with both the president and his chief of staff. She would have preferred to keep the president securely tucked away at Site R until they had a better understanding of what they had just thwarted, but there were huge economic and political issues at play.

The economic issues were easy enough to understand. Financial markets thrived on stability. If the announcement of a hike in interest rates, or an increase in unemployment, could send the stock market plunging, it was not difficult to imagine how news of the evacuation of America's political leadership from Washington would be received. Hayes didn't mention the political repercussions, but Kennedy knew what he was thinking. He was not going to sit safely in a secure military bunker while average citizens went to work, thus opening himself up to charges of cowardice by his opponents.

Hayes had been very adamant that the quickest and best way to avoid any type of panic was for him to be seen behind his desk at the White House running the country. For the most part Kennedy agreed, and when asked by the president she said so. An impromptu plan of sorts was then initiated by Hayes. He ordered the vice president and the Secretary of Homeland Security to stay put at the Mount Weather facility and Treasury Secretary Keane to meet him at the White House. Secretary of State Berg was to remain at Site R with National Security Advisor Haik, and Kennedy and Jones were to accompany him to the White House.

Kennedy couldn't remember how many times she'd been on Marine One, they were too numerous to count, but she could tell they were flying faster than normal as they came in low over the National Mall. She looked out the small window at the World War II Memorial. Workers were busy erecting bleachers and getting ready for the dedication ceremony on Saturday.

Rapp was already on his way back, expected to arrive sometime this evening. In the morning she would have him start looking for any possible link between the thwarted attack and the ceremony.

The helicopter banked hard and everyone in back reached for their armrests. Kennedy looked up at Warch, who was sitting in a jump seat by the cockpit. Like most Secret Service agents he tended to carry himself in a very stoic manner, but Kennedy knew him well enough to elicit from him a roll of the eyes and a crooked frown. Warch was not in the least bit happy with the president's decision to come back to the White House.

Gripping his leather armrests the president leaned out into the aisle and said, "Jack, are you trying to punish me?"

"Wouldn't think of it, Mr. President. Just trying to make sure we get you back to the White House without getting you shot out of the sky."

Hayes looked over at Kennedy and flashed her one of his engaging smiles. For the second time this morning he said to her, "Great job, Irene. I don't know what I'd do without you."

"Thank you, Mr. President," Kennedy allowed herself a smile, "but it's Mitch who you should be thanking."

"Don't worry, I plan on it."

He reached out and grabbed her hand with almost boyish enthusiasm and said, "We stopped the bastards, Irene! We stopped them cold. They took their best shot at us and we stopped them."

Kennedy's smile grew. "Yes we did, sir. Yes we did."

The director of the CIA was not one to gloat, but it was hard to suppress the heady, almost intoxicating feeling of having just foiled a terrorist attack that would have destroyed Washington, D.C.

THE MOTORCADE STEADILY pushed its way through the heavy downtown traffic; three big black Chevy Suburbans with government plates, lights flashing, sirens whooping, and no police escort. When the vehicles pulled through the heavy black gate of the White House, the pack of reporters standing on the north lawn dropped everything and ran to get into position. It was rather comical watching the pencil-thin TV journalists jostle with the more sturdy photographers and cameramen. Normally there was a pecking order, and reporters who had the most seniority in covering the White House were politely allowed to the front, but not this morning. The pressure was on. Producers were barking over ear pieces and editors were screaming into mobile phones. The rumor mill was in overdrive, and a scoop mentality was driving the pack.

The dark tinted windows of the trucks frustrated even the brightest flashes of the cameras as the photographers tried to get a glimpse of who was inside the middle vehicle. Through experience they all knew to disregard the first and last truck, which would only contain burly men in suits, with short haircuts and guns. If you hung out in Washington, let alone at the White House, this type of setup was common place. Important people being driven about in dark vehicles, with dark windows and bodyguards, was very Washington.

To these savvy reporters, such a sight would normally elicit no more than a passing curiosity, but not this morning. The lack of information or usable footage of anyone either entering or leaving the White House drove the reporters, photographers, and cameramen into a paparazzi-like frenzy.

The doors to the first and third vehicle sprang open and a group of men wearing lapel pins, sunglasses, and flesh-colored earpieces stepped onto the curb and made a path for their boss. Attorney General Stokes got out of the backseat of the middle vehicle with Peggy Stealey on his heels.

Reporters began shouting questions, photographers snapped photos, and cameramen jostled everyone in an attempt to get more than one second of unobscured footage.

Stokes strode through the phalanx without flinching. He been through this enough times to know it was important to stand tall, maintain a neutral expression, and ignore the cameras. Shielding your eyes from the flashes only made you look like you were trying to hide something.

"Attorney General Stokes!" one of the reporters shouted. "Is it true the president was evacuated from the White House last night?"

"Where is the president right now?" another reporter shouted.

Stokes stayed the course. His years of lawyering had taught him to usually ignore such questions, but this morning, after what they had just been through, he decided to have a little fun. "I'm headed inside to meet with him."

The attorney general and the tall blonde entered the building, and left the press looking at each other skeptically. They'd been on the White House press secretary all morning demanding to know where the president was, and they'd gotten nowhere. The fact that the press secretary refused to answer their questions was proof that the president wasn't where he was supposed to be.

A few reporters continued to shout questions after Stokes had entered the building, but stopped as soon as the heavy white doors were closed. When the din of griping had died down they grew aware of another noise. A noise they were all familiar with. They ran northward, away from the building, and began searching the sky. The distinctive thumping was that of a helicopter, and there was only one helicopter in the world that was allowed to penetrate the airspace around the White House.

One by one they began cursing Tim Webber for not allowing them to cover the arrival of the president from wherever the hell it was that he'd been.

FORTY-EIGHT

Peggy Stealey was more than aware that this was her first time in the Oval Office, and she wished her appearance matched the occasion. She found her hair, makeup, and choice of clothes severely wanting. As always, Attorney General Stokes was dressed impeccably in one of his three-button Hugo Boss suits. Stealey was sure one of his people had gone over to his house where Martin's perfect little wife had everything packed in the attorney general's Orvis garment bag.

Stealey didn't have people, not yet anyway, so she was still stuck in the boring gray Talbots pantsuit that she'd thrown on in the middle of the night. The outfit was to women's clothing what vanilla was to ice cream. There was absolutely nothing exciting or memorable about it, and if that wasn't bad enough she didn't even have anything to dress it up with. No necklace, no earrings, not even a bracelet, a watch, or bejeweled hair clip. She was stuck with a plain elastic band to hold her signature blond hair back and a nondescript pair of black Jill St. John flats on her feet.

Stealey had been in the White House dozens of times to meet with other senior administration officials, and had even sat in the back row of a few cabinet meetings. But on those occasions she was just one face among dozens. This morning was different in so many ways. This was history in the making, and Stealey was planning on helping shape it. Stokes had told her about his rebuke of the vice president and the approving look he'd received from the president. The opportunity was there. All they had to do was take it, and Stealey had a plan that would suit everyone's needs.

President Hayes entered the Oval Office with a spring in his step. Jones and Kennedy followed a few steps behind. Stealey felt a little better upon noticing that the president was in a pair of khaki pants and a white button-down shirt. That brief reprieve vanished a second later as a diminutive man in a starched white jacket whisked into the room from the opposite direction. He was holding a dark blue suit, pressed shirt, tie, and a pair of shiny dress shoes.

The president ignored his two guests and said, "Carl, you're the best."

With a beaming smile the president's Navy steward, who had stood his post for twenty-two years, said, "It's nice to have you back at the White House, sir."

Hayes had no doubt that Carl knew more about what had transpired over the last twelve hours than all but his top advisors. "Thank you, Carl. Would you please hang that stuff in my bathroom and bring us some coffee?"

"Absolutely, sir."

Hayes turned to face Stokes and Stealey, who were standing by the fireplace. He glanced at Stealey, and she noticed the brief questioning look as he tried to place her. The look was very subtle. He tried to mask it with a smile, and then his eyes moved quickly to Stokes. Stealey guessed miserably that given her appearance, it was likely that the president thought her a member of the attorney general's security detail and not one of his top lawyers.

The president clapped his hands together and said, "Martin, you and your people did a phenomenal job this morning."

"Thank you, Mr. President. It was a great team effort."

"It sure was."

"Mr. President," called out Kennedy as she walked behind the president's desk, "would you mind if I used your phone to contact General Flood?"

"Of course not."

There was a knock on the door and this time a woman entered carrying a garment bag. "Excuse me, Mr. President." The young woman immediately turned her attention to the president's chief of staff who was in the corner talking on her cell phone. "Val, I've got your stuff."

Jones covered the phone. "Put it in my office."

Stealey made a mental note to pack that "go bag" the first chance she got. Never again would she be caught so utterly unprepared.

"Mr. President," said Stokes, "I'd like to introduce you to my deputy assistant attorney general in charge of counterterrorism, Peggy Stealey."

Hayes smiled as he walked across the office, his right hand extended. "I think we've met before, haven't we?"

"More or less . . . yes, sir."

"Peggy," said Stokes, "was a big part of what went down this morning. She was the one bringing everything together on the domestic front."

"Well then you have my gratitude and my thanks." The president clasped her hand with both of his.

Her boss had just exaggerated quite a bit, but Stealey wasn't about to argue with him. If they wanted to give her credit, who was she to argue? "Thank you, sir."

Kennedy hung up with General Flood and joined the group. "Hello, Peggy."

"Good morning, Doctor Kennedy." Stealey was surprised that Kennedy had remembered her name. They had met only twice before, and both times in a large group.

"General Flood says SEAL Team Six found a sizable amount of molded C-4 plastique explosives. Based on the initial estimate they are guessing that the explosive charge was designed to be placed around the bomb's physics package we found in Charleston."

"An implosion device."

"Exactly."

"What about the other two ships?" asked the president.

"The search is underway, but nothing so far."

"We're not thinking a second bomb at this point, are we?" asked Hayes.

"It's too early to rule that out completely, but based on the pattern we're seeing my guess is we're going to find other key components used to assemble a full-up nuclear weapon."

"How far are the other two ships from the coast?"

"Over sixty miles. The Coast Guard is handling the situation with the Navy providing backup."

"When can we expect an answer?"

"Within the hour. The initial sweep on each vessel came up negative for nuclear material. Now they're moving cargo around to get at the specific containers."

"Let me know as soon as we find anything out."

"I will." Kennedy checked her watch. "If it's all right

with you, sir, I'd like to go down to the Situation Room, and get caught up on the complete picture."

"By all means. I'll join you in a little bit."

Kennedy left, and Jones came over to the group, a look of exasperation on her face. "The press . . . I swear there are times when I think the Communists had the right idea."

Everyone laughed.

"What's the problem now?" asked Hayes.

"Nothing. At least nothing I need to concern you with at the moment."

"You sure?"

Jones hesitated. "I've called a strategy meeting in thirty minutes. It can wait until then. The simple fact that you're physically here at the White House has taken the wind out of their sails for the moment." The chief of staff ran a hand through her tousled hair.

"Val," said Stokes, "I'd like you to meet Peggy Stealey, my deputy assistant attorney general in charge of counterterrorism."

Stealey shook Jones's hand and noted the dark circles under the chief of staff's eyes. Suddenly, she didn't feel so bad about her appearance.

"Peggy Stealey," Jones repeated the name as if she'd heard it before. There was a spark of recognition in her eyes and she said, "Pat Holmes."

"Yes." Stealey smiled. "Pat says you're the sharpest person in town."

Jones nodded in agreement and gave the president a little backhanded pat to the stomach. "Did you hear that?"

"You don't hear me arguing, do you?" Hayes threw up his hands.

"You'd better not." She turned her attention back to

Stealey. "You and I need to talk. Pat told me about your dinner the other night, and I couldn't agree more."

Hayes ebbed and flowed on the issue of wanting to know what his political handlers were up to. Often, their preparation and strategizing were nothing more than background noise, but there were times when their thirst for victory turned to outright foolish scheming.

As he looked back and forth at Jones and this striking Stealey woman, Hayes decided he wanted to know what the chairman of the Democratic National Committee and these two women were up to. "What are you plotting behind my back now?"

Stealey was a perfectionist who fretted about details only up to a point. It was all part of her constant quest for victory. The details mattered in preparation, but once the trial or debate started she focused on the big picture and took charge.

Stealey didn't wait for Jones to field the question. "There's a consensus over at Justice, sir, that the Patriot Act is too big a reach. We've got some landmark cases working their way through the system toward the Supreme Court. The way the calendar looks right now those decisions will be handed down late summer through early fall."

"In the final months of your reelection campaign," Jones added.

"The consensus, sir," Stealey said, "is that the court is going to embarrass us. And not just once. We're looking at a series of stunning defeats."

The president thought that after what had almost happened this morning, the Patriot Act should, if anything, be strengthened. "Your timing on this isn't so hot." Hayes fired his rebuke with a stern frown on his face. "I don't know if either of you noticed, but a group of terrorists just came awfully close to sneaking a nuclear weapon into our country."

Stealey stood tall, fixed Hayes with a look, and said, "Mr. President, I respectfully disagree. The timing couldn't be better to address this issue."

Attorney General Stokes took a half step back and watched his old lover go to work. Stokes noted that she was hiding her tendency to condescend. Her words were firm but respectful. Pleading, but not desperate. She piled up fact after fact and in the end brought in the political angle in a very deft manner. Stokes had seen her do it before, and he knew the president well enough to understand that he stood no chance. Stokes and Jones exchanged a quick look, and the president's chief of staff raised an impressed eyebrow. Stokes allowed himself to think about the Democratic National Convention this summer. He pictured himself making one of the key primetime speeches, and then he pictured the president announcing to the fevered crowd his new running mate. It was all there for him to grab.

FORTY-NINE

ALABAMA-GEORGIA STATE LINE

Manny Gomez felt like he was coming down with something. One minute he was sweating, then the next minute he was freezing. He tried to remember if he'd drunk anything while in Mexico, but he could have sworn he hadn't. He was always careful to bring his own water. He hadn't even stayed the night. He'd simply crossed over the border at Laredo, picked up his load, and then crossed right back.

He now found himself going 80 mph down Interstate 20 with Alabama in his rearview mirror, Georgia dead ahead, and a general discomfort all over. He'd been behind the wheel for nearly fifteen hours, and if he was going to make it back to his son's baseball game, he would have to dump his load, get out to the distribution center in Forest Park, pick up the new load for the trip back to Texas, and then get out of the city before the afternoon rush hour started.

He had it all figured out. He'd made the trip along I-20 enough times to know where the troopers set their speed traps, where the good food was, where to stop for sleep, and even more importantly where not to stop. There was a nice little truck stop outside Vicksburg,

Mississippi, where he could eat, shower, and grab four to five hours of sleep before he made the big push across Louisiana and Texas the next day. He'd deliver his load in San Antonio and be home to Laredo in time to pack the cooler and maybe even play a little catch with his son before the game.

Tomorrow night was the first round of the big Memorial Day weekend baseball tournament. His son, Manny Jr., was to take the mound at 9:00 p.m. for a classic Southwest Texas baseball game under the lights. His wife and daughter were almost as excited as the boys were. A baseball nut since he was a kid, Gomez had never bought into the line that football was the heart of Texas. Anyone who thought that should get out and drive around Laredo on a summer night. You could scarcely make it a mile without coming across an illuminated ball field, occupied by players ranging in age from four to sixty. From little league to senior league, baseball ruled in Texas.

Gomez took a drink of water and mopped his brow with a bandana he'd dug out of the center console. He was sweating again. He shook it off and told himself that it was passing—that he'd be fine once he got the rig pointed west again and back toward home. The road sign on the interstate told him his exit was just ahead. Gomez grabbed the map he'd printed off the internet and checked the directions one more time.

He took the exit ramp and turned onto the country road. A mile and half down he turned again and saw the construction site just up ahead. There was a big yellow tractor and a grader parked in an area of cleared trees, next to a construction trailer. Before turning in, Gomez surveyed the area to make sure he could get back out. The ground looked fairly dry and they'd been smart enough to lay down some gravel. He swung the big rig into the semi-narrow lane and pulled to a stop in front of the construction trailer.

Two men appeared from the trailer almost immediately. Gomez climbed down from the cab with paperwork in hand and was relieved that his slight nausea had passed.

"How ya'all doing?" asked Gomez.

"Fine," one of the men answered with an accent that Gomez couldn't place.

As Gomez looked around he grew slightly concerned. The construction site didn't look as if it was ready for a whole flatbed filled with expensive granite. Whatever they were building didn't even have a foundation yet.

"We have been waiting for you," said the other man as he looked at the load with a pleased expression.

Gomez took this as a good sign and handed over his clipboard. "I need one of you to sign at the bottom where the red X is."

The taller of the two men took the board and quickly scratched out his name. Gomez took the clipboard back, tore off one of the copies, handed it back to the man who'd signed, and asked, "Where would you like me to drop it?"

"Right there is fine."

Gomez looked at the trailer and frowned. It was kind of a funny place to leave it, but he wasn't going to argue. The sooner he dropped the feet and unhooked it, the sooner he could be back on the road. He did just that, and a couple of minutes later he was up in his cab and pulling back onto the road. Without the heavy trailer the truck felt like a sports car. Not more than a mile further on, Gomez started shaking. He flipped down his visor and looked at himself in the mirror. There were red blotchy marks all over his face.

Shivering, Gomez got back on the highway and headed for the distribution center. The thought occurred to him that it might be a good idea to find a truck stop on the outskirts of Atlanta and grab a couple hours of sleep. The only problem was, the temp was supposed to hit the mid-nineties, which meant sleeping in the truck wasn't an option. He'd have to get a room, and that wasn't in the budget.

No, Gomez told himself, *he'd tough it out.* He probably just had a little bug that he'd picked up in Mexico. He could hear his wife talking to him. Telling him to lay off the coffee and drink a lot of water. Up ahead he saw a sign for a truck stop and decided to top off the tanks and get some water and food.

The chills had passed by the time he'd pulled up to the diesel pumps and had been replaced with another wave of fever. Gomez got out of the rig mopping his glistening brow and neck with his bandana, and cursing the wave of nausea that was sweeping over him like a bad dream. As he staggered to the pumps, the thought occurred to him that he was really lucky that he'd decided to pull over when he did, because this one didn't feel like it was going to pass.

He put one hand out to steady himself, and then the sickness rose up from within him like a big unstoppable wave. A spasm gripped his entire body and then he projectile vomited a good six feet. Gomez tried to lean forward to prevent any of it from getting on his shoes. There was a slight pause but he could tell he wasn't done. Another wave was coming, and in preparation for it he told himself this was good. His body was just trying to get rid of whatever he'd caught in Mexico. That thought carried him through the next three gut–wrenching heaves, and then he dropped to his knees in unimaginable pain. Gomez knew something was horribly wrong when he saw the blood on the ground, but there was nothing he could do. He felt himself losing consciousness. His last thought before going limp was that he might miss his son's baseball game after all.

FIFTY

WASHINGTON, D.C.

Skip McMahon found himself sitting in a room with three people he did not like. One of them was a terrorist, despite what the man's attorney was saying. McMahon would bet his entire pension on it, and the smug little prick was sitting in front of him claiming that he was completely innocent, that he was only doing his job, and that he had no idea what was inside the container he was picking up in Charleston. McMahon could tell that he was lying.

It was easy enough to understand why he didn't like the other two people either. They were both lawyers. One of them, the really flashy one, represented the terrorist. His name was Tony Jackson, aka the Mouth of the South, and he was a civil rights attorney, a plaintiff's attorney, and a defense attorney all rolled into one. He was formidable, polished, obnoxious, and very good at his job. Barely fifty, the native Georgian had amassed a small fortune by winning several highly lucrative class-action lawsuits, the largest against a national food chain for race discrimination. Jackson had become one of those ever-available talking heads on the 24/7 cable news outlets. Refusing to leave his beloved Atlanta to go represent the various high-profile misfits in L.A. and

New York, he nonetheless felt free to comment often and unhelpfully in regard to said misfits and their persecution and poor legal representation.

The man had style, McMahon had to admit. He would be very difficult to beat in front of a jury. Six and half feet tall, he kept his afro short and allowed a touch of gray to show at the temples. The effect was to give him the appearance of a wise old sage. His suit, tie, and shirt were in impeccable taste, his cuff links and watch expensive. He understood the importance of appearance and exuded an air of complete confidence and competence, even if at times he could seem a bit outrageous and over the top. McMahon had seen it all before. In front of the right jury this man would be extremely formidable.

The fourth and final person in the room was Peggy Stealey, and McMahon was beginning to think that she had aspirations to try this case herself. There were many more experienced prosecutors than Peggy over at Justice. He could think of at least two who would go ballistic if they were passed over for his trial, but such was the unpredictable and often cruel world of Washington. Politics was the lifeblood of the city, and Stealey was the attorney general's golden girl. She lacked the real trial experience that Jackson had, but she was no fool and she was attractive, tenacious, and smart. It would be quite the courtroom battle.

The case, contrary to what Stealey had originally thought, was not a simple slam dunk. McMahon had warned her that the CIA would be loath to share its methods of collection and information in open court. He hadn't even bothered to guess how Rapp would react when he found out that this clown had a lawyer, but he knew for certain it wouldn't be pretty. Stealey had thought they would find all the incriminating evidence they'd need at the trucking company in Atlanta, and at this al-Adel's apartment, but so far they had come up with nothing.

The smug little Saudi immigrant had covered his tracks very well. The only slam dunk so far was holding the other man in the truck on several gun charges. Neither man was cooperating, and as long as the Mouth of the South was their lawyer, he doubted they would start any time soon.

"When are my clients going to be charged?" Jackson asked for the third time.

"If he tells us why he erased the hard drives on his computers, we might just let him go." Stealey looked from Jackson to his client.

Al-Adel looked at her in disgust. "You will stop at nothing to persecute me and my people. What have you done to my computers?"

McMahon shook his head scoffingly at the accusation.

"What are you laughing at, you racist?" Al-Adel stared at McMahon. "You people are nothing but fascists and thugs. You planted that gun on Ali, and you have ruined my computers. I have known him for years. He has never owned a gun and would never buy one. Your people planted that weapon on him, and you know it."

McMahon looked at the terrorist and said, "Ahmed, you and I both know who the liar is, so let's dispense with the theatrics and move on. Now where were you going to take that container?" The federal agent picked up his pen as if he assumed the prisoner would actually answer the question.

Jackson's arm shot out. "Don't answer that question.

For the last time, when is my client going to be charged?" The lawyer looked at Stealey. "You'd better say tomorrow."

"There are certain special circumstances surrounding this case." Stealey smiled, knowing there was no way Jackson knew the truth about his clients. Because if he did, he'd already be on a plane headed back to Atlanta. "I'm expecting the arraignment to take place on Tuesday at the earliest."

"You can't do that! That's seven days away!" Jackson bellowed in his deep voice.

"Actually I can. There are national security issues at stake here."

"And there's also the law. I swear, if my clients aren't formally charged before a federal judge by tomorrow at the latest, you are going to have a huge media disaster on your hands."

Stealey knew she had the ultimate ace in the hole. A twenty-kiloton nuclear warhead. There weren't many jurors who would be sympathetic once they found out al-Adel was arrested while in the process of trying to pick up a nuclear bomb.

"Tell me, Ahmed," Stealey said, "where were you planning on taking that trailer?"

"This is over." Jackson waved his hands in the air. "Don't say another word," he warned his client.

"You haven't told him what was in the trailer, have you?" McMahon looked right at al-Adel.

"My client doesn't know what was in that trailer, and this interview is over."

McMahon wanted to give the self-righteous little al-Adel something to think about. He picked up his file and stood. "The CIA wants to question you, Ahmed. Don't be surprised if you get woken in the middle of the night and transferred to a different location."

Jackson was out of his chair like a shot. "You just threatened my client with torture! That's it. I don't want anyone else talking to my client. You people are done, and when I tell the media, let alone a judge, what this idiot just said, heads are going to roll."

McMahon ignored Jackson and kept his gaze fixed on al-Adel. Satisfyingly, he saw genuine fear in the terrorist's eyes at last. In that moment he could tell the Saudi was not a man who could handle pain.

He turned his attention to Jackson and offered him a grim smile. "And when you find out the truth about your client, you are going to wish that the two of us had never crossed paths."

FIFTY-ONE

The G-V landed at Andrews Air Force Base just before midnight on Wednesday evening. The sleek jet taxied to a remote part of the base and into a simple gray metal hanger. As soon as the tail was clear, the doors closed. A few seconds later the stairs to the exe-cutive jet folded down revealing an extremely tired and unshaven Mitch Rapp. The CIA operative was still dressed in his combat fatigues and holster. With a bag under each arm, he exited the plane and walked across the smooth concrete floor. Four men passed him without comment and boarded the plane to retrieve the two prisoners he'd brought back. Rapp kept his blood-shot eyes fixed on Bobby Akram, the CIA's top interrogator. Once again, he was dressed in a dark suit and red tie.

Rapp had spoken to him at least four times on the long flight home from Afghanistan. The focus of the calls was to develop a strategy for squeezing every last bit of information from the two captured terrorists. Akram was an incredibly thorough person who was adamant that the best way to elicit valuable information from prisoners was to start the interrogation with a well researched and thought out plan. Akram wanted to know, in advance, every conceivable detail about the subjects he was to question. Establishing the appearance of omnipotence was crucial to setting the stage for success.

"Mitch, I hope you don't take this the wrong way, but you look like shit."

Rapp walked right past Akram, to his waiting vehicle. "I feel like shit."

Akram walked over to Rapp's car. "I thought you were going to sleep on the plane."

"I couldn't." Rapp popped the trunk and threw in his two bags. "Every time I got close, that damn Abdullah would start moaning for more morphine, or CTC would call and want something. How's it going with the two guys they picked up in Charleston?"

"I wouldn't know. I haven't seen them."

"Why?" asked Rapp.

"The Feds have them in custody, and so far they haven't offered us access."

Rapp slammed the trunk shut. "What?"

Akram could tell he was really pissed off. "Don't worry about it right now. Irene says she'll bring you up to speed in the morning. You're supposed to be at the White House at nine a.m. for a briefing." Akram folded his hands in front of him. "Until then, she wants you to go home and get some sleep."

Rapp laughed in a mocking manner.

"She said you'd do that."

"Do what?"

"Laugh at the thought of anyone ordering you to go home and sleep. Irene said it stems from your deep-seated problem with authority. I told her I understood completely, and we agreed that if you argued I'm supposed to order you to go to Langley and help with the translations, at which point she predicted that you would curse at me some, and then go home and sleep."

Rapp laughed sincerely this time. Kennedy knew him too well. "All right . . . you guys are real funny. I get the picture."

The first prisoner came off the plane. It was Ahmed Khalili, the young computer man from Karachi. He had a hood over his head, but this time it was clean—nothing like the filthy burlap sack that he had sported in Afghanistan. Rapp and Akram had talked at length about Khalili. Either he was going to be extremely helpful, or he had completely deceived them to this point. He'd talked freely throughout most of the flight. Rapp had recorded everything, and then every few hours he would send the information back to Langley via an encrypted burst transmission.

Khalili's revelations were helping to peel back the layers of com-munication within al-Qaeda, revealing the way they used the internet to contact cells in America. They were getting much smarter, having learned the hard way about the power of American spy satellites. They still used high-end encryption software and placed messages within known websites to be retrieved by their disciples abroad, but for every two real messages, a fake one was sent to confuse the Americans. To frustrate the listeners and watchers even further, they'd also begun a campaign of disinformation, flooding sites that they knew were monitored with messages claiming that an attack was imminent. Khalili told of times they sat in cafes in Karachi watching CNN and laughed with hilarity as the terror alert in America was raised in the wake of one of their frenzied message-sending campaigns. These feints were classic guerilla tactics, designed to water American security forces down. Al-Qaeda was no longer one-dimensional. In order to survive they had been forced to adapt.

Every system of communication had its weakness, and Khalili had given them a crucial piece of information concerning al-Qaeda's. In the mountainous border region between Afghanistan and Pakistan, the al-Qaeda leaders no longer used phones or radios to talk to each other. The American satellites were always overhead looking down, watching and listening, spy drones could often be heard circling overhead in the dark sky with their distinctive low-pitched hum, and jet fighters and helicopters with well-trained commandos were never far off.

To beat a high-tech enemy, al-Qaeda simply went low tech. Hand-written messages were couriered between commanders. This delivery system would often take days, and restrict the speed with which al-Qaeda could plan and react, but it was better than getting a 2,000-pound laser-guided bomb dropped on the place where you were sleeping.

Khalili told Rapp they were now using a similar low-tech strategy with the internet. Instead of using high-end encryption software, which was all but useless against the National Security Agency's supercomputers, they were now communicating with their American cells using teenage internet chat rooms. It had been Khalili's idea. The volume at these sites was overwhelming and it wasn't encrypted. In Khalili's mind it was the last place the supersnoops in America would look. After a phone call back to the CTC, Rapp found out Khalili had been right.

Rapp looked at his car keys and said to Akram, "I want Marcus to meet with him first thing in the morning." Rapp was referring to Marcus Dumond, the CIA's resident computer genius. "I understand maybe a quarter of what he's talking about, so for all I know he's been selling me a load of crap."

"But you don't think so?"

"No . . . but what do I know?" Rapp shrugged. He was at the end of his rope.

"You have great instincts," Akram told him. "Based on everything you've told me, I think you're on the mark."

Abdullah was carried out of the plane by two men. It was obvious to Rapp that since the Saudi wasn't screaming, he was fully dosed on morphine. "I gave him another shot about thirty minutes ago." Rapp grabbed a piece of paper from his pocket and handed it to Akram. "Just like you told me . . . I wrote down every dosage and the time they were administered."

Akram looked at the sheet. No wonder Rapp hadn't slept, he'd had to give the man a shot every sixty to ninety minutes.

"Good luck with him," said Rapp. "I think he might be a pathological liar."

Akram smiled ever so slightly. He loved a good challenge.

Car keys in hand, Rapp pointed at his Pakistani friend, and said, "After you've got these two tucked in, I want you to take a crack at the two guys they picked up in Charleston, and if you get any crap from the feds, let me know and I'll expedite things."

Akram nodded. A master at concealing his emotions, he gave nothing away. Kennedy had told him under no circumstances was he to tell Rapp of the events that had transpired between the White House and the Justice Department. Telling Rapp at this late hour would only ensure another sleepless night for him and anyone else he decided to roust out of bed.

Akram reached out and nudged Rapp toward the driver's seat. "Don't worry about anything. Just go home and get some sleep. You look like hell."

FIFTY-TWO

ATLANTA

It was the dead of night as the cab drove past a dormant Turner Field. It continued east down Atlanta Avenue for three quarters of a mile, before it turned into the parking lot of a nondescript two-story motel. The neon vacancy sign was dark, as was the manager's office. A few cars dotted the relatively small parking lot, but other than that the place looked deserted.

The cabbie turned around and looked at his fare through the smudged Plexiglas divider. "You sure you want to be dropped off here?"

Imtaz Zubair swallowed nervously and nodded. He, in fact did not want to be left here, but his handler had called and given him specific instructions.

"Yes, this is the right place," the Pakistani scientist said with more confidence than he felt.

The driver simply shrugged his shoulders and threw the car in park. Most of his fares made sense, but not this one. Picking someone up after midnight at the Ritz in Buckhead and taking him to a low-budget motel by the baseball stadium didn't make a lot of sense, but as long as the guy paid, he could care less what was going on.

The cabbie grabbed the large suitcase from the trunk

and set it on the curb. When the fare had paid him he got back in his car and left.

Zubair stood nervously on the curb and watched the cab drive away. In the distance he could hear the noise from the freeway and the sound of a dog barking. The Pakistani scientist looked around anxiously and then set his computer bag on the ground. The big red Coca-Cola machine was right where it was supposed to be. Following the orders he'd received over the phone, Zubair grabbed a dollar bill from his wallet, smoothed it out, and fed it into the vending machine. He pressed one of the ten buttons and then reached in and grabbed his can of soda, along with a room key that had been left for him. Zubair looked at the number and slid it into his pocket.

He stood there for a moment, next to the soda machine, and took a few swigs while he casually looked around as if he was waiting for someone. After clearing customs in Los Angeles, Zubair had found the rest of the journey less stressful. Flying to Atlanta had still been nerve-racking, but the knowledge that he was done having to lie his way through customs made everything easier. The most difficult part after landing in Atlanta had been taking the gigantic escalators down to the underground train and then up again when he'd arrived at the main terminal. If it wasn't for the fact that he'd been swept up in a sea of people and virtually shoved onto the sadistic metal stairs he doubted he could have made it to the baggage claim area.

His recruiter had taught him only the basics of spy craft, but Zubair took them seriously. He'd stopped to use the bathroom twice in the airport, both times checking to see if any of the same faces either entered or waited outside for him. When he was confident no one had followed him, he left the airport, and as instructed by his Saudi handler, took a cab downtown to one of the major hotels where he walked through the lobby, out a side exit, and down the block to a second hotel where a room had been reserved for him and paid for in advance by a fictitious corporation.

Zubair stayed downtown and out of sight on Monday night. On Tuesday he took a cab to the airport, and then instead of getting on a flight he jumped back in another cab and was taken to the posh Ritz Carlton in Buckhead. On Tuesday evening he ventured out to the local mall where he spent most of his time marveling at the items in two electronics stores. America was a very seductive place. The breadth and availability of consumer goods was amazing. Zubair could have spent an entire week examining the electronics, but he was so disturbed by the atmosphere of the mall that he had to go back to his hotel and pray. Only through prayer could he block out all the distractions and temptations and try to regain his purified mind.

He had finally seen with his own eyes just how corrupt America was. Young girls walked about in public with barely a stitch of clothing and no male escort. They roved around the mall like packs of dogs, flirting with boys, and no one did a thing about it. Here, indeed, was proof that America was an evil place. It was a country firmly in the grip of Satan himself, and if something wasn't done, the Americans would drag the rest of the world down with them.

After praying for several hours, he'd slept well through the night. The next morning he awoke late and ordered room service. While eating he turned on CNN and was alarmed to find out that the U.S. government had intercepted four ships headed for America. Zubair spent the entire afternoon in his room glued to the news coverage of this unfolding story. He did not know the specifics of his entire operation, but he did know that the weapon was being transported to America by ship.

It was just before five in the evening when the phone in his room rang loudly. Zubair answered tentatively, and was both relieved and frightened to hear the voice of his handler. There had been a change of plans, and the man gave him specific instructions concerning them. Zubair tried only once to ask what had happened with the ships, but had been so severely admonished that he dared not ask again.

Now he found himself standing in this dark parking lot in a city he did not know, following the orders of a man who scared him to death. Zubair took another swig of soda and looked at the various rooms of the L-shaped motel. Only a couple of lights were on, otherwise it appeared everyone was sleeping. As instructed, the Pakistani scientist threw the rest of the soda in the garbage can and looked at the number on the key he held. As luck would have it, the room was on the second floor. Zubair extended the handle on his big suitcase and began dragging it up the stairs one step at a time. When he reached the balcony he stopped, slightly out of breath, and looked around to see if anyone was watching him.

Room 212 was at the end of the balcony. Zubair slid the key in and held his breath. Perhaps his handler would be waiting for him in the dark, or perhaps the game was up and it would be the police. He opened the door and turned on the light. The room was a far cry from the one he had just left at the Ritz, but it was still better than almost anything he'd find in his native Pakistan. The scientist closed and locked the door and then checked to make sure no one was hiding in the bathroom. Grateful to be alone and having been given no further instructions, he sat down on the bed, turned on the TV, and began to wait.

FIFTY-THREE

Mustafa al-Yamani waited in the shadows for more than an hour. Despite the general malaise caused by his radiation sickness, his survival instincts were as keen as they had ever been. They had to be. He had come too far, and sacrificed too much, to fail. Yet, despite his best efforts, something had gone disastrously wrong. He, too, had seen the television coverage concerning the ships. Even al-Yamani, who always planned for the worst, was shocked by the completeness with which the Americans had thwarted his plan. Intelligence disasters struck in two ways, or often a combination of both. Either you were penetrated by your adversary, or someone from within your group leaked information, wittingly or not.

Since leaving Charleston, al-Yamani had revisited this issue from every conceivable angle, and he had little doubt that there had been a leak. There was no way the Americans had penetrated al-Qaeda. It was far more plausible that someone had spoken too freely of the plan, and that their words were intercepted by American spy satellites. Al-Yamani had warned his colleagues of this possibility, but he knew that despite his best efforts they had ignored him. He was told there were finances to consider. Benefactors needed to be warned. If the plan succeeded, American investments, even abroad, would be decimated. Large amounts of money needed to be moved to safety. They had told al-Yamani that it could be done without the Americans noticing, but he had been skeptical.

Even worse, the Saudi knew all too well the inflated egos of his people. Stature was everything, and the temptation to brag to others that something big was about to happen would be very hard to resist. As a countermeasure, al-Yamani had launched a campaign of disinformation to try to mislead the Americans, but obviously something had gone wrong and the Americans had sensed that something was amiss. While following up on their suspicions, they must have captured and interrogated someone fairly high up in the organization. He saw no other way. If the Americans had intercepted all four ships, they had to be operating off of specific information.

Everything al-Yamani had put together was now in jeopardy, but at least he had been very careful to keep the mission compartmentalized. The left hand did not need to know what the right hand was doing. The Americans had dealt him a serious blow, but this operation was far from over. Al-Yamani didn't travel all the way to America with his hopes pinned on just one plan. He was a military tactician, and the best strategies were always multipronged.

After leaving Charleston, al-Yamani had driven to the airport in Columbia, South Carolina, where he had gotten rid of the Ford Taurus and picked up a rental car using a Florida driver's license and credit card. He left Columbia immediately and headed for Atlanta. On the way to Atlanta he heard that overnight the president and other leaders had been evacuated from Washington. It was later that he heard about the ships being stopped.

He had memorized the address of the trucking company his group had fronted, and when he reached Atlanta he approached the area with great caution. It was only midafternoon, and as he rolled to a stop at a light a block away, he looked to his right and paused briefly just as any normal person would have done. There was no mistaking what was going on. Police cars had the street blocked. Al-Yamani took his foot off the brake, accelerated through the intersection, and never looked back. There was nothing left to salvage. An entire year of work and the deaths of many of his brave Muslim warriors had amounted to nothing.

Al-Yamani did not let his anger get the best of him. There was no time for it. Someone had betrayed them, but he quickly resigned himself to the fact that he would never know who that person was. There wasn't enough life left in his poisoned body to go searching for those answers. No, he had come to America to die, and he was going to take with him as many infidels as possible.

It was now two in the morning on Thursday. Al-Yamani had been extravigilant in arranging this meeting with the Pakistani scientist who was crucial to his tattered but still salvageable plans. Al-Yamani had spent two hours checking the perimeter of the Ritz Carlton in Buckhead to make sure the Pakistani wasn't being watched, and then after making contact he had followed the cab from a safe distance to see if any one else might be tailing him.

As al-Yamani looked through the window of his rental car, he decided it was time. He picked up the cell phone he'd purchased earlier in the day and dialed the number. The nervous little Pakistani answered before the second ring.

"Hello."

"I want you to get rid of the large suitcase. Bring only what you need and be down by the soda machine in five minutes." Al-Yamani pressed the red button and noted the time on the clock. Four minutes later Zubair appeared outside the room with his shoulder bag and hurried along the balcony. When he reached the soda machine, al-Yamani watched for a few minutes and then started the car. He stopped in front of the hotel and rolled the window down.

"Imtaz, hurry up and get in." Al-Yamani could tell by the look on the scientist's face that he did not recognize him without his beard. "It is me, Mustafa." In a more authoritative voice he added, "Get in, you fool."

Zubair finally recognized the eyes of the man who had recruited him. He jumped in the front seat and stared at the Saudi in semi-disbelief. "You never said you were coming to America."

Al-Yamani checked the rearview mirror to see if any new cars had pulled out onto the empty street. "Very few people knew of my plans."

"What happened today?" asked the disheartened scientist. "How did they know?"

All the Saudi could do was shake his head. "I have no answers." If he thought for a second that the Pakistani had betrayed him, he would kill him, but that was impossible. Zubair knew none of the details about the four ships that had been intercepted.

"What do we do now? Do we go back?"

Al-Yamani glanced over at the young scientist and smiled. "No, we do not go back, Imtaz. Allah still has work for you. The Americans may have scored a victory, but we are far from done."

Zubair was more than a little surprised to hear this. "What is your plan?"

Al-Yamani shook his head. "I am done discussing my plans. Too many good Muslims died digging up that cursed weapon. I should have never allowed so many people to know about it." He shook his head again. "No . . . you will see soon enough, and until then you will just have to trust me."

FIFTY-FOUR

Rapp hadn't slept all that well, and he thought he knew why. After tossing and turning for most of the short night, he gave up on sleep and got out of bed at 6:00 a.m. His mind wouldn't shut down and his body, which was used to working out at least six days a week, was screaming for exercise. So he left his air-conditioned house on the Chesapeake Bay and went for a run.

He had no problem loosening up in the humid morning air, and his shoes pounded out their rhythm on the gravel shoulder of the county road at a pace that was closer to a sprint than a jog. Sweat poured down his shirtless chest, and he could literally feel the toxins leaving his body. Before the run, he'd considered going for a swim instead. It was easier on his joints, and lately he'd begun noticing some new aches and pains. The years of sports and competing as a world-class triathlete, not to mention his work for the CIA, had taken their toll on his body.

He was glad he'd decided on the run, though. When he reached his midway point he felt strong. He looked down at his watch and noted the split. He'd maintained a six-minute pace, despite the travel and lack of sleep. It wasn't too long ago that he could keep a five-minute pace, but those days were gone forever. Paces like that were meant for younger lungs, younger hearts, and most importantly, younger knees.

The second half of the run didn't go as well. His energy waned and his splits steadily worsened, to the point where the sixth mile was twenty-two seconds off his pace. As was his habit, he sprinted to the finish line at his driveway and then continued past it for about fifty yards slowing to a jog and keeping his clasped hands behind his head and his elbows up so he could breathe better. He walked down his long driveway cursing himself. He was starting to slip a bit.

Rapp went down to the dock and took off his shoes and socks as well as his fanny pack, which contained a water bottle and a compact Glock 30, 45 ACP. He dove in and after relaxing in the water for a good five minutes and allowing his body temperature to cool down, he decided to head into the Joint Counterterrorism Center before his meeting at the White House. He went back up to the house, showered and shaved, and put on a light-gray summer-weight suit. Before leaving the house, he had a quick breakfast and filled his travel mug to the brim with piping hot black coffee.

By 7:40 a.m. he was standing in the office of the FBI's Deputy Director for Counterterrorism. Rapp and Skip McMahon had known each other for only a few years, but they understood one another well. Certainly well enough for Rapp to see that McMahon was behaving a little oddly.

Rapp sat down in one of the two nondescript chairs in front of McMahon's desk. The space smelled like fresh paint and new carpeting. Rapp was not surprised, but nonetheless amused, to see that McMahon was wearing a short-sleeved white dress shirt and a loose tie. Fortunately, his fashion sense had no bearing on his abilities as a federal agent.

"You're back," was all McMahon managed to say.

Rapp nodded and took another sip of coffee. He noticed an uncharacteristically nervous expression on the FBI man's face. Something was going on, and he thought he might know what, but first they would have to indulge in some ritual ribbing. Rapp remembered what Khan had said to him last night.

"Skip, you don't look so hot."

"Well . . . we can't all be pretty boys."

Rapp laughed. "Yeah, right." The counterterrorism operative turned his head and drew his finger down the thin vertical scar on his cheek.

"You still whining about that thing?" McMahon shook his head in feigned embarrassment for the younger man. "That's nothing. You should see the scar from my vasectomy. It's at least a foot long."

Rapp laughed and said, "Any truth to the rumor that you're leaving?"

"Where'd you hear that?" McMahon asked cautiously.

"We have all your phones tapped." Rapp kept his poker face on. "I've known about your vasectomy for years."

McMahon smiled for a second but then asked, "Seriously?"

"Irene told me."

McMahon turned and looked at the blank undecorated wall. It was obvious he had asked her not to tell anyone about his plans for the future.

"Don't worry," Rapp offered. "It came up because I heard Reimer over at DOE was thinking about taking a job in the private sector."

"Really?" McMahon looked both comforted and surprised at the same time. "Who with?"

"I'm not sure."

Their situations were similar. Both men had put in thirty-plus years of service to the government, and even though mandatory retirement was right around the corner, they'd both been promised extensions due to the importance of their jobs, "Well . . . I can't say I'll blame him if he gets out." As an afterthought he added, "He sure will be missed, though."

"You both will be," Rapp said with sincerity.

McMahon dismissed the comment with a doubtful expression. "A month after we leave, you guys will have forgotten all about us."

"That's not true and you know it. We would all prefer you guys to stay right where you are, but we'll certainly understand if you decide to grab the golden ring."

Rapp knew McMahon had been offered a job as the head of security for a casino syndicate based out of Las Vegas. His expense account alone would be twice that of his government pay, not to mention all the other perks and a significantly increased salary. The guy deserved it.

"Yeah well, I haven't decided anything yet."

"You wanna know what I think?"

McMahon leaned back and placed a hand under chin. "Sure."

"As I said, I'd like you to stay. There's very few people at the Bureau as talented as you are. At the same time, however, there's a part of me that hopes you take the job. You've put up with enough bullshit. I'd like to see you get a little taste of the good life while you can still enjoy it."

McMahon smiled. Those were his sentiments exactly. "I appreciate that. It's not an easy decision."

Rapp shrugged. "It'll be easier than you think." Changing the topic he said, "As long as you're still employed by the government, would you mind bringing me up to speed?"

"Sure. You got in late last night?"

"Yep."

"Well . . . I've been up all night trying to sort this mess out, and it just keeps getting better."

"How so?"

"How much do you know about what happened stateside yesterday?"

"I've got a handle on the big picture. We found a fire set and cash on the two ships bound for New York, and the explosives on the ship bound for Baltimore. The consensus is that they were going to bring all this stuff together in one place and then assemble the device."

"That's right."

"The nuclear material," added Rapp, "is out in the desert getting tested, and the two men who tried to pick it up are hopefully in a dark cell somewhere having very bad things done to them." Rapp said this last part with a false smile on his face, doubting, as he did, that this was what was actually happening.

McMahon nodded tentatively, not quite knowing where to start. "Last night Charleston PD got a call on a John Doe who had been stabbed to death in a parking garage. This parking garage just so happens to look down on the dock where our little package arrived yesterday."

"Have we I.D.'d the guy?"

"No, but he's Middle Eastern."

Rapp's eyebrows shot up. "Any chance it's al-Yamani?"

"Not unless he figured out a way to grow his leg back."

Rapp remembered that little fact and winced at his own stupidity. "Any security tapes?"

"Yeah . . . but they're shit. We've got it narrowed down to about a dozen cars, based on the approximate time of death, and we're running them down right now."

"What else?"

"We think we know where your guy came ashore."

"Al-Yamani?"

"Yep. On Monday the Coast Guard plucks this guy out of the drink down near the Florida Keys. He's lost so much blood they don't even think he's going to live. Well, yesterday afternoon he wakes up and starts telling a pretty interesting story. The guy's a Brit who lives on Grand Cayman. He gets hired to captain this really expensive boat that just so happens to be owned by one of the five thousand members of the Saudi royal family."

Rapp shook his head. He could already see where this was going.

"The Brit," continued McMahon, "takes the boat over to Cuba and picks up a guy who he's supposed to take to the Bahamas. A couple hours out of port the Brit gets knifed in the back and thrown overboard for dead.

"The Coast Guard thinks this sounds like drugs, so they call in the DEA, and here's where we get lucky. The agent the DEA sends to talk to the Brit is part of the Joint Terrorism Task Force out of Miami. The DEA guy arrives at the hospital, just after reading the alert we sent out about al-Yamani, and he puts two and two together."

Rapp was now sitting on the edge of the chair. "He's sure it was al-Yamani?"

McMahon shrugged. "The only photos we have of the guy are shit. They're grainy, and he's got a big beard and a turban. You know the song."

Rapp did. "Let me guess . . . he was clean shaven with a high and tight haircut."

"Exactly."

"Did the guy remember a limp?" asked Rapp.

"He wasn't sure, but he did remember that the man stumbled a bit when he got on board the boat."

Rapp was already trying to come up with a way to lean on Cuba. They would have to trace this guy's steps, and hopefully catch him getting on a flight for Cuba that originated in a country they had a good relationship with.

McMahon wasn't done. "The Coast Guard put out an alert for the missing boat, and lo and behold, it had already been discovered on Wednesday morning by a game warden at the Merritt Island National Wildlife Refuge."

"Where's that?"

"Near Cape Canaveral."

"Great. We don't have a shuttle launch this week, do we?"

"No. I already checked on that."

Rapp frowned. "Why Cape Canaveral then?"

McMahon shrugged. "I don't know. We've alerted NASA and the local authorities, but so far nothing else has turned up. I do have something on another front, however."

McMahon started sifting through some files. He

found the one he was looking for and opened it. Holding up a black-and-white photograph, he asked, "You recognize this guy?"

Rapp looked at the security photo. "No."

"Well, you should. We never would have found him without you."

He looked at the photo again. "I still don't know who it is."

"That young man who, incidentally, is passing through customs at LAX is none other than Imtaz Zubair, one of your missing Pakistani scientists."

"When did he enter the country?"

"On Monday."

"And you have him in custody?"

"Unfortunately . . . no."

Rapp sat back, a disappointed look on his face. "I thought you said you found him?"

"Discovered," said a tired McMahon, "that he entered the country would be more appropriate."

"Any idea where he is now?"

McMahon knew he was approaching an awkward point. "We have him boarding a Delta flight at LAX and heading to Atlanta."

"I assume you've got him getting off the plane in Atlanta?"

"Not yet. There's a problem with the surveillance tapes, but we expect to have it sorted out this morning."

"What about these two guys you picked up in Charleston?"

There it was. Things were about to get really uncomfortable. "We have them in custody," answered McMahon somewhat evasively.

"Where?" Rapp tilted his head suspiciously, sensing something in his friend's voice.

McMahon didn't look away, but he wanted to. Instead he got up and closed his door. "They're being held in the Fairfax County Adult Detention Center."

"You're not serious? They're here in town?" Rapp pointed at the floor.

"Listen . . . before you fly off the handle . . . there's a few things you need to know. For starters . . . both these guys are naturalized citizens."

"I don't care if they're the president's long-lost brothers!" yelled Rapp. "They should be in the Navy brig down in Charleston or down in Guantanamo, or better yet, you should have handed them over to me."

"Mitch, they have a lawyer."

"A lawyer!" Rapp was suddenly on his feet. "You're not fucking serious."

"He's not just any lawyer . . . he's a hotshot civil rights attorney from Atlanta with a lot of connections here in Washington. He went to the media with this late yesterday and . . ."

Rapp cut him off. "I don't care who he is! This is ridiculous!"

"It wasn't my call," McMahon said defensively. "Trust me."

"Let me take one guess. They're Arabs, aren't they?" McMahon nodded.

"Saudi?"

The FBI man nodded again.

"So you're telling me that two Saudi immigrants, undoubtedly Wahhabis, showed up in Charleston yesterday to pick up a nuclear bomb and the FBI decides to back down because they hire a lawyer?"

"We're not backing down, and it wasn't the Bureau's call. This is coming down from Justice."

"The attorney general?"

"More or less."

"The attorney general takes his orders from the president. Are you telling me this was the president's idea?"

"No. I know for a fact it wasn't the president's idea. It started somewhere else."

"Where?"

McMahon hesitated, not out of fear that he could get in trouble, but out of caution. "I'm going to tell you how this all got started, but I want you to look at it from more than just your perspective."

"What's that supposed to mean?" Rapp fumed.

"You don't have to play by the rules," McMahon said firmly, "but the FBI does. All I'm asking is that you understand the legal and political implications of what happened yesterday. Hear me out and then do whatever you feel is right."

Rapp had neither the patience nor the desire to listen to one more word, but for the sake of finding out who was behind this monumentally stupid decision he was at least willing to keep his temper in check for a few more minutes.

FIFTY-FIVE

The midnight blue BMW series five darted through the morning traffic at a near reckless pace. Although angry, the man behind the wheel was very much in control of the vehicle. Instead of crossing the Potomac on the Theodore Roosevelt Memorial Bridge, he shot across two lanes of traffic and followed the exit sign for the U.S. Marine Corps Memorial. The limousine was easy enough to find. Rapp drove around to the north side of the monument and brought his car to an abrupt stop directly behind the limousine.

As always, he quickly checked the surrounding area while throwing the car in park and unbuckling his seat belt. Then he grabbed his keys and got out. While walking to the limo he continued to survey the landscape. The back door was open and he climbed in.

Dr. Irene Kennedy had the TV on and was reading a file. She didn't even bother to look up at the CIA's top counterterrorism operative. Kennedy hadn't been there when they'd convinced the president of this course of action, but as soon as she found out, the first thing that came to mind was that Rapp would be furious.

"Good morning."

"And what's so damned good about it?" snapped Rapp.

Kennedy closed the file and slowly took off her glasses. "I'm glad to see you made it back in one piece."

Next to Rapp's wife and his brother, Steven, Kennedy was perhaps the most important person in his life. In many ways, her influence was greater than the other two combined. Kennedy knew things about him that the other two would, and could, never know.

Despite his great affection for Kennedy, there were times when her levelheaded demeanor drove him insane. "Irene, my head's about to pop off . . . so let's dispense with the pleasantries. What the hell happened between the time I left Afghanistan and got back here?"

This was exactly why Kennedy had asked him to meet her here. She did not want him exploding at the White House. "The simple version, Mitchell, is that two U.S. citizens were arrested yesterday in conjunction with a suspected terrorist attack. As is their right, they retained an attorney and . . ."

Rapp closed his eyes and began shaking his head. "Don't give me the P.C. version. I want to know how in the hell you let this happen."

"To be blunt . . . I was outmaneuvered."

"How?"

"I had my hands full."

"He didn't even consult you?" asked a disbelieving Rapp.

"Not really. By the time I found out it was too late."

"Was this Jones's idea?" Rapp detested the president's chief of staff.

"She was involved in the decision, but I think it originated at Justice."

"Stokes?"

"Yes, and one of his deputies."

Rapp shook his head. "I don't get it. I thought we had solved all this nonsense with the Patriot Act."

"So did I, but I should have known better."

"How so?"

"There was no way the left was ever going to let that thing stand. I should've known that once the shock of 9/11 wore off they'd begin to dismantle it."

"Irene . . . you know me. I could give a rat's ass about politics and ninety-nine percent of the crap that goes on in this town, but come on . . . these guys were involved in a plot to set off a nuclear bomb in Washington, D.C., and now I'm being told by the FBI that I can't talk to them, because they've got a lawyer."

"Mitch, I don't like this anymore than you do, but right now I don't see any other choice. This thing is public now."

"I'll tell you how to handle it. We take away their U.S. citizenship, based on the fact that they came to America with the intent of launching a terrorist attack, and then we put the screws to them until they give up every damn accomplice and piece of information we need."

"Mitch, the train has already left the station." She pointed at the TV. The screen showed a reporter standing in the White House press room. "The background has already been given to the press. The president is going to read a statement any minute. This is election-year politics. The president wants it both ways. A tough public prosecution of these two guys will give him a lot of good P.R., while at the same time assuage the concerns of the far left over the Patriot Act."

Rapp shook his head at the TV. "Mustafa Frickin' al-Yamani is on the loose somewhere in America. We have a dead Arab in a parking garage in Charleston, we have a missing Pakistani nuclear scientist arriving in Atlanta on Monday, and coincidentally the two guys we picked up in Charleston yesterday also happen to be from Atlanta." Rapp paused, his silence exuding frustration. "Has it occurred to anyone else that the two men who the FBI have in custody just might be able to help us track down al-Yamani and this nuclear scientist?"

Kennedy shared his frustration; she knew there was no way the Justice Department would allow anyone from the CIA, let alone Mitch Rapp to get anywhere near their two precious prisoners. Her protégé was now officially on the warpath and she had no interest in stopping him. "You'll have to ask the president about it. Just try and be respectful," she said.

FIFTY-SIX

The second motel wasn't as nice as the first. The carpeting was stained and matted, and the bedspreads were stiff and shiny. Imtaz Zubair did not complain. To do so in front of al-Yamani would have been foolish, especially since the man was in the bathroom throwing up. He was dying of radiation poisoning, that was obvious.

Zubair had seen it before when he worked at the Chasnupp nuclear power plant in Central Pakistan. There had been a minor leak that had been missed by a faulty sensor. A technician had continued to work in the contaminated area for an entire shift before it was discovered. By then it was too late.

Within a day the man was vomiting and had blotchy burn marks on his skin. Then came the swollen eyes, the agonizing spasms of pain, and finally the man's hands had turned to gelatin and he had bled to death from the inside out. Zubair still remembered the screams. What a terrible way to die.

Zubair sat at the foot of the bed and stared at the TV. He had been ordered to tell al-Yamani when the American president came on. According to the reporter they were running behind schedule, but expected him any minute.

When the president finally stepped behind the podium, Zubair called to al-Yamani. A second later he came out of the bathroom, wiping his mouth with a towel. Zubair noticed a dab of blood on the white towel and asked, "Is there anything I can do to help ease your burden?"

Al-Yamani shook his head and sat down on the edge of the bed. He was very interested in what the American leader would have to say. The president was joined by several people—two men and a woman.

"I have a brief statement, and then I'll field one or two questions before I turn things over to Attorney General Stokes." The president looked down at the podium for a moment and then back up at the cameras. "Yesterday the Department of Justice and the FBI foiled a major al-Qaeda terrorist attack that was designed to target Washington, D.C. As has been reported by the press, this attack involved the shipment of explosive devices aboard multiple international container vessels. Through the hard work and quick actions of the Department of Justice, the FBI, the CIA, and Department of Defense, this attack was thwarted, and in the process al-Qaeda has been dealt a serious blow. Terrorist cells located here in the United States have been identified and arrests are ongoing. Now I will take only a few questions and then Attorney General Stokes has a statement to make." The president pointed into the crowd of reporters.

A slender man with prematurely gray hair stood and asked, "Mr. President, is it true that you and senior members of your administration were evacuated from the city on Tuesday night?"

"As a standard precautionary measure that falls under the continuity of government program, certain people were evacuated from the city and moved to secure undisclosed locations."

"Were you one of those people?"

The president grinned. "For security reasons I will neither confirm nor deny." He pointed to another reporter.

"Mr. President." A woman stood up this time. "Can you confirm that this attack was to take place on Saturday during the dedication of the new World War Two memorial, and if so what extra measures will you put into place to protect the foreign heads of state who will start arriving tomorrow to honor the men and women who fought in the war?"

"For starters, al-Qaeda is on the run. They just gave us their best shot, and we stopped them in their tracks. As far as specific intelligence pointing to this Saturday's dedication . . . we have seen nothing that would lead us to that conclusion. I'll take one more question."

A group of reporters began shouting questions and the president picked one. The others were immediately silenced and the one who remained standing asked, "What type of explosive devices are we talking about, sir?"

The president shook his head. "The investigation is ongoing, so I can't get into specifics."

A woman appeared from off camera and reached for the president. The president thanked the reporters for his time and then left. A man al-Yamani recognized as the attorney general stepped up to the podium and began to speak. Al-Yamani didn't need to hear any more.

He turned off the TV and said, "It is time to go."

"Are we coming back?"

"No."

Zubair offered to drive but al-Yamani declined. They got in the rental car and left the seedy motel. Al-Yamani was eager to get rid of the rental car. *Keep severing ties,* he told himself. As long as he did that, the Americans would have no chance of catching him, and he could prove the president's victory speech premature.

FIFTY-SEVEN

WASHINGTON, D.C.

Rapp rarely thought of his job in terms of love or hate. It was a vocation, a duty, and not something that was easily affected by his moods, good or bad. There was only commitment to a cause in which he truly believed. There were, however, aspects of his job that he did not enjoy and increasingly took steps to avoid. One of them was coming to the White House.

For starters, Rapp and the president's chief of staff could barely tolerate each other. She was an impediment to every strategy or action he tried to advise the president on. The fact that politics weighed so heavily in every decision simply did not compute for Rapp. It should not have come as a surprise to him that in a town like Washington and in a place like the White House, politics played such an important role but, in an irritating and undermining way, it did.

Add to all of that a convoluted, misguided, and rabid political correctness that permeated nearly every meeting, and you were left with an environment in which the inconsequential was debated and dissected, and the issues of real importance were obfuscated and put off for someone else to deal with at a later date. It was not the type of place where a man of action felt at ease, but it was nonetheless where Mitch Rapp found himself on this Thursday morning in May, sitting in the Cabinet Room with a painting of Teddy Roosevelt appropriately looming over his shoulder. His surly mood had not abated, but for Irene's sake he was working to conceal it. All but four of the eighteen leather chairs were occupied. The national security team was assembled and waiting on their commander in chief to join them.

President Hayes entered with a smile on his face and a jovial bounce to his step. Everyone immediately stood, even Rapp, though he didn't feel like it. As the president walked past him, he squeezed Rapp's shoulder as a sign of his gratitude. So far he had not had the chance to thank him personally.

Hayes continued around the table to his chair that was positioned facing portraits of Lincoln and Jefferson. Chief of Staff Valerie Jones, never far from her master, took the vacant chair to the president's right. The thought occurred to Rapp, not for the first time, that it would have been more fitting for her to be seated on his left. Attorney General Stokes entered next and was followed by a tall blonde who Rapp assumed was this Stealey woman McMahon had told him about. So intense was Rapp's resentment of this woman that he failed to notice her obvious beauty. The Department of Justice officials took their seats opposite the president and then everyone sat.

Rapp had watched part of the press conference in Kennedy's limo and it was obvious that Attorney General Stokes was riding high on the accolades he'd received from the president. After National Security Advisor Haik announced the agenda, Paul Reimer from the Department of Energy took over.

Holding a yellow legal pad in his hands the man in charge of the Nuclear Emergency Support Teams began on a very sober note by saying, "Our scientists have concluded that if the various components that we intercepted had actually been assembled, the device would in fact have obtained a yield in the twenty-kiloton range." Reimer cleared his throat and added, "A nuclear weapon of that size would have destroyed the capital and killed over a hundred thousand people in the initial burst. In the following month that number would double due to the radiation effects."

A morbid silence fell over the meeting. Somewhat used to dealing with these scenarios strategically, General Flood was the first to move on. "Have you figured out where this thing came from?"

"That's the million-dollar question," replied Reimer. "Twenty KT is not significant by nuclear bomb standards, but by no means is it small. Attribution for the special nuclear material could take up to six months, but there are certain design geometrics that lead us to believe the weapon is of Soviet origin."

The president sensed there was more. "You sound a little shaky in your assessment."

"We have a slight disagreement among several of our scientists at the moment, but we're ninety percent confident that the weapon is in fact Soviet made."

"What's the other ten percent saying?"

"There is a slight possibility that it is one of the Pakistanis' early prototype designs."

The president looked at his secretary of state, briefly, and then back at Reimer. "Based on some of the intelligence we've already gathered I would be inclined to think the chances of this thing being Pakistani would be much higher."

"It's that intelligence, sir . . . the missing scientists in particular . . . that is causing us to leave the door open on the Pakistani issue. From a purely scientific standpoint, we are very confident that it's Soviet."

"Why?"

Reimer looked at the other attendees before answering, and then turned his attention back to the president. "As I said, it will take us six months to figure out exactly where this material originated, to fingerprint, in other words, the exact reactor where the SNM was made, but that is not the only way to identify the origin. The other method is through design analysis. At first we were thrown by this weapon. We'd never seen anything like it, which led us to believe that it was possibly an early Pakistani design that we knew nothing about. This was where the minor dissent, if you will, originally started. With the design.

"We ran the design through the computers and came up with nothing. Typically weapons with yields in the ten to twenty range tend to be designed for torpedoes, cruise missiles, or artillery shells. This weapon does not fit that design geometry profile. We were running out of ideas when one of our senior scientists remembered a series of tests that the Soviet Union conducted during the late sixties and into the mid-seventies."

Reimer flipped through a thick file and asked, "How many of you are familiar with the Kazakh test site?"

General Flood and Director Kennedy were the only two people who raised their hands.

Reimer held up a map. "The Kazakh test site is located in western Kazakhstan on the northern edge of the Caspian Sea. From 1949 to roughly 1990 the Soviets conducted 620 known nuclear explosions at this site. That is approximately two thirds of all Soviet tests. Over

300 megatons of nuclear weapons were exploded at this one range alone. To put that into perspective, that's the equivalent of roughly 20,000 Hiroshima bombs and nearly twice the amount of all U.S. tests."

Rapp only heard the first part. His mind fixed on it. He leaned forward in his chair and raised his hand to get Reimer's attention. "Paul, you said this test site is located on the northern edge of the Caspian."

"That's right."

"You might be interested to know that when we raided the al-Qaeda camp in Pakistan one of the things we found was a map of the Caspian region."

Reimer's thick eyebrows arched in surprise. "Could you send it to me when we're done?"

"Absolutely."

Reimer jotted a quick note and then continued saying, "From the late sixties to the mid-seventies the Soviets tested a series of atomic demolition munitions. ADMs. We don't know a lot about these be-cause they were not designed for military purposes."

"Then what were they for?" asked the president.

"A significant part of the Kazakh test site is rich in salt deposits. The idea behind these tests was to create extremely cheap and large underground storage facilities for oil, natural gas, and radioactive waste."

"Did it work?"

"No. A Soviet scientist who was involved in the program defected in 1979, and gave us detailed infor-mation about the results. Our scientific people looked into it and agreed that it was something that wasn't worth pursuing."

"So how would al-Qaeda get their hands on this bomb?" the president asked.

In Reimer's mind there were only two possibilities.

One of them, that the Soviets had sold the material, was extremely remote, and he wasn't about to throw it out in front of this group until he knew more. The other possibility, that al-Qaeda actually retrieved the material from the test site themselves, was more likely, but there were others at the table who were in a better position to answer, so he said, "I'm not sure, Mr. President."

Secretary of State Berg leaned forward and looked at CIA Director Kennedy. "We need to get the Russians involved."

"I agree. They can lean on the Kazakhs better than we can."

The president looked across at Flood. "General?"

"I concur. They don't want this stuff floating around any more than we do. They might not tell us everything they find, but they'll deal with the problem."

"What does that mean exactly?" asked Jones.

"On something this big," Flood answered, "people will be marched in front of a firing squad, and if they want to save themselves and their families they'll be given one last chance to confess."

Rapp simply couldn't pass up the opportunity to make his opinion on a related matter known. "You mean like we should do with the two guys we picked up in Charleston."

If anyone other than Rapp had made the comment, there would have been a smattering of laughter, but because it was him, everyone assumed correctly that he meant it.

President Hayes decided to let the comment pass. He had been warned by Kennedy that Rapp wouldn't like the move by the Justice Department, but he knew when he had the opportunity he'd be able to talk some sense into him.

"It goes without saying that we need to keep all of this very quiet," Hayes said. "So far the press has no idea just how destructive this weapon could've been, and I stress the word *could*. I've talked to Paul about this." The president glanced at Reimer. "This device was never fully assembled, and even then, it would have had to have been put together by someone highly skilled or it would have never reached its full destructive power. Therefore, it is highly likely it would have been nothing more than a subatomic yield. So . . . for reasons that should be apparent to all of us, from this point forward the device will be referred to only as a dirty bomb in official circles."

Rapp clenched and then flexed his hands in agitation. A disaster had been averted, but there was still real work to be done and instead they were playing word games. He couldn't resist pointing out the obvious.

He looked down the length of the table. "Paul, would Dr. Imtaz Zubair be skilled enough to assemble the weapon so that it could obtain its optimal yield?"

Reimer nodded, "Yes."

Chief of Staff Jones asked, "Who is Dr. Zubair?"

"He's a Pakistani nuclear scientist who entered the country on Monday using a false passport." Rapp looked directly at the president and then Jones. "You haven't heard of him?"

"Yes, we've heard of him," snapped Jones. "We've got a little bit more to worry about than the name of every terrorist who's trying to attack us."

"Val, after he arrived at LAX, do you know where he went?"

"No." Jones began jotting down notes as if Rapp had already lost her attention.

"Atlanta." Undeterred, Rapp turned to the attorney

general and his deputy. FBI Director Roach, who was sitting next to Stokes, thought he knew what was coming and slid his chair back a bit to get out of the way.

"Do we know anyone else from Atlanta?" asked Rapp in an ominously calm voice. "Maybe a couple of Saudi immigrants who tried to pick up a nuclear bomb yesterday?"

Before the attorney general could answer Peggy Stealey asked, "What's your point, Mr. Rapp?"

Rapp was caught slightly off guard that the blonde had answered for her boss but he returned her unwavering stare. "Do you think that just maybe those two guys you have locked up out in Fairfax might be able to tell us where to start looking for Dr. Zubair?"

"Mr. Rapp, our investigation is proceeding just fine, so I still don't see your point."

"Have you found, Dr. Zubair?"

"No, Mr. Rapp, we haven't, but rest assured we will."

Rapp was not about to give up. "Forgive me if I don't share your confidence."

Stealey chose to ignore the jab.

Rapp wasn't inclined to quit just yet. "What information have you gotten out of the two men in jail?"

Stealey looked at him as if she had tired of this line of questioning and was just barely able to conceal her impatience. "Mr. Rapp, this is a domestic issue that is already in front of the courts."

"And your point is . . ."

"The two suspects in question have a lawyer," she said now with a healthy dose of irritation in her voice.

"Surely you are not suggesting torture as a method to get these men to talk?"

"I don't give a *shit* what you use to get them to talk. Just get them talking, and do it fast."

Stealey's face flushed, but her piercing eyes never left Rapp's. "This is entirely ludicrous."

Rapp was beyond the point of caring. "I'll tell you what's ludicrous. Mustafa al-Yamani, one of al-Qaeda's top lieutenants, is in America right now, and I'll guarantee you the two men you have in custody have information that could help us capture him."

"Mr. Rapp, the Justice Department doesn't tell you how to conduct your business outside this country, so I suggest you return the favor and let us handle things here in America."

"Actually you do try to tell me how to do my job. I just choose to ignore you."

"Well, I guess we'll just have to do the same."

"How do you know they don't have another bomb? How do you know they don't have another attack planned? We can't take the chance. Those men you have in jail need to be interrogated, and don't tell me you can't find a federal judge to revoke their citizenship, because if you can't, I can think of one that'll have it all taken care of in thirty minutes."

"And we'll have a media nightmare on our hands," growled Valerie Jones. "I am fed up with these outbursts." She looked to Rapp's boss. "If you can't control him, don't bring him to these meetings anymore."

Rapp stood up so fast his chair toppled over. He slammed his left hand down flat on the table. "Outbursts," he shouted at Jones. "These two pricks were planning on wiping Washington, D.C., off the map! I think the American people might cut us a little slack if we decide to deny them their day in court!"

"That's it." The president stood and pointed at Rapp and then Kennedy. "My office! Right now!"

FIFTY-EIGHT

Rapp marched down the hall and seriously considered walking right out the door and never looking back. People who didn't share his commitment were one thing, but actually getting in his way was another. Before he could decide, Kennedy caught up.

"You said what needed to be said."

Rapp shook his head and kept moving. "I'm getting sick of this bullshit, Irene."

"I know you are, but hang in there." In a quieter voice she added, "He needs to hear you. Don't back down."

Surprised, Rapp turned his head and stared at her. Kennedy usually told him to keep his mouth shut. They turned into the Oval Office and a moment later were joined by the president and Jones. The four of them faced one another in front of the president's desk.

Jones started to speak and the president held up his hand and stopped her cold. It was obvious he was trying to remain calm. "This is the White House. I need levelheaded advisors, and I will tolerate nothing less."

Rapp was beyond caring. He was incensed at the lunacy of such decisions in the face of something so serious. "Levelheaded," he repeated. "Okay, how about this for a levelheaded assessment?" He took in a deep breath and then in a very calm voice said, "The next time a group of Islamic radical fundamentalists try to blow up Washington, D.C., you might want to consult your entire national security team, including the director of the CIA, and place a little less emphasis on the advice you receive from your attorney general, who by the way is looking to make a name for himself so he can be your running mate in the upcoming election."

Hayes's fair complexion had grown flushed. "You are on thin ice, Mister."

"Oh . . . I forgot one other thing. You should also place a little less emphasis on what your chief of staff tells you since she doesn't have the slightest idea what she's talking about when it comes to terrorism."

Hayes's face was now beet red. "Mitch, I have a lot of respect for you, but I'm getting sick and tired of you walking around here like you're the only person who cares . . . the only person who's contributed."

Rapp's anger reached a steady boil. Barely able to conceal his fury he kept his eyes locked on the president and said, "The next time you compare the contributions I've made in the fight against terrorism to that of your political appointees, you won't have to worry about firing me."

"Everybody contributes in their own way. Just because they aren't out in the field doesn't mean they aren't as committed to the war on terror just as much as you." Hayes pointed his finger at Rapp. "You need to start respecting other people's opinions, and realize you're not the only one with the answers."

Rapp didn't wonder for even a second if he was in the wrong. He had his faults, and he was more than aware of them, but what he had just heard from the president was absolute unadulterated bullshit. "Mr. President, you sit here in this vacuum with all of these sycophants and so-called experts running around advising you, but have you stopped to realize that you came within a whisker of being incinerated by a nuclear bomb?"

"Of course I have."

"Mr. President, there are a lot of things that I don't tell you about. Stuff that you're better off not knowing, but maybe now's a good time to give a you a glimpse into what it takes to win this war. Do you have any idea how we found out that the nuclear material was on the ship headed for Charleston?"

Hayes shook his head.

"We pulled five prisoners out of that village in Pakistan, sir, and none of them were willing to talk. I lined them all up, and started with a man named Ali Saed al-Houri. I put a gun to his head, and when he refused to answer my questions I blew his brains out, Mr. President. I executed the bastard, and I didn't feel an ounce of shame or guilt. I thought of the innocent men and women who were forced to jump out of the burning World Trade Center, and I pulled the trigger. I moved on to the next terrorist and blew his brains out too, and then the third guy in line started singing like a bird. That's how we found out about the bomb, sir. That's what it takes to win this war on terror. So don't lecture me about commitment because I doubt anyone else on your national security staff would have pulled that trigger, and don't ever forget that if I hadn't, we wouldn't even have the luxury of this argument. That is for certain."

FIFTY-NINE

ATLANTA

It was midmorning by the time they reached the construction site. Al-Yamani drove past the entrance twice before turning in. He even stopped once and scanned the sky to make sure there were no helicopters following him. He had very bad memories when it came to helicopters. They reminded him of the early years in Afghanistan when the Soviets had dominated the battlefield with their lethal flying machines. Al-Yamani loved the bitter irony that it was the Americans with their shoulder-launched Stinger missiles who had helped them to beat the godless communists. To al-Yamani it was further proof that Allah was on their side.

When they pulled into the clearing, the sun was already peeking over the tops of the easternmost stand of tall Georgia pines. Al-Yamani got out of the car wearing a cheap pair of sunglasses that he had bought to help shield his increasingly sensitive eyes.

Two men came out of the construction trailer with broad grins on their faces.

Al-Yamani took this as a good sign. He quietly embraced each of them, relieved beyond measure that they had made it. He pointed to the trailer and all four of them went inside where they could talk more freely.

"Imtaz," al-Yamani said, as he took off his sunglasses. "This is Khaled and Hasan."

The three men exchanged greetings. Al-Yamani had thought of his two old friends often since he last saw them in Cuba almost a week ago. He was relieved that they had avoided detection by the Americans.

"Have our shipments arrived?" al-Yamani asked.

Hasan, the taller and older of the two men answered. "Yes, the main component arrived yesterday."

"Take me to it. I wish to see it."

All four men went outside. Hasan led them to the back of a pickup truck and lowered the tailgate. A wooden crate approximately three feet square sat in the middle of the coated bed. Hasan climbed up and offered a hand to his weakened friend. He then pried the top off the crate with a crowbar and unpacked a balled-up canvas tarp. The two men stood there for a moment looking at the object of destruction that they had worked so hard to acquire. Basking in the warm sun they looked up at one another and shared a smile. They were about to do something great.

Zubair, standing on the ground below them, was like a child trying to see what the grownups were looking at. His contribution to the project had been to design the fire sets and help shape the explosive charges. For security reasons he had been kept at a separate location from the nuclear material, and had yet to lay eyes on it. Unable to hold back any longer he climbed up into the truck bed and looked into the crate.

What he saw horrified him. Zubair had expected to see a shiny, stable core of nuclear material in a properly shielded case, but was instead greeted with the sight of a corroded hunk of metal the size of a basketball. His eyes opened wide with fear, and he jumped from the back of the truck, almost spraining his ankle in the process.

Zubair scurried to his feet and ran back toward the construction trailer, leaving the other three men staring after him in surprise. "You need to get away from that object right now." Without the proper equipment, Zubair had no idea just how hot the nuclear material was, but he guessed it was extremely dangerous.

Al-Yamani glared at the cowardly Pakistani. He was just like the other three. The Saudi had recruited all of the scientists and killed each of them as soon as he had completed his task. He had hoped this one would show a little more bravery in the face of such magnificence, but it appeared he was as weak as the others.

"What are you so afraid of?"

"That is extremely unstable material, and it isn't even shielded. How did you get it into the country?"

Khaled, who was standing between the scientist and the pickup, pointed to the trailer that the semi truck had delivered yesterday. "We hid it in a shipment of granite."

Zubair spun around and looked at the truck. Of course. Not only would granite shield the device, but it emitted natural radiation that would confuse any sensors. He looked back at al-Yamani and said, "I'm not joking. You need to get down right now."

"Stop overreacting. It cannot do any more harm to me than has already been done."

"Oh yes it can. If you stand up there much longer you'll be dead before the sun sets."

Al-Yamani looked down into the box and decided to hear the scientist out. He climbed down from the truck and Hasan followed.

"Explain to me your fears."

"That has no shielding and it is showing signs of severe deterioration. Anything other than brief exposure could be fatal."

"I am already dying."

"But that will hasten your radiation poisoning. In order for us to transport and assemble the weapon it must be properly shielded or it will kill us all."

"How quickly?" asked al-Yamani. All he cared was that they made it to their target.

"Most likely before we reach Washington."

Al-Yamani frowned. "So what do you propose we do?"

"As I said, we need to shield it properly."

"Is that difficult?"

"Not with the right material . . . either lead or depleted uranium will do."

"How long will it take?" Al-Yamani had some extra time built into the schedule but not much.

Zubair thought about it for a minute and said, "A couple of hours."

"Do we have an alternative?"

"Not if you want to take it all the way to Washington."

There was a backup plan to detonate the device in Atlanta, but al-Yamani was not willing to settle for that. Especially after listening to the president this morning.

SIXTY

WASHINGTON, D.C.

It was standing-room-only in the bar at Smith and Wollensky's and every table in the restaurant was occupied. Pat Holmes sat at his usual corner table with his back to the wall looking out onto as much of the restaurant as possible. As chairman of the Democratic Party he needed to see and be seen. On a normal night, a half dozen people would have already stopped by to shake hands and say hello, but not this night.

Holmes had a pretty good idea why, and it involved one of the two women at his table. Valerie Jones had the unique ability to repel people by her mere presence. She was, to put it bluntly, a ballbuster of the first order. Jones had religion when it came to her beloved Democratic Party. So thorough was her commitment that there wasn't a Republican who she liked, and she made no effort to hide her feelings. She even despised independents for their spineless inability to pick sides. Her behavior toward the so-called enemy was more characteristic of a fanatical campaign volunteer than a senior White House official. Her pugnacious reputation caused the more civilized players in town to steer clear of her.

Truth be told, when the cameras weren't around, and if it wasn't election season, the vast majority of Democrats and Republicans got along, and in most cases actually liked each other. Holmes fell into that majority. When he had to, he could get out in front of the camera and accuse the Republicans of outlandish selfishness and incompetence, and then go play a round of golf later the same day with his Republican counterpart.

Sometimes he wondered if the president's chief of staff even noticed that she was so disliked by reasonable people. He doubted it. Jones was a very focused person, who had great organizational skills and uncanny political smarts, but who was severely challenged in the people skills department. At the end of the day, though, he supposed every administration needed someone like Jones—a pit bull to keep people in line.

Peggy Stealey was an entirely different story. She had that star quality about her. She had classy good looks; she was smart as hell; she was cunning, and he guessed very dangerous to be on the wrong side of. He wanted to get her into bed in the worst way, but he'd experienced enough dickteases over the years to know the best way to do that was to make her chase him.

The waiter approached, and before he got too close, Holmes gestured for another bottle of Silver Oak. Given the delicate nature of their current conversation, he didn't want anyone coming within ten feet of the table.

"I have no objection to anything I've heard." Holmes leaned in a bit closer and lowered his voice. "I think it will energize the party."

"I agree," said Jones, as she attacked her steak with a knife.

"Vice President Baxter is a dud," Holmes continued. "Stokes is younger, he's better looking, and he's got a pretty wife. He's a little light on experience, but all in all I think he'd be a nice addition to the ticket."

Stealey was about to take a bite of her Chilean sea bass when her fork stopped inches from her lips. "His wife isn't pretty."

"Sure she is." Holmes grabbed his glass of wine. "She's very attractive."

The sea bass was now in her mouth so Stealey just shook her head forcefully.

Holmes took a swig of wine. "Unless you're a lesbian, Peggy, I think I'm in a better position to judge this one. She's a good-looking woman . . . trust me."

Even though she wanted to argue with him, she knew it was unwise to let her hatred of her boss's wife be known. "Just a difference of opinion . . . that's all." She took a sip of water and then stabbed a green bean with her fork. "So we have a deal."

Holmes looked at Jones and wondered if they'd bothered to include the president in any of these discussions. "Robert's on board with this?"

"Absolutely. You know he hates the little weasel."

"All right, I know they're a bad fit, but I want to hear it from him personally."

"Why?" Jones took a sip of wine. "You don't trust me?"

"I trust you . . . I just want to make sure he's thought this all the way through. It isn't every day the president bounces his vice president off the ticket."

"It's been done before," Jones replied airily, trying to stress that it was no big deal.

Holmes knew it had, but it had to be done right. "I said I think it's a good idea. It just needs to be handled right. The last thing we need is Baxter airing our dirty laundry during the middle of a campaign because he feels we gave him the shaft."

"We are giving him the shaft," said Stealey. "And I don't see how he'll view it any other way."

"The party is bigger than any one person," said Jones. "He'll understand that, and if he doesn't, we'll just have to make it clear that if he decides to go crying to the press we'll bury him."

"You're absolutely right," said Holmes. "We play to his party loyalty, and if he doesn't get on board we'll let it be known that things could get really tough. It's absolutely crucial, though, that we get him to go quietly."

Holmes reminded Jones of something and she pointed her fork at him. "Do you know who else needs to go?"

"Who."

"Mitch Rapp. That's who."

Holmes almost choked on the piece of New York strip that he was trying to chew. When he'd chased it with gulp of red wine he said, "What are you talking about?"

"You know who Mitch Rapp is . . . don't you?"

"Of course I do. He's a walking legend, and he's married to that beautiful NBC reporter Anna Rielly."

"Have you ever met him?"

"No, but what's your point? Why in the world would the president want to get rid of him?"

"The man is a ticking bomb," answered Jones. "Sooner or later he's going to embarrass this administration, and I don't mean some little scandal . . . I'm talking full-blown Congressional investigation . . . people being fired and people ending up in jail."

She had gotten the chairman of the DNC's attention. Holmes set his fork down and wiped his mouth with his white linen napkin. "You're going to have to give me specifics, Val."

"I could go on for hours, but for starters, you're not going to believe what happened at the White House this morning. We're sitting in a National Security Council meeting and out of nowhere he starts attacking Peggy."

"About what?"

"He demands that we start torturing the American citizens that we arrested yesterday in connection with the terrorist plot."

Holmes was immediately suspicious of how Jones was relaying the facts. "Val, Mitch Rapp is a pretty serious guy. I doubt that he just out and out demanded that we torture American citizens."

"He pretty much did," Stealey weighed in.

"That's not even the half of it." Jones looked at Stealey. "Peggy, I was waiting to tell you this. Remember when the president, Kennedy, Rapp, and I left the meeting?"

"Yes."

"Well, we went into the Oval Office and things got really hot. The president told Rapp he would no longer tolerate any more of his outbursts and the abuse of his staff and do you know what Rapp said?"

"I can't wait to hear."

"He went on to tell the president that the only reason we found out about the impending attack was because he flew over to Afghanistan and lined up five al-Qaeda terrorists and started executing them one at a time until they talked."

Peggy Stealey's blue eyes were bugged in disbelief, "You can't be serious."

Holmes looked on with a furrowed brow.

"He told the president that he put a gun to their heads and blew their brains out, and that he didn't feel an ounce of guilt or shame about it. I kid you not. Now if that isn't reckless . . . I don't know what is."

"He admitted this in front of you?" Stealey asked in shock.

"Yes, and the president and Kennedy."

"It's not only reckless, it's illegal. He's a federal employee. He should be in jail."

"Well . . . that would be one way to get rid of him."

"Slow down, you two." Holmes placed an elbow on the table and looked from Jones to Stealey and back again. "Are you both out of your minds? Do you two have any idea who you're messing with? You're talking about locking up an American hero."

"He's an *assassin* in a suit," snarled Jones.

Holmes pointed at the president's chief of staff. "There are people in this town . . . very powerful people . . . who will have your heads on a platter if you even think about attempting something so foolish."

"Pat, did you hear anything I said?" Jones was clearly irritated. "We're not the ones running around breaking the law and risking the future of this administration."

Holmes looked at Jones in utter disbelief. He threw his napkin down on his half-eaten steak and said, "Investigating Mitch Rapp is one of the dumbest ideas I've ever heard." He glanced at Stealey and then back at Jones. "You two need to take a step back and look at the big picture. Stop worrying about the *party base* and the *Patriot Act* and start thinking about just who in the hell you're fucking with."

Jones started to speak, but Holmes cut her off with a harsh glare. "Don't say another word. There are things you two don't know . . . things you don't want to know. People you don't want to cross. Drop this nonsense right now, or our deal is off. In fact, drop this nonsense right now, or I'll make sure you're both out of a job by tomorrow morning, and I am dead serious."

SIXTY-ONE

Mustafa al-Yamani looked forward to dying with each passing mile of road. There wasn't an inch of his body that didn't hurt, and more and more his thoughts turned to giving up—to letting the others see it through to the end. He couldn't quit, though. There was still too much to be done, and he could not trust this weak Pakistani scientist to light the fire. He would pee down his leg like a scared child at the first sign of trouble.

Al-Yamani could ignore the pain for a little while longer. A few days of agony were nothing when compared to the struggle of his people. He was on a crusade, a continuation of the thousand-year-old battle between the Arab people and the infidels. Never at any time in history, though, had so much been at stake. It was time to ignite a true global jihad and show the other believers that America could be brought to her knees.

Al-Yamani could not do it alone though. He barely had the strength left to walk, and his vision was getting worse by the hour. He hated to think what would have happened if he hadn't met up with Hasan and Khaled. His fellow warriors were a great comfort to him. They had been through so much together. Their devotion

357

was unflinching. They would do everything in their power to make sure this mission reached its glorious conclusion.

Even Zubair, despite all of his worrying, had proven useful. Al-Yamani was not a man of science. He had no medical knowledge of how radiation affected the human body—only practical knowledge. He had watched as dozens of his devoted Muslim warriors fell victim to the unseen killer. They had dug for months in that barren wasteland at the north end of the Caspian in search of crumbs discarded by a careless Soviet giant. The cost had been great, but in the end it would all be worth it.

Having seen firsthand what the unseen killer could do, al-Yamani listened to Zubair's warnings. The Pakistani's estimate that it would take two hours to shield the weapon had proven wrong. It had actually taken six hours, but al-Yamani saw the wisdom of their actions from more than just a health aspect. Washington, D.C., was ringed with sensors that detected radioactivity. Every bridge that went into the city and every major road was equipped with the sensors. If al-Yamani wanted to get the weapon to the point where it would do the most damage he would need to get past them, and to do that the weapon would have to be shielded. He had originally thought that traveling by water would prevent detection by the sensors, but Zubair had now made it clear, that this bomb would never escape detection without proper shielding.

Under the direction of Zubair, Hasan had tracked down a sizable amount of depleted uranium in the form of discarded elevator weights. The scrap yard where he found them was unfortunately on the other side of town. While Hasan went to pick up the depleted uranium, Khaled escorted Zubair to a medical supply store where the Pakistani scientist purchased four lead aprons, of the variety used by X-ray technicians, some heavy-duty chemist's gloves, and a batch of dosimeters or film badges for measuring the doses of radiation they were receiving. As a further precaution an enclosed trailer was rented using Hasan's pirated credit card.

At a nearby Wal-Mart they purchased water, soap, new clothes, and a massive white fishing cooler. Back at the construction site the fishing cooler was lined with the elevator weights, and then Zubair used blocks of foam picked up at a packing store to create a nest for the nuclear material. From a safe distance the scientist watched as Hasan and Khaled transferred the nuclear material from the crate to the cooler, and then covered it with foam and more depleted uranium. Zubair repeatedly told them to work quickly but carefully. When they were done, the cooler was placed in the trailer and everything else was discarded, including their clothes. Zubair made the now naked Hasan and Khaled wash down behind the construction trailer with the water and soap they'd purchased. After they'd put on their stiff new clothes, they all left Atlanta.

That had been nearly twelve hours ago. Now as the sun came up they were nearing their next destination. It was Friday morning, and they had a little less than a day and half to get into position. They stopped for breakfast in Bracey, Virginia, and waited until 7:00 a.m. to make the call. Al-Yamani found a payphone and dialed the number from memory. A man whose voice he had not heard in years answered.

Al-Yamani asked, "Is Frank there?"

There was a moment of hesitation on the other end

and then the voice said, "I'm sorry, you must have the wrong number."

Al-Yamani hung up the phone and walked out to the waiting truck. Zubair and Khaled were in the backseat and Hasan was in the driver's seat. Al-Yamani climbed in and picked up a map. He pointed to a spot and said, "That is where we are to meet him. At noon. The Richmond National Battlefield Park."

Hasan nodded and put the truck in drive. "We'll have no problem getting there early."

"Good."

Al-Yamani stared out the bug-spattered windshield, desperately wanting to get this last step over with. The man he had called was to have asked him what number he had dialed if he felt he was being watched. Fortunately, he had not uttered those words, for if he had, al-Yamani did not know what he would have done. If they could not link up with this man, all hope really would be lost. So much had been sacrificed, surely Allah would never let that happen.

SIXTY-TWO

Rapp sat in the conference room at the Joint Counterterrorism Center and listened half-heartedly to the briefing. Walking away from it all was starting to seem like a good idea. There was just too much bullshit, too many rules, and too many people who weren't willing to do what it took to get the job done. Yes, he understood that this was America, and there were laws to be followed, but if there was ever a time to at least bend them—this was it.

It wasn't going to happen though, because that six-foot-tall blond ballbuster from the Justice Department had showed up with an army of lawyers to make sure everything was done by the book. In their minds, they were going to trial, and they sure as hell weren't going to let some spook from the CIA, or a bunch of thick-necked special agents from the Bureau, screw things up. The entire thing had turned into a farce. It pained him to no end to listen to these people yammer on about obtaining search warrants and running down leads, when they should be kicking in doors and rounding up suspects by the vanload. Even his own boss had deserted him.

Kennedy had passed down the order that they were

to give the FBI everything they had regarding Rapp's recent cross-border raid in Southwest Asia, and that included Ahmed Khalili, the young computer expert from Karachi. His cooperation had provided them with some good leads on the internet accounts and chat rooms that al-Qaeda had used to contact the U.S.-based cells.

Waheed Ahmed Abdullah, whom Rapp had shot in the knee and tortured, was still in the CIA's custody, but he was providing mostly dated intelligence of no great significance. Rapp and Dr. Khan had both come to the conclusion that Abdullah's IQ was located somewhere near the lower end of the chart. It seemed his main function for al-Qaeda had been to raise funds from other wealthy Saudi families.

They now had an artist's sketch of al-Yamani based on the description provided by the British captain who had been fished out of the water by the Coast Guard. That sketch, and Imtaz Zubair's passport photo, had been sent to nearly every law enforcement officer in the country. Right now Atlanta was the focus of much of the investigation. Zubair had been tracked there after his arrival in Los Angeles and a hotel employee at the Ritz in Buckhead had identified him. An army of agents had descended on the trucking company owned by one of the men picked up in Charleston, and they were going over every square inch of the place and contacting everyone they'd done business with.

They'd also connected the dots on the man they'd found in the parking garage in Charleston. He was a Kuwaiti who was attending the University of Central Florida on a student visa. Interestingly, his e-mail address at school turned up on Khalili's laptop, and the type of knife wound the Kuwaiti had died from was very similar to the one which the British captain had sustained.

On another front, the Cubans had turned out to be predictably unhelpful. Both Kennedy and the secretary of state had put in calls to their Russian counterparts who were now leaning on the Cubans to hand over everything they had on al-Yamani. They expected to hear something within the hour, and they were sure it would involve Fidel asking for compensation of some sort—most probably American dollars.

It was nearing noon, and Rapp was thinking about getting out of town early. He was to catch a 4:00 p.m. flight to Milwaukee and then rent a car for the drive up to his in-laws' cabin for the Memorial Day weekend. Kennedy had asked him to stick around and help monitor what was going on, at least until his flight left. She was taking off early with her son and mother for a weekend getaway at the beach, her first vacation in more than a year.

Rapp was not looking for medals or public accolades. He wanted to be listened to and taken seriously. In this regard, the president's apology at least kept him in the game, but for how long he wasn't sure. He was of no use in this current manhunt. Rapp did not operate well within the confines of large government bureaucracies. They moved too slowly, and again, there were too many rules. He was best left to apply his skills autonomously through a combination of stealth and brutal, efficient force, if needed.

Maybe it really was time to get out and save himself the headache. He'd have to give it some serious consideration, but for now he should at least check into taking an earlier flight. He missed his wife dearly, and saw no point in wasting a minute more of his time on an investigation that he considered a monumental waste of time and resources.

The big blonde from Justice announced that they'd take a quick thirty-minute break for lunch, and everyone got up to return phone calls, check e-mails, and stuff their faces with whatever they could find down in the lunch room. Rapp had been so well behaved and so resigned that this thing had grown beyond his control that he'd failed to notice Stealey's desire to avoid any further tussles with him.

After Valerie Jones had left dinner last night, Stealey had pressed Holmes to explain what he'd meant about Rapp. She made it clear that she knew very little about the man. Indeed, everything she had heard or read about his wild exploits she had chalked up to journalistic exaggeration. Holmes had responded that he didn't know what she had heard or read, but he doubted that any of it was exaggerated. Yes, the media got many of the facts wrong, but in Rapp's case they didn't know the half of it. "In fact," said Holmes, "if anything, they barely scratched the surface."

Holmes would give her no details. He told her only that there were a lot of very powerful people in Washington who supported what Rapp did. People whom presidents, Democrat and Republican alike, went to for advice. Holmes warned her that one of the quickest ways to ruin her career, and possibly her boss's, would be to pursue this foolish course against Rapp. In addition, he told her to watch her step around Rapp's boss, Dr. Kennedy. Despite her genteel ways, the director of the CIA wielded significant influence in circles where even he did not walk.

Offering proof of Kennedy's influence, Holmes told Stealey that someone very high up in the Hayes administration would not be around much longer, and the president himself didn't even know it yet. Stealey tried to speculate, but Holmes wouldn't entertain any guesses. "Trust me," he told her. "Someone big, and I'm not talking about the vice president, will be gone by next fall and it will have been Kennedy's doing."

Stealey, a skeptical person by nature and trade, decided to heed the chairman of the DNC's warning, but only to an extent. There was something about Mitch Rapp that was infinitely appealing. A certain recklessness. He was like an animal who refused to be tamed. The audacity that he had shown in front of the president and his senior cabinet members was breathtaking.

But she had brought men like Rapp to their knees before. They all had a singular weakness. So filled were they with testosterone that the slightest hint of a breast or the accidental stroke of a hand in the right place could send them down a path that had only one destination. Stokes had been like that at one point, but his mother and that little wife of his had culled it from him. They'd neutered what had once been an extremely attractive and aggressive man. Now he was nothing more than a full-grown eunuch in a suit.

Even at his peak though, Stokes didn't hold a candle to Rapp. The CIA man's rugged, handsome features combined with the knowledge that he'd killed other men made him an intoxicating, dangerous object of sexual desire. Stealey stood by the door and watched him, as people filed out of the conference room. He moved with a distinct athletic grace.

At that moment, he caught her looking at him, but Stealey didn't care. She kept her gaze fixed on him, her expression open and warm. She watched as he looked away and then came back to her a moment later. She'd noticed he did that often—kept his eyes moving. He was perpetually alert.

As he drew near, Stealey reached out and gently took hold of his wrist, careful to place her forefinger on the palm of his hand—skin on skin. His reaction was instant, and if she hadn't been studying him so intently, she might not have caught it. His head came around quickly, but not so quickly that he seemed alarmed. It was very smooth, as was the way he withdrew his hand and stepped to the side. His dark eyes turned on her and sized her up. She had never before seen eyes like this, and they caused her to momentarily forget what she was going to say.

Rapp did not like being touched by pretty much anyone other than his wife. Proximity and physical contact was an occupational hazard and not something he associated with casual social or business encounters. He stared at the DOJ official guardedly, wondering what this woman could possibly have to say to him after what had transpired yesterday. He had come here today and kept his mouth shut. He had detached himself from the hunt and realized it was out of his hands. If she wanted another confrontation, though, he would not shy away.

"I'd like to start over." Stealey stepped back so Rapp could get out of the way of the other people who were still trying to leave. "It was unfortunate that things had to get so heated yesterday." She held out her hand.

Rapp shook it and nodded once while he continued to study her. She was the same height as him. Maybe even a bit taller with her heels on. He chose to say nothing.

"It's been a crazy few days," she added.

"Yeah."

"Well," she smiled at the last person who was leaving and looked back to Rapp. "I know you're only trying to do what you think is best. I just hope you understand where I'm coming from."

Just where in the hell are you coming from? Rapp thought to himself. He wasn't going to provoke a fight. He'd come to the conclusion that he'd simply have to work doubly hard to keep information from these hard-core law-and-order types. The bureaucracy was too big to take on. He'd have to go around it.

In a conciliatory tone, giving her what she wanted, he said, "I understand exactly where you're coming from. In the future I'll try to be more well mannered."

Stealey smiled warmly, showing a perfect set of white teeth. "I appreciate that, and I just want you to know that I have a lot of respect for your passion and commitment. You're a hard-working man who's given a lot to this fight."

Rapp smiled slightly. It was more of a reflex than a sign of appreciation. This woman wanted something else from him. What, he wasn't sure, but he'd play along for a while. "How are your two prisoners?"

"Defendants." She corrected him with a grin.

"Defendants."

"Yes . . . well, they're not saying much. At least not to us."

"Who are they talking to?"

"Their lawyer."

"I forgot about him. Are you taping their conversations?"

Stealey folded her arms across her chest. The movement was intentional, in that it caused her breasts to swell and peek out of the open neckline of her blouse.

She sighed and said, "Oh, you're a troublemaker."

"Yeah, but I get results."

"I bet you do." Stealey gave him a coy smile. "I bet you do."

Rapp started to get the idea that this blond-haired, blue-eyed legal eagle was flirting with him. He glanced at his watch, flashing her a clear view of his wedding ring. "Well . . . I've got to get going, but thanks for making the effort."

"My pleasure." Stealey held out her hand again. "If they tell us anything of interest, I'll let you know."

Rapp sincerely doubted that they would get anything useful from the two men, but didn't say so. He shook her hand and said, "I'll see you later."

Stealey watched him walk away, and thought to herself, *Yes, you will.*

SIXTY-THREE

Rapp didn't make it far. Skip McMahon caught his attention from across the sea of desks and waved him over to his office. Rapp walked around the perimeter and joined the FBI man. McMahon didn't say anything, he just turned around and went back into his office with Rapp following. Paul Reimer was sitting in one of the two chairs in front of McMahon's desk. McMahon closed the door and walked around behind his desk.

"What's up?" asked Rapp. "You guys comparing notes on the cushy jobs you've been offered?"

"Yeah, we're talking about taking a celebratory cruise together," snarled McMahon.

"Hey . . . don't get defensive. I think it's great. In fact I might join you guys in the private sector."

"What's that supposed to mean?" asked Reimer.

"Let's just say, I'm getting a little burnt-out."

"You're too young to quit," McMahon said, dropping down in his chair.

"Age has nothing to do with it. It's all the bullshit."

The former Navy SEAL and the FBI special agent shared a worried look. Reimer said, "You're not really serious, are you?"

"Yep."

"You can't. Someone's got to hang around and tell them how it is."

Rapp tilted his head and asked, "Weren't you at the White House yesterday?"

"I'll never forget it."

"Well, I don't know if you noticed, but they don't seem to be listening to me."

"Don't let this turn you sour, Mitch," McMahon said. "You're better than that. You did some great work this week. Without you, I'd hate to think what could have happened."

"I'll be honest. Things were a hell of a lot easier when I worked in the shadows."

McMahon, never one to listen to anyone complain for more than a second or two said, "Yeah, well you're not anymore, so suck it up. You're too damn young to go quitting on us, and besides, what in the hell would you do?"

"Have babies, play golf . . . I don't know. I'll find something."

"You'd be bored out of your mind in two months," said Reimer. "The only reason I'm leaving is because I'm tapped out after putting three kids through college. I need to make some serious money before my wife and I sail off into the sunset."

Rapp eyed Reimer disbelievingly. "You're not sick of all the B.S. with Homeland Security?"

"Of course I am, but I'm fifty-six. You're only in your mid-thirties. You've got a long way to go before you can say you're burnt-out."

McMahon looked at his watch impatiently. "All right . . . now that we've got all the career counseling out of the way, and we've decided you're staying, can we get down to business?"

"Sure." Rapp smiled.

"Paul's got some interesting information. Stuff he doesn't want disseminated through official channels, and after you hear it, I don't think you're going to be quitting."

McMahon had his attention. Rapp turned to Reimer. "What's up?"

"The Russians have been quietly helpful. The truth is they are every bit as concerned by these Islamic radical fundamentalists as we are. In some ways they're more concerned."

"They should be. Most of them are in their own backyard."

"Yeah, well anyway . . . I've had some interesting conversations with one of my counterparts over in the motherland. All off the record . . . all unofficial. I sent him the particulars on the nuclear material, and he agrees that it's one of theirs."

"Interesting. Does he have any idea how al-Qaeda got their hands on it?"

"He's looking into it, but he has a theory that sounds plausible to me."

"Let's hear it."

"First of all, he confirmed as best he could without actually seeing the nuclear material, and conducting the tests himself, that the material is in fact one of their prototype atomic demolition munitions that they tested at the Kazakh range in the late sixties. Without looking up the numbers he seemed to remember that approximately twenty of these weapons were tested during that time. Now here's where things get interesting. The Soviets don't advertise this little fact and neither do we." Reimer took on a more serious tone. "Not all of the tests that we conducted worked."

"That doesn't shock me," said Rapp. "Isn't that why they're called tests?"

"Yes, but it's the next part that will shock you. When I say they didn't work, that means that some of them reached critical mass, but didn't obtain their maximum yield, and that there were also others that simply didn't work properly in another way."

"You mean they didn't blow up?"

"Not exactly. The duds, as we so scientifically refer to them, often did blow up. They just never reached critical mass."

"In English, please."

"The physics involved in these weapons is very precise. If," Reimer made a ball with his hands, "the explosive charge that is placed around the nuclear material fails to detonate perfectly, critical mass cannot be obtained. Does that make sense?"

McMahon and Rapp nodded.

"Well, on occasion, the conventional explosive would misfire. We wouldn't reach critical mass, and we'd move on to the next test. If it wasn't too much work, we'd try and retrieve the nuclear material from the hole, but more often than not we simply left it buried down there. Now, knowing how the Soviets operate, my guess is they never even thought of retrieving the material from their failed tests."

"Why not?" asked a surprised McMahon.

"In the fifties and sixties we were churning out so much of this stuff that it was a lot easier to start with a fresh batch than go down into a collapsed, radioactive hot hole to salvage a hunk of junk that was extremely dangerous and that might or might not have been cost effective to reprocess."

"So," Rapp was starting to piece things together, "this Kazakh test site is littered with how many duds?"

"We're not sure," Reimer answered.

"Take a guess?"

"Maybe a dozen. Maybe more."

Rapp's mouth opened in disbelief. "Why the hell have I never heard of this threat before?"

"Because it wasn't actually deemed a threat. This Kazakh test site is a radioactive wasteland. The idea of someone trying to dig one of these things up is ludicrous. If you don't have the proper equipment, you're going to die. And even if you do have the proper equipment, you'd better be quick about it."

Rapp buried his face in his hands. "Or you could just promise a bunch of young Islamic radical fundamentalists an express ticket to paradise." Rapp stood and looked at his phone.

"Is this test site still in operation?" McMahon asked.

"No."

"Is it guarded?"

"It's over two hundred thousand square miles."

"So it's not guarded?" asked a disappointed McMahon.

"No."

"Oh, this is bad," said Rapp.

"Maybe . . . maybe not." Reimer tried to keep an upbeat attitude. "The Russians are looking into it. My counterpart is on his way down there right now with a team to investigate."

"Who else have you told?" Rapp asked.

"Just you two. Considering the circus we went

through earlier in the week, I didn't want to get people too riled up."

Rapp nodded. "I don't blame you. Skip, what do you think?"

"Did you find anything on that raid that would point to a second bomb?"

Rapp thought about it for a moment. "No."

McMahon contemplated the manhunt that was already underway. "Virtually every law enforcement officer in the country has seen the sketch of al-Yamani and the photograph of Zubair. Thanks to the info you got over in Afghanistan, we've got a good lead on the terror cells here in America. We're going to be serving a batch of arrest warrants this afternoon from here to Atlanta and beyond. I say we wait to hear back from the Russians, and see if we catch any breaks on the home front."

"I agree," replied Rapp. "Let's keep this between the three of us until we know more. I don't need any more lawyers from Justice telling me what the rules are, and the president and his people are busy enough getting ready for tomorrow's dedication."

SIXTY-FOUR

RICHMOND

They got to the rendezvous point early, and al-Yamani had Hasan drop him off. He gave them instructions not to wait for him. If he did not call them back by 12:30, they were to leave for Washington without him and do their best. Al-Yamani honestly didn't know what to expect. His faith told him one thing, but his practical experience told him something else. The Americans had penetrated his organization, but how far he did not know. So far it appeared that only one cell had been compromised. If his old friend had been discovered, al-Yamani was confident he would have held up under torture and warned him by passing along the prearranged signal. That was of course if he knew he'd been discovered. These Americans were tricksters, and his ally from the early days in Afghanistan was much older now. He might not even know the Americans were on to him.

Despite his deteriorating health, the walk through the park was strangely refreshing. Just being out of the confined space of the vehi-cle and away from the nervous chatter of the Pakistani scientist did wonders. Al-Yamani found the bench next to the cannon. He'd seen photos of it and recognized it instantly. The historical significance of the artillery piece meant nothing to the Saudi. There was a bronze plaque near the cannon. He thought about going over to read it and decided not to. Instead he would use these last few minutes alone to center himself. To pray to Allah for the strength to make it through the next twenty-four hours. That's all he asked for. That and some luck.

A short while later he heard a car pull up and the door slam. Al–Yamani looked over his shoulder and saw a man get out of the green-and-white cab and begin walking toward him. He was not a passenger. He was the driver, and thankfully he was alone. Al–Yamani should have gotten up, but suddenly he didn't feel so good, so he sat there conserving energy and waited for his old comrade to come to him.

The cabdriver stopped about ten feet away and looked disbelievingly at the man sitting on the bench. "Mustafa?"

Al–Yamani took his sunglasses off. Hopefully his eyes would bring a spark of recognition. "It is me, Mohammed."

"You have changed so much." The man's voice was laced with concern.

"And so have you my friend." Al–Yamani's voice was weaker than he would have liked. "Your beard no longer has any pepper. Only salt."

"It has been a long time. More than a decade."

Al–Yamani nodded. They had last seen each other in Afghanistan in 1987. Mohammed, one of the bravest warriors al–Yamani had ever seen, had almost died in a fierce battle with the Soviets. A CIA man who they had been working with for nearly two years saw to it that Mohammed got evacuated to Germany where real doctors could work on him. After nearly a full year of convalescence the CIA man then helped him immigrate to the United States. He had settled in Richmond, Virginia, and had been driving a cab ever since. Al-Yamani had corresponded with him over the years, and sensed that his fellow warrior had kept his fervor.

"What is wrong with you?" the man asked.

"I am dying."

"We are all dying."

"Yes. Some faster than others, though."

"Is there anything I can do to help?"

"No." Al-Yamani shook his head only once and stopped. It hurt too much. "I am ready to die."

"What is wrong with you?"

"Nothing that can be cured. Enough about me. How have you been, my friend?"

The cabdriver fingered his prayer beads. "These are difficult times. Our faith is under attack."

"Yes, it is. That is why I am here."

"The boxes you sent me?"

"Yes. Have you kept them safe?"

"I have. Just as I promised."

"Did you open them?" Al-Yamani looked his old friend in the eyes.

"No."

"Good." Al-Yamani believed him. "Will you take me to them?"

"Absolutely. I will take you to my home first, though, and we will eat and talk."

Al-Yamani would have liked that, but it wasn't going to happen. "I'm sorry, Mohammed, but I cannot. I am on a mission from Allah and time is short."

THE STORAGE FACILITY was only twenty minutes away. Al-Yamani rode in the cab's passenger seat to make sure things looked normal. Mohammed had not pressed him further about taking time to relax and talk. The two had served side by side for nearly five years in the bloody war against the Soviets. Mohammed knew al-Yamani was a serious man of few words, a man who he respected greatly, and a true believer who had left his native Saudi Arabia to come fight the aggressors in Afghanistan. Mohammed had been amazed by the devotion of his fellow Muslims and their call to arms—especially al-Yamani.

He was the bravest and toughest of all the mujahideen Mohammed had fought alongside. Mohammed had been there the day that al-Yamani stepped on the mine that tore his lower leg from his body. He had never witnessed anything like it. There were no screams and no tears. Al-Yamani handled the grievous injury in a manner brave men hoped they would, but rarely did. Barely a month later al-Yamani was back in action, hobbling around the difficult terrain on a wooden peg. He was unstoppable. The most fearless man he had ever known.

Mohammed told him all those years ago that he prayed a day would come when he would be able to repay his Islamic brother in arms. Four months ago, al-Yamani had contacted him. A letter appeared under the door of his apartment one morning asking for his help. The letter contained instructions on what to do if he was willing to assist his old friend. Mohammed hadn't hesitated for a moment.

The favor, in fact, proved disappointing. He was only expected to do two things, neither of them difficult. The first one involved renting the storage locker and waiting for the packages to arrive, and the second favor required him to arrange for a boat to be chartered. He was to keep the packages in storage until al-Yamani himself arrived to pick them up. He was also told not to open the packages or discuss them with anyone. The mission was of the highest priority, and Mohammed had honored his old friend's request without hesitation.

The storage facility comprised one large, two-story block building surrounded by rows of orange and white garages. As they drove through the open gate, al-Yamani looked behind them for the truck. He had ordered Hasan to follow at a discreet distance. As they passed into the yard, he glimpsed the truck pulling off to the side of the road.

Two turns later they stopped in front of one of the smaller storage lockers, with a four-foot-wide orange metal door. Al-Yamani and Mohammed got out. While Mohammed inserted the key in the lock, al-Yamani looked around cautiously. This was once again one of those moments when he half expected the American police to jump out and handcuff him. Mohammed slid the door open, and sitting right there on the floor were three boxes. Al-Yamani recognized them immediately, for he had been the one to pack them. He had been unwilling to trust anyone else with this part of the operation. One of the boxes was fairly light. Al-Yamani grabbed the light one and allowed Mohammed to wrestle with the other two.

In less than a minute they were back in the cab and leaving the storage facility. When they pulled out of the yard, al-Yamani was once again in the backseat. He told Mohammed to turn left. They had barely made it across the lane of traffic when al-Yamani noticed something that caused him to stop breathing.

Up ahead on the left he could clearly see the truck and trailer pulled over to the side of the road and parked behind it was a police car with its lights flashing. Al-Yamani stared out the window as they passed by, searching for a clue as to what might have gone wrong. A police officer was at the window of the truck with his right hand resting on his gun. If the Americans were on to them, they surely would have more than one police car involved.

He made his decision in an instant. Without sounding alarmed he said, "Mohammed, turn the car around, please."

"Right here?" They were on a two-lane road with the next stop-light approximately a quarter mile away.

"Down a little further. We have a problem."

Mohammed drove a little further and swung the cab around. "What is wrong?"

There wasn't a lot of time to explain, so al-Yamani decided on the truth. "Some of my men have been following us, and they have been stopped by the police. "Up ahead on the right."

"What are you going to do?" The cab started to slow.

The police officer was back by the trailer now. He touched the padlock on the door, and then started walking back toward his vehicle. He was reaching for something on his shoulder and a split second later al-Yamani realized what it was. The cab was going less than twenty miles an hour.

Al-Yamani looked at his old friend's reflection in the rearview mirror. "Mohammed, do you trust me?" he said urgently.

"Of course."

"Then I need you to do something for me, and you have to do it immediately and without hesitation."

SIXTY-FIVE

Hanover County deputy sheriff David Sherwood was looking forward to his weekend off. He'd just purchased a new Jet Ski that could do eighty miles an hour, and this would be his first chance to really open it up. This was his first Memorial Day weekend off since joining the department four years ago, and he planned on spending it down on Lake Gaston on the Virginia–North Carolina border. One of his high school buddies had purchased a little place with five beds, and Sherwood planned on getting one of them. More than twenty people had been invited and told to bring tents and sleeping bags. Sherwood didn't do the tent thing. Not unless some little hottie wanted him to share her sleeping bag.

No, he definitely had his eye on one of the beds, and that meant when his shift was over at 2:00 he would have to get his ass out of town quickly or it would be tent city. His truck was all gassed up and his shiny new wet bike was hooked up and ready to go. All he had to do was pick up a case of beer on his way down and he'd be in great shape.

The pickup truck and its trailer had caught his attention several miles back down the road. Sherwood had a theory. Most people who pulled trailers were morons, himself excluded, of course. For starters they thought that the two-wheeled box they were pulling gave them an excuse to dispose with all common sense and the rules of the road.

This particular moron had pulled off in such a way that the tail end of his trailer was practically hanging out in traffic. And, of course, he hadn't bothered to turn his hazards on. Sherwood had had no idea just how many stupid people there were in the world until he got into law enforcement.

As Sherwood pulled his cruiser to a stop he hit his lights and radioed in that he was making a routine traffic stop. A lot of people would die on the road this weekend, and just maybe he could talk some sense into this idiot before he caused an accident.

Sherwood noticed the Georgia plates on the trailer and shook his head. He got out and walked up to the already open driver's window of the vehicle. He kept his right hand on the butt of his gun and stopped just short of the driver as he'd done a thousand times before.

"Is there a problem here?" he asked.

"No. No problem," the man answered, sounding no more nervous than the average motorist.

Sherwood noticed a slight accent. He couldn't place it but it definitely wasn't southern. "License and registration, please." The man handed it over immediately, which was always a good sign. Sherwood studied the Georgia license, and then looked over the top of his wraparound sunglasses at the driver. The photo matched the face.

"Where are you from, David?"

"Atlanta," Hasan answered.

"I can see that . . . I mean, where are you from originally?"

"Oh . . . I'm sorry. Greece." Hasan was suddenly grateful that al-Yamani had made them rehearse their stories over and over.

Sherwood nodded and then looked at the other two men in the vehicle. Something about the man in the backseat struck him. He was small, like a teenager, and he looked jumpy.

"Did I do something wrong?" Hasan wanted to distract the police officer's attention from the nervous scientist.

Foreigners, Sherwood thought. "This isn't exactly the best place to pull over."

"Sorry."

"You should be more careful when you're pulling a trailer like this. Your tail end is hanging out in traffic." Sherwood would probably let him off with a verbal warning, but he'd make him sweat a bit. "Sit tight while I run your license, and I'll be back in a couple of minutes." Sherwood took another look at the passenger in the backseat. There was something about the guy, but he couldn't put his finger on it.

Sherwood began walking back to his cruiser. He paused briefly and memorized the plate on the truck and then stopped at the trailer and looked at the heavy padlock. The padlock and the Georgia plates caused something to click. And then he thought of the dark skin and the accents. Greece wasn't the Middle East, but it was close and besides, Sherwood didn't have the foggiest idea what a Greek guy was supposed to sound like. He'd been tired when he came into work at 5:00 a.m., but he seemed to remember some stink that the Feds were making about a couple of foreign guys they were looking for who had been in the Atlanta area. He couldn't remember specific features from the photos he had glanced at, but he did remember that one of the guys looked a little young to be a terrorist.

Sherwood stepped away from the trailer and looked back at the truck. The driver was watching him intently in the big side-view mirror. The twenty-five-year-old deputy put his right hand back on his gun and with his left hand he toggled the transmit button on his radio.

Tilting his head toward the shoulder mike he said, "Dispatch . . . this is . . ."

The deputy never finished his sentence. Nor did he see what hit him. A passing car swerved from the right lane of traffic and struck him in the left leg, sending him bouncing off the trailer and to the ground, where his head hit violently. His eyes fluttered briefly and then closed.

SIXTY-SIX

The decision to head to the airport had been relatively easy. Reimer hadn't heard back from the Russians, and the bevy of search warrants that had been served had yet to produce any explosive evidence. They were at a standstill in an investigation that Rapp had no real control over. In addition, Rapp's people were telling him that they thought al-Yamani was already gone. The upper echelon of these terrorist organizations didn't martyr themselves. They let the new recruits do that. Several of the CIA's top analysts were predicting that al-Yamani had already left the country and was on his way back to his cave.

Rapp checked the clock. It was 3:08, which meant he'd be cut-ting things a little close for his flight. He was just pulling into long-term parking at Dulles when his digital phone rang. He checked the number before answering. It was McMahon at the Counterterrorism Center.

"What's up?"

"You at the airport yet?"

"Yep. Just pulling into the parking ramp."

"Well . . . we've got an interesting development that I thought you might want to hear about."

Rapp rolled down his window and grabbed the ticket. "I'm listening." The arm popped up, and Rapp drove under it.

"The Virginia State Police called. We've got a possible I.D. on Imtaz Zubair."

Rapp eased up on the gas. "Is he in custody?"

"No, and this is where the story gets a little confusing. The report is that he was I.D.'d by a deputy sheriff who pulled a vehicle over for a routine traffic stop. Apparently the deputy was on his way back to his car to run a check on the driver when he was hit by a passing car and knocked unconscious."

"When and where?"

"Just north of Richmond at approximately one this afternoon."

Richmond was only an hour and a half south of D.C. "Have you talked to the deputy?"

"No, and we can't. At least not for a while. They just rushed him into surgery to relieve the swelling on his brain."

Rapp knew from the security tapes at the Ritz in Atlanta that Zubair had been there on Wednesday evening, and had left in the middle of the night. *Why was he headed toward Washington?* "Do we have a description of the car?"

"Yes. It's a Ford F-150 extended cab, late nineties model, hunter green and tan. He was traveling with two other guys, and the report is that the driver had an accent."

"Was there anything in the bed of the truck?"

"Not that we've heard, but we're getting our information third- and fourth-hand, right now."

Rapp stopped the car. "They could already be in Washington."

"The State Patrol doesn't think so. They had a trooper on the scene just four minutes after the deputy was hit, and they got out a description of the vehicle almost immediately. Within twenty minutes they had a plane and a helicopter in the air, one patrolling ninety-five and the other searching the surrounding area. My agent who spoke to them says they're fully staffed for the holiday weekend. They are virtually guaranteeing that this truck is still in the Richmond area."

"Any chance one of the other guys in the truck was al-Yamani?"

"I have no idea. This deputy isn't due out of surgery for at least another hour."

"Is he going to make it?"

"I have no idea, but listen. I know your wife is going to be pissed at me, but I need you to get back here. There are some things . . ." McMahon hesitated. "Some things that Paul and I need you to help us with."

Rapp could tell that whatever it was, McMahon didn't want to talk about it over an unsecure line. "She won't be half as pissed at you as she will at me. I'll be there in twenty minutes."

Rapp pushed the end button, swore to himself three times, and didn't move for nearly ten seconds. He just stared at his phone and tried to figure out how he was going to explain this to his inquisitive wife without giving her any details. He tossed the phone onto the passenger seat and decided he'd put it off for a little while longer. If he was lucky, by the time he got back to the office, the fugitives would already be in custody. If that was case, he could probably wrangle Kennedy into arranging transportation on one of Langley's executive jets. Rapp knew this was all

SIXTY-SEVEN

RICHMOND

It was the scanner that had saved them. The little black box attached to the underside of the cab's dashboard began squawking not more than two minutes after they'd left the scene. Al-Yamani hadn't even noticed it. He was too busy talking to Hasan on his mobile phone, but Mohammed had heard every word of the drama as it unfolded, and it nearly gave him a heart attack. Like a lot of cabbies, Mohammed carried a police scanner. At first he did it to help avoid traffic tie-ups when there was an accident, but after a while the scanner became a source of entertainment. When he worked nights, the police chatter was often more interesting than the radio.

The initial report was that a motorist had reported an officer down. Mohammed knew that nothing got the cops more riled up than hearing that one of their brethren was hurt. Not more than two miles away from the incident a police car zipped past them headed to the aid of the fallen officer. Less than a minute later, a second and a third police car passed them. Just when Mohammed felt that they were going to get away, the voice of the officer he had hit came over the radio, giving a description of the truck he had pulled over and rambling on about some man the FBI was looking for.

Mohammed had to think fast. The plan was to take Interstate 295 over to Highway 301 and then up to Dahlgren on the Potomac River. That was where he had chartered the boat, paying for it in advance. Mohammed knew from experience, though, that 301 was a heavily patrolled road. His other option was to take Interstate 95, but that was even worse. Mohammed was once caught speeding on that road by an airplane. There was no way they could make it all the way to Dahlgren without being caught.

Mohammed told al-Yamani that they had to abandon the truck. He was then informed very succinctly that this was not an option. Since they could not get rid of the truck and knowing for sure that they would be caught if they went north or stayed on the main roads much longer, Mohammed made a quick decision and told al-Yamani to tell the others to follow him. He led them at high speed over several lightly traveled and tree-lined country roads away from both Richmond and Washington, D.C. Mohammed liked to fish, and he knew of an isolated spot where they could regroup and sort things out.

Mohammed and al-Yamani hung on every word that was uttered over the scanner. By the time they reached the York River, additional information about their caravan was being reported. A description of the trailer as well as the truck was now out, and to make matters worse, the police were also looking for a green-and-white Metro Cab.

With every mile they traveled, they risked getting caught. Finally, after passing through the town of Plum Point, al-Yamani decided it was time to stop running scared and take a gamble. It was the sight of water through the trees that gave him the idea.

"What is that body of water on our left?" al-Yamani asked Mohammed.

"That is the York River."

"Where does it lead?"

"To the Chesapeake Bay and then the Atlantic Ocean."

"And these roads we keep passing . . . do they lead to homes on the river?"

"Yes."

"Take the next one."

Mohammed, obviously hesitant, looked over his shoulder.

Al-Yamani raised his voice and repeated the command. This time his friend followed orders, and they turned off the paved road onto a gravel drive and into the woods. Several hundred feet in, the drive split off in two directions. To the left there was a sign for two families and to the right only one. *The Hansens.* Al-Yamani told Mohammed to turn right. They followed the slightly rutted gravel drive for several hundred more feet. Intermittently they caught glimpses of the river as its surface sparkled in the afternoon sun, and then they saw the house.

It was a two-story Cape Cod with gray siding and white window trim. Next to it was a detached three car garage with a bunk house above it. Beyond both, there was a perfect carpet of lush grass that sloped down the river and a dock. Al-Yamani smiled when he saw the boat.

"What do you want me to do?" asked Mohammed.

Al-Yamani couldn't tell if anyone was home. It

would be easier if they weren't, but either way he would get what he wanted.

"Stop in front of the house."

Mohammed brought the cab around the circular drive and parked it by the front door. Al-Yamani asked him to get out with him. Hasan and Khaled joined them on the front steps and al-Yamani told the scientist to wait in the truck.

"Go around back," he said to Khaled. "See if there is anyone down by the water." Then looking to Hasan he said, "Go with him and check the back door. If it's open wait a few seconds and then enter."

They nodded and took off. Al-Yamani tried the door. It was unlocked, but he did not open it. Instead, he rang the doorbell and waited to see if anyone was home. About ten seconds later a woman who looked to be in her mid-sixties came to the door in a pair of shorts and a tennis shirt. Al-Yamani was careful to stand back a few feet so as to not alarm her. Mohammed was standing by his cab.

The woman opened the door but not the screen. "Yes?"

"Hello, you must be Mrs. Hansen. I'm looking for Doctor Hansen."

The woman gave him a confused look. "I'm Mrs. Hansen, but my husband isn't a doctor."

"I must have the wrong house. Do you know of any other Hansens on the river?"

Mrs. Hansen thought about it for a few seconds and then said, "No . . . not that I know of, but it's a pretty big river."

Al-Yamani put a disappointed look on his face and took a step back as if he was leaving. "Would your husband know if there was a Doctor Hansen on the river?"

"He might, but he's not here right now."

Al-Yamani put his hands on his hips and shook his head. "That's too bad." He saw Hasan coming down the hall behind the woman and said, "Sorry to have bothered you." A second later Hasan was within striking distance. Al-Yamani made eye contact with his man and nodded.

SIXTY-EIGHT

WASHINGTON, D.C.

There was an accident on the expressway. Traffic was thick in both directions with people who felt the need to gawk at the crash, and it was nearly 4:00 by the time Rapp got back to the Joint Counterterrorism Center. He wasn't so sure he'd made the right decision to miss his plane. He wanted al-Yamani in the worst way, but at this point it was law enforcement that was going to have to catch him. There was something in McMahon's voice, though, that had been slightly pleading and very uncharacteristic for the thirty-plus-year veteran.

Rapp found McMahon standing in the elevated glass-enclosed bridge located at the rear of CT Watch. He was monitoring the situation in Richmond and trying to separate the facts from the white noise. Without speaking, McMahon signaled for Rapp to follow him, and the two men entered a small conference room at the back of the bridge and closed the door. Rapp plopped down in a gray fabric chair and rested an elbow on the shiny wood-laminate conference table.

"I assume from the look on your face that they haven't found the truck."

"No, they haven't."

Rapp glanced at his watch. "It's been what . . . almost three hours since the traffic stop? That's not good."

"You're not telling me anything I don't already know."

"Has the deputy come out of surgery yet?"

"He just made it out, but he's not awake yet."

Rapp tapped the shiny surface with his forefinger. "They're sure our guys are still in the Richmond area?"

"They're convinced."

Rapp looked at him skeptically. "I find that a little hard to believe."

"I know. I feel the same way, but let me show you." McMahon briefly left the room and returned with a map of Virginia. He laid it out on the table and said, "Here's Richmond and here's D.C. The traffic stop occurred over here on the northeast side of town. The State Patrol says they had all the major roads already covered when the call went out. They checked the traffic cameras on ninety-five and two-ninety-five and came up with nothing. That means they didn't get on the interstate, which is by far the quickest way to travel the hundred miles between here and there."

The FBI man tapped the four points of the compass around Richmond and said, "Everything was covered. This is one of the busiest traffic weekends of the year. People headed to the beach, people headed to the mountains, people headed up to D.C. for the memorial dedication. The roads are packed."

"I know. I was just out there."

"Well, there's something else that we didn't hear right away, but it went out over the police net. This Ford pickup was pulling a trailer. The head of the State

Patrol tells me there's no way his people or the locals would miss something like that."

"Trailer?" Rapp repeated in a concerned tone.

"I know . . . I know what you're thinking. What's in the trailer? Paul and I have already talked about it."

"Has he heard back from the Russians?"

"They're at the test site and beginning their search."

Rapp stood and let out a long exasperated exhale. He studied the map. He thought about the trailer. "What if these assholes have another bomb?"

"We don't have any intelligence that would point to that. You know it yourself. You guys didn't find a thing in Pakistan that would point to a second bomb."

Rapp knew he was right, but he had to assume these guys weren't driving around in a pickup with a covered trailer for nothing. "How can the State Police be so sure they aren't already in Washington?"

"They had a plane patrolling ninety-five and Highway One when the call went out. They had a helicopter over Richmond within fifteen minutes, and they had over one hundred cops, deputies, and troopers on patrol between just D.C. and Richmond alone. They think these guys are holed up somewhere, and I happen to agree with them."

"Or they switched vehicles."

"Or we could have a jumpy deputy who got himself run over, and has no idea what he's talking about."

Rapp studied the map, and then glanced up at McMahon. "Then why'd you call me back here and ruin my vacation?"

"Because I don't believe in coincidences, and I think before the night's over I'm going to need you to do some things that . . . well let's just say . . . I can't."

"You mind telling me what they are?"

of a true believer. He'd had seen plenty of
during his life, and compared to what he'd
the battlefield this was mild.
e in the evening, and according to the
and her now-deceased husband weren't
visitors until one of their children was to
hiladelphia with her husband and kids in
Al-Yamani wanted to know the details.
d when?

d be five of them and they were to arrive
he morning. Al-Yamani had been in the
ned to the answering machine when the
led to check in. The daughter's message
woman's story. She ended by saying
d to call back, and that they'd see them
So good was their recent turn of luck
ar as always to al-Yamani that Allah
ng their mission.
d man on the floor in front of his wife
ving room. Al-Yamani looked at the
"How long will it take you to get
taken the packages out of the back

Al-Yamani w
sucked from hi
began to drai
and knew
with the
disapp
hea
h
was being
etachment and

"Not yet, but you'll know soon enough."

"Have you kicked this up to the White House yet?"

McMahon shook his head. "I brought Brian up to speed on it, but that's it." McMahon was referring to his boss, FBI Director Roach.

Rapp looked surprised.

"Listen . . . I've got every cop in the five-state area looking for these clowns. Telling them," McMahon pointed to the ceiling, "means that I'll have to drop everything I'm doing and run over to the White House and brief the entire damn cabinet, and then the next thing you know the Department of Homeland Security will be trying to run the show, and we'll all be tripping over each other."

Rapp nodded in agreement. "So what's your plan?"

"The tape of the traffic stop is on its way up here right now. I want to review it, and I want to talk to this deputy when he wakes up. Other than that I want to stay out of the way of the locals and let them run these guys down."

"And would you mind explaining to me again why I missed my flight?"

"I told you already. Trust me, if we don't find these guys pretty quick, your talents are going to be very much needed."

SIXTY-NINE

Virginia

Mrs. Hansen's first name was Julia. It turned out she was the mother of four kids, all of whom now lived in other parts of the country. Mr. Hansen's first name was Tom, and by the time he arrived home the vehicles had been stashed and they were waiting for him. The cab was parked in his spot in the garage and a riding lawn mower and several bikes and trikes were moved to make room for the pickup truck. The trailer was left outside on the far side of the detached three car garage.

It had been fairly easy to subdue Tom Hansen. He was after all seventy years old, and not accustomed to having to defend his home. This was civilization, not some remote frontier outpost back in the 1900s. He had driven down the hill in his big Cadillac, returning from the local hardware store where he'd gone off in search of a bolt to repair a loose section of the dock. Tom Hansen was a fastidious man, and with several of the grandkids coming tomorrow, he wanted things just right.

They got him when he opened his garage door, during that moment when he stared in perplexity, wondering why in the hell someone had parked a cab in his spot. They appeared quickly, one man on each side

of his big Cadillac. Th
was pulled from the
to defend himself. T
on each arm, dra
warning him to ke

By the time
Hansen was in ca
attack at the age
too much fatty
the smoking,
completely. E
angioplasty, a
cardiologist t
while he wa
was never g

They dr
feet of hi
Tom Ha
bewilde
refrige
child
uni
a t
u

moral clarit
people die
witnessed o

It was fi
woman, she
expecting any
arrive from P
the morning.

How many an

There woul
around ten in t
kitchen and list
daughter had ca
confirmed the
there was no nee
in the morning.
that it was as cle
himself was guidi

They left the ol
and went into the
and asked
the bomb ready?"

Zubair had already
of the trunk and ex
explosives charges th
surreptitious stay in
should take no more t
assembled and ready fo

"Can you do this by
"No." Zubair shook
"Of course not."
coward when he s
expose himself that ready?"
Khaled. "Is th

SIXTY-NINE

VIRGINIA

Mrs. Hansen's first name was Julia. It turned out she was the mother of four kids, all of whom now lived in other parts of the country. Mr. Hansen's first name was Tom, and by the time he arrived home the vehicles had been stashed and they were waiting for him. The cab was parked in his spot in the garage and a riding lawn mower and several bikes and trikes were moved to make room for the pickup truck. The trailer was left outside on the far side of the detached three car garage.

It had been fairly easy to subdue Tom Hansen. He was after all seventy years old, and not accustomed to having to defend his home. This was civilization, not some remote frontier outpost back in the 1900s. He had driven down the hill in his big Cadillac, returning from the local hardware store where he'd gone off in search of a bolt to repair a loose section of the dock. Tom Hansen was a fastidious man, and with several of the grandkids coming tomorrow, he wanted things just right.

They got him when he opened his garage door, during that moment when he stared in perplexity, wondering why in the hell someone had parked a cab in his spot. They appeared quickly, one man on each side

"Not yet, but you'll know soon enough."

"Have you kicked this up to the White House yet?"

McMahon shook his head. "I brought Brian up to speed on it, but that's it." McMahon was referring to his boss, FBI Director Roach.

Rapp looked surprised.

"Listen . . . I've got every cop in the five-state area looking for these clowns. Telling them," McMahon pointed to the ceiling, "means that I'll have to drop everything I'm doing and run over to the White House and brief the entire damn cabinet, and then the next thing you know the Department of Homeland Security will be trying to run the show, and we'll all be tripping over each other."

Rapp nodded in agreement. "So what's your plan?"

"The tape of the traffic stop is on its way up here right now. I want to review it, and I want to talk to this deputy when he wakes up. Other than that I want to stay out of the way of the locals and let them run these guys down."

"And would you mind explaining to me again why I missed my flight?"

"I told you already. Trust me, if we don't find these guys pretty quick, your talents are going to be very much needed."

of his big Cadillac. The doors were yanked open, and he was pulled from the vehicle before he could do anything to defend himself. They handled him roughly, one man on each arm, dragging him toward the house and warning him to keep his mouth shut.

By the time they reached the front door, Tom Hansen was in cardiac arrest. He'd suffered his first heart attack at the age of fifty-two. Too many cigarettes and too much fatty food, his doctor had told him. He quit the smoking, but didn't give up the unhealthy diet completely. Eight years after that he underwent an angioplasty, and just recently he'd been told by his cardiologist that it was time to consider bypass surgery while he was still young enough to recover fully. That was never going to happen.

They dropped him on the floor of the kitchen at the feet of his bound-and-gagged wife of forty-six years. Tom Hansen looked up at her, clutching his chest, a bewildered expression on his face. Behind her, on the refrigerator, he could see the photos of their grand-children, nine adorable faces, the center of their universe. Not his or hers, but theirs. They were a couple, a team who shared everything, especially a devoted and unyielding love for their children and grandchildren.

Julia Hansen struggled against her bonds frantically, but could not break free. She knew it was his heart. She had been subtly trying to help him for years, cooking healthier, engineering long walks together, giving him disapproving looks when he lit up those damn cigars with their two boys. Now she saw the agony on his face and knew that he would not make it. When the color began to drain from his face, as if his very life was being sucked from him, she began to weep.

Al-Yamani watched this with the detachment and

moral clarity of a true believer. He'd had seen plenty of people die during his life, and compared to what he'd witnessed on the battlefield this was mild.

It was five in the evening, and according to the woman, she and her now-deceased husband weren't expecting any visitors until one of their children was to arrive from Philadelphia with her husband and kids in the morning. Al-Yamani wanted to know the details. How many and when?

There would be five of them and they were to arrive around ten in the morning. Al-Yamani had been in the kitchen and listened to the answering machine when the daughter had called to check in. The daughter's message confirmed the woman's story. She ended by saying there was no need to call back, and that they'd see them in the morning. So good was their recent turn of luck that it was as clear as always to al-Yamani that Allah himself was guiding their mission.

They left the old man on the floor in front of his wife and went into the living room. Al-Yamani looked at the scientist and asked, "How long will it take you to get the bomb ready?"

Zubair had already taken the packages out of the back of the trunk and examined both the fire set and the explosives charges that he had crafted during his brief, surreptitious stay in Iran. "Everything looks good. It should take no more than two hours to have everything assembled and ready for transport again."

"Can you do this by yourself?"

"No." Zubair shook his head nervously.

"Of course not." Al-Yamani could recognize a coward when he saw one. The Pakistani didn't want to expose himself to the poison. He looked to Hasan and Khaled. "Is the boat ready?"

"Yes," answered Hasan. "It is fully gassed and in good working order."

"Good. Grab a blanket off one of the beds upstairs and use it to wrap up the old man, then go out to the garage and help Imtaz with the assembly of the weapon. We'll leave as soon as it is dark and dump the old man's body in the river."

The three men left, leaving al-Yamani and Mohammed alone. Mohammed looked at his old friend and said, "Mustafa, what are you up to?"

Despite the dull pain coursing through every vein in his body, al-Yamani smiled. "We are about to strike a glorious blow for Islam, Mohammed. A glorious blow."

In Mohammed's wildest dreams, he would have never guessed that his friend possessed the destructive power of a nuclear bomb. "Who are you going to kill?"

"The president," al-Yamani said proudly. "The president, himself."

SEVENTY

All four TV stations in Richmond led the evening news with the story, as well as two of D.C.'s network affiliates. There was a manhunt under way, and very few things got the viewing audience as fired up as a good old-fashioned manhunt. Reporters and camera people were at the hospital, where the fallen officer was recovering from brain surgery; they were at the scene of the crime; and they were at the Hanover County Sheriff's Department.

During the six-o'clock broadcast Sheriff Randal McGowan released the video of the hit-and-run that had been captured by the camera mounted on the deputy's dashboard. So startling and violent was the collision that it was virtually guaranteed to be picked up by every station from Charlotte to Baltimore come the eleven-o'clock news. Sheriff McGowan told the reporters that they were looking for a green-and-white Metro Taxi Cab, most probably driven by a Mohammed Ansari, a resident of Richmond. A photograph of Ansari was released, as well as a brief description of a second vehicle that had left the scene of the crime. Sheriff McGowan made it very clear that the second vehicle, a green-and-tan Ford F-150 pickup pulling a trailer, was only wanted

for questioning in relation to leaving the scene of the crime.

Skip McMahon had been adamant about the last part. He'd been in close contact with Sheriff McGowan and the special agent in charge of the FBI's Richmond office for the last several hours. The roadblocks set up by local law enforcement had yet to turn up a lead, and there was major pressure to go to the media for help. The big break was the tape of the traffic stop.

The license plate wasn't caught, but the cab company was identified. After some quick checking, the dispatcher for the company confirmed that they had one cab that had been AWOL for the better part of three hours. When McMahon and his team heard that the driver's name was Mohammed Ansari, the pucker factor doubled. A quick check of the CIA's counterterrorism database proved even more ominous. According to their records Ansari had immigrated to America from Afghanistan in the late eighties with the help of the Agency. He had been interviewed post 9/11 by the CIA and asked about his relationship with none other than Mustafa al-Yamani. At the time, he went on the record to say he loved America and was embarrassed by al-Qaeda.

Somehow, Rapp doubted the veracity of that statement. The facts were beginning to add up. A deputy stops a truck, thinks he recognizes Zubair, who they know was recruited by al-Yamani, and suddenly the deputy gets run over by a cab driven by a guy who fought alongside al-Yamani twenty years ago in Afghanistan. There was no way it was a coincidence.

They were starting to fear the worst when Reimer's counterpart in Russia called with some good news. He and his team had just conducted a thorough search of the area where the atomic demolition munitions were tested. Only one of the four holes where failed tests had occurred had been compromised. The Russians were apologetic, but at the same time confident that the Americans had intercepted the only missing piece of nuclear material. In addition, an FBI WMD team out of the Richmond office did a cursory inspection of Ansari's home and his locker at the cab company and came up with no hint of radiation.

What was in the trailer then? Both Reimer and McMahon argued that it was most likely an improvised bomb, made out of fertilizer and fuel. In the counterterrorism business they called it a poor man's bomb, the modern-day and much larger version of a Molotov cocktail. A dirty bomb was a possibility, but more difficult to pull off and hence more remote. The consensus was that al-Qaeda was trying to carry out an attack despite the setback in Charleston. A strategy was decided on by McMahon and Rapp and they both consulted their bosses before proceeding with it.

Spooking Zubair and al-Yamani by letting them know they were onto them was a bad idea. It might cause them to prematurely detonate the weapon, or change targets, or simply abort and disappear. Rapp was adamantly opposed to running the risk of alerting them, so it was decided that the best way to advance the investigation without tipping their hand was to make Ansari and his cab the focus of the search.

Not long after the story aired on the six o'clock news the Hanover Sheriff's department received two phone calls. The first one was from a man who was out walking his dog near Tunstall at the time in question. He reported that he specifically remembered a green-and-white Metro Cab passing him heading east, and that it was going very fast. That was why he remembered it. When he was pressed about the Ford pickup with a trailer, he couldn't be sure, but he did seem to remember a second vehicle. The man sounded old, his voice was a little shaky, so the deputy who took that call didn't have a lot of faith in the lead until he fielded another call a few minutes later. It was from a woman near Plum Point, and she was very specific.

This woman had walked to the end of her driveway to pick up the mail. She knew the exact time, because she went out to get the mail at the same hour every day. She was standing at the end of her driveway when both the cab and the truck came racing around the bend. The deputy asked her if she was sure, and she said she was because she remembered thinking two things. The first was, *What in the heck was a Metro Cab doing way out by Plum Point* and the second was *What was her seventeen-year-old son doing chasing it*. It turned out her son also drove a green-and-tan Ford F-150 pickup truck. As further proof of her sharp mental faculties she told the deputy that she and her son had watched the six o'clock news together. After the story on the hit-and-run aired, her son commented that that must have been why he'd been pulled over twice this afternoon.

McMahon himself called the woman, a Mrs. Molly Stark, and spoke to her. After hearing Mrs. Stark tell her story, McMahon asked to speak to her son. Two minutes on the phone with her and one with the boy was enough to convince him. Like most career law enforcement types he didn't need a polygraph to tell him if someone was lying, just a few well-phrased questions and a discerning ear.

When McMahon announced this new development, there was a collective sigh of relief at CT Watch. The terrorists had fled east and south, away from D.C. Upon further discussion with the Virginia State Police they learned that Interstate 64 between Richmond and Norfolk had been fully covered during and after the hit-and-run. With the Chesapeake Bay and its tributaries providing a natural roadblock to the east it was now quite a bit easier to narrow the search. It was starting to look more and more like they had pulled off somewhere, and were indeed holed up.

The FBI's Hostage Rescue Team was on alert status down in Quantico, no doubt pissed off that their Memorial Day weekend was being delayed, but that's what they were paid for. With their helicopter transports they were only thirty minutes away from the area. Rapp took the opportunity to point out that SEAL Team Six was even closer, down in Little Creek, Virginia. This comment would have been vigorously challenged by the other FBI special agents present if it had been uttered by anyone other than Rapp. American soil was the FBI's territory, not the military's. It was that simple.

As they stood staring at the map of Virginia, McMahon decided to turn up the heat. He told one of his deputies to draw up a press release. He wanted the new information on the last sightings to be included, and he wanted it to state that the suspect or suspects were to be considered armed and dangerous. As the woman left, McMahon told her to send it to every news outlet between D.C. and Virginia Beach.

SEVENTY-ONE

Rapp slipped away to consult with Kennedy. She had left town around four with her son and mother to spend the weekend at a house they'd rented on the beach in Ocean City, Maryland. They were only a few doors down from her cousin, who had a whole flock of kids for Tommy to play with. Kennedy never showed it, but Rapp knew she was stressed. They'd been planning this trip for a year. Kennedy's cousin had invited them to stay at her house, but that was impractical. She had a security detail, broad-shouldered men with big appetites and big guns, who needed to be housed and fed.

Kennedy had tried to get Rapp to leave for Wisconsin by saying that she could delay her trip and keep an eye on the recent developments down in Richmond. Rapp's thoughts immediately turned to her son Tommy. The kid had suffered more than his fair share of disappointments in life. His mother worked sixty hours a week minimum, and his father lived on the opposite coast. He had been talking about this trip for months. In his typical rough fashion Rapp pointed all this out to Kennedy, and in turn she became uncharacteristically defensive. Eventually, though, she saw Rapp's point and left with her son, mother, and security detail.

Rapp had spoken to her about an hour and a half ago just after her small motorcade had crossed the Bay Bridge. Now one of her bodyguards answered her secure phone, and a minute later Kennedy was on the line.

"How's Tommy?" Rapp asked.

"Great. Couldn't be more excited. He's running around down on the beach with the other kids looking for wood to build a bonfire."

Rapp could tell by her voice that she was relaxing. "Good. Make sure you tell him I said hello."

"I will. What's up?" she asked.

Rapp brought her up to speed on the manhunt, and told her about Reimer's conversation with his Russian counterpart. Both pieces of news seemed to give her some comfort. They were the first bits of good news she'd received since finding out the CIA had helped Mohammed Ansari immigrate to the United States. Once that little tidbit was made public, she would be beaten over the head with it even thought she'd only been a junior-level case officer at the time.

Throughout the afternoon one thing had given Kennedy great concern. Tonight was the state dinner honoring the Big Three of WWII: America, Great Britain, and Russia. It would be the perfect time to launch an attack. The only thing that prevented her from calling the president was that he was already up at Camp David with the British prime minister playing golf. At that location they were not a target. She agreed with Rapp that it was best to stay out of the way of the FBI and the locals. As a precaution, though, she stayed in close contact with Jack Warch, the special agent in charge of the president's Secret Service detail.

She knew that now the president was at this moment returning to the White House aboard Marine One with the British prime minister. They were apparently running late for their own state dinner. None of this was a surprise to Warch, since the president had turned tardiness into a habit recently. The Russian president was also running late, having been delayed by some unusually strong headwinds on the way over. He had just made it to the Russian Embassy and wasn't expected to arrive at the White House until nearly 9:00, an hour and a half late. Additionally, Kennedy had spoken directly to Reimer, and he guaranteed her that based on the material they found in Charleston, the sensors in and around the capital would have alerted them to any nuclear weapon being smuggled into the city.

Rapp had just finished giving her the details of the manhunt when she asked, "What's your gut telling you, Mitch?"

"I think they're holed up somewhere. We're talking about five Middle Eastern–looking men in a part of the country where there's a ton of retired military . . . if they'd stolen a vehicle we would've heard about it."

"That's if someone saw them."

"That's the other thing. You've been down there. It's not far from the Farm." Rapp was referring to Camp Perry where the CIA trained all of their new recruits. "There's a lot of woods. A lot of dirt roads and trails where someone could disappear."

"And you still think the locals can handle this?" she asked.

"They're our best option right now, but if we find the vehicles abandoned in the woods I'd like to bring in the SEALs and track them."

"Well," she said thinking about the repercussions, "you know how that'll go over."

"I've already had one go around about it, but you and I know it's not even close. HRT is really good in a controlled environment, but not that used to running patrols in the woods."

"I agree. We'll cross that bridge when and if we have to. In the meantime keep me posted on any new developments."

"I will."

Kennedy disconnected the line and stood there in the kitchen staring out through the big double sliding-glass doors at the deck and the water beyond. Somewhere down on the beach she could hear the laughing and yelling of her son and her cousin's children. She wished that just once she could get away from it all. Shut it off, and live like a normal person. The head of her security detail was standing in the hallway by the kitchen watching her.

"Carl," she said, "would you call Langley and tell them I need a helicopter put on standby."

"Sure."

Kennedy dialed the next number from memory and looked at her watch. It was almost 7:30. Special Agent Warch answered after the first ring. "Jack, it's Irene. Are you back at the White House yet?"

"Almost. I know it's a real shock, but we're running late."

"So you're on Marine One right now?"

"Yep."

Kennedy thought about it for a second and said,

"Jack, I need you to do me a favor. It's more of a precaution really." Kennedy went on to explain what she wanted, and with a little bit of cajoling, the agent in charge of the presidential detail agreed.

SEVENTY-TWO

Peggy Stealey arrived at the dinner in a black stretch limousine with DNC Chairman Holmes. As she was helped from the backseat, the long slit of her evening gown parted to reveal a naked, toned leg that caught the attention of even the military Honor Guard arrayed on each side of the door. She took Holmes's arm and elegantly strode up the steps under the North Portico of the White House. Flash bulbs erupted to catch the stunning blonde who looked like she would be more at home on the red carpet at an awards ceremony than a state dinner at the White House.

The two entered the White House and were immediately offered a glass of champagne. Stealey took one, but Holmes declined. He'd already declared his intention to avoid the pond scum that they served at these types of things and stick to Belvedere vodka, which of course meant that he'd be tanked by ten. To Holmes any bottle of wine, sparkling or otherwise, was to be avoided unless its price tag had at least three digits prior to the decimal. For an evening like this, four would have been preferred, but Holmes hadn't been consulted. If he had been, it probably would have meant he was expected to pay for it, or worse, provide a dozen cases from his private collection. That would never happen. The only sin worse than drinking a cheap bottle of wine was wasting a good one on people who couldn't appreciate it.

Holmes looked like a fullback blocking for a halfback as he pushed his way through the Cross Hall toward the East Room and the bar. Between them he and Peggy created quite the stir, half the men beseeching Holmes for a favor and the other half gawking at his date. Holmes refused every attempt to engage him in conversation.

"You know the rule," he said at least three times. "Not until I have a drink in my hand." As chairman of the DNC he was in control of the party's purse strings, and there was never enough money to go around.

When they finally reached the bar Holmes went around the side and waved the bartender over. Two rows of people were neatly cued up and patiently waiting their turn. Holmes didn't wait in lines, especially when he was thirsty. Several of the people muttered to each other over the break in decorum.

The bartender came over and Holmes slapped a folded hundred-dollar bill in the man's hand and whispered in his ear, "Belvedere on the rocks, double, and a tall Vodka tonic, double."

The man glanced down at the crisp bill and said, "Sir, it's an open bar."

"I know it is. That's your tip."

"But I can't . . ."

"Yes, you can," Holmes said impatiently. "Now hurry up. I'm thirsty."

The bartender left to make the drinks.

Stealey turned her bare back to the people in line.

"You're getting some awfully dirty looks, Mr. Chairman."

Holmes glanced over her shoulder and plastered an ugly smile across his face. "They're not looking at me. They're all looking at you. They're thinking you're a movie star."

Stealey smiled warmly. "What a nice compliment, Pat."

"Yeah, either that or they think you're a high-priced call girl."

The smile vanished and was replaced with a scowl.

"You should be flattered. Have you ever seen how hot some of the call girls are in this town?" The scowl remained, so Holmes kept digging. "All I'm trying to say is that you are an extremely beautiful woman. You look fantastic tonight."

Stealey sighed and shook her head. "Patrick, there are nicer ways to say that than comparing me to a prostitute."

Thankfully the drinks arrived, because Holmes couldn't see her point. He didn't say *prostitute,* he said *call girl,* and in his mind, and in this town, there was a big difference.

He took the drinks from the bartender and told him he'd be back in about ten minutes to reload. He handed Stealey her drink and with a British accent, said, "As I mentioned, you look *raaavishing* this evening." He raised his glass in a toast. He looked handsome in his tux, and she looked stunning in her shimmering robin's-egg blue evening gown. If all went well he'd finally get her into bed tonight. They both took a drink and smiled at each other. He knew she knew, and she knew he knew and round and round they went.

Stealey set her champagne glass on the tray of a

passing server and turned to take in the magnificence of the East Room. Weddings, wakes, and countless functions, some historical and some meaningless, had all been held in this, the grandest room of the People's House. The ambiance was intoxicating. This was power. This was the closest thing modern-day America had to a King's Court.

A senator, whose name Stealey couldn't recall, approached and extended his hand. Stealey returned the gesture and was surprised when the man took her hand in his and kissed it.

"Pat," the senator said to Holmes, while keeping his eyes locked on Stealey's, "please introduce me to this lovely woman."

"She's my fiancée, Harry, so take your mitts off her." Holmes grabbed Stealey by the arm and led her away. "I'm not one to talk about morals, but that man is the scum of the earth."

"Where are you taking me?" Stealey asked, as she was whisked across part of the dance floor and between several tables.

"I see our next vice president over here with his wife."

Stealey went rigid, but it was too late. Stokes and his wife, the mouse, were both waving at them. Holmes took a big gulp of vodka and then held up his drink. A split second later they were standing right in front the attorney general and his wife, Stealey as stiff as a board and Holmes as gregarious as ever.

"Libby, so good to see you." Holmes was well over a foot taller than the woman. He bent over and gave her a warm kiss on the cheek.

"Good to see you too, Pat." She rubbed his arm warmly. "You look very handsome tonight, and . . ."

She paused as she turned her big brown eyes on Stealey.

Stealey stood there with her best fake smile plastered across her porcelain face. *Here it comes,* she thought. *She's going to kill me with kindness like she always does.*

"Look at this beautiful woman." Elizabeth Stokes took a half a step back and looked Stealey over from head to toe. "Peggy, I swear you're the only woman I know who gets better looking each year."

"Elizabeth, you're too kind." The women exchanged air kisses so as to not disturb their makeup.

"For the last time, Peggy, call me Libby."

Stealey nodded and kept the fake smile in place. It drove her nuts that here this woman was, close to fifty, and she still wanted to be called by her childhood nickname. "Libby," she over annunciated the name like she was speaking to a child. "You look very nice also."

"Nice," growled Holmes. "You look gorgeous."

"Why, thank you." Libby did a miniature debutante twirl and batted her big brown eyes and lush eyelashes at Holmes.

That was her best weapon, Stealey knew. She'd seen her do it before. The big bedroom eyes and those naturally thick eyelashes drove the boys crazy. Stealey wanted to tell her in the worst way that she had slept with her husband and finally be done with this insincerity, but she knew deep down where that would lead. Libby was the mother hen and she would do anything to protect her nest. Martin was too gutless to stand up to her. There was no way he would leave and she knew she didn't really want him anymore anyway.

"So," Holmes said in much quieter voice. Everyone leaned in a few inches. "Has your husband told you the big news?"

Stokes looked almost instantly uncomfortable. "I think it's a bit premature, don't you?"

"Oh, I don't think so," Holmes said with a big grin.

"What big news?" Mrs. Stokes asked excitedly.

Stokes took another sip and shook his head.

"Oh, come on," Holmes chided him. "Won't you let me tell her?"

Stokes finally smiled. "All right, go ahead, but, honey, I want you to know the only reason I didn't tell you was that it's not a hundred percent yet."

"It ain't over until the fat lady sings, of course. But then again you're here tonight and the vice president isn't."

"What's going on?"

Stealey watched as Libby Stokes sidled up to her husband like a cat in heat.

"Please let me tell her?" asked Holmes.

Stokes nodded.

"Good." Holmes offered his arm. "Would you like to accompany me to the bar, Libby? I need to freshen my drink and along the way I will share with you the good news."

Libby shivered like an excited child and they were off. Stealey watched them with a mix of disgust and amusement. She hoped Holmes told her she looked as nice as a call girl. She felt her boss's breath on her bare neck and slowly turned. He had that look in his eye. That look that he only got when his wife was not around.

"You look fabulous," he whispered, "and you smell great too."

If they were alone Stealey would have considered another blow to his groin, but this was obviously not the place for her to fully express the hate side of their love-hate relationship.

"It's too bad you brought your wife tonight."

Stokes stood there guardedly, knowing she was toying with him, but unable to help himself. "Why do you say that?"

Stealey leaned forward, her lips almost touching his ear. "Because I was going to bring you back to my place tonight and tie you up." Then leaning away from him she nonchalantly said, "Oh look, there's Valerie. Well, maybe some other time." And just like that she was gone, leaving her boss and former lover standing alone to sort out the mix of emotion and desire that was coursing through his brain and other parts.

SEVENTY-THREE

I t was just after 9:00 when Reimer walked into CT Watch looking more than a little concerned. Rapp had just gotten off the phone with his wife for the second time today. He apologized again, and she said she understood, even though she didn't sound like she did. He didn't like disappointing her and promised he would catch the first flight out in the morning. She said she'd be waiting for him at the end of the dock in her bikini. He laughed, she didn't. She was sick of sharing her husband, and he couldn't argue with her.

The Virginia State police, along with the various county and local authorities, had set up a series of checkpoints around the area where the vehicles had last been seen. Now that it was nightfall they were stopping every vehicle that was headed in and out of the area. If nothing turned up they were prepared to start going door-to-door come morning.

Reimer opened the door to the bridge, and instead of entering, he motioned for Rapp and McMahon to follow him. He walked straight into McMahon's office and didn't bother taking a seat. When McMahon and Rapp had joined him he closed the door firmly and said, "I just got a call from one of my people, and you're not going to like this." Reimer looked extremely unhappy.

"Apparently the CDC in Atlanta called some dipshit over at the Department of Energy this afternoon and reported a death at one of the local hospitals due to radiation poisoning." The veins on Reimer's neck were bulging. "This jackass paper pusher was more worried about getting out of town for the holiday weekend than national security, so instead of picking up the phone and calling me directly, he sent me an e-mail . . . One of seventy-eight that I received today, and the little idiot didn't even bother to mark it urgent."

Other than the word *radiation* and the reference to the Centers for Disease Control, Rapp hadn't a clue as to what any of this meant. "Paul, I'm not following."

"This guy died from ARS . . . Acute Radiation Syndrome. I just got off the phone with the hospital. The doctor who treated him thinks he was exposed to a minimum of twenty thousand rads."

"And what does that mean?" asked McMahon.

"It means he was in contact with something very hot. Something you don't just stumble across in everyday life."

"Is the guy Arab?" Rapp asked.

"No. He's a Mexican American from Laredo, Texas. Apparently he picked up a load in Mexico earlier in the week and drove it to Atlanta. He dropped off his load and then went to fill up on gas, and passed out at the pumps."

"Don't tell me he brought it to the warehouse owned by the two guys we've got sitting out in Fairfax."

"Not that we know of, but I doubt it. If something this hot was in that warehouse, the WMD Teams would have picked up a whiff. We do know where the cab is, though, and the CDC has a team on the way to check it out."

"And the trailer he brought across the border?"

"We're trying to get someone on the phone from the trucking company, but their offices are closed for the weekend."

"But we know where the truck is, right?" asked McMahon.

"Yes."

"Well, he should have paperwork in the cab." McMahon picked up the phone to call the Atlanta office. "I'm going to send some agents out there to look around. You got the address?"

Reimer handed over a piece of paper with the information on it.

Rapp asked him, "So are you trying to tell us that you think there's a second bomb?"

"I don't know that for sure, but I sure as hell don't like this coincidence."

"I thought your Russian counterpart was sure only one of the bombs was missing?"

"He was sure that only one of the *unexploded* atomic demolition munitions was missing."

"What are you trying to say?"

"There's dozens of duds buried under the ground on that test range. Everything from demolition munitions to the big megaton weapons designed for inter-continental ballistic missiles."

"The city killers?" Rapp asked in shock.

Reimer nodded but said, "I don't see how they could have dug one of them up. We buried those things miles underground when we tested them. I'm sure the Russians did the same. It would take a pretty big operation to go after one of them."

"Does your Russian friend know about this?"

"Yeah, I already talked to him. He agreed with what I just told you so they're shifting their search over to a part of the range where they tested some of the smaller warheads for cruise missile and torpedo designs."

McMahon hung up the phone shaking his head. "The Atlanta office already knew about it, and have two agents on the way. This damn bureaucracy. We can't even communicate within our own or-ganizations. What are we going to do when DHS gets involved in this?"

"Once that happens we're screwed," Reimer said. "They'll want to start locking down cities, and evacuating people, and in the process all they're going to do is get in the way. I've already got one of my Search Response Teams on the way to Richmond. I think we've got a real shot at finding this thing. If that truck driver died from the exposure he got from this device while it was sitting in the trailer behind him, it's got to be pretty damn hot. That means my people should be able to get a bead on it."

"What if somehow they got around this manhunt and are in the city?" Rapp asked. "You know there's a state dinner tonight."

Reimer shook his head confidently. "They'd never get it past the portal sensors. The entire city is ringed with them, and we're tied into the traffic cameras. The slightest whiff and we're on them like that." Reimer snapped his fingers.

"I sure hope you're right," Rapp said.

McMahon was a bit more hesitant. "I don't know, Paul. We've got the whole continuity of government thing to consider."

Reimer frowned. "You saw what happened earlier in

the week. One little hint that the leaders had been evacuated from the city, and the press was on the story like hyenas on a half-rotted carcass. We pull him out of that state dinner right now, it'll be all over the news, and then what's to stop these terrorists from simply blowing up Richmond or Norfolk? Fifty thousand people is fifty thousand people whether it's up here or down there."

"I know, but we're talking about the president and key cabinet members and the leaders of the House and Senate."

"The vice president is out in California," Reimer began ticking names off one finger at a time. "The secretary of the treasury is in Colorado, the president pro tem of the Senate is in Kentucky, most of the Supreme Court is out of town, and almost all of the Senate and House are gone. It's a holiday weekend. We have de-facto continuity in place."

"But we're talking about the president and the secretary of state, secretary of defense, the leaders of the House and Senate and the damn leaders of Great Britain and Russia."

"I know that, but I'm telling you if we evacuate them, the press will report it, and the terrorists will find out, and once they do that, why risk coming to Washington when they've all flown the coop? Add to that the likely panic by the public, and my people have almost no chance of finding this device. The terrorists will just blow the damn thing."

Rapp thought of something Ahmed Khalili had told him during his interrogation—that they planned on killing the president. "Paul's right. They want the president, and if they know they can't get him, they'll just kill as many people as they can."

"And if they manage to get this thing into

Washington and end up killing the leaders of America, Great Britain, and Russia?"

Rapp shrugged. "At least there won't be any more ambivalence about the war on terror."

McMahon looked at his friend from the CIA and frowned.

Rapp reached out and nudged his shoulder. "Relax . . . this state dinner isn't going to last all night. As soon as it's over I'll make sure that the president is very quietly taken back to Camp David . . . and if we don't find this thing by noon tomorrow he won't be coming back for the dedication."

McMahon thought about it for a moment and somewhat reluctantly said, "All right, I'll go along with it, but there's something else I think we should do." McMahon looked at Rapp. "Something I think you'll have no problem agreeing to."

SEVENTY-FOUR

VIRGINIA

He wanted to kill the scientist, but at the moment did not possess the strength to do so. Al-Yamani was on the couch in the living room resting. The disease was in its final stage. The weakness, fatigue, and nausea were nearly constant. No matter how much water he tried to drink it could not soothe his parched and swollen mouth. His throat ached and his nose, gums, and rectum had begun to bleed. Several open sores were now visible on his forearms, and his top layer of skin had begun to slough off. Part of him, the weak part, wanted to simply fall asleep and never wake up. But that could not be allowed to happen.

For too many nights to remember, a beautiful vision had come to him in his sleep. He always sailed around the same river bend from left to right. The sky was a glorious clear blue, with not a cloud in sight. Boats large and small, some with sails and some with engines, were everywhere. Large groups of people were gathered on the river bank. The mood was festive, and beyond the tree-lined banks he could see the alabaster domes and spires of a great city. The capital of his enemy. That was his destiny. That was why he was fighting to stay alive for just one more day. He wanted to come around that bend in the river, he wanted to look on the unsuspecting faces of the nonbelievers, he wanted to sail right into the very heart of them and ignite a jihad that would show the true believers the path.

Hasan and Khaled would have to be his strength. That was why he had allowed the weak scientist to order them around. When they had finished assembling the weapon, and stored it on the boat, Zubair had made them strip naked in the yard while he hosed them down with water. Using a rake Zubair had then collected their clothes and thrown them behind the garage. Then the little Pakistani had marched them into the house and forced them to take long showers and scrub themselves with soap. Unbeknownst to Zubair, his efforts to prolong the lives of his fellow Muslims would be for nought.

Now his two warriors were walking around the house in the clothes of the seventy-year-old man who had died of a heart attack. The shirt and pants that Hasan had picked fit him reasonably well, but Khaled, who was both taller and more muscular, had been forced to put on a ridiculous track suit that was too short in the arms and legs. The two of them were now in the kitchen gathering some food and water for the trip.

Al-Yamani had seen the newscasts. Mohammed had become extremely concerned when the photo and description of him appeared on the television. The decision to help his old friend was proving to be disastrous. He even went so far as to at one point tell al-Yamani that he had ruined his life. Al-Yamani began to realize that his friend lacked the conviction he'd once had. The final disappointment, though, was yet to come.

Hasan came and told al-Yamani that everything was prepared. Provisions and extra gas were on board and the boat was ready to go. Since no one else was around, al-Yamani asked Hasan to help him stand. When he was on his feet Mohammed entered the room and asked to have a word alone with him. Al-Yamani granted his wish.

Mohammed spoke without looking his old friend in the eye. "I know you have said you would like me to come with you, but I think I would prefer to stay here."

"Are you sure?"

"Yes. Someone needs to stay anyway and watch the woman."

Al-Yamani nodded as if he hadn't thought of that. "What will you say to the police?"

"I will claim ignorance. An old friend called and asked me to meet. As far as all of this other stuff is concerned . . . I knew nothing."

It was clear to al-Yamani that Mohammed had been thinking about this, but hadn't thought it through well enough. There were certain things he would not be able to explain. Certain things that would put the police back on their trail, and al-Yamani couldn't afford that. They had nearly 200 miles to go, and according to Hasan that would take them approximately fourteen hours.

"I am sorry you will not be accompanying us on the final leg of this mission." Al-Yamani put his hand on his friend's shoulder and the two men walked slowly into the kitchen. The woman had been moved upstairs and was tied up in her bedroom.

"I think I have gone far enough. You will be in my prayers."

"Will you stay the night here?" al-Yamani asked as he

very subtly made a gesture to Hasan with his free hand.

"Yes, I think so."

Al-Yamani stopped and faced him. He placed both hands on the man's shoulders and said, "May Allah watch over you." From the corner of his eye he could see Hasan moving.

"And you my . . ." Mohammed never finished the sentence. Hasan had just plunged one of the long kitchen knives into the older man's back.

Mohammed slid to the floor and died in precisely the same spot that the owner of the house had earlier in the day. Al-Yamani looked at the face of his old friend and shook his head. Even those who had once been brave and great could grow weak. Mohammed was further proof of America's ability to corrupt.

"Go upstairs," al-Yamani said to Hasan, "and kill the woman. Then put the bodies on the boat with the old man. We'll dump them all in the river after we leave."

SEVENTY-FIVE

Peggy Stealey found herself seated at the singles table in the corner furthest from where the president and his esteemed guests of honor were seated. She was joined by her quasi-date, DNC Chairman Holmes, Chief of Staff Jones, Press Secretary Tim Webber, and four other people who she didn't know and didn't care to meet. These were the cheap seats, where they put the hired help and political devotees. She should have been happy for simply being invited to a state dinner, but she found herself a bit tanked and in a bit of a foul mood.

She knew why she was tanked. It was once again the festival of Pat Holmes. He had everyone at the table laughing. He remembered everyone's name, engaged each person in conversation, and entertained all with his endless supply of witty stories. He'd even gone so far as to arrange for a tray of shooters to be brought to the table. Before dinner he'd ordered vodka and green apple schnapps, and asked all ten of them to drink to the Democratic Party as he hoisted his own glass of chilled vodka. No one dared disobey. Not in front of Valerie Jones. Not if they wanted to keep working for this administration.

Stealey also knew why her mood had soured. It was the little five-foot-nothing brown-eyed mouse sitting at the head table next to the British prime minister of all people. Her boss and his wife were basking in the bright light of their lofty dinner companions. Stealey held her head up high and caught Stokes trying to get a glimpse of her. She would always have that hold over him. He desired her far more than he had or ever would desire his wife. If he became vice president, she would sleep with him, but only once. They'd have to do it on some overseas trip where she could really work him over. An all-nighter that would leave him exhausted.

Then she'd cut him off and wait to see if he ever got the top job. That was the key to controlling Martin. She'd give him a little taste and then if he became president in four and half years, she'd give him another night to remember. What a rush it would be, to tie up the most important man in the world and dominate him.

For tonight, though, she'd have to settle for Holmes. She'd make him forget little Libby Stokes. She didn't want to go to his place, though. That would give him too much control. Her place was also out of the question. She wanted to do the leaving, not wait around for him to slide out of bed in the morning and disappear. Then she would have to deal with the obligatory note or even worse, flowers sent later that day. No, she'd have him get a nice hotel room, and if he brought up Libby Stokes again she would make him pay. In fact she knew just the move. It would take a chiropractor a year to fix him after she was done with him.

The ringing of her cell phone brought her back to the moment. Stealey opened her beaded clutch purse and extracted the phone. She was more than a little surprised to see who it was. For a moment she considered not answering, but then decided it too delicious of an opportunity to pass up. It would be oh so nice to tell the infamous defense attorney Tony Jackson that she was at the White House for a state dinner with the president of Russia and the prime minister of Great Britain.

She pressed the green send button and put the phone to her ear. "Peggy Stealey here."

The confident smirk on her face vanished almost immediately, as she listened to an absolutely apoplectic Tony Jackson explain to her in great detail, and with horrendous profanity, what he was going to do to her personally, and to the Justice Department in general.

SEVENTY-SIX

Ahmed al-Adel had been sitting alone in his cell with the lights off for about an hour. No one had spoken to him in more than ten hours by his estimation. No reading, no radio, no TV, and no communication since he'd last talked to his lawyer after lunch. He had no watch, no way of telling time, but it seemed that they turned the lights off at 10:00 each night.

He was in solitary confinement and so had no contact with any other prisoners, and only sparse contact with his guards. They dropped off and picked up his food three times a day. He assumed they watched him from the camera mounted on the wall opposite his cell. All of this was fine with him. He had no desire to talk to anyone. Even his lawyer was irritating him. Jackson was beginning to question his story.

Worse, though, was that Jackson had already been proven wrong. The lawyer had told him that there was no way they would be able to hold him in jail over the long weekend unless they charged him formally. Instead of charging him, though, the feds had decided to hold him as a material witness. Jackson told him that the American Arab community in Atlanta, Miami,

Baltimore, and New York had all been hit with a flurry of arrest warrants. This was not good news, but al-Adel didn't let Jackson know it bothered him. It was crucial that he feigned ignorance for another day. Whether he lived did not matter, just so long as his death came quickly and without pain. Al-Adel was ready to be martyred. They had promised him that his pivotal part in this operation would be properly recorded. All of Arabia would soon know of his greatness.

The clanging noise of a heavy door opening and closing pulled him from his thoughts of greatness. He could hear footsteps coming down the hallway. He wasn't sure if it was more than two people, but it was definitely more than one. Two men suddenly appeared on the other side of his bars. Al-Adel couldn't see much more than their backlit silhouettes, but he could tell by the uniform that one of them was a guard.

The guard unlocked the door to the cell and left without uttering a single word. The man who was left did not open the door right away. Instead he pulled a phone from his pocket and dialed a number.

"Are you in?" the mysterious man asked. He listened for a second and then said, "Cut the video feeds and erase anything that shows us entering or leaving the building."

The man put the phone away and began addressing al-Adel in flawless Arabic. Al-Adel sat up in his bed clutching his blanket, terror coursing through every vein. "I am an American," he said with what little courage he could muster. "I want to see my lawyer."

The man on the other side of the bars did not answer him with words, but with laughter, laughter that showed no fear of anything that al-Adel could say or do, laughter tinged with a deep anger that spoke of unpleasant things to come.

SEVENTY-SEVEN

The turning point came after the second call from Atlanta. The CDC Hazardous Material team found the truck, and it was really hot. As predicted, there was paperwork pertaining to the trip from Mexico to Atlanta. The truck's location was not far from the truck stop and upon arriving the Hazmat team quickly located the trailer. It was also contaminated but even more telling was the pile of discarded clothes, lead aprons, and radiation badges that they found behind a nearby construction trailer.

Reimer had relayed all of this to McMahon and Rapp. The team identified the source of radiation as Pu-239, or plutonium, the primary isotope used in reactor fuel and weapon-grade nuclear material. On a more positive note, Reimer was saying that, as predicted, this device was extremely unstable and throwing off a ton of radiation, which would make it easy for the sensors around D.C. to pick up.

It was after Reimer's call that McMahon had surprised Rapp. Rapp knew the veteran agent was capable of looking the other way, but what he had just proposed went way beyond looking the other way. This was breaking the law, something that Rapp was not in the slightest bit opposed to, but there would be no turning back if they decided to move forward. It would be a definite career ender for McMahon and maybe even for Rapp himself. Knowing all that, Rapp still decided to go for it. Too much was at stake to not take the risk.

Only one thing gave him pause. He could deal with accusations and deflect media scrutiny, but not if they had him on video tape. One phone call to Marcus Dumond, the CIA's resident computer hacker, allayed his concerns. A short while later Rapp and McMahon were flying Route 123 toward Fairfax.

It was after 10:00 and the area around the federal courthouse and county jail was pretty quiet. McMahon drove his FBI sedan around to the rear of the building and honked his horn. One of the big garage doors opened and they entered the sally port where prisoners were transferred to vehicles. The port was empty with the exception of one man, and he did not look pleased to be there.

McMahon and Rapp got out of the car and walked over to the man. McMahon stuck out his hand, "Joe, I appreciate this."

The man shook his head. "I hope you know what you're doing."

"If I'm wrong, which I'm not, I'll take all the heat." McMahon pointed to Rapp. "Joe, meet Mitch Rapp. Mitch, this is Joe Stewart, U.S. Marshal's office."

The two men shook hands. "Thanks for sticking your neck out like this," Rapp said.

"Yeah, well, I've known Skip for a long time and I know he wouldn't ask if it wasn't serious."

"It is, trust me."

"We'd better get going then." The Marshall led them over to a heavy steel door. After a second it buzzed and they were let in. A Fairfax County deputy was waiting for them. Stewart looked at the younger man and said, "We need Ahmed al-Adel. You've got him in solitary."

"What for?" the deputy asked.

Stewart was short, but imposing. He glared at the young deputy and said, "Don't worry yourself with what for. He's a federal prisoner. When I say go get him, you just go get him."

The deputy backed down immediately. Rapp stepped forward. "I'll go with."

The deputy shrugged. "Suit yourself."

Another heavy door was buzzed and Rapp and the deputy entered. As they walked down the hallway, the deputy looked over his shoulder and said, "Hey, aren't you that Mitch Rapp fellow?"

Rapp shook his head. "Nope. You're not the first person to say it though. I'm with the Justice Department." Rapp didn't actually think this would work as an alibi, it was just better than having to answer all the man's questions about what it was like to work for the CIA and kill bad guys.

They went down a flight of stairs and through another locked door into a quiet and darkened cell block. At the very end of the passage the deputy unlocked a cell and before he opened the door Rapp said, "I can take it from here."

The deputy hesitated. "I have to put cuffs on him. It's the rules."

Rapp smiled confidently. "Don't worry about the cuffs. I can handle him."

The deputy didn't move. "I could get in big trouble."

Rapp shoed him away. "Don't worry about it. Go back upstairs. I can take it from here."

The deputy studied the face of the man standing in front of him. He'd already noticed the bulge of the weapon slung under the guy's right arm and the thin scar on the side of his face. He was athletic and in his mid-thirties. This guy was Mitch Rapp, not some lawyer from the Justice Department.

The deputy relented and left. He knew what to do. Brian Jones was twenty-two years old and had worked at the jail for not yet a year, but in that short time he'd learned to hate the hotshot Feds who came and went almost as much as the loudmouthed animals they housed behind the thick steel bars. Jones walked back upstairs and went into the security room where he monitored the prisoners via their new digital camera system. A short while later the man claiming he wasn't Rapp came upstairs with the prisoner. He had the man by the scruff of his orange jumpsuit. The prisoner looked scared, and if that was in fact Mitch Rapp, he was absolutely right to be scared.

Jones watched on the monitors as al-Adel was put in the backseat of the sedan and Rapp got in with him. The big jerk, Deputy U.S. Marshal Joe Stewart, talked to the other man for a second and then they shook hands and the tall guy from the FBI got in the car and started backing up. Fairfax County Deputy Sheriff Brian Jones punched the button to raise the garage door and as soon as the sedan was clear he closed it. A second later his entire video surveillance system crashed and his monitors went black.

Deputy Jones didn't move and didn't dare touch a thing. He just held his breath hoping the system would reboot itself. Five seconds passed, then ten, then twenty, and then finally the cameras started coming back online. Jones wiped the sweat from his brow and sighed in relief. The system had been installed around the time Jones had started, and it had never malfunctioned like that before. The timing of the crash made him a little suspicious, so he logged into the system and began checking the archives. Everything was stored digitally.

Roughly five minutes of surveillance footage was gone. Erased from the server. *Lawyer, my ass,* he thought to himself. *Just who in the hell did they think they were coming into his jail and pulling this shit?* Jones grabbed his wallet and found the card. He had been planning to call the man anyway. The Mouth of the South was famous. He'd passed his cards around the detention center telling deputies that he was going to be looking to hire out a lot of off-duty security for the trial. Fifty bucks an hour for sitting around and reading paperback novels on his days off sounded pretty good.

Jones bet the Mouth of the South had no idea his client had just gone for a ride with the CIA. He thought about how nice it would be to make fifty bucks an hour. If he let the Mouth know what was going on, he'd have the inside track on that off-duty job for sure. Jones was already counting the money he'd make as he dialed the number.

SEVENTY-EIGHT

VIRGINIA

They left the jail, took U.S. 50 west and cut off on Highway 28 north. McMahon drove close to eighty mph the entire way. When they hit the Hirst Brault Expressway by Dulles they passed a State Trooper on the side of the road who started to pull out. McMahon hit his emergency lights that were concealed in the front grill and back window, and never slowed. The only thing Rapp had told him was that they were going to a place that didn't exist, that McMahon could never talk about to anyone.

Dr. Akram had always told Rapp that the threat of torture was often more persuasive than actual torture itself, and based on what he'd seen so far with al-Adel that theory was likely to hold true. Rapp had consulted briefly with Akram on how to proceed and he had given Rapp a protocol to follow. Don't let al-Adel sense that you are desperate, was his first piece of advice. Make him believe that you are a patient, fair, and in control person who knows far more about him and his operation than he could possibly imagine. Let the threat of torture hang ominously in the back of his mind. Make him feel that he is insignificant.

The only part of this plan that was difficult for Rapp

was not laying a hand on him. McMahon had been right in his assessment that al-Adel had an infuriatingly smug air about him. In the twenty-some minutes that Rapp had been in the company of the Saudi-born immigrant, he had asked for his lawyer approximately once every minute. Each time the ludicrous request was made in the Saudi's arrogant tone, Rapp had been forced to resist the urge to break the man's nose. He knew that if they had to resort to torture, there were more subtle ways to hurt him, equally unpleasant, and even more important, fully deniable.

No physical marks could be left. If things didn't work out, and this second bomb was nothing more than a paranoid delusion, they would need to hand al-Adel back over to the Justice Department, and if there were obvious signs of torture, there would be an investigation. Physical abuse was very hard to prove if there were no marks. It would be Rapp's word against an Islamic radical fundamentalist who was involved in a plot to detonate a nuclear warhead in Washington, D.C. The public would undoubtedly believe Rapp was capable of such brutality, but everybody with the exception of the press and a handful of lefties and activists would be more than willing to side with him against the terrorist. Even if they left marks on al-Adel, the majority of Americans would probably give Rapp a pass considering what they were up against, but for now Rapp was willing to heed Akram's advice.

So Rapp sat in the backseat with the Saudi immigrant and spoke to him in his native tongue. He told him things that he knew would shock him. Rapp talked to him about his family, and even went so far as to say he had spoken to his father.

Al-Adel was unable to conceal his surprise at this. "You are lying to me."

Rapp shook his head. "I talked to him only an hour ago. Earlier in the day I placed a call to the crown prince and asked that your family be brought in for questioning. Even the women."

The look on al-Adel's face was one of both shock and disbelief.

Rapp said, "The crown prince and I have done a lot of business over the years."

"What kind of business?" asked a skeptical al-Adel.

"The business of eliminating threats, Ahmed. The crown prince profits from his business dealings with America. The eradication of people like you helps him ensure those dealings continue. He sees you Wahhabis for what you are . . . a bunch of backward religious fruitcakes who are embarrassed to admit you're wrong. Zealots who want to live in the past."

"I do not believe you. You do not know the crown prince."

"Think about it, Ahmed. The crown prince and the Saudi royal family have billions of dollars invested in the American economy. If you and your little band of whack jobs succeed in setting off a nuclear weapon in Washington, D.C.," Rapp paused when he saw a glimmer of recognition in the man's eye. "Yes, Ahmed, I know there's another bomb, and part of me hopes your friends succeed."

Al-Adel was caught off guard and showed it. "I do not know what you are talking about."

Rapp studied him intensely. He reached out and put his arm around the Saudi immigrant. Al-Adel closed his eyes tightly as Rapp whispered in his ear. "Yes, I really hope they succeed. Do you know why?"

Al-Adel shook his head.

"Because if they do, the United States of America will end this war in one fell swoop. We will nuke your beloved kingdom all the way back to the stone age. Mecca, Medina, all the holy sites gone just like that, and it will all be on your shoulders, Ahmed. You will go down in history as the man who destroyed a religion. The man who buried the Wahhabi scourge once and for all."

All al-Adel could do was shake his head in disagreement.

"Ahmed," Rapp laughed, "that puny twenty-kiloton bomb you tried to pick up down in Charleston is nothing. We have a single submarine sitting in the Arabian Sea right now that has enough nuclear missiles on board to destroy all of Saudi Arabia, and that's only a tiny fraction of our nuclear arsenal."

Al-Adel tried to show some confidence by smiling, but he was less than convincing. "Your president is too weak. He will never authorize such an attack. And even if he wanted to, the United Nations and Europe would never let him do it. And what about the oil?" he said in a taunting tone. "You will never bomb our country. You would be slitting your own throat."

"Oh, Ahmed, you really are stupid. The U.N. and Europe will have absolutely no say in the president's decision. France and Germany will publicly plead for restraint, but only because they have to. This will be a history-changing event. They will privately agree that a precedent must be set, that those who trade in terrorism will be dealt with in the most extreme way possible. And as far as the oil is concerned, we would never be so foolish as to nuke your oil fields. More than eighty percent of your population is along the Red Sea and in

Riyadh. The oil fields will remain unscathed, and the crown prince knows this. That is why he is having your family tortured as we speak. He knows if you fools succeed, his kingdom will be taken from him."

"My father is a respected man. The crown prince would never torture him."

"For starters the crown prince will do whatever it takes to save his own ass, and that includes torturing your little pissant father. Fortunately, though, your father is cooperating. He says you are an embarrassment to your family."

"You are a liar." Al-Adel refused to look at Rapp.

"We'll see." Everything Rapp had said was a bluff, but not an outright lie. He did know the crown prince, and he knew if the president called him and laid all his cards on the table, the crown prince would gladly round up al-Adel's family and begin torturing them. He also knew that if these guys actually set off a nuclear weapon on American soil the president would be under immense pressure to nuke somebody and something, and Saudi Arabia would be at the top of that list.

The driveway to the facility was blocked by a twelve-foot steel gate with an all-weather camera mounted off to the side. After only a second the gate opened and they made their way down the long, winding tree-lined drive. The main house was a two-story redbrick federal style with matching wings on either end. When they pulled up to the front door Dr. Akram was waiting on the front step looking dapper in his dark suit and red tie.

Rapp, McMahon, and al-Adel got out of the car. Rapp did not bother to make any introductions. Dr. Akram politely greeted al-Adel in Arabic, but said nothing to McMahon. He then turned and entered the house, expecting the others to follow. They continued through the house and out the back door to a slightly elevated terrace that looked down on a long rectangular pool. Akram walked over to a table where a tray of food and a pitcher were waiting.

He pointed to a chair and said, "Mr. al-Adel, if you will kindly sit." Akram looked to Rapp and McMahon, "I would like to have a moment alone with Mr. al-Adel."

Rapp and McMahon walked to the far end of the patio, where McMahon asked, "What in the hell is this all about, and who's the guy in the fancy suit?"

"Don't ask. Just observe. He's going to get him talking and if he doesn't learn anything of value he'll turn him back over to us and we'll get to play bad cop for a while."

"Good. I can't wait."

Rapp wasn't sure if McMahon was serious or not. "Skip, you don't have to participate in this. In fact, I'd prefer it if you didn't."

McMahon looked past Rapp at their prisoner and the man in the suit. "No. I'm not going to ask you to do anything I'm not willing to do myself."

"You're not asking me to do anything."

"You know what I mean."

Rapp nodded. "It might get ugly."

"I'm no boy scout, Mitch."

Rapp's phone rang and he snatched it from his hip. Before opening it, he looked at the tiny display. He hesitated for a second and then decided reluctantly to answer. "Yeah."

He held the phone to his ear and listened. After about five seconds he said, "I'm the middle of something right now. I'm going to have to call you back." Not waiting for the other person to respond he closed the phone, and said to McMahon, "We're going to have to work fast."

"Who was that?"

"Irene." Rapp winced. "Somehow the word's out that I pulled al-Adel out of the Fairfax jail."

"We've only had him for a half hour!"

Rapp shrugged. "Irene says that Justice Department is furious. She started to say something about Valerie Jones, and I just hung up."

Rapp's phone rang again. It was Kennedy trying to call back. He stared at the phone for a moment and then silenced the ringer and put it away. "We'll have to hurry. We don't have a lot of time."

SEVENTY-NINE

Rapp walked across the terrace, and placed a hand on Akram's shoulder. "We need to talk."

They left McMahon to watch over al-Adel and walked far enough away so that they couldn't be heard. Rapp said, "I'm out of time. Has he said anything to you?"

"I've barely had a chance to get started. The only thing he's said is that he's an American and he wants his lawyer."

"Yeah . . . he's like a parrot that way. Here's the deal. The word's already out that I have him, so we've got to get him talking quickly and as you said earlier, it would be best if he left here without any marks on him. What do you suggest?"

Akram thought about it for a brief moment. "The lemonade he's drinking has a stimulant in it. It will help heighten his sense of fear when you throw him in the pool."

Rapp looked at the lit pool and then back at Akram, a questioning expression on his face.

Akram explained, "Swimming isn't real popular in Saudi Arabia."

The thought had never occurred to Rapp.

"If by chance he does know how to swim, you'll just have to get in with him and force him under." Akram looked at his watch and said, "I'll be back in ten minutes to see how you're doing."

Akram turned and went back to the table. "Mr. al-Adel, I'm afraid we've run out of time. I'm going to ask you one question. If you refuse to answer, or lie to me, I'm going to have to turn you over to these two gentlemen. And I can promise you it will not be a pleasant experience." Akram had been thinking of this moment for sometime. It was important that he didn't reach too far right away, so he started with something simple. Something they already knew. "The bomb that you picked up in Charleston . . . where were you to bring it? What city?"

Al-Adel shook his head defiantly. "I am an American citizen. I know my rights. I don't have to talk to any of you. I want to see my lawyer."

Akram gave him his most sympathetic expression. "I am very sorry for what is about to happen, but it must be done." He then turned to Rapp and whispered in his ear, "The key with this one will be to get him talking. Start out small. Get him talking about anything other than his lawyer, and then you can go for the gold." Akram walked away and went back in the house.

Rapp walked over to the prisoner and said, "Get up."

Al-Adel didn't move. Rapp reached down to grab his wrist, but al-Adel clamped down on the chair's armrests, refusing to budge.

"I'm not going to ask again. Get up."

Al-Adel remained stubborn.

Rapp delivered a lighting-fast blow to the man's solar plexus. Al-Adel doubled over instantaneously, releasing his grip on the chair. It would have been far more gratifying to break the man's nose, but this would have to do for now. Rapp grabbed a fistful of hair and yanked him from the chair. Al-Adel remained bent over, clutching his stomach, as Rapp dragged him along the terrace toward the steps that led to the pool.

"Do you like to swim, Ahmed?" Rapp marched him down four steps to the lower terrace and the pool. Al-Adel began to fight fiercely at the sight of the water.

"What's the matter?" asked Rapp. "You're not afraid of the water are you?"

Al-Adel leaned back at first, locking his knees in an attempt to stop his progress toward the water. Rapp yanked harder on the man's hair and stood him up. With only a few steps to go al-Adel let his legs go limp, and collapsed to the ground. McMahon showed up just in time and grabbed him by the feet. Rapp grabbed one hand and then the other, and after two swings they launched the terrorist into the middle of the deep end, orange prison jumpsuit and all.

Rapp watched him flounder as he walked around to the other side of the pool to grab the skimming pole. Al-Adel definitely did not know how to swim. He was thrashing about, flailing his arms in every direction, gasping for air and getting mostly water instead. Rapp took off his suit coat and grabbed the long aluminum pole. He swung the basket out over the pool and put it right in front of al-Adel's face. For a second he thought the idiot wouldn't realize it was there, and that he'd actually have to jump in the pool and save him. Fortunately, one of his flailing arms hit the basket and he grabbed on.

Rapp leaned back on the pole with his right hand and

used his left hand like a fulcrum to lift al-Adel's head and shoulders out of the water. The terrorist hung onto the basket like rat clutching a piece of flotsam from a shipwreck.

"Ahmed," Rapp said in a loud voice. "If you say you want your lawyer even once, I'm going to rip this away from you and let you sink to the bottom. Alright?"

He didn't answer right away so Rapp shook the pole.

"Yes! Yes! I understand!"

"Now, Ahmed, listen to me very carefully. Where were you taking the bomb that you picked up in Charleston?"

Al-Adel clutched the basket at the end of the pole, his eyes shut tight, his entire body shaking with fear.

Rapp repeated the question even more forcefully and then started counting. When he got to five and al-Adel hadn't answered he released all tension on the pole and drove the basket and the clutching terrorist down under the surface of the water. Rapp held him under for only two seconds, but he knew it was an eternity to a man who didn't know how to swim. He leaned back hard on the pole, and a sputtering al-Adel popped to the surface. Rapp shouted the question again, but this time didn't even bother to wait for an answer. He saw al-Adel open his mouth wide, gasping for air, and drove him right back under.

Rapp pulled him back up a split second later, and this time he was rewarded with an answer. Al-Adel screamed the two words, spit out a mouthful of water, and sucked in a gulp of air for his starving lungs. Rapp couldn't believe what he'd just heard. He looked across the pool at McMahon and then repeated his question yet again.

Al-Adel gave the same answer again, and when Rapp threatened to send him back under he began blabbing in earnest, spewing out detail after detail as he clutched for dear life to the aluminum pole.

EIGHTY

Rapp and McMahon had a plan. They'd had thirty minutes to discuss it and to try to poke holes in it. They had spoken briefly to their bosses; Rapp to CIA Director Kennedy, and McMahon to FBI Director Roach. They would discuss nothing over the phone. No, they would not tell them where the missing prisoner was. They were on their way to the White House where they would meet them in the Situation Room at midnight. Neither boss was happy about this, but neither Rapp nor McMahon cared. They would face all their accusers in one room, and truth be told, it wasn't their bosses who had them worried. They would do the right thing. It was the others, the president included, who they were wary of.

The president needed to see firsthand that there were people in his administration, people who had been chirping in his ear, whom he should not be listening to on issues of counterterrorism and national security. Once Rapp told the president what they had found out, these very people would inundate him with bad advice, bad advice that could lead to the premature detonation of the second weapon.

It was for that reason alone that Rapp and McMahon

had decided to keep everything from their bosses until everybody was in the same room. To do this right they needed to give their detractors the chance to go berserk and lose their cool, to promise to take away their jobs and pensions, and to threaten them with prosecution, and they needed them do it all right in front of the president. Because when the other shoe dropped, they would be left looking like utter fools.

Secret Service Agent Jack Warch was waiting for Rapp and McMahon under the awning on West Executive Drive. Rapp had called Warch and asked him to meet them. He was wearing his tuxedo from the state dinner, and he looked worried. As Rapp and McMahon stepped onto the curb he said, "Just what in the hell is going on?"

"Too much to explain, Jack. You're just going to have to trust me on this one."

"You know I'm not supposed to get involved in stuff like this, but you've got some really pissed-off people in there. Jones wants your balls on a platter, and so does that other broad from the Justice Department. Even your bosses don't sound too supportive, and the president . . . well, let's just say I haven't seen him this mad in a long time."

"Good," Rapp said and he meant it. "Is the president in the Situation Room?"

"He's on his way over."

Rapp checked his watch. "I need you to do me one other favor, Jack. Irene told me Marine One is here."

"That's correct."

"How long before it's ready to take off?"

"Five minutes."

"And how late does the president usually stay at this type of event?"

"Normally about midnight is his limit, but this one's a pretty big deal. Where the hell are you going with all of this, Mitch?"

"In about five to ten minutes, the president is going to come out of this meeting and he's going to tell you he wants to go up to Camp David tonight, because he wants to get up early and play a round of golf with the British prime minister and the Russian president."

"The Russian president doesn't play golf."

"Then he's going to ride in the cart. I don't give a shit. All I'm telling you is that I want all three of them and their wives on Marine One in fifteen minutes. I want them safely out of the city, and I don't want the press to get the slightest whiff as to the real reason why they're leaving. Do you get my drift?"

The head of the president's detail slowly nodded. "I think so."

"Good, and, Jack, you never heard this from me. This was the president's idea. He thought it would be a good idea to spend some time alone with his fellow leaders in a more low-key environment. Spread that around to your agents. That way if they get hit up by the press they'll be none the wiser."

Rapp could tell Warch was thinking of something else. Taking a stab at it he said, "Relax, you live up by Rockville, right?"

"Yeah."

"Your family's fine. Just make sure they don't try to come downtown tomorrow."

Rapp's phone rang. He checked the number and answered it. "What's up?" He listened for about twenty seconds and then said, "Thanks," and hung up.

Rapp looked at McMahon. "They just finished the polygraph. Everything checked out."

"Any chance he beat it?" McMahon asked.

"No way. I don't think even I could fool these guys."

Warch put his hand up and touched his flesh-colored earpiece. Both McMahon and Rapp knew someone from his detail was talking in his ear. Warch turned and said, "Let's go. The president is in the Situation Room."

They followed him through the door, past the uniformed Secret Service officer standing his post and down the hall toward the White House Mess. Two turns later they passed two tuxedoed agents and entered the Situation Room. All chatter ceased for one brief moment and then a torrent of accusations, insults, and threats spewed forth.

EIGHTY-ONE

As they had planned, both McMahon and Rapp stood in silence and took the abuse. In the room were both their bosses, National Security Advisor Haik, Attorney General Stokes, the president, Chief of Staff Jones, and Peggy Stealey. Everyone was sitting with the exception of Rapp, McMahon, and the two people doing most of the talking, or more accurately, the yelling.

National Security Advisor Haik didn't say a word, and their bosses were also silent, but by the looks on their faces they'd just gone through one hell of a tongue-lashing. Attorney General Stokes sat next to the president, and although he wasn't talking, he looked extremely disappointed that two men who should clearly know better would be so reckless. The president for his part was clearly angry. His tense jaw and the fact that he made absolutely no effort to rein in the two screaming women on the other side of the table told the whole story.

Rapp actually enjoyed it. Knowing what was coming next allowed him to do that. To make matters even more interesting, he was beginning to get the impression that both Jones and Stealey were not quite sober.

The Situation Room wasn't that big, and from across the table he could smell the alcohol on their breath. In addition they'd each slurred a few words and their eyes had that semiglassy look that people get when they're either tired or have had one too many cocktails.

Rapp waited for a pause and then asked in a confident, nonemotional tone, "Are you done?"

The manner in which he asked the question sent the two women to new heights of indignation. Jones thrust a ringed finger at him from across the table and yelled. "That's it!" She turned her attention to the president. "I have been warning you for two years that he is a loose cannon! I told you that he was going to do something that would embarrass you and this administration, and now he's done it!" She looked back at Rapp. "Do you have any concept of the law? Do you have any idea the position you have put the president in?"

Stealey must have felt left out because she picked this as the moment to glare at McMahon and shake her head in disgust. "I would expect more from a man who has put in thirty years at the Bureau, a man who has sworn to uphold the law."

"It's a foregone conclusion," yelled Jones. She looked right at Director Kennedy and Director Roach. "They're both fired! Right here! Right now! It's over! I want them both fired right now!"

Kennedy watched all of this carefully. She had not yet had the chance to tell the president or the others about the events in Richmond and Atlanta. Rapp had asked her to wait until he arrived at the White House. Director Roach had received the same request from McMahon.

Kennedy knew Rapp could be reckless, but that was part of the territory. She knew he had a problem with following rules, but she also knew he was no fool. He was holding something back, for if he had truly screwed up as badly as these two women were claiming, there was no way he'd stand here and take it. In fact there was no way he'd be here at all. He had a healthy dose of pride that precluded him from suffering the criticism of anyone he did not respect. Even more telling was McMahon's participation. Kennedy knew him well enough to understand that there was no way he would ever take part in anything so drastic unless there was good cause.

"Well," Jones said to Kennedy and Roach, "I'm waiting."

"Okay," announced Rapp as he looked at his watch, "Amateur hour is over. You two can either sit down and shut your mouths, or leave. It's up to you."

The president slapped his hand down on the table and yelled, "Damn it, Mitch, I have had enough your reckless antics. I don't care what you've done in the past, I can't protect you any longer. You have become a major liability, and your irresponsible behavior can no longer be tolerated."

"Do you have *any* idea what the media is going to do to us over this?" asked Jones.

"Do you have any idea that al-Qaeda has smuggled a second nuclear weapon into the country?" Rapp leaned forward, placing both hands on the table. "That's right, Mr. President, so before you get rid of me, please allow me to save your ass one last time. While you've been busy listening to these two idiots," Rapp pointed at Jones and Stealey, "chatter in your ear about the ills of the Patriot Act, and the upcoming election, and how good a running mate Attorney General Stokes would make, we've been out busting our asses trying to figure out what these terrorists are up to, and you are not going to like what we found out.

"Earlier this evening, we received a call from the CDC down in Atlanta. A local hospital had called to inform them that they had an out-of-state truck driver who had just died from Acute Radiation Syndrome, an illness that is very rare. The CDC, DOE, and FBI located this man's truck and trailer and found that they were contaminated with Pu-239, which is the isotope used in the production of weapons-grade nuclear material. We found out the truck driver picked up a load in Mexico and crossed over the border on Wednesday morning headed for Atlanta."

Rapp turned his attention on Stealey. "Atlanta, if you will remember, was also the destination of Imtaz Zubair, the missing Pakistani nuclear scientist. It also happens to be the home of Ahmed al-Adel, who was arrested in Charleston this week. The same man you decided to prosecute rather than deport and hand over to the CIA."

Stealey stood so she could face Rapp eye to eye and started to lecture. "You have no idea what you're talking about. We can't simply deport American citizens and hand them over to the CIA for torture."

Rapp cut her off with a booming voice that was almost a full-blown yell. "The debate portion of the evening is over. You are an idiot! You have no idea what you are talking about, and you have no idea what it takes to wage this war. Now sit down, and don't interrupt me again or I will throw you out of this room by the scruff of your neck." Rapp pointed his finger at the president's chief of staff and said, "And that goes for you too, Valerie."

Stealey slowly sat back down and Rapp continued.

"As I was saying . . . considering the gravity of the situation, I took it upon myself to interrogate Ahmed al-Adel, who has refused to talk to anyone except his lawyer, and who has proclaimed he is a patriotic American. Before anyone tries to get back on their constitutional high horse, I'd like to remind all of you that this was the same man who tried to pick up a twenty-kiloton nuclear weapon, which would have killed upwards of 100,000 people and destroyed this building and most of the city.

"After just five minutes of persuasive questioning, Mr. al-Adel admitted that he was in fact part of a terrorist cell that was planning to detonate a nuclear weapon on American soil. There is only one problem, though. The bomb that Mr. al-Adel picked up in Charleston was not meant for Washington, D.C. It was meant for New York City. The second bomb is intended for Washington, D.C. The one that came across the border from Mexico on Wednesday morning."

The room was dead silent for at least five seconds and then the president, concern and embarrassment represented equally in his voice, asked, "Do we have any idea as to the location of the second bomb?"

"Yes," said Rapp, "but I'm not going to tell you. Not until you're on board Marine One with the British prime minister, the Russian president, and your wives, and on your way to Camp David."

The president started to protest, but Rapp shook his head firmly. "Not until you're up at Camp David. I know the time and the specific target of the attack. The only chance we have of stopping them is to make everything appear as if it's business as usual. That is why your press secretary is going to announce that you and your fellow leaders decided to head up to Camp David tonight so you could play an early morning round of golf, before coming back into the city for tomorrow afternoon's dedication ceremony."

The president gave Rapp a disapproving look. He was not used to taking orders, but knew he had put himself in this situation by not heeding the advice of Kennedy. He turned to his director of the Central Intelligence Agency. "What do you think?"

"I think you should go to Camp David."

"What about Operation Ark?"

Kennedy did not think an evacuation of key people was a good idea, but decided that she would keep that to herself for now. "I think the most important thing right now is to get you and your fellow leaders out of the city. Once you are up at Camp David we can discuss the rest."

EIGHTY-TWO

POTOMAC RIVER

Saturday morning dawned with heavy gray skies and a steady rain that peppered the calm surface of the bay. The hypnotic effect of the rain falling on the water served as the perfect backdrop for their morning prayer. They'd made their way down the York River and out into the Chesapeake under the cover of darkness, and were now headed north. The thirty-seven-foot cabin cruiser owned by Mr. Hansen was more than up to the task, especially on calm seas. Its GPS navigation system helped them to maneuver through these foreign waters.

Like al-Yamani, Hasan and Khaled had also learned basic seamanship on the Caspian. They had been in charge of receiving and preparing the fresh martyrs who were shipped in from around the region. They would house them for a day or two, waiting for al-Yamani to return with the flat-bottom barge, and then they would have nothing to do until the next batch arrived. During those inactive times they were ordered to learn the ways of the water. Money was not an issue, so whenever the opportunity arose, they would rent a boat and practice on the calm waters of Gorgan Bay at the southeast edge of the Caspian.

Despite everything they'd learned, though, there was no way they could have memorized the craggy outline and bays and inlets of the Chesapeake. The GPS and chart that was onboard had been lifesavers, for they had never planned on navigating this body of water at all. The original plan had called for them to put in at Dahlgren on the Potomac River forty miles due south of Washington. The route following the river was a bit longer, but not significant compared to the 200 miles they now had to travel in the rain and with poor visibility.

Al-Yamani was on his knees, but he was not praying. He was in the head, throwing up yet again and it was not a pretty sight. He could no longer keep down even a morsel of food. His thirst was insatiable, but with every cup of water came more vomiting, and the fluid had gone from a pinkish tinge to dark crimson. He placed his hand on the edge of the tiny toilet and locked his elbows as he braced himself for another stomach-tearing hurl.

The wave of nausea passed, and al-Yamani was left hovering over the toilet, a thick dribble of blood and spit hanging from his mouth. His entire body was covered in sweat and he was shaking. This would be his last day on earth, whether they succeeded or not, but he did not believe they would fail. Not after yesterday. Allah was guiding them, showing them a safe passage to their destiny.

They were all going to die. He had been forced to lie to the scientist about that, but he felt no shame in doing so. Certain people were not strong enough to handle the truth. The scientist had spent most of the trip sitting in the bed up under the bow of the ship, as far away from the bomb as possible. Zubair had been adamant that the bomb be lashed to the fiberglass swim platform at the aft of the vessel. Even though they'd gone to great lengths to shield it, the weapon was still giving off significant radiation. Because of that it had to be placed downwind and as far away from them as possible.

The scientist had asked what the plan was once they got to Washington. Al-Yamani told him they would set the timer on the bomb, dock the boat, and then leave. *How would they get away?* the Pakistani wanted to know. Al-Yamani told him someone would be waiting for them. It was another lie, but one that the Pakistani would never know, because he would be dead before they reached the city.

Khaled came down the stairs into the small cabin and stood over al-Yamani. "We are nearing the river."

Al-Yamani barely had the strength to stand. He held up his arm so Khaled could help him to his feet. "Is it still raining?"

"Yes."

Even with the help of Khaled it was a struggle to stand. Al-Yamani began working his way up the stairs with Khaled both pushing and holding him from behind. When they reached the helm he sat down on the bench seat next to Hasan who was driving.

Al-Yamani peered through the rain-spattered windshield and waited for the wiper blade to come around and give him a glimpse of what lay ahead. "Any sign of trouble?"

"No, but we aren't quite there yet."

"Where is the river?"

"According to the GPS it's up there on the left about another mile."

Al-Yamani couldn't see anything but he trusted his fellow warrior. "If you see any sign of trouble we will continue past the mouth and then decide whether we should proceed to Baltimore or try again."

"I know. Maybe we should have the scientist arm the weapon."

Al-Yamani had thought of this, but was reluctant. He did not know if the bad weather would end up forcing a postponement of the dedication of the memorial or not, and until he knew for sure he wanted to wait. "Have you learned anything of the weather?"

Hasan kept his eyes on the water, but pointed to the radio controls. "They don't know if it is going to clear or not. They are giving it a fifty percent chance by this afternoon."

Less than a minute later they came up on the channel marker to enter the Potomac. The going had been slower than anticipated during the night, and Hasan had had to compensate by running at a faster speed while they were out in the bay. He pulled back on the throttles taking the boat down from its cruising speed of thirty mph to around five mph. There wasn't a boat in sight.

Both men smiled. "How long until we lay our eyes on the city?" asked al-Yamani.

"We will be there by noon. A full hour before the ceremony is to commence."

Al-Yamani grinned with anticipation. "Good."

EIGHTY-THREE

It was a long night, and morning brought with it more questions than answers. The president had boarded Marine One with the leaders of Great Britain and Russia and their wives and left for Camp David. Irene Kennedy, National Security Advisor Haik, Secretary of State Berg, and Chief of Staff Jones had all taken a separate helicopter from the Pentagon's heliport and met the president at the secure underground Site R, near Camp David, where they were now safely monitoring the situation. Before they all left the Situation Room, though, Rapp had forcibly commandeered Jones's mobile phone.

At daybreak Rapp had dispatched Secretary of Defense Culbertson to Site R to help bolster Kennedy and Haik's sway over the president and negate that of Berg and a diminished Jones. Even though Jones had been severely embarrassed at the midnight meeting, she was not the type of person to just quietly fade away. Rapp had a feeling before this was all over she would once again be chirping in the president's ear poisoning his judgment with her usual politically tainted advice. Rapp appraised Secretary Defense Culbertson of this concern, and Culbertson gave Rapp his word that he would deal with Jones harshly if she tried to pull anything. He also promised that the military would monitor all calls she made or received from Site R.

The remaining attendees of the midnight meeting in the Situation Room, FBI Director Roach, Attorney General Stokes, Peggy Stealey, McMahon, and Rapp, all left for the Joint Counterterrorism Center. Rapp made it crystal clear to everyone that there were to be no personal calls. Absolutely no one outside of the core group was to know the real reason why the president and his guests had returned to Camp David. If the press got wind of what was going on they would simply have to endure a repeat of what had happened earlier in the week. Only this time it might precipitate the premature detonation of the device. With that in mind he also commandeered Stealey's mobile phone.

When the president was safe at Camp David, Rapp honored his word and explained to him over the phone the details of what he'd discovered. The terrorist they had captured in Charleston had confessed that the bomb was to be detonated at noon this coming Tuesday in New York City, not Washington, D.C. It was to be the second act in a terrorist attack that was to wreak havoc on the American psyche, economy, and very soul. The first act was to take place at 1:00 p.m. today during the dedication of the WWII memorial. It was designed not only to destroy the city but to decapitate the federal government by killing the president and the other senior officials and politicians who were to attend the event. The allied leaders who were set to attend were a bonus. The follow-up attack on Tuesday was designed to make sure the American economy slipped into a depression. Shockingly, the planners of the terrorist attack had not taken into consideration a possible nuclear retaliation by America. Such was the thinking of martyrs.

Rapp, McMahon, and Reimer all argued forcefully that any evacuation of either city would hinder their search for the weapon and more than likely precipitate the attack. As morning approached, the Russians now found a second test site that had been excavated, despite their initial report that only one site had seen compromised. Records showed that this portion of the range had been used to test warheads for the Russian navy. This spot in particular had been the location of a failed test for a fifteen kiloton warhead to be used in a torpedo. Near the excavation they found a shallow grave containing at least fifty bodies and probably more.

Based on the radiation signatures at the site in Kazakhstan and those found on the trailer and truck in Atlanta, Reimer believed that they were dealing with a very unstable configuration of nuclear material, a warhead that was throwing off large doses of radiation. It would be much easier for his NEST teams to find than he had originally feared. That had been the assessment at three in the morning, but now as the clock inched toward midmorning Rapp's assuredness, at least, was beginning to wane.

A combat air patrol was up over the city, surface-to-air-missile batteries were activated at both the Pentagon and the Capitol, the no-fly zone around the city had been expanded to forty miles, and every airport within 200 miles was under close scrutiny by an airborne early-warning AWACS. The door-to-door search by the local law enforcement agencies down by Richmond had so far come up blank, and the NEST teams, contrary to what they had hoped, had yet to get a hit on the device. Reimer explained that it had something to do with the rain affecting the sensors that were carried aboard the helicopter that was patrolling the area south and east of Richmond.

On a more positive note, though, the rain was keeping people from coming into the city for the dedication of the new WWII memorial and the festivities that were to culminate with a rock concert and fireworks display after dark. The Park Police estimated that upwards of 500,000 people would attend the event from start to finish. It was slated to begin at 11:00 a.m. So far, the only people who had showed up on the Mall were the vendors, event security, and a handful of die-hard fans who wanted to stake their claim to a front-row seat for the various acts that were to start midafternoon and continue well into the evening.

Every law enforcement officer on the East Coast had the sketch of al-Yamani, the passport photo of the Pakistani nuclear scientist, the photo of the cab driver, and the fake driver's license that had been left behind at the traffic stop in Richmond. After pouring through the CIA's terrorist database with facial-recognition software, they were now confident that the man on the fake license was Hasan Abdul-Aziz, a Saudi national who hailed from the notorious al-Baha province.

The area between Richmond and Norfolk was flooded with cops, all looking for the fugitives. Nowhere though, were the words *nuclear,* or *weapon of mass destruction* mentioned. This was strictly a manhunt for a group of suspected terrorists who were considered extremely dangerous. The fact that they were terrorists was kept out of the press releases. The media were told only that the men were wanted for questioning in the attempted murder of a law enforcement officer. The tape of the deputy getting run over by the cab was getting a lot of air time and was the lead story on every local Saturday-morning newscast.

Despite all the news coverage and the blanket thrown down by local law enforcement, they had come up with nothing. Not a single break since yesterday evening. McMahon was standing by the eyewitness accounts of the two people who had seen the cab and the truck, but Rapp had his doubts. Either *they* were mistaken or the police were. McMahon had relayed the fact that the local sheriff thought these guys were probably holed up in the woods somewhere.

Again, Rapp had his doubts, and he was growing more nervous with each passing tick of the clock. The president had laid down a noon deadline. If they hadn't found the weapon by then, he would implement Operation Ark to ensure full continuity of government and operations. Once that happened, the cat would be out of the bag. It was simply impossible to ask that many people to keep a secret.

Rapp was sitting in the conference room off to the side of CT Watch with his feet up on the table. The shower he had taken only an hour ago down in the locker room, and the change of clothes, helped revive him a bit. He'd ditched his suit and was wearing a pair of khaki cargo pants, a dark blue T-shirt, and a tactical vest stuffed with two mobile phones, spare batteries, a headset, and other important items. He was used to going without sleep, but he was starting to get a little jumpy. He was drinking a cup of coffee an hour on average and the gut rot was beginning to set in.

He ignored the jumpiness and told himself that either way this thing would be over in three to six hours. He scratched the thick black stubble on his face and looked at a fresh sheaf of documents in his other hand. Dr.

Akram had just faxed him the transcripts from the session he'd had with al-Adel. Apparently, the man was cooperating. Akram had him hooked up to a polygraph while interrogating him and had so far only caught him lying once. The good doctor stopped the interrogation and told al-Adel that unless he wanted Mr. Rapp to take over with the questioning, he should refrain from any more lies. From that point forward Mr. al-Adel had chosen to tell the truth.

Rapp was in the midst of a section detailing how the attack in New York was to be carried out when McMahon and Stealey appeared in the doorway. They were an awkward-looking pair, McMahon in his short-sleeve white button-down shirt and dull tie that stopped a full inch above his belt buckle, and Stealey in her shimmering robin's-egg blue evening gown. She had tried to go home earlier to change, but Rapp had said no. CT Watch was under lockdown. He'd already taken her mobile phone, and he wasn't about to let her out of his sight. He'd finally relented an hour ago to send someone else to gather some things for her.

"We've got a problem," McMahon said.

Rapp laid the transcript on the table and asked, "What's up?"

"Tony Jackson," said Stealey, as she folded her arms across her chest, causing her breasts to swell. "Mr. al-Adel's attorney is raising quite a stink."

Rapp couldn't help but notice that this lawyer liked to show off her cleavage. "Right now I'm a little more concerned about finding a nuclear bomb. Mr. Jackson is not a problem."

"Yes he is," said Stealey in a combative tone. "I've already assured him three times since last night that his client is safe and unharmed. He is unharmed, isn't he?"

Rapp shrugged. "He's missing a few fingers, but other than that he's fine."

Stealey's eyes opened wide. "You're not serious?"

"No, I'm not. He's fine. Not a mark on him."

She tapped her foot on the ground, and glared at Rapp. "The attorney general's office is getting bombarded by calls asking where al-Adel is, and why we're not allowing Tony Jackson to see his client."

"Peggy, let me be real clear about this. I don't give a shit." There was an edge of irritation in Rapp's voice. "Tell this attorney to go fuck himself. I've got more important things to deal with."

Stealey glared right back at Rapp. "You can go ahead and tell him yourself, Mr. Big Shot. I told him you're the man in charge. Go ahead," she pointed at the phone, "he's holding on line three."

Rapp hesitated for only a second and then grabbed the phone and pressed the red blinking light. "Mr. Jackson, this is Mitch Rapp."

Stealey's stern face turned into a grin of anticipation. She could already tell that Jackson was unloading on Rapp. She watched eagerly, wanting to see how the notorious Mitch Rapp handled one of the best trial lawyers in the country.

"Mr. Jackson, if you shut your mouth for a second I'll explain. Are you recording this call?" Rapp listened to the lawyer's reply. "Good. Here's the deal. Your client is guilty. Come Tuesday morning certain information will be made public, and when that happens I can promise you that you will wish you'd never met Ahmed al-Adel." Rapp listened for a few seconds and then laughed. "No, Mr. Jackson, that wasn't a threat. If I thought you were a real problem, I wouldn't waste my time threatening you . . . you'd just simply disappear."

Rapp hung up the phone and looked up at Stealey. "There, are you happy?"

As Stealey looked back at Rapp she decided right then and there that she wanted to sleep with him. She had never seen anyone so confident and sure of himself, and at the same time so utterly reckless. There was a laserlike focus about him. He simply didn't care what anyone else thought. The fact that he was married didn't bother her in the slightest. In certain ways it made the proposition even more exciting, more dangerous. Before she had the chance to come up with a good line, one of McMahon's agents came running up.

The young female agent announced, "The New Kent County Sheriff's Department just called. They think they've located the cab and the truck."

EIGHTY-FOUR

The NEST helicopter came in over the garage, hovered for approximately ten seconds, and then departed. A deputy stood in the driveway with his slicker on watching the entire thing. About a minute later a second deputy arrived and then a third, and then they just kept coming. Within ten minutes the long driveway was lined with police cruisers, government sedans, and SUVs.

Debbie Hanousek and her Search Response Team were already on their way when they got the call from the tech onboard the helicopter that the site had come up positive. They arrived in two Suburbans and barged their way past the vehicles that nearly blocked the driveway. When they got near the house they drove right across the lawn to the garage.

Hanousek had her door open before the truck came to a full stop. She grabbed her Baltimore Orioles cap from the dash and hit the soggy ground running. She found her way through the throng of law enforcement officers and saw the trailer. She turned to the group and said, "I need everybody to back up at least a hundred feet."

None of the men had any idea who she was and instead of moving, they just stared at her.

"Guys, I'm a federal agent, and we have reason to believe that trailer contains toxic material. If any of you are still thinking about fathering children, you're going to want to back up right now."

That did the trick. All of the men backed up except one. She surmised that he was probably the owner since he was in shorts. "Sir, are you the owner?"

"My parents are."

"Well, I'm going to need you to back up." One of her techs came running over wearing a backpack that contained a sensitive gamma neutron detector. Hanousek pointed at the trailer and said, "Get right to it."

The man still hadn't budged. "I want to know what's going on right now."

"I can't tell you because I'm not sure, myself, but for your own health you need to back up right now."

"I show up here this morning with my family. My mom and dad aren't here but their car is, and I've got a cab and a truck sitting in their garage and that trailer over there." He came closer. "I have three little kids inside who want to know where their grandparents are, and all of these cops are scaring them to death."

Hanousek could see this guy wasn't going to simply walk away. She grabbed him by the elbow and walked him over to the first man she saw wearing an FBI windbreaker. Hanousek pointed at the agent and looked at the guy in shorts. "Tell this agent everything you just told me and answer his questions." She then looked back at the agent. "I want you to relay everything he tells you directly to Assistant Director McMahon up at CT Watch."

Hanousek marched back to the trailer and hooked up

her earpiece and mike for her secure mobile phone. She hit the speed dial for her boss and a second later he was on the line asking her in his typical SEAL talk for a "sit rep," which to the nonmilitary types was short for situation report.

"It appears to be the trailer. We're running a quick check with the gamma neutron detector right now."

The tech finished his sweep and said, "Gamma five, neutron three."

Hanousek repeated the reading to Reimer.

"That's a little lower than I expected."

"Well, they might have shielded it," replied Hanousek.

All of the sudden a voice Hanousek didn't recognize came on the line. "Paul, what's going on?"

"Debbie, we've got Mitch Rapp from the CIA, and Skip McMahon on the line."

"This is the trailer we've been looking for and it's hot . . . just not as hot as we expected it to be."

"What's that supposed to mean?" Rapp asked.

"They've either shielded it, or the device is no longer in the trailer and we're seeing contamination."

"Debbie," said Reimer. "Get an HPG count and skip the X-ray. Have the FBI drill a hole in the side of the trailer. Do it nice and high. You know the routine."

Hanousek relayed the order to one of her techs who grabbed a black case and ran over to the trailer. Another man pulled out a cordless drill and Hanousek pointed to a spot on the top third of the trailer. It took little effort for the drill to pierce the thin metal skin. A small fiber optic camera with an infrared light on the end was fed through the fresh hole like a snake.

Hanousek cupped the small video screen in her

EIGHTY-FIVE

Rapp and McMahon had both been hovering over the speaker phone, one on each side of the conference table. Neither man asked Hanousek to repeat herself. They'd heard the disappointment in her voice as well as her words. They both stood there in deafening silence, too caught up in trying to calculate the implications of what they'd just learned to respond. The bomb could be anywhere.

McMahon finally straightened up. He placed his hands on his hips and let out a sigh of frustration. "Do you want to call the president, or do you want me to do it?"

Rapp didn't answer right away. He hovered over the speaker phone, palms flat on the table, arms locked, brow furrowed. There was no way these men had simply vanished. Rapp looked up at McMahon. "They didn't just walk out of there. They had some mode of transportation."

Hanousek's voice came out of the speaker. "I don't think so. The son of the owner just told me his parents' car is still here."

"Where are the parents?" asked Rapp.

"No one knows."

"What's their car look like?"

"It's one of those big four-door Cadillacs. Brand-new."

"That doesn't make any sense. Why wouldn't they just take the car and drive out of there?"

"Maybe they met someone there?" McMahon guessed.

Rapp shook his head. "Not likely. They were on the run."

"What about the neighbors?" asked Reimer. "Has anyone checked with the neighbors?"

"That's a good idea," replied McMahon. "I'll make sure the Sheriff's Department gets on it right away."

Rapp finally stood. He turned around and looked at a map on the wall. They were missing something. He'd been on the run before in a foreign country, and none of this made any sense. The Cadillac was a golden opportunity to change vehicles and get away. "Are we sure they only had one vehicle?"

There was a moment of hesitation and then Hanousek said, "I never thought of asking. Hold on a minute."

About five seconds later Rapp could hear Hanousek repeat the question, and then he heard a man say, "No. They only had the one car."

Rapp was still staring at the map trying to get an idea of the lay of the land. He only had a general idea of the house's location. "Debbie, describe for me what the setting is like there. How big is the lot, how close are the neighbors . . . anything that might be useful?"

"It's a nice place . . . big. Probably around ten acres or more. You can't see the neighbors. The road in is real private. You cut through the woods and down a sloping drive to the house and then beyond that there's the river."

Rapp froze for a second, and then returned to hovering over the phone. Something she had just said struck a note of familiarity. "Did you say *river?*"

"Yeah."

"What river?"

"I don't know."

"Ask the son?" Rapp turned back to the map.

"The York River."

Rapp found it on the map and traced it with his finger. He turned quickly and picked up the transcript of al-Adel's interrogation that he had been reading when McMahon and Stealey had come in the room just ten minutes ago. He flipped through the pages searching for the passage that he couldn't quite remember. Rapp ignored both Hanousek and McMahon who tried to ask him what he was doing.

He found the passage and skimmed it. "Debbie," Rapp said earnestly, "ask the son if his dad has a boat."

Her reply came two seconds later. "Yes, he does."

Rapp pinched the bridge of his nose. "Has anyone bothered to check and see if it's there?"

Rapp could hear Hanousek ask the question, but he could barely make out the man's answer. He was saying something about his father never leaving his car parked outside, and that was why he noticed the cab and the truck in the garage right away and he'd heard about it on the news so he called the police right away, and no he hadn't had time to check on the boat.

"The boat!" yelled Rapp. "Go see if it's there."

Rapp grabbed his secure mobile phone and punched in Dr. Akram's number. Someone else answered and told Rapp Akram was busy. "I don't care what he's doing, put him on the phone right now."

Less than five seconds later Akram was on the line. "Mitch."

"Are you with al-Adel?"

"Yes."

"Ask him why they planned on attacking New York by boat." Rapp turned around and looked at the map again, shaking his head and silently cursing himself for not seeing it sooner. It made no sense. Why would a man who couldn't swim decide to get on a boat, when he could simply drive the bomb into the city? The answer was obvious. Because he feared detection.

Akram came back on the line. "He said something about sensors at all the bridges and tunnels leading onto the island."

"Just like D.C." Rapp looked back up at the map.

"What sensors?" asked Akram.

"Never mind, I'll tell you later." Rapp ended the call and a second later Hanousek was back on the speaker phone. He already knew what she was going to say.

"The boat is gone."

EIGHTY-SIX

They were only twenty miles from their destination. The wind had picked up a bit, so it was difficult to tell if the rain had diminished or not, but it looked as if it was clearing to the east. Al-Yamani had been worrying about the weather all morning. His greatest fear was that the entire event would be canceled. Losing the weapon that was to destroy New York was enough of a setback, he did not need another. He had journeyed all this way, and he desperately wanted the president and the other American leaders to suffer Islam's fiery vengeance. The rain would reduce the number of people who were predicted to show up for the event, but al-Yamani would gladly spare thousands of those people their lives if it meant he could kill the president.

Today would mark the beginning of a true global jihad. Al-Yamani would show his fellow Muslims that America was not so mighty after all. He would show them that with great sacrifice even America could be brought to her knees. Al-Yamani knew that America would strike back. He doubted they would have the courage to retaliate with nuclear weapons, but if they did it would still be worth the sacrifice. They would be drawn out from behind their relatively safe borders and forced to fight.

Muslims from around the world would resent them for the godless people that they were. The destruction of the American capital and its leaders would have disastrous economic effects mostly here in America, but in today's global economy everyone would be affected. The master plan, with a strike in Washington and then a follow-up attack in New York, would have undoubtedly shattered the American economy and sent the rest of the world into a global depression. But even so, a nuclear attack in Washington was no small feat. At a bare minimum, it still had the potential to create great economic hardship.

Muslims were used to hardship. They would flourish in a global recession, whereas the fat, lazy Americans would not. They would be seen for who they were in the face of such hardship, and resentment for them would continue to grow. Al-Yamani took great solace in knowing that he was about to ignite a revolution. It was the one thing that helped him ignore the pain that had spread to every single inch of his body.

They were now approaching what looked to be a large bend in the river. Hasan, who was driving the boat, pointed to the left. "I think that is what they call Mount Vernon."

"What is it?" asked al-Yamani who was sitting next to him.

"It is where George Washington lived. The man they named the city after. And up ahead is Sheridan Point. Once we clear it I think we will be able to see the city."

Al-Yamani smiled. "Where is Khaled?"

Hasan yelled for his friend and a moment later he was

at al-Yamani's side. "Get the scientist and have him arm the weapon."

Khaled lowered his voice to a whisper and asked, "When he's done, can I kill him?"

Al-Yamani would have liked to do it himself, but he doubted he had the strength to dispatch even someone as weak as Zubair. "Yes, you may."

"Thank you." Khaled turned and went below. A moment later he returned with the scientist.

Zubair had one of the lead aprons on and was holding his laptop. Al-Yamani was about to tell him to take the apron off, but decided it wasn't worth it. They had seen only a handful of boats all morning, and right now they were the only boat in sight.

"Do you need any help?" asked al-Yamani.

"No. I only need to know when you would like the bomb to go off." Zubair checked his watch. "It is eight minutes past eleven right now."

"Two hours from now."

Zubair tilted his head in a questioning manner. "How much longer until we reach the dock?"

"We should be there in an hour."

"That will not leave us much time to get away."

"It should be more than enough."

Zubair was about to argue and then thought better of it. These other two soldiers of the jihad had been giving him dirty looks for two days, and he got the distinct impression they would like to hurt him. "Very well."

Zubair walked to the stern, stepping out from under the canvas cover and into the falling rain. He had spent months designing the fire set so that he was the only person who could both arm and disarm the weapon. With the aid of his computer it would take only a few seconds to start the countdown. Zubair opened the cooler and briefly admired his work. No longer was the oxidized hunk of poison visible. It was concealed by an outer shell of plastique explosives and a complex maze of blasting caps and six separate firing circuits. If by chance anyone found the bomb, there was no way they would be able to defuse it in time. Each firing circuit was independent of the other, and each one used its own unique set of wiring with multiple false leads built in.

The Pakistani scientist plugged a cable into the data port he'd placed near the top of the weapon and plugged the other end into his laptop. Holding the computer with one hand he pecked the keys with the other. He entered two separate sets of passwords to get to the proper screen and then punched in the count-down sequence. He wanted to be as far away as possible when this filthy weapon exploded. The numbers 02:00:00 appeared on all six detonator screens. Zubair smiled at the knowledge that only he could now stop this explosion from occurring. He entered one last password and then watched as all six screens began counting down in unison.

Zubair closed his computer, unhooked the cable, and then shut the cooler. He turned around to get out of the rain and ran smack into the chest of the imposing Khaled.

"Are you done?"

"Yes," Zubair answered a bit nervously. He did not like the way these two men treated him.

The scientist's spastic demeanor, the laptop, the lead apron, and the rain-slick surface of the deck, all contributed to what happened next. Khaled reached out and grabbed the Pakistani by his free arm. His other arm plunged up and out with the four-inch blade that had been at his side. Instead of piercing the Pakistani's chest like he'd planned, the blade hit the lead apron and stopped dead.

The Pakistani screamed and tried to spin away. In the process, the laptop came up and hit Khaled in the chin, stunning him for a half second. He recovered quickly though and reached out to grab hold of the back of the Pakistani's shirt. This time he would not be thwarted by the apron. He swung his blade viciously and plunged it into the side of the man's neck. When he withdrew his blade the entire back of the boat as well as Khaled were sprayed with bright red blood.

The geyser of blood hit Khaled in the eye, and he lost his balance for a second on the rain-soaked deck. At the same time the Pakistani jerked wildly and broke free of the larger man's grip. With blood spraying out between his clenched fingers, Zubair reeled, stumbled, and then fell over the side of the boat and into the river.

The boat was traveling at twenty mph. Hasan turned to al-Yamani and asked, "What do you want me to do?"

Al-Yamani looked through the rain at the body in the water. Zubair was already sinking, though his arms were slapping the surface, and he was struggling to stay alive. No one could lose that much blood and survive. He looked down at an embarrassed Khaled. He was covered in blood as was a good portion of the deck and the side of the boat, though the rain was already washing it away.

Al-Yamani looked straight ahead and said, "Keep going. Even if they find his body they won't be able to stop us."

EIGHTY-SEVEN

Rapp burst through the door and sprinted across the rain-soaked parking lot to the waiting helicopter. The wind had picked up a bit, and the sky was clearing to the east. The rain would not last much longer, and as soon as it stopped, people would start flocking to the river and the National Mall. Rapp opened the starboard door of the Bell 430 helicopter and jumped in. The door to the executive helicopter clicked shut sealing out the noise of the twin Allison turbine engines and the five spinning rotors.

Four men were sitting in back dressed in plain clothes just as he had requested. One of them carried a long Special Purpose Rifle and the other three carried MP5 submachine guns. All four of the weapons had silencers affixed to the barrels. Rapp would talk to them in a minute when he was done briefing the pilots.

Rapp handed the pilot the photo he'd pulled off the manufacturer's website and said, "This is the boat we're looking for. She's thirty-seven feet long and has *Scandinavian Princess, York River, VA* written in gold letters on the stern."

The pilot handed the photo to the copilot and asked, "Where do you want to start?"

"Let's hit the Key Bridge and work our way down-river from there."

The pilot nodded and the fast executive helicopter lifted off the ground. It's landing gear retracted smoothly up into the belly of the craft and it began slicing eastward.

When they discovered that the boat was missing, Rapp had asked to speak directly to the son. He got a full description of the boat and they pulled it up on the manufacturer's website. The guy's father had named it the *Scandinavian Princess* after his wife. The son had asked Rapp if he thought his parents were all right. Rapp didn't have the heart, or the time, to tell the guy that his parents were most certainly dead, so he lied. Al-Yamani was on a quest to kill thousands, and Rapp doubted he would show compassion for two elderly people, no matter how kind they might be.

When Rapp hung up with the son, he made three phone calls. The first was to General Flood at the Pentagon. Rapp told Flood precisely what he needed, and where he wanted the particular assets staged. Flood listened patiently. Having worked with Rapp many times, the four-star general had complete confidence in the younger man's analytical and tactical ability. He told Rapp the assets would be in place as quickly as possible. Rapp's second phone call was to the CIA. He wanted the helicopter and a four-man security team dressed in plainclothes sent over to the Joint Counterterrorism Center ASAP. The third and final call was to Kennedy. He did not want to talk to the president. He was not going to try and explain what he wanted to do and then have to ask for permission. There was no time for that. Kennedy said she would pass everything on to the president and get back to him.

Rapp looked up at the four men sitting in the back of the helicopter. All of them were reasonably fit and they had that ex-military look. If there was more time, Rapp would have called in a freelance team that he was used to working with, but time was something they were running short on. "Who's in charge?"

Three of the men were sitting directly across from him facing the front and one was sitting next to him with his back to the pilots. The one sitting next to him put a finger in the air and said, "I am."

Rapp stuck out his hand. "Mitch Rapp."

"I know who you are, sir. John Brooks." The man who looked to be about Rapp's age shook his hand. "It's an honor to be working with you today."

"You might not think so after I tell you what we're up to. Are you guys SOG or SWAT?"

"SWAT."

The CIA had a top-notch security force with its own SWAT team as well as a little-known paramilitary outfit called Special Operations Group. Both were staffed predominantly by men and women with military experience. "What's your background?"

"Two tours Green Berets. Stan and Gus here served with the Rangers and Sam was a sniper for the Corps."

Rapp looked at the last man. "You ever killed anyone with that thing? And I need an honest answer." The guy looked to be in his early twenties.

"Not this rifle in particular, sir, but I did a tour in both Afghanistan and Iraq. I've got recorded kills up to six hundred yards."

"You ever shot anyone from over a hundred yards from a helicopter?" A long aerial shot from a moving, vibrating helicopter was one of the most difficult tasks in the business.

"No, sir."

"Have you ever practiced it?"

"No, sir."

This could be a problem. Before Rapp could ask any more questions his phone rang. It was Kennedy.

He flipped it open and said, "Yeah."

"Where are you?"

"I'm airborne and headed toward the river."

"The president wants to implement Operation Ark."

This did not come as a great surprise, but it was irritating nonetheless. Attorney General Stokes had already snuck off to Mount Weather. "I thought we had until noon." He looked at his watch. It was 11:32.

"All things considered, Mitch, I think it's the right move. It would be impossible for the media to get wind of this and go public with it before one o'clock."

"I suppose you're right."

"The bigger problem is that he's considering alerting all the embassies in Washington so they can evacuate their staffs."

"Absolutely not," Rapp yelled.

"I know . . . I know. It's a bad idea. It started out with requests from the British prime minister and the Russian president and grew from there."

"If you evacuate the foreign embassies the press *will* find out for sure, and then all bets are off. Tell the president to honor his word and give me until noon."

"I think I can do that, but there's something else you need to be aware of. Secretary McClellan and Attorney General Stokes are pushing to have the Coast Guard close the river down and block all traffic coming into the city."

"Irene, you have to convince the president to wait. If we tip our hand, al-Yamani will just blow the damn thing. Tell him I'll be over the river in a few minutes, and I'll call you back."

"All right, but I can't promise anything. You're going to have to move fast."

Rapp ended the call and quickly dialed McMahon's number. When the agent answered he asked, "What's up?"

"We're calling the marinas and getting the word out. The good news is boat traffic has been really light and they're fully staffed for the holiday weekend. The bad news is the weather is about to clear and things are starting to pick up."

"What about the Park Police?"

"Their helicopter should be up any minute and over the river about the same time you get there."

"Have them start on the Anacostia just south of the Capitol and work their way down to the Potomac. They can focus on the east side of the river and we'll stick with the west, and don't forget to tell them, I want them flying over land, not over the river, and if they spot the boat, just call out the position and keep on flying. I don't want to do anything that will spook these guys."

"I already told them. What do you want to do with the D.C. police? Should we have them hit the marinas?"

"Not yet. We've got a little time to work with. What else do you have?"

"The Harbor Police has a couple boats in the water and they've been alerted. Reimer has his people searching the city, and he says he should have a helicopter up with all of the sensing equipment soon. This rain has been a real blessing. The Coast Guard says boat traffic is really light on the river."

Rapp looked out the window of the helicopter.

"That's not going to last, unfortunately." Rapp had a house out on the Chesapeake Bay and he knew what happened on holiday weekends when the skies cleared. "As soon as the rain stops, they'll all head out at once. The river will be packed."

"Yeah, I know. Homeland Security wants to shut down the river and close all roads coming into the city."

"I heard. I swear they're going to screw this whole thing up." Rapp ran a hand through his thick black hair and shook his head. "What else do you have?"

"I've got the Hostage Rescue Team on their way back from Richmond. They should be here in about thirty minutes, but in the meantime we've got the Washington Field Office's SWAT team on alert."

"Skip, I don't want to argue with you over this, but unless this boat is beached somewhere, SEAL Team Six is going to handle the takedown. They train for this type of stuff more than anyone else. Vessel takedowns are their specialty."

"You're going to have problem then, because Attorney General Stokes made it very clear to everyone before he left that he wants the Bureau to handle this situation. Not the military and definitely not the CIA, and according to my boss, the president agrees."

"Well, the attorney general doesn't know his head from his ass."

"Mitch, you'd better be real careful here," warned McMahon. "This isn't your jurisdiction, so don't go running off like some cowboy."

"If you want these guys, you'd better find them before I do, because I'm not going to wait around for HRT to get their asses in position, and I sure as hell am not going to wait for a bunch of people sitting in a bunker sixty miles from ground zero to give me the green light."

"Those people you are referring to were elected by the American people to make these decisions."

"Skip, the last thing I fucking need right now is to be micromanaged by a bunch of fucking people who don't know the first thing about running a takedown, so do me a favor and keep them off my back. If HRT gets there first, they can have the honors, but if the SEALs are in position first, it's their show and I can guarantee you the president will agree with me."

"Then you'd better get him to tell my bosses because they think this is all FBI."

"I will. Call me if you learn anything. We're almost to the river."

EIGHTY-EIGHT

POTOMAC RIVER

Mustafa al-Yamani had tears in his eyes. It was exactly as he'd dreamt it would be night after night for nearly a year. They rounded a slight jog in the river, the clouds parted and beams of sun shown down brightly on the massive dome of the U.S. Capitol. The swordlike Washington Monument shot upward, marking the center of the National Mall, and the cap of the Jefferson Memorial lay in the foreground, partially concealed by a row of trees. He could not see the White House but he knew where it was, just beyond the Washington Monument. He had studied the maps over and over until each detail was seared into his memory, and now he would destroy it. Everything in sight would be leveled in a little more than an hour.

The fathers of America had designed their capital city to form a crucifix. The Washington Monument marked the center, with the Capitol and the Lincoln Memorial forming the longer center line while the Jefferson Memorial and the White House formed the shorter horizontal line. The Americans were modern-day crusaders trying to stamp out Islam. They'd even backed the Jews in retaking the Holy Land. It was time to begin a new crusade. A *crusade* for the people of Islam.

Al-Yamani smiled at the view in front of him. It was just as he had dreamt it would be; the sun shining down through the parting clouds, the green trees and blue water. For the sun to come out at the exact moment when he laid eyes on the city was further proof that Allah was guiding them.

Al-Yamani placed a frail hand on Hasan's shoulder. "You have done well. There is nothing they can do to stop us now. Continue to the spot by the Tidal Basin and drop the anchor. I am going below to pray. You and Khaled may join me when you are ready."

Al-Yamani called out for Khaled. The man came up the stairs to the bridge area and stood by al-Yamani.

"I do not think I have the strength to walk. Would you please carry me below?"

Khaled nodded, choking back tears. He bent over and cradled the bravest man he had ever known. Looking like a man clutching his decrepit and dying father, he walked him down the stairs and into the cabin where he gently set him on the floor. Al-Yamani kneeled on the floor, brought his palms together, and began reciting a *sura*.

EIGHTY-NINE

The blue-and-white helicopter flew through the sky a mere 300 feet above the treetops of the lush Potomac River Valley. When they reached the tall Francis Scott Key Bridge, they slowed from 140 mph to 80 mph and dropped down another hundred feet. The boat would not be able to navigate the river any further upstream than this. The pilots cut around the east side of Roosevelt Island and took the Georgetown Channel. They passed a series of docks on the east bank where large tour boats where docked. So far the *Scandinavian Princess* was nowhere in sight.

Rapp continued looking out the port window and called General Flood on his phone. "General, we're coming up on the Roosevelt Bridge. Can you give me an idea what the picture looks like downriver?"

"The AWACS is tracking twenty-six contacts within ten miles of the capital. That's up from eighteen just five minutes ago."

"How many of those contacts are headed north?"

"I don't know. Let me check."

Rapp could hear the chairman of the joint chiefs talking to someone. He came back with an answer in short order.

"Twenty-one of the twenty-six are headed upriver."

"General I want the AWACS controller to vector us in on each contact. Find out what channel they want my pilot on." Flood came back with a quick answer. Rapp passed the information on to the pilot and then asked for the status on SEAL Team Six.

"They're about twenty minutes away, but we've got a slight problem."

Rapp noticed a note of hesitation in Flood's voice. "What's that?"

"The president just informed me that Team Six is to be used only if the FBI's Hostage Rescue Team is not in position."

"And what did you say to that?"

"I said, yes, sir, and informed the CO of Team Six of the situation."

Rapp swore and looked out the port window at the Lincoln Memorial. "When is HRT expected to be in position?"

"I'm hearing thirty minutes."

It matched the same information he'd received from McMahon. "All right. I might be calling you back and asking to be patched directly through to Six's commanding officer. Any problem with that?"

"That depends on what you want to talk to him about."

"You know exactly what I want to talk to him about."

"Then we're going to have a problem. I can't simply insert you into the chain of command. Not after what the president just said."

"General," interrupted Rapp, "someone has to be calling the shots. You tell me . . . do you think that person should be on-site or sitting in a blast-proof bunker up by Camp David?"

"Mitch, I know what you're saying, but it's the way it has to be. If you find that boat before HRT gets up there I'll patch you through to Six's CO, and I'll tell the president we should let you make the call, but as soon as HRT is on the scene, you and I are going to have to step aside."

Rapp had no intention of stepping aside, but there was no point in telling Flood that. "All right, general, I'll be in touch." Rapp ended the call and continued scanning the river.

They passed over a boat headed north and his heart began to race a bit. The vessel fit the general description of the one they were looking for. As they continued past it Rapp used a pair of binoculars to try and get a read on the boat's name. The writing was in blue and he could only make out the first word. The boat was the *Maryland* something. It was not the one they were looking for.

The helicopter climbed slightly as they passed over a series of four bridges and then dropped back down. Reagan National Airport was a half a mile ahead on the starboard side and they now had to contend with commercial air traffic. They were coming up on Hains Point where the Anacostia River split off to the East.

The Park Police helicopter entered the picture flying along the opposite bank about a mile ahead of the CIA helicopter. Rapp spotted several boats, one too small and the other too big. Twenty seconds later they passed the Washington Sailing Marina. The parking lot was full, and he counted at least four boats leaving the marina. This search would get more difficult with each passing minute. They passed several more sail boats and then Rapp winced as he saw the emergency lights sitting atop the Harbor Police boat below. Rapp hoped they'd been given the right orders. Anyone who saw these guys was to make no attempt to stop them. They were to call it in and go about their business as if nothing unusual had been noticed.

Up ahead was the Woodrow Wilson Memorial Bridge. It spanned the river carrying the Beltway traffic back and forth between Virginia and Maryland. They flew over the tandem bridge and a few more boats. None of them was the one they were looking for.

About another mile down river the pilot turned around and said, "The Park Police chopper just said they have a possible I.D. on the boat. They couldn't get a read on the name but they said the length and make appear to match."

Rapp looked through the front windshield at the other helicopter and then looked down at the river. There were two boats in sight. "Which one is he talking about?"

"The one closer to us. Right in the center."

"Slow up a bit and work your way inland a little more so we don't spook him."

Rapp continued looking over the pilot's shoulder until they were within a quarter mile and then he went back to the port-side window. With binoculars in hand he knelt on the ground and looked down at the boat. At first he didn't think it was their boat and then realized it was the canvas sun top that made it look different.

The two vessels passed each other, one headed north and the other south. Rapp peered through the binoculars trying to catch the name, but something was in the way. He could only catch the first letter. The writing was gold but all he could see was the letter 'S.' Nor could he make out the man who was driving the boat. He was concealed by the canvas top. Almost as an afterthought he realized what the object was that was obscuring the boat's name. Rapp focused in on the large white cooler lashed to the swim platform, and then lowered the binoculars.

He thought of something that Paul Reimer had said and then calmly told the pilot, "Tell the AWACS controller to mark that boat, and then start doubling back far enough away from the river so they can't see us."

NINETY

Rapp tried to recall the bomb-damage assessment Reimer had given him while he waited for the senior energy official to answer his phone. This thing was supposed to be in the fifteen-kiloton range, with a warhead roughly the size of a volleyball. It would leave a crater a half mile across and vaporize everything above ground for one and a half miles. The blast effects would cause damage as far away as ten miles, and the radioactive plume would go as far as the prevailing wind could take it.

When Reimer finally answered, Rapp asked, "Paul, we've found the boat, and I spotted something lashed to the aft swim deck. Would this device fit in one of the those big fishing coolers?"

Reimer was at the DOE's Germantown facility with his top people. "It would depend on what they were using for an explosive charge, but yes . . . I suppose it would."

"All right . . ."

"Where is the boat?"

"It's about a mile south of the Woodrow Wilson Bridge traveling north."

"Hold on, let me look at the map. A mile south of the

Woodrow Wilson Bridge," Reimer repeated. "That's eight miles from the White House and the Capitol, and seven from the Pentagon. Mitch, we have to stop this boat as soon as possible. I won't waste your time giving you the details, but there is a consensus between our scientists and the Russians that this thing will not reach its full yield of fifteen kilotons. If we can keep the device outside a six-mile radius, I think we can save everything north and east of the National Mall. The Pentagon also stands a good chance of surviving the blast because of the way it's designed."

"What about the radiation?"

"The wind is from the east and it's picking up. Rural Virginia and possibly West Virginia would get hit hard with fallout, but if the wind stays constant, downtown Washington should be spared."

"So the sooner we stop this thing the better."

"Absolutely."

"Where's your Search Response Team?"

"One's on their way back up from Richmond, and the other one's downtown by the National Mall."

"Get the one downtown a helicopter ASAP, and I'll call you back with further instructions."

Rapp closed his phone and poked his head up into the cockpit. "The AWACS give you a speed yet?"

"Twenty mph."

"Ask them how long it'll take for the boat to reach the Woodrow Wilson Bridge."

The pilot asked the question, and about five seconds later he had an answer. "They'll be at the bridge in three minutes and twenty seconds approximately."

"Where's that Park Police chopper?"

"He's still headed downriver."

"Tell him to turn around and hightail it back up here.

I want him flying low and fast right up the east side of the river."

SEAL Team Six was still a good fifteen minutes away, and the HRT would take even longer. At twenty mph they would cover a mile every three minutes. By the time SEAL Team Six was here, the boat would be within three miles of the White House. He looked out the cockpit window at the Beltway and the Woodrow Wilson Bridge and said, "All right, here's the plan."

RAPP EXPLAINED IN detail to the pilots exactly what he wanted to do, and then did the same with the four men from the CIA's SWAT team. The helicopter landed at Jones Point Park on the western bank of the Potomac, just north of the Woodrow Wilson Bridge where they were well concealed from the river traffic. Two men got out and ran down to the river's edge while Rapp and Brooks hit the quick-release latches on the helicopter's starboard and port doors so they could take them off and get them out of their way. Rapp then jogged down to the riverbank with his phone to his ear. He didn't have time to call all the people who he should, so he decided to just call one.

When Flood came on the line Rapp said, "General, I'm down here under the Woodrow Wilson Bridge, and I think I've found our boat."

"The Woodrow Wilson Bridge? Where in the hell is that?"

"It's where the Beltway crosses the Potomac River about six miles south of you."

"And where is the boat?"

"About a mile south headed upriver."

"Jesus Christ!"

"I know. I just went over everything with Paul

Reimer. He says it's crucial that we stop this bomb before it gets any further north. I've got a four-man tactical team with me from Langley and I'm going to take this boat down when it comes under the bridge. That is unless you want me to wait around for the HRT to arrive . . . in which case you should be able to look out your window at the Pentagon and watch the takedown in person."

"If you think you have the assets to handle the job, Mitch, then do it and do it quickly."

"I thought that's what you'd say. Just in case something goes wrong, your AWACS has a bead on this boat. So if we fail, have them vector Six's strike team in on the target, and tell them not to hit the cooler sitting on the aft swim deck because I think that's where the bomb is." Rapp reached the edge of the river and looked out past the bridge's concrete supports. Traffic was whizzing by overhead on the six-lane interstate. "I've got to go now, general. I'll call you back in a few minutes when I'm in control of the vessel."

Rapp closed the phone and shoved it into his breast pocket. He could see the boat heading their way and behind it the Park Police helicopter was closing fast. He checked his watch and then said to Brooks's men, "I'd grab that spot right over there in those bushes."

"I was thinking the same thing," answered the former Marine sniper.

"All right, get ready, and don't shoot unless you see a gun or we give you the word." Rapp took one last peek at the oncoming boat and then ran back to the helicopter.

He climbed in on the starboard side and poked his head up in the cockpit. "You guys have any questions?"

Both pilots shook their heads.

"Good. What's their ETA?"

"Just under a minute."

"And the Park Police helicopter?"

"I don't know."

"See if you can find out. The last thing we want is a midair collision."

While the pilot checked with the AWACS controller, Rapp sat down in the aft-facing portside seat. He loosened the seat belt as far as it would go and then fastened it. With one of the silenced MP5s in hand he sat on the edge of the seat, shouldered the weapon, and leaned against the seat belt. He was left-handed, so the position allowed him to clear the door frame with little difficulty. He looked at Brooks, who was sitting directly across from him. The team leader did the same thing, and both men flashed each other the thumbs-up sign.

Rapp looked at the former Ranger who had given him his silenced MP5. "Stan, remember . . . don't draw your pistol until you hit the deck. We'll cover you. Go straight for the helm, and don't pull back on the throttles until the helicopter is clear. The pilot is going to be matching speed at twenty mph going sideways, so if you pull back on the throttles too fast you might get your head chopped off."

The former Ranger nodded.

"Here we go," yelled the pilot.

The helicopter lifted slowly from the rain-soaked grass and moved into a hover twenty feet off the ground. They were now perfectly parallel with the bridge. Slowly, almost imperceptibly, they began to move forward, staying hidden behind the bulky concrete span that carried traffic from one state to another. They moved out over the river foot by foot and then stopped a little over a third of the way across. Even though it was expected, the arrival of the Park Police helicopter was startling. It blew over the bridge and then dipped back down to a mere fifty feet off the water, its engine and rotors roaring.

The CIA helicopter began inching its way forward again, in an effort to get to the exact place where the boat would appear. Rapp was leaning out as far as he could to try and get a view of the boat as it came under the bridge. A few seconds later the bow poked out from the shadows, and then the windscreen. As the boat came into the clear the helicopter began to descend and then slide sideways. The pilots did a perfect job bringing them in right behind the boat and then matching its speed and course.

Rapp looked through the hoop sight of his submachine gun and zeroed in on the head of a man who was staring through the windscreen of the boat at the Park Police helicopter that was racing upriver. The man slowly turned, realizing that something was now behind them. Rapp watched him intently, looking for the slightest reason to squeeze the trigger. The helicopter was closing distance on the boat. They were no more than thirty yards away. Only a few seconds had ticked by, but for Rapp, the scene was unfolding in slow motion.

The man, who was tall and dark-skinned with short black hair, turned and looked directly at Rapp. In that fraction of a second, the man did something that was entirely unexpected given the situation. He smiled.

Rapp had his weapon pulled firmly against his left shoulder and at the very first hint of the smirk he squeezed the trigger twice in less than a half second. Instantly, the muzzle of the submachine gun moved to

NINETY-ONE

POTOMAC RIVER

The boat started a lazy right turn that would only get worse if they didn't get control of the helm quickly. Fortunately, the two CIA pilots were good. They adjusted to the new heading and brought the portside door of the chopper right over the aft sundeck. Rapp kept his weapon trained on the cabin, and when they were hovering a manageable six feet from the deck he yelled, "Go! Go!"

The man leaped from a squatted position and landed as he'd been taught in jump school, with his weight evenly distributed on both feet and his knees slightly bent. He rolled to his left and came up reaching for his pistol. As soon as he was on his way up the steps to the helm, Rapp yanked his seat belt free and jumped after him. He hit a little harder than he had planned, but he ignored the pain that shot up through his left knee and moved for the steps that led to the cabin.

His thick black silencer probed the shadows first. He could see someone on the floor, but the figure had its back to him. Rapp knew there would be a head down the steps and to his right. Other than that, there were no other places to hide, with the exception of the storage compartment tucked up under the bow. Not having the time or the backup, he jumped to the bottom of the steps, let loose an eight round burst into the closed door of the head, and then yanked it open. It was empty.

Rapp spun and kicked the man who was prostrate on the carpeted floor. His foot caught the man square in the stomach and flipped him onto his side and then back. Rapp leveled his weapon at the man's head and studied his face. The first thing he noticed was the blood dripping from the corners of the man's mouth. Then he noticed the bulging, bloodshot eyes and the burned, blotchy, peeling skin. The guy looked like someone had stuck him in a microwave.

Even so, there was something vaguely familiar about him. Rapp's brow furrowed and then he said, "Mustafa al-Yamani."

Al-Yamani smiled the vacant smile of a true believer, and coughed up more blood. "You are too late," he said as blood oozed from the corners of his mouth. "There is nothing you can do to stop us."

"Where is Zubair?" Rapp placed the tip of the silencer against al-Yamani's forehead.

"He's dead," al-Yamani smiled, showing his bleeding gums, "and he's the only one who can disarm the weapon." He began to laugh. Almost immediately, though, his entire body was racked with a convulsive spasm that sent more than just blood spewing from his mouth.

Rapp forced al-Yamani's head into the ground with the tip of the silencer and said, "Have a nice time in hell, Mustafa." He squeezed the trigger just once and left the twitching corpse to go back topside.

Rapp burst back onto the deck and signaled for the helicopter to back off. He then took over the helm, turned the boat around, and pushed both throttles to the stops. The engines groaned loudly and the bow came out of the water a few feet. Rapp looked back at the cooler and feared the worst. What a hell of a way to die.

Rapp grabbed his secure digital phone and called Reimer. When the voice on the other end answered he said, "Paul, we've got control of the boat, and we're heading away from the city. You got any bright ideas?"

"Is the weapon armed?"

"I think so."

"How do you know . . . have you seen it?"

"No. I asked al-Yamani where Zubair was and he told me he was dead. He also said Zubair's the only one who can disarm the bomb. So I'm assuming it's armed." Rapp turned around and looked at the cooler again. "Do you want me to open it up and look at it?"

"No!" Reimer shouted. "Whatever you do don't touch it! I've got a team on the way. They're lifting off from the Mall right now. Where are you?"

"We're going back under the Wilson Bridge."

"Seven miles from the White House," said Reimer. "How fast are you going?"

Rapp looked at the dashboard. "Thirty-five miles an hour, and I think I'm topped out."

"A little over a mile every two minutes. That's good. The further away you get the better."

"Paul, I'm not some damn Kamikaze. I hope you have a better plan than me simply taking this thing as far down river as possible until it blows."

"I do . . . I do, but just getting you ten miles away could make a huge difference. My people are coming and the Blue Team is on its way up from Little Creek. Keep heading south at top speed for at least six minutes. My people will come up on your six and they'll find a place for you to dock. Then we'll take it off your hands."

Rapp looked back at the cooler again. The two men he had shot were lying one on top of another where Sam had dumped them. For the moment, Rapp saw no better option than to maintain course and speed. "All right, I'll keep an eye out for them."

Rapp hung up and looked at Sam, "Radio the chopper and tell them to follow us."

Rapp kept one hand on the wheel, and with the other he began unzipping the canvas top. When he had it halfway across the windscreen Sam took over and finished the job. The top flapped free and floated away to land in the river. Rapp checked his speed and fuel level and hunkered down for the six-minute dash.

THE MARINA WAS almost exactly three miles from the bridge on the Virginia side. Rapp watched the DOE Bell 412 helicopter circle and come in for a landing. Rapp came in hot, running the engines at full throttle until the last possible moment. He nearly swamped two smaller boats that were on their way out through the channel. The drivers gestured wildly and cursed the crazy son of a bitch who was driving the thirty-seven-foot cabin cruiser so recklessly. Rapp was headed straight for the marina office. Those who hadn't gone to watch the helicopter land in the parking lot looked at the oncoming vessel with fear in their eyes.

Rapp yanked back on the throttles, left them in neutral for only half a second, and then slammed them into reverse. The engines groaned as they strained to slow the forward movement of the boat, and people scrambled in every direction. The boat stopped just twenty feet from the main pier, but its building wake kept coming, rising up over the wood planks and slamming tethered boats against pilings and gangways.

Rapp immediately eased up on the port engine while slipping the starboard engine back into the forward gear. The boat began spinning until its aft was pointed toward shore and then Rapp reversed the starboard engine, sliding the boat backward toward the boat ramp.

A middle-aged man in plaid Bermuda shorts, docksiders, and a polo shirt came out of the office and started yelling. "Who in the hell do you think you are?"

Rapp put the engines in neutral and ignored the man. "Sam, grab those lines and tie us up."

Three men came running across the parking lot, each of them loaded down with a case or bag under each arm. They stopped at the top of the ramp and set their equipment down. The man in the ridiculous Bermuda shorts wasn't done though, and he stormed down the dock shaking his fist at Rapp.

"Listen here, you jackass. In all my years as a sailor I have never seen a bigger bonehead move." The man came right up to the edge of the boat. "Just who in the hell do you think you are?"

"I'm a federal agent," replied Rapp, as he pointed at the dead bodies laying on the aft sundeck. "I killed those two right there, there's a third one down in the cabin, and unless you want to be number four I'd advise you to get your ass off this dock and out of my face right now!"

Dumbfounded, the man just stood staring at the two bodies.

"Now!" Rapp yelled. The man turned and walked as quickly away from the dock as his skinny legs could carry him. A crowd of people were beginning to gather near the top of the boat ramp. Rapp looked up at them and said to Sam, "Radio the helicopter and tell them to land in the parking lot. Have them help you get these people out of here and secure a perimeter."

One of Reimer's guys was wearing a backpack. He walked down the boat ramp and right into the water. By the time he reached the swim platform the water was almost up to his crotch.

"They had to put the doors back on. They'll be here in less than two minutes."

Rapp nodded. "Go up there and tell those people to get the hell out of here."

The tech stood sideways in front of the cooler for several seconds and then yelled back to the other two men, "Gamma eleven, neutron six."

Rapp watched with great interest. "What in the hell does that mean?"

"It means it's hot." The SRT tech walked quickly back up the ramp, his pants soaked.

Rapp looked up at the still-gathering crowd. Sam was trying to push them back. Several people were pointing and asking questions, while others were looking at the CIA helicopter that was now circling overhead looking for a place to land.

Rapp pulled out his pistol and fired two shots into the water. The loud reports got everyone's attention. They all stopped what they were doing and turned to look at him. "I want this parking lot cleared right now Goddammit! This is an emergency!"

Everyone finally got the hint and began scrambling for their vehicles. Rapp grabbed his phone and dialed Reimer's number. "Paul, it's Mitch. I have an idea. Why don't we load the device on a helicopter and get it the hell out of here?"

"That's not how we do it, Mitch."

"Why?"

"We have to conduct diagnostics first. Ideally we don't want to move it at all, especially by air."

"Why?"

"An aerial burst increases the range and destruction of the blast. Just sit tight and let my people work. The Blue Team should be there in five minutes, and we'll have the device defused in no time."

Rapp glanced down at the bomb. "Excuse me for not sharing your confidence, but when al-Yamani said that only Zubair could defuse this baby, I think he meant it."

"Mitch, these bomb techs from SEAL Team Six are the best. They'll be able to figure out the fire set."

"And what if they can't?" asked a clearly skeptical Rapp.

"It's never happened before, Mitch."

"Is that in practice or reality?"

"Both."

"Bullshit. You're telling me these guys have defused live nukes before?"

"No . . . not live nukes, but they deal with working exercise devices all the time. The principle is the same."

"I hope to hell you're right."

NINETY-TWO

The Blue Team arrived aboard two gray U.S. Navy Seahawk helicopters. The large birds set down in the parking lot and a half dozen men piled out of each helicopter. At least six of them were dressed from head to toe in black combat gear and heavily armed. These men immediately fanned out to secure a perimeter. Two of the men were wearing light blue anticontamination suits, with sealed boots, helmets, and gloves. The other four men were dressed in desert fatigues.

Rapp was still at the helm of the *Scandinavian Princess*. He watched the SEALs unload their equipment and consult with the members of the DOE Search Response Team. He checked his watch. It was 12:08. Rapp had gotten over the jitters that this thing was going to blow any second. He was sure that al-Yamani wanted to get it as close as possible to the heart of the capital, and also to kill the president and the rest of the leaders who were to be present at the dedication of the new WWII memorial. That event was to begin at 1:00, so if Rapp was forced to bet, he'd say they probably had another fifty-two minutes until the bomb was set to go off.

In his mind, though, those were crucial minutes that could be used to get the bomb further away from the city. Rapp looked at the four helicopters in the parking lot, and decided to call Reimer back. "Paul, listen to me. I'm guessing the weapon is set to go off at one o'clock. I still think we should put it on a helicopter and get it as far away from the city as possible."

"Mitch, I already told you, we need to do the diagnostics first."

"Can't they do that in the air?"

"What if the terrorists placed an altimeter in the fire set and the second this thing gets a hundred feet off the ground it blows?"

Rapp hadn't thought of that. "All right, but what's the plan if the SEALs can't defuse it?"

"We're working on that right now."

Rapp watched the two men in the sealed suits walk down the boat ramp carrying a piece of equipment. "What do you mean, you're working on it?"

"Our first choice would be to take it out to sea."

"That's assuming you'll have enough time. It's at least a hundred miles to the Eastern Shore."

"And the beaches are packed right now, and the wind is blowing to the west, and that's just for starters, Mitch. We game this stuff all the time. The environmental impact, the economic impact, we've looked at it from every angle."

"If taking it out to sea isn't going to work, then what's the other option?"

"The only other option is to take it someplace remote, where the blast and fallout will do the least damage."

"That's it?" said a shocked Rapp. "That's our last and best option?"

Reimer didn't answer right away. "There is one other option, but it has never been fully studied. I don't think the president would ever authorize it. I know the Pentagon would flat out say no."

"Why?"

"Because it involves destroying a multibillion-dollar government facility."

One of the SEALs in desert fatigues came jogging down the dock toward Rapp. "What facility?" asked Rapp.

"Mitch, that's the president on the other line. I'm going to have to call you back."

"Don't . . ." The line went dead and Rapp cursed.

"Mr. Rapp?"

It was the SEAL who was now standing next to the boat. Rapp let out a long sigh and said, "Yes?"

"Lieutenant Troy Mathews." The officer stuck out his hand. "General Flood told me to keep you in the loop."

He shook the officer's hand. "What's the status with this thing?" Rapp pointed at the cooler. The two men in space suits were moving a device around the outside of the cooler, pausing every few feet and then moving on.

"That's a portable X-ray machine. They're snapping some photos for us so we know what's inside."

"Lieutenant," one of the men in the space suits yelled. "I'm counting six separate firing systems."

"Six?" the officer asked in a shocked voice.

"Yes, and I think they used plastique for a molded charge. It's covered with at least two dozen blasting caps."

"Six firing systems? You've got to be shitting me." Mathews looked toward the parking lot and shouted,

"Mike, I need the drill and the fiber-optic camera right away."

Rapp found none of this comforting. "What's going on?"

"I'm not sure." The lieutenant started rolling up his sleeves as he climbed in the boat.

As the lieutenant stepped over the dead bodies Rapp asked, "How long is it going to take you to defuse this bad boy?"

"It all depends on how they're wired, but I can tell you it isn't going to be a cakewalk."

Rapp watched as one of the lieutenant's men ran down the ramp and into the water, where he handed over a cordless drill and a black bag. A hole was carefully drilled through the top of the cooler, and then the pencil-thin camera head was delicately inserted. The lieutenant knelt down over the cooler and watched the small TV screen as his men took several minutes to try and glimpse as much as possible.

Finally, they pulled the camera out and one of them said, "No trip wires, sir. I think it's safe to open."

The lieutenant placed both hands on the top of the cooler and slowly lifted the lid. Rapp stood behind him looking down into the jumbled mass of wires and counted the six separate sets of red numbers. They had fifty-three minutes until the bomb blew.

Rapp swore and then said, "Lieutenant, I need a no bullshit assessment. Can you and your team disarm this thing in less than fifty-three minutes?"

The lieutenant studied the wiring, looking at it from the left and then the right. "I'm not sure."

"Well, *I'm not sure* isn't going to cut it. You see any altimeter in there, or anything else that would preclude us from putting the device on a helicopter, and getting it farther away from the city?"

"No." Mathews looked at his two men in the space suits. "Guys?"

They both shook their heads.

Another minute ticked off on all six screens and it was Mathews who swore this time.

They'd never make it to the ocean in time. Rapp's hands were suddenly covered in sweat. "Lieutenant Mathews, this is what we're going to do. I want your men to place this cooler in the back of that blue-and-white helicopter sitting in the parking lot."

"I'm going to have to call the Pentagon for an okay on that."

In a very calm, but firm voice, Rapp said, "Lieutenant, we don't have time to argue. While your men are putting the device on the helicopter, you are going to assess your chances of defusing it, and I'm," Rapp held up his phone, "going to call the president and General Flood. If you can't tell me with absolute certainty that you can stop this bomb from going off, the most important next step is to get it as far away from the city as possible."

The lieutenant stared down at the jumble of multi-colored wires and then nodded. "Okay . . . it sounds like a reasonable precaution."

"Then let's move it quickly and carefully."

"Mike . . . Joe," Mathews yelled. "Bring down the lead blankets. We're going to move it."

Rapp got off the boat and started walking down the dock. He dialed a number and put his phone up against his ear. He was going to call the president, but not just yet. There was one other person he needed to talk to first.

NINETY-THREE

The rope that held the cooler in place was cut, and with Lieutenant Mathews supervising, a lead blanket was draped over the cooler and it was carried up the boat ramp and placed in the back of the Bell 430 helicopter. Two older members of the Blue Team as well as one of the Search Response Team members climbed in the back of the chopper and studied the device. Then one-by-one the three of them exited the helicopter, shaking their heads.

Rapp watched all this while he stood in front of the helicopter, his phone stuck to his ear. He guessed correctly that the two older members of the Blue Team were both master chiefs. Master chiefs were the backbone of the SEAL Teams, and when it came to explosives they were some of the most knowledgeable people in the world.

Rapp looked at the two pilots who were still in the cockpit of the CIA helicopter. He held up his right index finger and began twirling it in the air. The pilots nodded and started flipping switches and checking displays. Rapp's mind was already made up. Every second was going to count, and he wasn't going to sit around wasting a single one of them.

He began walking toward the helicopter and said into the phone, "So one of your scientists thought this up?"

"Yes," answered Reimer.

"And you think it'll work?"

"I know it'll work. We've run all the calculations."

The engines on the helicopter fired up and a second later the rotors began turning. "Paul, you get all the facts you need to convince the president. I'll call you back in a minute when I'm in the air."

Rapp didn't have to go find Lieutenant Mathews because he was already on his way over. "I need an answer. Can you do it or not?"

"My chiefs say we've got a fifty-fifty shot at best."

"Not good enough," said Rapp, who immediately turned away from the lieutenant and toward the helicopter.

"What did the president say?"

"He said if you can't guarantee success, he wants this device as far away from the capital as possible." Rapp hadn't spoken to the president, but he was sure that at least on this, they would share the same opinion.

Mathews followed Rapp, "Where are you taking it?"

"I'm not sure just yet," Rapp lied. He got in the back of the helicopter, closed the door, and asked the pilots, "What's the top speed of this baby?"

"She's rated for one hundred and sixty miles per hour, but at that speed we can only stay up for approximately one hundred miles, depending on wind conditions."

"We're not going that far. Okay, let's get the hell out of here. Head due west as fast as you can and as low as you dare. Once we clear the city by at least ten miles we'll start heading north. I'll give you an exact heading in a few minutes."

Rapp sat down, and as the helicopter lifted off the ground, he did the math in his head. They had to go approximately sixty miles. At top speed the helicopter would cover 2.66 miles every minute. That meant it would take less than thirty minutes, not counting takeoff and landing, to get there. He rounded it up to thirty-five just to be safe, and then moved the heavy lead blanket and lifted the lid to the cooler. The closest LED told him the bomb would detonate in forty-six minutes. That wouldn't give him much time to handle the rest but it was doable. Rapp set the timer on his watch and covered the cooler back up with the blanket.

His phone rang and he answered it instantly. "Yep."

"Are you ready?" It was Reimer.

"Yeah, we're already in the air."

"I'll patch us through."

There were a couple of clicks on the line and then Rapp heard the president's voice. "Mitch?"

Rapp leaned his head against the leather headrest. "Yes, Mr. President."

"Good work today."

Rapp was caught slightly off guard. For some reason he was expecting to get his ass chewed out. "Thank you, sir."

"Paul tells me that our technical people aren't sure they can stop this thing from going off. Is that what you're hearing?"

"Yes, sir. I was told defusing it was a fifty-fifty proposition at best."

"How much time do we have?"

Rapp looked at his watch. "Forty-five minutes, sir."

Reimer quickly interjected, "That's not enough time to take it out to sea, Mr. President."

"Then what do you propose we do?"

"We have two options, sir. We can dump it in the Chesapeake, in which case the immediate fatalities will be limited to the number of boaters in the area, though due to the fact that the bay is not very deep the fallout will be significant. We'd end up with a sizable cloud of radioactive vapor that would spread for hundreds of miles, and since the wind is coming from the east, it would move toward the more populated areas."

"Could it reach Washington?"

"Possibly."

"How many fatalities?"

"Initially . . . probably somewhere around a hundred, but the fallout could drive that number easily above a thousand as cancer rates would skyrocket. It would also take decades for the Chesapeake to rebound, as well as the contaminated surrounding areas that take the brunt of the fallout."

There was silence. "What's the second option?"

"The second option, sir, is a bit controversial, but it is also the one that would result in the fewest casualties, and do the least harm to the environment."

"Let's hear it, then."

"Take the bomb by helicopter to Mount Weather and put it inside. Then close the blast doors to limit the fallout."

Mount Weather was a secure hardened facility built in the 1950s, located fifty-five miles from the White House. It was the main location in the Federal Relocation Arc, a system of just over a hundred shelters in five states designed to house key government employees in the case of a nuclear attack or other emergency.

"Mount Weather!" someone shouted. "I'm at Mount Weather! You can't bring the damn thing here!"

Rapp recognized the voice as belonging to the attorney general. Rapp pictured the look of panic in the man's face and smiled. Every cloud had a silver lining.

"Mr. President," said the Director of Homeland Security, "Mount Weather is the backbone of our emergency command-and-control system. The replacement cost would be staggering . . . it would be at least several billion dollars."

"We're a rich country," answered Valerie Jones. "We'll build a new one. Mr. President, you can't drop this thing in the Chesapeake Bay."

Rapp was slightly taken aback. He thought this was probably the first time he'd ever agreed with Jones on anything.

"FEMA has offices located on that mountain, sir," countered Secretary McClellan. He was referring to the Federal Emergency Management Agency. "And the Blue Ridge Mountains are as much a national treasure as the Chesapeake Bay. The Appalachian Trail runs within two miles of the place."

"I think the FEMA facilities will survive the blast, Mr. President," Reimer said. "Mount Weather is carved out of the most dense rock on the East Coast, and it has two sets of vaultlike blast doors that are each five feet thick."

Before Reimer could continue, the conference call broke out into a free-for-all with invective and opinions flying back and forth. All of the sudden Rapp felt really tired. The leather chair was comfortable, and the slight vibration from the helicopter was putting him in a trance. He let out a yawn and almost put his feet up on the cooler but he caught himself at the last second.

Rapp shook his head and looked at his watch. After another moment of listening to the arguing he said, "Mr.

President." The free-for-all continued, so he repeated himself a little more loudly. Again, no one yielded so Rapp yelled, "Everybody shut up! Right now!"

The arguing trickled to a stop, and Rapp said, "Mr. President, you need to make a decision. I'm already in the air with the bomb headed west away from the city. Now, if you want me to dump it in the Chesapeake, then you'd better tell me quick, because I'm going to have turn around and haul ass back over the city, and hope I can get there in time."

"You're already on your way to Mount Weather?" asked a shocked Attorney General Stokes.

"Yes, and quit your whining, I'm the one whose been baby-sitting this thing for the last hour."

The president's voice was calm. "I don't want to hear anyone else speak unless I ask for their opinion. Mr. Reimer, how far away would we have to get the people at Mount Weather to protect them from the explosion and fallout?"

"Not far at all, sir. Our worst-case blast damage analysis indicates that as long as the main blast doors are closed, the facility will contain all of the blast. There is a slight chance of some venting but it will be minimal."

"How far?" The president sounded impatient.

"A mile would be sufficient."

"Mitch, how much time do we have left?"

Rapp looked at his watch. "We're down to thirty-eight minutes, Mr. President."

"How long will it take you to get to Mount Weather?"

"Approximately twenty-five minutes."

"General Flood . . . your thoughts on this?"

"We do have other facilities, sir, such as Site R, where you are right now."

"But," interrupted Secretary McClellan, "Mount Weather is the most important facility in the system."

"Kendall," the president snapped, "I'm talking to General Flood right now. When I want you opinion, I'll ask for it. Now, general, as you were saying."

"For starters NORAD is the most important facility in the system, and from the Pentagon's point of view Site R is of greater importance than Mount Weather. Even more appropriate, though, is that there's a shared opinion among the brass that these bunkers are good for command and control, but if we actually go to war with the Russians, or some day the Chinese, Mount Weather will be taken out in the first salvo with either multiple strikes or one of their big, deep underground megaton bombs."

"So you're saying it's obsolete."

"Sir, I think it was obsolete about a year after it was completed."

"How long would it take to evacuate the mountain?"

"I have no idea, but I do know it takes ten minutes to close the blast doors."

Ten seconds of silence ticked by and then the president said, "I want Mount Weather and the surrounding area evacuated immediately! And, General Flood, I want my cabinet members on the first helicopter out."

"Yes, sir."

"And make sure Mitch gets whatever he needs."

"Thank you, Mr. President," said Rapp. "General, I'll call you back in a minute with an exact ETA."

Rapp closed his phone and poked his head into the cockpit. "You guys know where Mount Weather is?" They both nodded. "Good. Get us there as fast as you can."

NINETY-FOUR

Virginia

Mount Weather is located in the craggy northwest corner of Virginia near the West Virginia border, five miles south of the town of Bluemont, Virginia, on Blue Ridge Mountain Road. The site occupies a mere hundred acres, but can be seen for miles around due to the large communications towers that spike up from the peak of the mountain, one of which is owned and operated by AT&T. Since its inception in the fifties, the facility has been shrouded in deep mystery. Not even Congress gets to look at the annual budget, and over the years the facility has even changed names in an effort to keep its location and purpose a secret. Those names have varied from its first code name, which was High Point, to Crystal Palace, the name for the president's quarters within the facility, to a long list of mundane names that mean different things to different government agencies. In the end, though, it is most commonly referred to as Mount Weather.

The place is a living, breathing dinosaur of the Cold War. Much like Site R, it was built to survive a nuclear war, back when the bombs were bigger in design, smaller in yield, and significantly less accurate.

Fortunately for the people who were intended to occupy the facility in the event of a nuclear war, Mount Weather never got the chance to take its place beside the Siegfried and Maginot lines in history's trash heap of well-intended, but short-sighted, fixed fortifications. Now it would serve a purpose, though, and in the end become the tomb it was always destined to be.

As they approached the mountain from the east, Rapp could see cars moving down the mountaintop's switchback road like ants streaming out of an anthill. Four military transport helicopters were also taking off from the small landing strip at the top of the mountain and another helicopter was vacating the helipad by the east portal. The Mount Weather facility had two main roads leading into the underground bunker, one on each side of the mountain. Traffic was moving well down both roads. There were a couple of stragglers still getting in their cars, but the bulk of the people were well clear and already past the mile mark.

Just as General Flood had promised, a pickup truck was waiting for them next to the helipad. It was pointed toward the concrete reinforced tunnel entrance that led into the mountain. Rapp checked his watch. They were down to twelve minutes. He yanked the lead blanket off the cooler and checked the timers. They read 00:12:26. A little less than twelve and a half minutes.

Reimer had informed him that the calculations had been based on taking the device into the center of the facility and putting it in an elevator that would drop it down another hundred feet into the bedrock. He promised Rapp there would be plenty of time to accomplish this. Rapp hoped he was right.

The CIA helicopter set down in the center of the pad. Rapp pushed the door open immediately, and grabbed the handle of the cooler. He dragged it to the edge, and the four men dressed in blue battle dress uniforms from the Federal Protective Services came to his aid. Like attendants from a mortuary hauling a casket, they took hold of the cooler and loaded it into the bed of the idling pickup truck. Three of the men then jumped in the back with the cooler, and the officer in charge of the group slid in behind the wheel. Rapp got in the passenger seat and they took off.

The sunny afternoon disappeared behind them as they entered the long tunnel. The man driving the truck glanced over and said, "You must be the man Secretary McClellan and A. G. Stokes have been bitching about for the last twenty minutes."

"That would sound about right."

The tunnel narrowed a bit and they passed some type of decontamination station. The driver honked the horn and kept his foot on the gas. "We have to start closing the doors now."

Rapp looked at his watch and nodded. They were cutting it close.

"McClellan says you're a real pain in the ass." The man said this with great amusement.

Rapp smiled and shook his head. "Yeah . . . well, actually, McClellan doesn't even know his head from his ass, so I'm not sure he's the best judge."

"You ain't going to get any argument out of me." The driver nudged his way around an abandoned golf cart and hit the gas. "So what's in the cooler?"

Rapp kept his eyes focused on the tunnel. He still couldn't see an end to it. "They didn't tell you?"

"Nope."

"Here's the deal, Lieutenant, when we get to the elevator I'll tell you what it is."

"Well, whatever it is, it can't be good. Here comes the elevator right up here."

The truck began to slow and then skidded to a quick stop on the concrete floor. Everyone piled out. The head of the security detail opened the freight elevator and Rapp helped the other three men carry the cooler. They placed it in the middle of the large elevator, closed the gate, and hit the button for the bottom floor. Rapp watched it disappear and then jumped back in the truck just as it had finished turning around.

As they peeled out he looked at his watch. They had a little over eight minutes to go.

"So what's in the cooler?" asked the driver.

Rapp laughed. He supposed the young man was going to find out sooner than later. "A bomb."

"What kind of bomb?"

"A nuclear bomb."

"You're kidding me?"

"Nope. You'd better step on it, because it's going to go off in about eight minutes, and if those blast doors don't hold we're screwed."

The young man punched the gas and they accelerated down the tunnel. Less than a minute later they skidded to a stop in front of the first blast door, which was already half closed. They abandoned the vehicle, and everyone hit the ground running. They ran one by one past the second blast door and up the road out into the bright afternoon sun. The head of the FPS detail told his men what was in the cooler. The news was received with shocked looks. All Rapp could do was laugh in the face of such insanity.

They reached the helipad with just under three minutes to spare and everyone piled in. The helicopter lifted off and raced eastward. Rapp called Reimer and told him the device was safely tucked away. Reimer advised Rapp that if they were more than a mile away by the time the device blew they wouldn't have to worry about the electromagnetic pulse of the weapon, which could potentially down the helicopter. Rapp told the pilots to keep flying and stay low.

Rapp looked at his watch, counted the seconds, thought of his wife, and willed the helicopter to fly faster. With ten seconds left before detonation he yelled to everyone in the helicopter, "Cover your eyes—don't open them until I tell you."

Rapp counted the seconds in his head. He got to ten and still hadn't heard anything, so he kept going. After twenty seconds he grabbed his phone and dialed Reimer. "What happened? Did it blow?"

"It sure did. We felt the tremor all the way over here across the state line."

"Did the mountain contain the blast?"

"I don't know. You're in a better position than I am."

Rapp asked the pilot to turn around so he could have a look. Rapp gazed out across the beautiful tree covered range in search of any sign that the bunker had failed to contain the blast. There wasn't a plume in sight—not even a puff of smoke.

Rapp smiled and said, "Tell the president we did it. It worked."

"I think you should be the one to make the call," Reimer insisted. "You're the one who did all the heavy lifting."

"It was your idea, Paul. You call him. I'm going to take a quick nap." Rapp closed his phone before Reimer could argue further. He suddenly felt the need to talk to someone.

He looked up the number for the cabin on his phone and punched send. After six rings the familiar voice of his wife answered.

"Don't tell me you're not coming." Her voice was full of disappointment.

"Come on, honey, have a little faith."

"You're going to make it?" she asked excitedly.

"Yep, I'll be there by dinner." Rapp figured after what had just happened he could wrangle the Agency's G-V executive jet for a little personal trip.

"So, everything's all right?"

Rapp looked at the communications towers that were still standing atop Mount Weather. "Yes, honey. Everything is just great."

EPILOGUE

Monday Morning; Memorial Day

The birds were singing, the sun was peeking through the sides of the window shade, and somewhere off in the distance the thrum of an outboard engine punctuated the still morning air. It was summer. Rapp stirred and reached out expecting to find the smooth, soft skin of his wife. All he found was a lumpy pillow. He clutched it and rolled over, not yet sure if he wanted to keep sleeping or get up. The guest cabin at his in-laws' north woods retreat was a great place to sleep. It sat a mere twenty feet from the water's edge, and when there was a slight breeze the water would lap up against the shoreline rhythmically, sending you into a prenatal slumber. It was nature's version of a mother's heartbeat.

On this particular morning, however, there was no breeze, which presented an entirely different problem. In addition to the thrum of the outboard engine, which was fading, there was the sound of another boat on the water—a boat he was very familiar with. Rapp's in-laws were big water skiers, and when at the Rielly cabin, there were only two times to ski: either early in the morning or late in the evening. Early in the morning was always preferred. The evenings were a bonus.

On Saturday, Rapp had left D.C. almost immediately. He'd talked briefly to Kennedy, and it didn't go very well. The full reality of what they had narrowly avoided had begun to gnaw at him almost immediately. In his typical straightforward manner, he told Kennedy what he thought of certain high-ranking people in the U.S. government. She asked him to keep his opinions to himself, and he hung up the phone without responding.

He left D.C. on a private jet and flew to Rhinelander, Wisconsin, where his wife was waiting to pick him up. They had sat by the campfire that night with his in-laws and told stories. At no point were the events of the last week brought up. Rapp had slept hard that night and then right through the morning ski ritual. Anna and her three brothers had ribbed him about it the rest of the day. That was the other thing about the Rielly family—if you didn't ski you were a wimp. Rather than suffer through another day of verbal abuse he threw back the covers and got out of bed.

In the small galley kitchen he found a pot of coffee and a note. It read: *Honey, went skiing. You'd better get your butt down to the dock or you'll never hear the end of it.* Rapp smiled. He poured himself a cup of coffee and looked out at the lake. Through the tall pines he got a glimpse of them skiing down the north shore of the lake. He went back to the bedroom and threw on his swim trunks and an old faded sweatshirt.

On his way back to the kitchen his satellite phone rang. He picked it up and looked at the screen. It was Kennedy. This was the fourth time she'd tried to reach him since he'd left D.C. There was no TV at the cabin, and he'd made no effort to turn on the radio and find out what was happening in the world. He stood there staring at the screen and after a few seconds reluctantly decided he'd better find out if something was going on. He unplugged the charge and brought the phone up to his ear.

"Hello."

"Good morning," Kennedy said in a slightly guarded tone.

"Everything all right?" Rapp's voice was gravely from sleep.

"Yes, everything's fine. I'm sitting on the deck, watching Tommy build a sandcastle. Any reason why you haven't been answering your phone?"

Rapp grabbed his coffee and stepped outside, the screen door slamming closed behind him. "I wasn't in the mood to talk." Rapp worked his way across the dew-laden grass toward the dock.

"And why is that?"

After he left Washington on Saturday, Rapp's resentment toward those who lacked his fervor had worsened significantly. "Why do you think, Irene?" Rapp stepped onto the dock. "You think, just maybe, I'm fed up with all the bullshit?" Despite his choice of words there was no cynicism in Rapp's voice, only resignation.

"Could you be a little more specific?"

"For starters, we came within minutes of losing a half million people and the nation's capital." The old dock squeaked under his weight.

"But we didn't, Mitch. Thanks to you and Paul Reimer and Skip and a whole lot of other people, we stopped them."

Rapp sat down in an Adirondack chair at the end of the dock. "It should've never gotten that far, Irene. We got lucky."

"But we stopped them, and the president is extremely grateful for what you did."

Rapp looked at the water. There wasn't a ripple on the lake. He wanted to tell Kennedy that the president could kiss his ass, but he decided to instead say, "At the moment I don't really care too much about what the president thinks."

"That's unfortunate, because you are probably the only person who can talk him out of acknowledging you when he addresses the nation tonight."

Rapp was dumbstruck. "What are you talking about?"

"You haven't read the papers or seen the reports on TV?"

"No. I'm in the middle of Northern Wisconsin. The nearest town is fifteen miles away."

"Well, the blast at Mount Weather was picked up by seismic installations around the globe. The French government is complaining that we have reneged on the test-ban treaty, the Germans are saying that there was a nuclear accident west of Washington, and rumors are running rampant in the American press that there was a terrorist attack on a secret government facility near Washington."

Rapp set his coffee cup down. "Irene, tell the president that I do not need, or want, the public acknowledgment."

"I already told him that, but he won't listen. He says whether you like it or not you deserve it."

"Absolutely not."

"Then you'd better tell him yourself."

Rapp looked across the length of the lake. "I have no desire to talk to the president. In fact, tell him I'm already thinking about quitting, and if he so much as mentions my name it's a done deal. And tell him that not only will I quit, but I'll tell every last reporter in Washington that while the rest of us were trying to stop these terrorists, he was more concerned with election-year politics and listening to Valerie Jones and Martin Stokes and that Stealey woman from the Justice Department."

There was a long pause on the line, and then Kennedy asked, "You're not serious about quitting?"

"You're damn right I am."

"Mitch, let's not overreact here. I'm sure I can convince the president not to . . ."

"It's not that, Irene. I'm fed up with the whole mess. All the politics and the P.C. bullshit. I'm sick of working with people who have no idea how to fight this battle. I'm sick of trying to convince political appointees how serious the threat is, and I'm sick and tired of people who want to treat this as if it's a law enforcement issue when we're in the middle of a damn war."

"Mitch, I share your frustrations, but you are far too valuable to this fight. We need you."

"Then you'd better convince the president to make some changes. I don't want a medal, I don't want any public recognition . . . I want some people fired. Remember when we used to fire people, or better yet, remember when people used to resign? Well, I don't care if they leave on their own, or if they're shown the door, but some people need to go."

Kennedy didn't answer right away. After a long pause she said, "Would it help if I told you Valerie Jones will be stepping down within the month?"

"I'd say it's a nice start. What about Stokes and Stealey?"

"I'm not sure about Stokes, but I don't think he's the problem. If we tell him to crack down, he'll do it."

"Then what about Stealey? She's the idiot who convinced the president to lock those two guys from Atlanta up in a jail, when they should have been stuffed in some hole."

"I think between the two of us we can make that happen. Will that help?"

"Again . . . it's a nice start."

"So, I'll see you at work soon?"

Rapp looked out across the serene lake. The ski boat was headed back in his direction. They were still several hundred yards away, but he could tell it was his wife who was flying across the wake. She was practically lying down on each cut, throwing up a wall of water.

"Mitch," said Kennedy, "this thing is far from over. You know they're going to come at us again."

Rapp knew better than anyone that the Islamic radical fundamentalists were not about to pack up and quit. He let out a tired sigh and closed his eyes. "Irene, I'm tired, and I'm sick of butting heads with people who are supposed to be on our side."

"Believe me, I understand. I've already spoken to the president about this, and he knows that he hasn't listened to us enough. The enormity of what almost happened has shaken him to the core." Kennedy's voice had taken on a surprisingly optimistic tone. "Mitch, if there was ever a time to get him to declare open season on terrorists—this is it."

"But will he? When it comes down to it, will he actually turn us loose?"

"This time . . . yes, I think so."

Rapp looked out across the water and sincerely wondered if he could walk away from it all. He doubted it. He was too passionate about the fight. He didn't need to admit that to Kennedy and the president, though. He would push for everything he could get.

"Irene, I want carte blanche. Tell the president I'm going to hunt down every last son of a bitch who had a hand in this attack, and I don't want anyone from the White House or the Justice Department looking over my shoulder."

"I think there's a very real chance he would welcome that strategy."

"Good . . . then I'll be in sometime this week." Rapp ended the call, his mind already a thousand miles away, coming up with a plan of attack. A mental list was forming of who and what to hit first. Soon the religious zealots would regroup and come at them again. The outcome of this war, Mitch knew, was far from certain. There was no walking away from this fight. No sidestepping it. There was only one way to wage it—head-on and with brutal and overwhelming force.

Don't miss the following exclusive
extract from Vince Flynn's explosive
next bestseller

CONSENT TO KILL

coming soon . . .

PRELUDE

To kill a man is a relatively easy thing – especially the average unsuspecting man. To kill a man like Mitch Rapp, however, was an entirely different matter. It would take a great deal of planning and a very talented assassin, or more likely assassins, who were either brave enough or crazy enough to accept the job. The latter was more than likely the type who would take on the challenge, for any sane man by definition would have the sense to walk away.

Even with the element of surprise on their side, though, they would need to catch Rapp with his guard down so they could get in close enough to finish him off once and for all. The preliminary report on his vigilance did not look good. The American was either hyper alert or insanely paranoid. Every detail of their plan would have to come together perfectly, and even then, they would need some luck. They'd calculated that their odds for success were probably seventy percent at best. That was why they needed complete deniability. If whoever they sent failed, Rapp would come looking, despite their positions of great power, and they had no intention of spending the rest of their lives with a man like Mitch Rapp hunting them.

ONE

Rapp stood in front of his boss's desk. He'd been offered a chair, but had declined. The sun was down, it was getting late, he'd rather be at home with his wife, but he wanted to get this thing taken care of. The file was an inch thick. It pissed him off. There was no other way to describe it. He wanted it gone. Off his desk so he could move on to something else. Something more important, and probably more irritating, but for now he simply wanted to make this particular problem go away.

His hope was that Kennedy would simply read the summary and hand it back to him. But that wasn't how she liked to do things. You didn't become the first female director of the CIA by cutting corners. She had a photographic memory and a hyper-analytical mind. She was like one of those high end mainframe computers that sit in the basement of large insurance companies, churning through data, discerning trends and risks and a billion other things. Kennedy's grasp of the overall situation was second to none. She was the depository of all information, including, and especially, the stuff that could never be made public. Like the file that was on her desk right now.

He watched her flip through the pages with great speed, and then backtrack to check on certain inconsistencies that he had no doubt were there. Preparing these reports was not his specialty. His skill set had more to do with the other end. There were times when she would read his work with a pen in hand. She'd make corrections and jot down notes in the margins, but this was not one of those times. This particular pile of crap was one of those things that could turn out to be toxic. The type of thing that would ruin careers like a tornado headed for a trailer park. Kennedy knew when he came to her office, either early in the morning or late in the day, and refused to sit, that it was a good idea to keep the cap on her pen. She knew what he wanted, so she kept reading and said nothing.

Kennedy wanted final review on things like this. Rapp wasn't so sure that was a good idea, but she had a better grasp of the big picture than he did. She was the boss and ultimately it was her pretty little neck on the chopping block. If it blew up, Rapp would jump on the grenade without hesitation, but the vultures on the Hill would want her hide too. Rapp respected her, which was no small thing. He was a loner. He'd been trained to operate independently. To survive in the field all on his own for months at a time. For some people that type of work would be unnerving. For Rapp it was Valhalla. No paperwork, no one looking over his shoulder. No risk-averse bureaucrat second guessing his every move. Complete autonomy. They had created him and now they had to deal with him.

Guys like Rapp didn't do well taking orders unless it was from someone they really respected. Fortunately, Kennedy had that respect, and she had the clout to make things happen, or as in this case, simply look the other way while he took care of things. That's all Rapp wanted. What he preferred, actually. He didn't need her to sign off or give him the green light. She just needed to give him the file back, say goodnight, and that would be the end of it. Or the beginning, depending on how you wanted to look at it.

Rapp had the assets in place. He could join them in the morning and be done with it in twelve hours or less if there weren't any surprises, and on this one there wouldn't be any surprises. The target was a moron of the highest order. He would never know what hit him. The problem was in the stir it might create. The aftermath. Personally, Rapp could care less, but he knew if Kennedy hesitated that would be the reason.

Kennedy closed the file and removed her reading glasses. She set them down on her desk and began rubbing her eyes. Rapp watched her. He knew her well. As well as he knew anyone. The rubbing of the eyes was not a good sign. That meant her head hurt, and in all likelihood the discomfort was due to the pile of crap he'd dumped on her desk.

"Let me guess," she said as she looked up at him with tired eyes, "you want to eliminate him."

Rapp nodded.

"Why is it that your solution always involves killing someone?"

Rapp shrugged. "It tends to be more permanent that way."

The director of the CIA looked disappointed. She shook her head and placed her hand on the closed file.

"What do you want me to say, Irene? I'm not into rehabilitation. This guy had his chance. The French had him locked up for almost two years. He's been out for six months, and he's already back to his same old tricks."

"Have you bothered to think of the fallout?"

"Not really my forte."

She glared at him.

"I've already talked to our French colleagues. They're as pissed off as we are. It's their damn politicians and that goofy judge who let the idiot go."

Kennedy couldn't deny the fact. She'd talked to her counterpart in France at length about this individual and several others, and he was not happy with his country's decision to set the radical Islamic cleric free. The counterterrorism people in France didn't like it any more than they did.

"This guy is a known entity," Kennedy said. "The press has written about him. They covered his release. If he turns up dead, they're going to jump all over it."

"Let them jump. It'll last a day or two . . . maybe a week at the most and then they'll move onto something else. Besides . . . it'll serve as a good message to all of these idiots who think they can operate in the West without fear."

She looked back at him, her eyes revealing nothing. "What about the president? He's going to want to know if we had a hand in it."

Rapp shrugged. "Tell him you don't know anything about it."

Kennedy frowned. "I don't like lying to him."

"Then tell him to ask me about it. He'll get the picture, and he'll drop it. He knows the game."

Kennedy leaned back in her chair and crossed her legs. She looked at the far wall and said, more to herself than Rapp, "He's a cleric."

"He's a radical thug who is perverting the Koran for his own sadistic needs. He raises money for terrorist groups, he recruits young impressionable kids to become suicide bombers, and he's doing it right in our own backyard."

"And that's another problem. Just how do you think the Canadians are going to react to this?"

"Publicly . . . I'm sure some of them will be upset, but privately they'll want to give us a medal. We've already talked to the Mounted Police and the Security Intelligence Service . . . they wish they could deport the idiot, but their solicitor general is hell bent on proving that he's Mr. PC. We even have an intercept where two SIS guys are talking about how they could make the guy disappear."

"You're not serious?"

"Damn straight. Coleman and his team picked it up this week."

Kennedy studied him. "I have no doubt that our colleagues will privately applaud this man's death, but that still doesn't address the political fallout."

Rapp did not want to get involved in the politics of this. He'd lose if that's where they ended up going. "Listen . . . it's bad enough when these religious psychos do their thing over in Saudi Arabia and Pakistan, but we sure as hell can't let it happen here in North America. To be honest with you, I hope the press does cover this . . . and I hope the rest of these zealots get the message loud and clear that we're playing for keeps. Irene, we're in the middle of a damn war, and we need to start acting like it."

She didn't like it, but she agreed. With a resigned tone she asked, "How are you going to do it?"

"Coleman's team has been in place for six days watching him. This guy operates like clockwork. No real security to worry about. We can either walk up and pop him on the street, in which case we might have to hit anyone who's with him, or we can take him out with a silenced rifle from a block or two away. I prefer the rifle shot. With the right guy, the odds are as good and there's less downside."

Her index finger traced a number on file and she asked, "Can you make him disappear?"

"With enough time, money and manpower I can do anything, but why complicate things?"

"The impact of it will be significantly reduced if the press doesn't have a body to photograph."

"I can't make any promises, but I'll look into it."

Kennedy began nodding her head slowly. "All right. Number one rule, Mitch, don't get caught."

"Goes without saying. I'm very into self preservation."

"I know . . . all I'm saying is if you can come up with a way for him to never be found, it might help."

"Understood." Rapp reached down and grabbed the file. "Anything else?"

"Yes. When you get back I need you to meet with someone. Two people actually."

"Who?"

She shook her head. "When you get back, Mitch. Meanwhile, you have my consent. Make it happen, and call me as soon as you're done."

TWO

"I want a man killed."

The words were spoken too loudly, in front of far too many people and in a setting that hadn't heard such frank talk in decades. Twenty-eight men, bodyguards included, were standing or sitting in the opulent reception hall of Prince Muhammad bin Rashid's palace in Mecca. This was where he held his weekly *majlis*, or audience, in the desert sheik tradition. Some came to ask favors, many more came just to stay close to the prince, and undoubtedly there were a few who came to spy on behalf of Rashid's half brother the crown prince. Now, any pretense of discreet eavesdropping, normally an art form at these weekly audiences, was dropped. Heads swiveled in the direction of the prince as words hung on lips half spoken.

Prince Muhammad bin Rashid did not look up, but could feel the collective gaze of the men around him. He had shown only the briefest discomfort at his friend's brazen request, and it wasn't because it involved killing. Rashid had expected that. For some time now he'd been feeding his friend the information that would incite this desperate plea. In truth the only thing that annoyed him was that his old friend would be so reckless as to utter such a thing in front of so many who could not be trusted. The Kingdom had become a very dangerous place, even for a man as powerful as Muhammad bin Rashid.

Rashid clasped the kneeling man's hand and carefully considered his reply. The request, and what was said next, would be repeated all over the kingdom and beyond by sunset. There was a division in the House of Saud. Brother had been pitted against brother and Rashid knew he needed to be very careful. Royal family members had already been killed and many more would die before it was over.

Resisting his natural urge to flaunt his Arab bravado he said, "You must not speak of such things, Saeed. I know the loss of your son has been difficult, but you must remember Allah is mighty, and vengeance is his."

The man replied angrily, "But we are instruments of Allah, and I demand my own vengeance. It is my right."

The prince looked up from the pained face of his old friend, who was kneeling before him, and gestured for his aides to clear the room. He then reached out and touched the knee of a man sitting to his right, signaling for him to stay.

After the room was cleared, the prince looked sternly at his friend and said, "You lay at my feet a very serious request."

Tears welled in the eyes of Saeed Ahmed Abdullah. "The infidels have killed my son. He was a good boy." He turned his anguish filled eyes to the man Rashid had asked to stay: Sheik Ahmed al Ghamdi, the spiritual leader of the Great Mosque in Mecca. "My son was a true believer who answered the call to Jihad. He sacrificed while so many others do nothing." Saeed looked around the large room hoping to direct some of his anger at the privileged class who talked bravely, threw around money, but gave no blood of their own. He'd been so immersed in his own pain he hadn't even noticed they'd all left.

Sheik Ahmed nodded benevolently. "Waheed was a brave warrior."

"Very brave." Saeed looked back to his old friend. "We have known each other for a long time. Have you ever known me to be an unreasonable man? Have I ever burdened you with trivial requests?"

Rashid shook his head.

"I would not be here now asking for this if the cowards in Riyadh had honored my simple request and stood up to the Americans. All I asked for was the body of my youngest child, so I could give him a proper burial. Instead, I am told he was defiled by Mitch Rapp so as to intentionally bar him from paradise. What would you expect me to do?"

Rashid sighed and said, "What is it you ask of me?"

"I want you to kill a man for me. It is no more complicated than that. An eye for an eye."

He studied his friend cautiously. "That is no small request."

"I would do it myself," Saeed said eagerly, "but I am naïve in such things whereas you, my old friend, have many contacts in the world of espionage."

For sixteen years Rashid had been the head of Saudi Arabia's Ministry of Intelligence. Then after 9/11 he was shamefully dismissed by his half brother, the crown prince, when he caved into pressure from the Americans. Yes, Rashid had the contacts. In fact he had just the person in mind for the job. "Who is this man you want killed?"

"His name is Rapp . . . Mitch Rapp."

The prince concealed his joy. Caught by surprise, most men with enough sense would have choked on the name, but Rashid had been planning for months. It had started when his friend had asked him to find out what had happened to his son who had left the kingdom to fight in Afghanistan. Rashid had used his sources in the intelligence community and discovered a great deal more than he intentionally let on to. Slowly, he fed his old friend the information that he knew would lead him to demand nothing short of vengeance.

"Saeed, do you know what you ask of me?" The prince spoke in a well rehearsed and dire voice. "Do you have any idea who this Mitch Rapp is?"

"He is an assassin, he is an infidel and he is the man responsible for the death and defilement of my son. That is all I need to know."

"I must caution you," Rashid said very deliberately, "this Mitch Rapp is an extremely dangerous man. He is rumored to be a favorite of the American president and the crown prince as well."

"He is an infidel." The bereaved father repeated as he turned to the religious man. "I have listened to your sermons. Are we not in a war for the survival of Islam? Have you not told us to take up arms against the infidels?"

What little face that could be seen through the thick gray beard showed nothing. The sheik simply closed his eyes and nodded.

Saeed looked back to the prince, his old friend. "I am not a politician or a statesman, or a man of god. I am a businessman. I don't expect either of you to publicly or privately support what I am going to do. All I am asking, Rashid, is that you point me in the right direction. Give me a name. Someone who is wise in these ways, and I will handle the rest."

With the exception of Saeed's public proclamation, Rashid couldn't have been more pleased with how things were proceeding. He had predicted his friend's response almost perfectly. He sat stolidly, not wanting to appear too eager. "Saeed, I know of a man who is very skilled in these things. He is extremely expensive, but knowing you as well as I do, I doubt that will be an issue."

Saeed nodded his head vigorously. He had easily made billions, first by putting up phone and power lines around the kingdom and other countries in the region and now by laying thousands of miles of fiber optic cable.

"I will send him to see you, but you must make no mention of this . . . our meeting here today. Especially to the man I send. I share your anger, and I wish you success, but you must give me your word as my oldest friend that you will never speak of this to anyone. The Kingdom is a very dangerous place these days, and there are brothers of mine who would not be as sympathetic to your plight as I." Rashid's reference to Saudi Arabia's pro American government was obvious.

Saeed sneered. "There is much I would like to say, but as you said the Kingdom is a very dangerous place these days. You have my word. I will speak of this to no one. Not even the man you send."

"Good," smiled Rashid. He stood and helped his friend to his feet. The two began walking across the cavernous room, leaving the cleric sitting alone. "Saeed, operations of this nature are very dangerous. You are entering a cut-throat world and I advise you to deal only with the man I send. For your own safety, and the safety of your family, speak of this to no one. If you succeed in killing Mr. Rapp, and the Americans find out you were behind it, the crown prince will cut off your head. If you fail, and Mr. Rapp finds out you were behind it . . . he will visit you and your family with more pain than you can imagine. Do you understand how important your silence is?"

Saeed nodded. "How will I recognize the man you send?"

"He is a German. There will be no mistaking him. He is infinitely capable. Just tell him what you want, and he will take care of the rest."